THE FINAL
DILEMMA

JAMES BARTLESON

PAGE PUBLISHING, INC.
New York, NY

First originally published by Page Publishing, Inc. 2018

ISBN 978-1-64350-450-6 (Paperback)
ISBN 978-1-64350-451-3 (Digital)

Printed in the United States of America

Dedicated to William Samuel Summers and his genuinely loving family. You helped change the course of my life in more ways than are evident. I miss you.

James Bartleson, October 25, 2017
Book Dedication

CONTENTS

One of Those Days 7

Adolescence...19

Serving the Machine...45

The College Years..68

Life Begins 92

Betrayal 114

Jailed 137

Reality 184

No More 209

Montana 235

Dilemmas..264

ONE OF THOSE DAYS

The Edge ... there is no honest way to explain it because the only people who really know where it is are the ones who have gone over.
—Hunter S. Thompson

Pushpins should do it. At least that was what he thought. Hard to tell in this pieced-together house with paneling matched to Sheetrock and all perfectly textured to blend. Pins were easy to push into the sheetrock, but not so much into the paneling, and he could never tell where one began and the other started due to the blending of the texture and paint. Someone had even painted over the outlet covers and windowsills to avoid any extra or, more appropriately, necessary preparatory labor. Even with the half-assed repair work performed by the previous owners, they were very skilled in the art of wall texturing and painting. He just hoped that he would get lucky and select the appropriate section of overly painted splendor that would have Sheetrock underneath and the pins would slide in with minimal effort, although *lucky* would never be a word he would use to describe any part of his life.

Michael Stevens looked down from the wall with a half-disgusted, enraged glare on his face while gazing down on his birth certificate that he held gripped in his left hand. This was an actual recording of the shameful event that brought him here—this world that he now considered his prison. He looked at the names of his mother and father on the form. How he did love his mother so much, but the controlling, compassionless, judgmental, negative energy of his father was too much to overcome. He didn't even celebrate his birthday anymore, as he equated it to a convict celebrating the day of their conviction.

He had managed to accept and forgive a lot of things when he sobered up, but thoughts of revenge now filled his head. He knew that none of his problems were caused by his father. Everything that happened to him was because of how he reacted to situations using his own free will to make hard decisions. Michael accepted that, but he didn't really care anymore. Right now, he could think of nothing and no one that was worth sticking around this place for. He was done, and this was payback time. All he wanted to do was make them all feel his pain.

The four multicolored pushpins in his right hand were starting to pierce his palm as he clenched his fist tighter and tighter in anger. His eyes were forced closed with a slight snarl on his lips. Michael was seeing visions of all the wrong that he had done to others in this life as well as the suffering he had to endure. It was like rapid fire of memories of pain combined with visions of his father and the many times Michael thought that he helped devastate his life. He ignored the pain in his palm as tiny droplets of blood began to drip from between his fingers. As his rage swelled, he let out a loud primal scream and squeezed the pins harder in his hand. He opened his eyes to a view of a motionless wall. Michael looked down as he opened his hand, exposing the pushpins, which were now even more multicolored with the addition of red smudges of fresh blood. A couple were even stuck deep in his skin.

He just laughed it off. *Who really gives a shit anyway?*

Michael held the birth certificate against the wall and pinned each corner, being very careful to center it appropriately on the wall behind his easy chair. Even in a state of giving up, Michael was a perfectionist. He gave a slight sarcastic chuckle as he inserted the final pin and realized that he had indeed managed to find Sheetrock for all four pins. Michael stared into the birth certificate on the wall and concentrated on all the designs and happy artwork around the edges. He started to float off into more visions of pain and suffering but quickly got control of it and snapped back to consciousness form realizing that he had to get on with things.

Michael zeroed in on the date of his birth: January 8, 1970. It was the same day (not year, obviously) as Elvis Presley, one of his all-time favorite recording artists. He had lots of Elvis memorabilia that he had collected over the last couple of decades and just about everything the rocker had ever recorded in one form or another. Michael's prize collectable was a dancing Elvis phone that his wife had given him for a birthday present a long time ago. He used it every day, and it still worked just fine. He could always relate to the King in some way. Perhaps it was some metaphysical thing to do with having the same birthday. Who knew? Michael always loved the Elvis movie that Kurt Russell starred in during the late 1970s. It was actually directed by John Carpenter, Mr. Horror himself—the one who created Michael Meyers and, quite possibly, Kurt Russell as well. No one harnessed the true essence of Elvis like Kurt Russell did.

Now, the pain receptors in his brain were starting to register the little holes in his palm. *Ouch!* He gave a slight grimace, but pain really didn't ever affect Michael too much. In fact, when pain got too extreme, he would always break into uncontrolled laughter. It was some sort of psychotic acceptance method for when pain was so bad and there was nothing presently that he could do to stop it. It was darkly humorous, but Michael had experienced so much disappointment in life that when things seemed hopeless, it was hilarious to him. This pain was nothing—nothing when compared to the pain of something like pancreatitis, which Michael had several times during his drinking decades. God, it was more like the asshole decades. He was two years sober now, but no longer could Michael take the pain of his awakening to the truth and reality. There was something about himself that he still didn't understand, and all the knowledge that he had wouldn't help him. Something evil remained in Michael, and he was out of options. There were no more dilemmas to ponder. He would never go back to drinking to drown out his exception level of feeling. He had once told his mother that he would swallow a bullet before he swallowed a drink again, usually in a jocular manner. The world simply called his bluff, and he was about to prove it.

Michael wiggled his way sideways back out from between his easy chair and the wall. He loved that chair and remembered how he had bought it on closeout at a large furniture warehouse. He always found it so funny that furniture stores were always having a "going out of business" sale. Just another thing in a long list of corporate scam techniques to get their hands on your money. That was one of many things that disgusted him about this world: the corporate greed and the consumers' thirst for more material goods that they didn't need but somehow seemed to improve their self-esteem for about two minutes. His hatred for materialism aside, this chair was the most comfortable thing that he had ever put his ass on in his life.

"I am going to miss that comfy thing," he said to himself.

He looked down at the couch and saw that Rikki was still a little shaken up by his primal scream that woke her from a well-earned nap a moment ago. She had that familiar "scared, hanging head with eyes staring up" look on her face that was a result of years of Michael's drunken fits of yelling and throwing shit around the house. Rikki, a ten-year-old Australian shepherd, had been the best companion that he had in this life. The only unconditional love that he had ever felt in this world was from a dog. He'd been backstabbed, used, and abandoned by every person he had ever known. It was certain to him that there were only three real guarantees in life: the sun rises, the sun sets, and sons of bitches. Cynicism had just become second nature to Michael.

"Sorry about that, old girl." Michael sat down next to her on the couch. "I had to get that yell out of the system," he said as he began to scratch the side of her neck and calm her down. He was confident that the benevolent soul that Rikki had within her would be present in the pet he would have in the next life, if there was one. He knew that with all his heart and was not afraid to die because he knew that he would go on in a better one. If his knowledge of reality showed him anything, it was the truth about existence. He was, however, a little concerned about the karma that would come from what he was about to do.

In all his years of reading, research, and spiritual growth, he could never come to a conclusion on suicide. There were many schools of thought on this as there was with anything else that was of the so-called unknown or controversial subject. Michael did not have any belief systems, only an open mind full of information. Most religions taught that you would go to some place called hell if you decided to cut your time here short. Forgiveness for your very existence could be acquired on Sundays, for a small fee. Michael was pretty sure that this was bullshit.

He had read Dante's *Divine Comedy* not too long ago, which was very Catholic and very, very Italian; more specifically, a composite of the people that Dante wanted to see punished was illustrated in beautiful poetry. Although Michael loved the story of the "Inferno," the "Purgatory," and the "Paradiso," he was convinced that we all came from a spiritual Creator but that there was no actual heaven or hell. If anything, this current three-dimensional existence on this earthly plane was the closest thing that resembled the hell of the Bible, and he could not take it for one more day. His willingness to die had now exceeded his fear of the unknown.

Michael left Rikki sleeping on the couch, and he went to his desk. He sat down and looked at the blank piece of paper. The Tim McGraw song about the sheet of paper was going through his head. It seemed so cliché to him to leave a note, but he just wanted to give one final "Screw you" to this world.

"I'll show them," he said, which gave him a little chuckle.

So many things became funny once one lost one's mind, and there was little else to clutter it up. He already had what he wanted to say in his head, so writing the note would be no problem.

He grabbed his favorite Zebra pen and began his final letter as he sung softly to himself, "I am just a blank sheet of paper. This fool's about to write you a letter ..."

Greetings.

Obviously no one will believe I was of sound mind after the events of today, but I would like this to serve as my last will and testament. I will not try to explain all the reasons why I am doing this. I think

11

that most of the people that know me well enough will know why, or at least they will think they do. Thinking is not really this world's strong suit, lately. I have accepted the fact that those who choose to walk the path of truth choose to walk in this world alone. The problem is, I don't want to live in this world alone.

I was raised with judgment and control because that is the way the Controllers have socially engineered us. The source of all human suffering is their unwillingness to learn and look inward to themselves to find true happiness. I can see just how simple the solution is and what is behind it, but I can't continue to live in a world that actually fights to remain in bondage. I cannot be a part of that. Everyone sits around and complains about what is wrong with their lives while idly hoping for change, all while lumped on a couch, drinking alcohol, being told what to think from a black mirror. With a society that looks like that, how can I expect another human to understand empathy? It is not possible for humanity to do that, and that is why I am doing this. I never wanted material things, just love and understanding. That is not what society is about anymore. I wonder if it ever was.

I would like my body to be cremated. Enclosed is a sealed envelope that contains enough cash to cover all the costs of such as well as the incidentals that may go along with it. I do not intend in any way for my death to financially impact anyone in a negative way. Since money is the only God of this wonderful rock, I wanted to make sure that I paid my way, even in death.

In closing, I would like my ashes to be dumped down the nastiest public toilet that you can find. That way, I can feel at ease that I was treated in

death the same that I was treated in life—used, for-
gotten, and dumped in the shitter.

Best regards,
Michael Stevens

As he proofread the note, a tear welled up in his eye, and he began to laugh until more tears just seemed to join in. Why couldn't he just have found love and appreciation from one person in this world without them leaving? Why did that not exist here? It seemed so simple to him. The human potential to love, thrive, and live in joy was there, but the lie of this world was so much more powerful. He came to believe that a certain level of evil was always going to be necessary. You would never be able to completely eradicate it.

The yin-and-yang balance of good and bad was the basis of all existence in nature. The problem was that the world was out of balance. Evil was out control, and good was at risk of extermination. A tear ran down the side of his nose and just hung on for a few seconds from his nostril. He resisted the urge to itch the spot where the tear had made its way. He could almost watch the tear drop in slow motion as it fell onto the note. The moisture swelled on the paper as if he was leaving his own personal watermark.

Michael paper-clipped the note to the sealed envelope that he had filled with cash previously. He held the ensemble out as he stood up from his desk chair. Michael just let the letter and envelope drop back on the desk with a disgusting flop, and he walked over to the stereo. He had already preplanned his final music. It was almost like he always knew what would be playing when he left here. Nothing else but "Fade to Black" by Metallica would do, one of his all-time favorites. He plugged the stereo cord into his Zune and selected the song, ready to go at the touch of a button. All he had to do was push Play at the right moment.

The Zune—wow, what a bunch of crap he took from everyone for buying that thing instead of an IPod. It was so amazing how he could see the herd mentality in society so clearly manipulated by corporate advertising. He had owned that Zune for ten years with no problems, and Michael considered that to be a worthy purchase. His friends used to make fun of how he was the only person that ever bought a Zune. That was Michael's buddies for you. If you couldn't trust your friends to spread gossip about you, use you, make fun of you, and stab you in the back, then whom could you trust?

He went back to the desk and pulled a red Sharpie from his cup full of miscellaneous pens, pencils, etc. He walked back over to the birth certificate that was hanging so perfectly centered on the wall. Michael uncapped the Sharpie in his teeth and began to write in big bold letters. He pressed so hard that the tip of the Sharpie was semicrushed against the wall. He probably didn't make it through all six layers of paint between the paper certificate and the Sheetrock, but he probably got through two or three of them. He stepped back a ways in front of his easy chair and admired his handiwork.

VOID

Michael knew that would get people's attention, aside from everything else that people would be talking about for quite some time after today. He glanced around the room to make sure that everything was in place. The birth certificate was on the wall behind the easy chair, the note and money were on the desk, and the music was ready to go. He walked over to the couch and knelt down next to his faithful companion. She opened her eyes and looked up at Michael. Rikki slept a lot more these days. She was really getting up there in years for an Australian shepherd.

He cupped her head in his hands, and she gave a soft, gentle lick on the tip of his nose as if to say, "Hey, I'm just resting, but I still love you."

He finally broke down in uncontrolled sobbing. He loved her so much. When there was no one else he could talk to, she would always listen. She had not been an easy dog to train in the beginning, but once the wheels were adjusted, she became the best friend he'd ever had. He chuckled despite the tears as he thought of something he had heard once. A man he knew once told him, "Take your dog and wife and lock them in the trunk of your car for an hour. After that, open the trunk and see which one is glad to see you."

"Goodbye, Rikki. I know you don't understand any of this, but I will see you again someday. I love you so much." Michael choked out the words between stuttering breaths and sobs.

He had already made sure that there was plenty of food and water out for her to last several days and that she would be able to go in and out of the house through the dog door and into the yard. Rikki was always fairly low maintenance, and she only ate until she was full. She would be fine until someone finally found his body. He didn't have many visitors and no "true" friends left, so it would take a few days, he imagined. As a backup, Michael had already placed a letter to the newspaper in his mailbox regarding his death. It would go out the next day.

He got up and looked away from Rikki toward the stereo. Everything was a little blurry until he wiped his eyes on his sleeve. "Time to get it done," he muttered.

He walked over to the stereo and pushed Play on the Zune and then turned and walked back to his favorite chair. The music started right up just as he had envisioned. Michael had already laid the shotgun on the floor next to the chair when he had climbed out of bed that morning, and he made sure to load shells into the magazine.

Michael had considered many firearm options before selecting the shotgun. He only owned three firearms: the shotgun, a pistol, and an AK-47. He originally thought about using the AK. The thing that was nice about the AK-47, above all other rifles, was that it was short and rarely ever jammed. The nice thing about being short was that the tip didn't dig into the roof of your mouth so bad when you tried to reach the trigger. Hey, comfort was an important consideration here. As far as jamming went—not going to happen.

He remembered a demonstration that he had seen on a Marine Corps base when he was in the Navy. The master-at-arms was demonstrating many different firearms, but when he came to the AK-47, it was a whole new demonstration. The marine took the AK-47 and immersed it in muddy, filthy, thick water and moved it around to make sure that it was nice and full of mud. He did this with the bolt open and then pulled the AK-47 out of the mud then locked a round home, and it performed like it was just out of the box. Incredible! Due to the history of this shotgun, it just seemed so much more fitting, but it would definitely leave more of a mess.

Life it seems to fade away, drifting further every day ... Metallica was coming on strong. He had to hand it to Lars and Hetfield. They really made a name for themselves. Michael remembered how he was the one to introduce Metallica to his little small town high school in the early 1980s. He had mail-ordered their *Ride the Lightning* album out of a *Hit Parader* magazine when he was thirteen. He had never heard of them before, but he really liked the picture of the album cover art with the electric chair and all the lightning coming out of the big blue background. It was so cool. Boy, was he pleasantly surprised, as it was the most incredible thing he had ever heard. Soon after, he brought it to school for everyone else to listen to. This was the time when cassettes were really coming on strong, and it was great to have portable music, although the school didn't like it so much. Michael had his Walkman confiscated at school many times due to Metallica. The band went on to be his favorite, and he even saw them twice in concert. There was nothing on this earth that could compare to a live Metallica show.

He suddenly remembered a passage from H. G. Well's *The Time Machine*: "I grieve to think how brief the dream of the human intellect had been. It had committed suicide." Exactly right. This was not the first time that Michael had considered suicide. This was actually the third (unless you counted that incident with Brad in the woods). The first couple of ways that he had contemplated would have actually been more of a cry for help. One was with pills, and the other was with gas. Blowing your skull all over a wall with a shotgun, however, was only for the really serious. Michael was not crying for help. That time had passed.

I was me, but now he's gone ...

Michael sat down in his chair and picked up the shotgun. He cradled the shotgun between his knees with both hands as he put the tip of the barrel in his mouth. The taste was not what he expected. It was just the cold metal that seemed to electrify his tongue. He had not oiled it for some time, but he could still taste that sour flavor of gun oil residue. He stuck his tongue in the hole of the barrel. Maybe he was trying to bring it to arousal before setting it off. He had not been with a woman in years, so this was the closest he was going to get in his final hour.

Michael could no longer make out the music as he closed his eyes in meditative thought; the tip of the barrel placed slight pressure on the roof of his mouth but was still quite comfortable as he continued to cradle the butt of the rifle in his knees.

The birth certificate on the wall behind him would be exactly in the blast path. He was now drifting into a memory of his early childhood, a time when he was happy, when he knew nothing of the real workings of the world. He was having an ice cream with his mother at a Baskin Robbins. He couldn't place the time and place, just the feeling of contentment that he was feeling at the exact moment. It was a feeling that he would have liked to have again, but never had.

He couldn't take the thought of the way he was about to break his mother's heart. He used to blame her (and his father) for bringing him in the world in the first place. Michael couldn't really hold her accountable for that; she had been just as ignorant of the real world as the majority of the population. He did blame her for choosing to remain that way, which was the one thing that had kept humanity enslaved for so long. Every time Michael would try to share facts of reality with her, she would get upset with him and walk away.

He never did understand why everyone shot the messenger, until he read a quote from Mark Twain so many years ago: "It is easier to fool people than to convince them that they have been fooled." Boy, how true he knew that was. Michael had lived that one for decades. If anything, he did have empathy for the world that had been fooled for so long. He understood how hard it was to realize, but that didn't mean that he had to continue to live among them.

His parents still drank every day, and after Michael had sobered up, he knew that definitely had something to do with it. They still had clouded views of this fake reality, of which his were clear now. No one would ever be able to see anything clear until they came out of the fog of drunkenness. He never figured that his mother would have been much of a drinker had it not been for his old man. Michael would bet everything that he owned that his father had not missed a day without drinking in over fifty years. That was no lie. Oh well, why was he getting sidetracked with those thoughts now?

"Fade to Black" had finished its run, and the room was dead quiet. Rikki had also gone back to sleep. He simply forgot to hit Repeat on the Zune, but it didn't much matter now. He placed his right thumb on the trigger of the rifle and closed his mouth tight around the tip of the barrel.

He leaned back and said to himself, *May the Creator spirit of humanity forgive me for what I am about to do.*

Flashbacks of his life were really starting to overwhelm him at this point. Was this a personal life review or second thoughts? His thumb began to form around the trigger. As he pressed harder, the skin on his thumb began to fade from pink to white as pressure was increasingly applied. Tears began to grow in the corner of his shut eyes as he pictured his mother's face.

Please forgive me, Mother, he thought, *but I had to do it this way so people would understand.*

Today was a very special day, he thought, and he said aloud, the words slurred by the tip of the barrel jammed in his mouth, "Haffy Fadder's Day."

ADOLESCENCE

Adolescence is a plague on the senses.
—Henry Rollins

Michael was only twelve years old when he first saw a dead body. It had been that of his paternal grandfather. His father had taken him to the funeral home into a private viewing room on the day before the funeral to personally say goodbye to Pappy. He looked down at his sleeping grandpa with confusion in his heart. Michael's face began to lose focus as his eyes slowly filled with tears. He turned his head to look away from Pappy's face and then up at his father in wonderment. How could someone he loved so much raise someone that he despised. Rather ironic?

His grandpa was only sixty-eight when he died. That kind of made sense when he thought more about it. Michael used to watch his grandfather eat bacon covered in sausage gravy, two helpings of grits, four eggs over easy, and sourdough bread dripping with farm-fresh butter—and that was just for breakfast. He also did not have the best table manners; he liked to talk with oozing mouthfuls of mixed-up, multicolored, half-masticated meat. He chewed with his mouth wide open, even when he wasn't talking between feedings. No one could really change it. That was just the way he was, and everyone just seemed to accept it. Michael always wished that his own family could understand his "flaws" in the same way.

He was just born different than everyone else. To Michael, it was definitely a "flaw." When people weren't able to fit in with the group—especially a child, to whom acceptance was really a big deal—

19

it could be devastating. He felt things much deeper than other kids, and he felt alone and isolated because of it. When he could easily see the solution to any given problem, Michael just couldn't get his point across to others, especially his immediate family. They just didn't understand. Sometimes he wondered if he was even human because of how few people he encountered understood him or even wanted to listen so they could understand. Pappy had been the only one in his early childhood that he felt completely comfortable around.

Although he was so young when his grandfather was in good health, Michael still remembered the fun times. Pappy was the one who taught him to shoot, work with livestock and agriculture, and enjoy nature as it should be. Maybe he was part of the reason Michael had such an affinity for the outdoors. He was just as happy in the driving rain as he was on a peaceful fall day, and Michael felt the same way. Pappy taught him that nature would never lie to you, cheat you, or try to deceive you like a man would. You always knew where you stood with nature. It was man that you couldn't turn your back on.

Pappy loved his slip-on rancher roper shoes, and they were always sitting on the floor by the back door, waiting for him to put them on so he could wander out to the fields or the barn for whatever miscellaneous farm chore that needed doing. He raised cows and strawberries, an odd combination and a very time-consuming one. The stench of cow manure was everywhere, and you just had to get used to it. Pappy had a bit of a slouch to his stance, which was a result of decades of stooping over the strawberry fields. The fields that the Beatles sung about might have been very mesmerizing and beautiful, but that would end if you ever had to work in one.

He was a very typical farmer, as Michael remembered. If it could not be fixed with bailing twine, duct tape, or an absolute overkill of nails, then in the trash it went. He recalled once when Pappy was pitching hay in the barn and Michael was crawling up and sitting on different levels of the haystacks, which he used to absolutely love. Grandma called Pappy to the house, while Michael kept on playing and climbing in the little cracks between the stacks to hide. When Pappy came back, he was irritated and had an angry look on his face.

"You okay, Pappy?" Michael asked from his wedged location in between two haystacks from about eight feet above his grandpa's head.

He looked up at Michael and said, "You know, Mikey, you can never trust anything that can bleed for a solid week and not die." It would be years until Michael understood the absolute truth of that statement. "Forget I said that," Pappy continued without haste. "I hope you're having fun up there, Mikey. Please be careful, though. I don't want to have to hear any more from her today." Grandpa looked back toward the ground and shook his head as he went back to forking hay into the cattle feeders.

Now, Pappy lay here in a box in front of him. He just looked so cold and still, but peaceful nonetheless. The short lid over his face was the only part of the casket that was open. Michael didn't really know how to feel. He would miss Pappy's company and teachings about life, but he just seemed to know at an early age that there was a beautiful place of joy beyond our version of this reality we were in now. He said his goodbyes to his grandpa. Michael had a deep feeling of joy that told him that Pappy was happy now. He just knew it somehow, and he could not tell anyone why, but his grandpa was finally at peace.

Michael's family had moved to the eastern part of Washington State from the western side when he was seven years old. Washington State was a strange phenomenon in itself. It was split in half by the Cascade mountain range into two sections that were complete environmental, geological, political, and economic polar opposites. There was a proposal at one time to split the state into two separate states, but the so-called powers that be shot that down in a hurry. Oregon was considering that too, Michael had heard somewhere.

They settled in a small country town just an hour from the Canadian border. It was Michael's guess that it was like any other small country town in America in the late 1970s. There was a main street with one stoplight, the only one in the entire county at that time. The stores were all Western mercantile style with large gable frontages to draw attention. A bakery, three taverns, two barber shops, and countless craft-and-antique stores were the local fare.

They had an annual town rodeo that drew in all the people from the surrounding cattle ranches and hay farms for the three-day party.

His family was about as standard as it could get. Michael was an only child with two working parents; in fact, it was his father's change in careers that had brought them to this dusty little town. The family prepared a home-cooked meal together every night, no matter the time, and always worked on their home-improvement projects together as a family. They went camping, fishing, hunting, and a two-week planned vacation every year. It seemed like the picture-perfect vision of an American family, but just like what George Carlin said, that was why it was called the American Dream, because you had to be asleep to believe it. How true that was, especially when everything was done out of duty and not necessary love as the motivator.

Starting school in a small town school as the new kid was just a horrible existence to be in. Michael came to town the summer before the third grade, where most students had established friend groups by then. He remembered sitting at a desk with all the wondering eyes staring at him as the teacher introduced him, "Class, this is Michael Stevens. His family has recently moved here from … where was it again?" She leaned over to Michael, and he whispered it to her. "Oh, okay, from Tacoma. Please make him feel welcome and introduce yourselves when you get a chance."

Small towns were really hard to make friends in. The social cliques were most noticeable, and they were hard to get into. As with anything else in life, there were good and bad to small towns and big cities. With smaller towns, people knew a lot more about you, or at least they thought they did. On the up side though, it was a lot easier to disappear and get away from human judgment in the wide-open country. That would prove to be quite handy for Michael in the coming years. In big cities, no one could care less about you. Anyone could remain fairly anonymous if they chose, but you couldn't get away from people very well.

No matter what people said about gossip, it was what small town Americans based their opinions about people on, even if it was a lie, which it usually was. Gossip ruled the air waves. Michael considered gossip to be Satan's breath. Some people started gossip to try to get revenge on someone, but most used it to make themselves look better for narcissistic reasons in order to get themselves into the right clique. Maybe it was just a problem with low self-esteem, where humans think they would feel better about themselves by hurting another. Maybe it could be that the majority of the population had no empathy and got a kick out of it—the beginnings of psychopathy. If it got bad enough, gossip could actually turn you into the very thing that you were not. For someone like Michael, it could eventually overtake who he was, and if he passed the point of no return, there was no coming back.

Within weeks of starting school, the students had begun to tease Michael about his weight. Michael was waiting outside of the classroom one morning with some of the beautiful students. He never really said much to them, but they always were nice to him—when they needed help with schoolwork, of course. Another great human quality: using people for their own selfish gain and then judging and teasing them along with everyone else. Noble.

Michael noticed something about a shirt one student was wearing and made a comment but was not trying to be insulting, just playful. He couldn't remember what that comment even was to this day, but he would never forget the result.

One of the princesses, Shelagh was her name, turned to him and said, "How would you like it if we call you Boob Man?"

Michael just looked at her. "Don't call me that!"

It was bad enough that he was one of the chubby kids in school, but he was the only one who had fat boy breasts.

"How about Tits?" some ignorant jock yelled out.

The name stuck, and then almost everyone in school would call him that until his senior year in high school. Just terrible.

His parents would never show compassion or even try to understand his problems at school with the teasing. He would try to tell them about his torment, and instead of sympathy, he received blame. His mom would tell him that he must be doing something to cause his peers to tease him in such ways. She did not want to understand, for fear of her son being different; this, of course, had rubbed off from the old man's lack of empathy. They could not understand that possibly humanity was just a cosmic sewer and that people got a kick out of hurting others.

Michael never could quite put together how people could treat him like they did. How mentally diseased was a race of beings that shunned the very ones that wanted to improve it and create something out of real love. Michael believed that people didn't want to be around and accept people that were smarter and better. Human ego was the biggest cause. The love of money was not the root of all evil; the human ego was. If it weren't for the ego, man would never be greedy and selfish in the first place. Or maybe they just couldn't stand to be in the presence of truth because they would have to accept how truly enslaved they actually were? Who knew?

For Michael, making friends would always be quite difficult, no matter what town he was in. It seemed to be that way for the intelligent and hypersensitive ones. Countless times, he had heard people say that the world did not make sense. But why? Michael possessed a benevolent soul and high level of intelligence, and he would be shit on throughout his life because of it. It wouldn't be until the fifth grade that Michael would make his first, and only, friend in this town, and what an interesting way that it happened.

Sometimes people just woke up in a bad way, and they were a firecracker waiting to go off all day. Michael's days were like that more frequently by the fifth grade. He was not well liked at school and was teased for just about everything you could think of. Being the smart kid never helped, but also the chubby one? Not fun. Plus, he was not an original local; so he was never, nor would he ever be, accepted as one of the original townsfolk even way into adulthood. School that day started as any other, but he could feel the chip on his shoulder growing as he stepped off the bus and approached the front doors of the school.

In elementary school in the early 1980s, all classes were in the same room with the same teacher. As Michael walked into the classroom, he noticed that Jimmy was sitting in his chair. Jimmy was the tall lanky kid in class with glasses and was also subjected to his share of teasing from the fortunate ones. For some reason, Jimmy wanted to sit in Michael's seat today. The students did not have assigned seating per se, but Michael had sat in the same seat all year, and he had liked the location away from the beautiful kids.

He looked down at Jimmy in his chair and said, "Hey, you're sitting in my seat. I always sit there. Yours is up front in the next row."

"You'll just have to sit somewhere else today," Jimmy said without even looking up at him.

Michael could feel the rage growing inside of him, the same rage that would plague him for most of his life. The thought of having to sit over among the mean kids was just not sitting well with him. He could feel his anger from all the teasing and bullying growing, and this poor sap in front of him was about to be the victim of his projected rage.

Jimmy was not trying to hurt him; he was just having a bad morning himself. Michael didn't even realize it when he drew up his right fist in the air above him and blindsided Jimmy on the side of the head, knocking him out of the desk and onto the floor. Jimmy's glasses had flown about six feet away and landed right in front of the teacher, who was standing in the aisle, watching the entire event unfold.

The teacher looked at Michael. "What did you just do, Michael? You two both go down to the principal's office. Are you all right, Jimmy?" She bent down and tried to help Jimmy up to his feet.

Jimmy stood up and looked at the teacher. "I'm fine," he choked out between partial sobs. He wasn't bleeding but would have a nice shiner on his cheek and eye the following day.

Michael turned and left the room for the principal's office with Jimmy quietly in tow, rubbing his tender cheek. He had stopped sobbing and was just staring at the back of Michael's head as they walked to the office. All was quiet, and not a word was said.

It seemed funny, but life usually was, if you liked dark humor. People who fought sometimes ended up being great friends. There was an actual psychological term for it, but Michael could not remember what it was called. Jimmy and Michael both sat in the chairs outside the principal's office with heads hung low. Michael looked up and saw Jimmy staring over at him with his hand on his cheek. He started to smile, and Jimmy couldn't help but return the gesture. With the unspoken communication of "I'm sorry," their smiles gradually grew to a small chuckle and then hard-to-suppress laughter. When they left the office after their sentencing for not conforming to the herd, they became best friends.

Michael had young boyhood acquaintances before he moved to the east side of the state, but none of them ever blossomed into a close friendship. This was the first friend that he had made in this town—a town that he lived in for almost three years. The very next day, after the skirmish, Jimmy and Michael sat in desks right next to each other, one with bruises on his knuckles from the edge of some geeky-looking glasses and the other with knuckle-shaped bruises on his cheekbone. What a pair to draw to.

Every Halloween Michael and Jimmy would stay up all night in their pajamas and watch the old Abbott & Costello horror flicks. *Abbott and Costello Meet the Mummy* was always their favorite. That particular one wasn't on every year, but it was a treat when it was. Most years it was included with the selected schedule for broadcast. Michael's mom would make them popcorn and Chex Mix for the evening, and they would put their sleeping bags on the floor in the family room in front of the TV. They loved it.

The two would ride their dirt bikes everywhere together. It turned out that Jimmy only lived a couple of miles away from Michael. BMX bikes and track racing were very popular in the 1980s. Michael and Jimmy both had Huffys, the more affordable of the bikes at the time. Everyone had to have all the accessories and safety pads too. The gooseneck pad, handlebar pad, crotch bar pad, and seat bar pad were just a must if you wanted to fit in. Hopefully, they would be stamped with Mongoose so you could cover up every-where that it said "Huffy" to make the rich kids think that you, too, had a Mongoose.

Michael and Jimmy lived out in the sand flats full of sagebrush, mesquite, and jumping cactus. They were constantly building their own super BMX race track, fully equipped with jumps, moguls, and the occasional muddy water hole. They finally figured out that you had to lay black plastic in the hole if you wanted it to hold water in the sand flats. The sagebrush provided a nice obstacle to lay the winding course out, but the jumping cactus had to be removed. These little jumping suckers would go right through the side of sneakers, not to mention thin bike tubes, and hurt like the dickens long after you pulled that sticky son of a bitch out. There was a toxin inside that itched for days. Since this was in the days before good tire slime, they went through bike tubes in the dozens. Their parents were never too happy about that, but they managed to get them replaced when needed. The tricky thing about finding the cactus patches was that they blended in so well with their surroundings that they could be tricky to spot unless you got one that had punctured the sneaker or the tire. Sometimes that was the only way to find them, but they did their best and would eventually get them all cleared away from the ever-expanding bike track.

The few neighborhood kids would come and race on the track as well, and every Sunday they would have races, with spectators and everything. Michael was always very industrious, and he would even create ribbons and small trophies for the winners of the races. The neighborhood kids sure liked those Sunday races, but they seemed to be hard to locate when the work for the track preparation was going on after school during the week. Michael and Jimmy did all the work, but they really didn't care, since they enjoyed spending time with each other.

One time in particular, Jimmy thought it would be a cool idea to build a ramp that would be of sufficient height to jump over each other. Michael actually liked the idea as well. With their trusty shovels, which got a lot of use over the years, they built up a jump at least two feet high. Of course, they tested the jump a few times to see how far away from the ramp the back tire was landing to make sure it would be enough distance to clear. They had to add brush and dirt to the jump a couple of times, but they eventually got the distance they were looking for.

Michael went first and lay down with his head toward the ramp, just in case Jimmy didn't quite make it. It would be better to have a broken leg than a crushed skull. Jimmy got up enough speed and just barely cleared Michael's feet. The rush of fear combined with adrenaline was always a fun experience. These two seemed to feed on it, but for Michael, it was always like a rush, literally. He could close his eyes and see a powerful white light and feel like he was floating in a kind of energy field.

Jimmy was always just a little more extreme but sometimes bordering on the stupid. He lay down the same as Michael did, while Michael peddled back to the starting point. As Michael was nearing the jump, he could see Jimmy quickly spin and slide in a half circle on the ground behind the ramp. He had switched positions and now had his head at the far end. Michael's eyes got wide because he knew there was no stopping his bike now. He was so close to the ramp that he had to make the jump or dump the whole bike on top of Jimmy, which would also be disaster.

Michael swung the bike slightly wide and then back in to hit the jump at an angle instead of straight on, with barely enough time to make the adjustment. The back tire of the bike landed a few inches to the right side of Jimmy's head. Michael looked back as he landed. The front tire of the bike twisted in the sand when it made contact at an awkward angle, causing him to flip into a big sagebrush bush with a nice cactus patch cushion for his leg.

After he managed to pick those painful sons of bitches out of the front of his thigh, Michael got up and turned around to see Jimmy just giggling on the ground. "What the hell were you thinking? I could have crushed your damn skull."

"I know," Jimmy responded after he quit laughing. "But you didn't, and it was a rush, let me tell you." Jimmy had a crazy streak like that. He didn't really want to die, not like Michael did some days. His home life was much better, and his parents didn't drink all the time and actually did things together that weren't always surrounded by drinking. He thought that maybe Jimmy just didn't really have a sense of fear like other people because he wasn't surrounded by it like Michael was.

Since Michael felt things deeper than most people, he could sense people's fears and frustrations at an early age. This would be the source of a lot of his troubles throughout life due to his inability to deal with it correctly or use it for the right things. He literally could not even sense any fear in Jimmy like he could with others, including himself. He knew that if people could just get rid of their irrational fears, then life would become a joyous experience.

It seemed that everything changed when you got to "that" age. It was no longer cool to do these things that you enjoyed in your youth. Intolerance of others, judgment, and self-destruction became the new righteous things to do. Michael had great training with that, growing up with his foolish, drunken father. Keeping his mother drunk also allowed him to be able to severely influence all situations like some sort of self-appointed king with no flaws at all, so Michael really had no ally at home.

Michael was not allowed to express feelings aside from what was programed into society's mind as being normal. He was made to feel bad by his family for thinking outside of the box. The propaganda and lies that society was brainwashed with did not work on Michael, like it did on his parents. Michael was a growing empath with spiritual intuition, but it would be far into adulthood before he would realize that. For an empath, being denied expression of your feelings was just like torture. It was like dangling a sandwich in front of a starving child that was locked in an electrified steel cage except, in this case, the "sandwich" was love and understanding.

His father could never make time to show love and affection to anyone in the family, but he always made time for his nightly happy hour. More than half of all recovering alcoholics would say they continued their problem drinking because they were "functional." Since you had a job and home and didn't drink until after five, then there was no way you had a problem. Right. Social programming, anyone? Alcohol was another great way to control people, just ask the Rockefellers.

It was impossible for an alcoholic to show compassion and understanding to anyone or to love anything except booze. They would make sure that they always had their bottle, and to hell with everything else. One also could not love if they accepted lies. Since his father was both the fool and the drunk, he was doubly not able to love and understand anything that was not exactly like him. What a sad existence that must be. To actually think that the Creator was not capable of making something that you didn't understand or that you would not accept in your heart; that was the same as renouncing the Creator itself.

His father would bring armloads of beers into the house refrigerator every night from his stockpile reefer in the garage, dropping a couple along the way since he would heap as many as he could carry in one load. By the time high school rolled around, it was more mixed drinks than anything. He would keep his mother's wineglass full at all times as well. Michael could not ever remember his mother making her own drinks. His father would bring them to her with a smile to keep her nicely controllable. That was the thing about his father; he had to control EVERYTHING! He controlled how the garbage was disposed of, what was in the refrigerator, what meals they ate, what time they ate, what time the dogs ate, what time the watering was done, what time they slept, and the list was endless; Michael literally felt like he was living in a prison within a prison and in a make-believe reality at that.

Michael's mother went out of her way to do many little nice things for him on a regular basis. Perhaps it was a denial technique of utilizing material things to try to make things seem better, having to live under the black cloud of control of his father, or maybe she just really loved him and wanted to make him as happy as she could. Michael knew in his heart that it was the latter. She made every Christmas VERY special—not just with the gifts. She made all the traditional Norwegian treats, like lefse and *krumkake*, all with love. She did that for all the holidays as well: special care in each Easter basket, the tooth fairy never missed, Halloween dress-ups, and many a Valentine's Day card.

Michael's father did not seem to connect to him in any soulful way. It was combustible when a well-programmed fool was trying to raise a free-thinking soul on the quest for truth. That was not to say that Michael didn't learn anything from his father. Quite the contrary. He learned almost everything he knew from him, except how to love. That one was not taught or even demonstrated. Think about it, did your teacher love you? No. Michael gave his father credit though. Although there was no love, he was raised up to be completely self-sufficient and respectful.

All the good semantics of proper swear usage, Michael also learned from working around his father during his teens. He remembered once when his dad was under the car, fixing the exhaust system in the garage and Michael was helping by handing him the wrong tools as usual. Dad was in rare linguistic form that evening, so much so that it brought Mom out to investigate.

"What is all the yelling about out here?" she asked.

This was his one opportunity to swear and not get in trouble. He couldn't pass this up. Michael looked at his mom with a wicked grin and said, "Well, apparently, Mom, the piece of shit will not fit into the whore in church."

While Michael kept smiling at his mother, she looked at him as if to say, "What did you just say?" Instead, the smile grew steadily into a belly laugh that got Michael going along.

Dad peeked his head out from under the car. "What is all the goddamn laughing about?"

"Nothing, dear," his mother replied. They both stopped laughing, and she went back into the house to finish supper. His father did not like to be laughed at because nothing he ever did was wrong in the first place. He had a strong control over his mother, and she would act differently when his father was around. Michael liked to talk to her, but it had to be just the two of them. Her judgmental ways were totally controlled by his father, not her.

Michael's mother was an orphan, but she had plenty of brothers and sisters from the same parents. He always liked his mom's side of the family, but no so much his father's. This was so odd considering how much he had loved his dad's father. Mom didn't get a lot of love from her foster family, so she always gave lots of hugs and affection to Michael. He always felt loved by his mother, but much more so in his younger years before she started drinking to the level that his father did.

Both of them were very materialistic, but more so his mother. God forbid they would accidently break or scratch something, and Michael's mother would come unhinged, and if the damage was costly enough, then Michael was overwhelmed with fear of his mother. He received many a spanking over just that very thing. His father would use the belt or his hand during one of his behavioral adjustments, but his mother would use whatever was within her reach. Kitchen utensils, shoes, curling irons, and firewood kindling were her weapons of mass obsession. She got worse as the years went on, which most likely coordinated with the increasing regular intake of gin and tonic.

His father drank to intoxication every night of Michael's life. There was no reasoning with him because the only truth that existed was what his father believed to be true, which were based on the lies he had been fed his entire life. Michael would refrain from saying things that he knew his father would not agree with. His father never went to any school function that occurred at night because that was his drinking time. On the other hand, if the affair had an open bar, he would be more than happy to attend.

Michael was at an intellectual level above most people. His frustrations at home and with the world around him caused Michael to have trouble accepting the fact that he could not explain himself to anyone. His family would not get him no matter how he tried to explain himself. If he didn't have Jimmy to talk to, he wasn't sure what would happen to him. Michael always wished that there was some way for him to connect his mind to his others so they could see what he was talking about. There was a way to do that, but the common man would not have the correct control of the human potential that made that possible. His father would not listen because it was outside of his realm of comprehension, thus weird and strange, so it was unacceptable to feel that way.

His frustrations grew to the point that Michael would begin hitting himself with closed fists as hard as he could on the side of his head, very similar to outbreaks of turrets or symptoms of violent autism. No one was sure what he was trying to accomplish, maybe suicide or hopefully a stroke. He did this quite frequently, mostly when he was alone, but sometimes by accident in front of his mother or Jimmy.

In his early teens, Michael began to feel that he wanted to hurt these people that, he believed, intentionally hurt him and teased him all the time, but he would hurt himself instead because there was no way that he wanted to hurt others. The sense of injustice all around him was too much to bear sometimes. He wanted to take revenge for people not wanting to understand him and alienating him because of it. Michael even started to feel that this world was always going to be a prison for him, and he would feel more and more like that with each passing day of his life.

High school was a breeze for Michael. Math was the subject that made the most sense to him. He didn't even need the teacher when it came to math and science. It was common sense to him. Occasionally, there would be something that he needed more clarification on from the teacher, but, quite often, the teachers did not have the answers to his questions. So he would use the library or what was already embedded in his brain from birth. It was funny, but whenever his math teacher would leave the classroom, he would tell the class that if they had any questions, they should ask Michael for help while he was gone.

Michael made the mistake of beginning to help others with their schoolwork since they all began to take notice of how smart he was. It wasn't really until high school that they had needed his assistance. He thought, *Why would I want to help people that got a kick out of my nickname, Tits?* Some of them were still calling him that on in to high school.

Public school was a joke. One thing stuck out in his mind more than any other. He was in history class, and the subject they were covering that day was the assassination of JFK. The teacher was going over the lone-gunman explanation, and he started to explain the way the "magic bullet" was supposed to have travelled.

Michael raised his hand while simultaneously speaking, "Wait a minute. That is complete crap. No rational mind in the world would believe that story that a bullet just did all those miraculous moves in one single instance."

"Well, Michael," the teacher responded, "that is the conclusion that your government made after their investigation."

"Well," Michael returned, "then the government is lying to you. Do you mean to tell me that they sold this bucket of lies to the entire American public? I think people need to start asking some more questions and digging a little on their own."

"Michael, this is the history lesson in class today, and I need you to participate in a helpful manner." The teacher tried to rationalize with a much more intelligent opponent. "I can't keep having these disruptions. Remember, Michael, there is no *I* in *team*." The teacher was a basketball coach as well and was trying to use some of his bull-shit team building jargon.

"No," Michael responded without haste, "but there's a *me*."

"That's just about enough, Michael," the teacher scolded back because he knew he had been beaten. "You will go down to the principal's office and explain your theories to him."

This was nothing new to Michael. The principal's office had become like a second home to him. He was very perplexed as he walked down the hallway in the direction of the office, and his mind wandered a bit. Why was the teacher so dense as to not see the lie even if it was recorded in history texts? Why did he get so angry at him for just thinking differently? What was the government trying to cover up, and why were people going along with it? For the first time in his life, he felt like he was living a lie, a monstrous lie. Michael had always had an easy time telling when someone was lying, but this was much bigger.

The principal was a pushover as usual. Humans were easy for Michael to figure out. They actually thought they had some control over their existence. If you just appealed to their sense of self and the ego, then you could get them to go a little easy on you and maybe even help you. Actually, Michael's only crime here was not agreeing with what was being taught, and he was being punished for that. How was that freedom? Controlling the way people thought was a sign of enslavement.

That was one of the big lies of the public education system. It wasn't education at all, more like a dumbing down. Albert Einstein once said, "Education begins once one has forgotten what they were taught in school." Truer words were never spoken. Michael would learn later in life that the public education system was actually one of the key tools used by the Controllers to instill conformity and igno-rance into the masses, and it had worked very successfully.

When Michael arrived home after school that day, he already knew that news of his nonconformity had reached his parents. He sat and anxiously awaited the punishment that was to come his way after they got home. Although his father didn't physically abuse him every day, his spankings were usually quite severe and carried out after Pop had plenty of liquid hate and judgment already coursing thought his veins. This beating would be one to remember, however.

Michael was sitting in his room when he heard his father arrive home and come in through the garage. It wouldn't be much longer now. He could sense a little courage as he was awaiting what was to come. He could constantly sense his father's resentment for him and the amount of mental torment that he put him through. Corporal punishment was the result of his parents not understanding him, which created their own fears, and they simply took their denial out on him. Sometimes he could sense the battle inside his mother when he was being spanked by his father, like she was still in there and couldn't bear to watch the punishment of her misunderstood child. It was kind of like Darth Vader watching Luke being fried by the Emperor.

His father burst into Michael's room, already enraged, but he didn't have time to get his nightly load on yet. "So you think you know more than our school systems, do ya?" His father had such a foolish, ignorant tone about him. "They tell me that you could have been suspended this time." He paused and shook his head in disgust. "Michael, I have really had enough of all your questioning of things. You are going to learn to do as you are taught and told. Now turn around and drop you pants." He was pulling his belt out of the belt loops on his pants as Michael turned around as usual.

He wasn't even sobbing this time as he turned around. Michael had really had enough of his father's ignorant and baseless philoso-phies of life. If he lived the life that his father had in mind for him, then it would really be no life at all, just a prolonged death. The spankings began as usual, and Michael was able to ignore most of the pain. He wasn't sure what possessed him to say something to his father after the spankings were over, but it just kind of slipped out.

He looked back at his father, with pants still around his ankles. "Is that all you got, tough guy?"

The rage that came out of his father was like nothing he had seen before. Michael could actually feel the fear in him. He was so fearful of accepting and dealing with reality in a courageous way that he was willing to cause immense physical pain to his only son that represented that reality. A true trait of a coward. He grabbed Michael by the back of the neck and shoved his face into the bedroom wall, splitting his lip wide open. Then he tossed him backward like a rag doll against the closet door, knocking it off its track.

"No, Pop," Michael said while putting his hands up to block his approaching father. "I won't do it again. I swear. Please, please stop." Unfortunately, the pleadings did not help. His father reached down and grabbed the top of Michael's hair and pulled him to his feet. He began slapping Michael across the face until he lost consciousness.

Michael woke up on the floor of his bedroom. He was only out for a few minutes. No one was in the room with him. Although his face hurt badly, his heart hurt much worse. This man that called himself a father had just broke his heart. He sat up and leaned against the broken closet door and just sat leaning on his knees for a while. He wasn't even crying. Michael didn't think that his mother was home yet, and he was sure that his father was not going to tell her this story. He figured that he would come up with his own story.

He went out into the kitchen to wait for his mother. Michael saw his father in the TV room, watching the daily lies on the news and not even bothering to look in his direction. He wasn't even worried, like he expected Michael would cover for him. He wouldn't be wrong, but it was a shitty thing for Michael to have to see. When his mother came in, she dropped her purse on the chair and instantly noticed Michael's face.

"Michael?" She said with a gasp. "What happened to your face?"

"I got in a fight today, Mom." Michael did not hesitate with the explanation. "I am just so tired of the teasing about my weight that I finally stood up. Kids here are just so mean." He never lied, so this was a stretch for him, but he pulled it off beautifully. "I'm okay though. It looks worse than it is. More of a bruised ego."

"Well." She immediately went to get a towel to put ice in. "I'm going to fix you up." She started to put together an ice pack for him. His mother had bought the whole story, and his father never moved a muscle in his easy chair.

After the famous JFK incident of his youth, Michael realized something. Almost none of what he was being taught by the school, his parents, and the Lutheran Church that they belonged to was making any sense to him. Most of it just seemed highly improbable when he researched things on his own and applied his rational thought and discernment to the information. In school, he began to question more things in class, like the real reason behind the Civil War, the sinking of the *Titanic* and its connection to the creation of the Federal Reserve Bank, the facts of the Holocaust, the Nazi infiltration of the US government after WWII, the Roswell crash, the suppression of technologies to keep the monetary system intact, and many other hard topics.

The information that he was getting was so easy to find at the library, and it made sense. So why was everyone else not looking into these things? This very question would remain unanswered until far into his adulthood. He never could understand people. If they actually listened to the information that the nutjob on the corner was telling them, used some discernment, and compared it to the information that they were getting from the attractive people wearing expensive suits, they would see that they were being lied to. Michael always thought that it was so naive to think that wealthy Controllers had their best interests in mind.

Yeah, that was it! People achieved wealth through good Christian morals and humanitarian activities. What a crock of shit. They achieved it through deception, lies, and distraction.

As Michael's classroom inquisitions became more frequent, he noticed that other students wanted to have less and less to do with him. The intelligent, outside-the-box thinker frightened them immensely. So what did they do instead of approach him and try to learn more about what he knew? They started to spit on his back when he walked down the school hallway. Just another notch in the belt of human depravity.

Since he couldn't see behind him, this could have been going on for weeks before he noticed. Jimmy was the one that pointed it out to him one day. "What's that on the back of your coat, Michael?"

Michael took off his jacket to have a look. There was a nice long slimy loogie that had made its way down from the top of the back of his coat, leaving a little slug-like saliva trail down to its final crusty resting place on one of the jacket folds near the waist.

"You have to be shitting me." He wiped of the hardened ball of phlegm and went over to the drinking fountain to wash off the dried spit with Jimmy in tow. "I really don't get this place, Jimmy. I only want to be nice and make friends, but humans are just so shitty to each other all the time. I am not going to say much around anyone anymore, just you. As long as I have you, then life is tolerable." He put his coat on and turned around to look at Jimmy.

Jimmy had a little tear in his eye and was looking around to make sure none of the other kids could see it. "I know, Mikey. Don't worry, I'll always be here for you. I love you." He made sure to say it in a low enough voice to not be heard. "Not in a fag way." They both smiled. "You are genuinely a good soul, and I feel good for knowing that. If we weren't at school, I'd give you a hug." They both smiled big and shook hands instead; that would be all Jimmy would ever say about how he felt about Michael.

Michael's life went on like that for the rest of his childhood years. He started to become reclusive at a young age, but he still had his one good friend through it all. Jimmy meant the world to him. Michael normally did not want other kids around at night during his parents' happy hours, but Jimmy seemed to understand it and just ignored it. Even in the saddest of situations, Michael was able to find some humor along the way no matter how gross. His father's bathroom breaks became rather legendary. Combining poor diet with more than generous amounts of alcohol was an explosive situation for any colon.

His parent's living room sat at one end of a long hall that ended with the main bathroom in the house. Acoustically, it could carry any sound down the hall and amplify it along the way to be enjoyed by all sitting comfortably in the living room. The closed door and fan would provide very little in the area of a muffling effect. Michael and Jimmy could always hear when his father was making a mad dash for the shitter and would grin at one another.

Within seconds of the bathroom door closing, a large deep reverberating toilet bowl sound could be heard. The echoing sound would seep out from the gap between the seat and the bowl. The two could literally hear the explosive spray coating the inside of the toilet bowl, and the sound would come in waves. It was almost like someone was trying to get the last bit of ketchup out of a two gallon bottle. The sound was literally stomach turning, and to these two sick senses of humor, absolutely hilarious. With the sound of the fan, which did little to help the odor, his father could never hear them laughing at the sheer grossness of this nightly chore. Sometimes Michael would raise up his finger like he was an orchestra conductor to the timing of his father's spastic colon. They would laugh so hard that sometimes they had to go outside to finish before his father would emerge so they could straighten up.

Michael did need other ways to battle loneliness other than his time spent with Jimmy. He liked books and movies, provided they were intelligent and thought provoking. He did like a good zany comedy or a spoof to lighten the load as well. Books helped him learn real truth about this world, and movies helped him to escape it. He also had a great memory, once again, provided the material was worth remembering. If a movie scene or a book quote hit home with him, then Michael would remember it for the rest of his life. People were amazed at how he could pull a movie scene out of his memory bank to fit almost any situation, and as he got older and had seen many more films, it became second nature for him.

In high school, it was no longer BMX bikes but dirt bikes that occupied Michael and Jimmy's spare time. Everyone had to have a YZ, which was made by Yamaha. It didn't really matter as long as it had those yellow stickers on it to let people know you were part of the "in" crowd. Michael and Jimmy were no different, except their parents were a little more frugal. They had to work for their own money to buy the bikes, but that was how it should be really.

Michael enjoyed dirt bike riding and racing, but Jimmy REALLY liked dirt bike riding and racing, so much so that he grew very confident on that bike of his. Jimmy would race with the local motor heads and fuel-injected rednecks, who seemed to look at death and say, "Kiss my sunburned ass!" Looney, some of them. It might go without saying, but some of them died at early ages; at least they died with a smile doing something that they loved to do.

It was a warm spring morning just ripe for a good ride, and the orchard flats in town would have plenty of fresh mud to play in. Jimmy was on his porch at the crack of dawn, just hammering the doorbell. His mother was not pleased, but she could see they were so excited to get the dirt bikes muddy. They could ride their bikes on the back roads and cross all the county and state roads to get to there. The orchard flats were on the cliffs above town, and Michael and Jimmy had ridden to the area many times. The two took off after breakfast; they couldn't go without fueling up the body first. Jimmy always led the way. Obviously, he was the more confident of the two, but today confidence would cross the line of stupidity.

Muddy was the word for it. They got out above the cliffs shortly before noon. The mud was thick but nothing that they hadn't ridden in before. They just played around in the mud for hours until they were sufficiently brown, and there was no way you were going to recognize any yellow stickers, let alone what brand of bikes they even were. They looked out over the muddy flats and saw all the tire prints, mud piles from spill-outs, and general splatter everywhere and realized that they had accomplished their goal. Jimmy looked at Michael and smiled. He had one more thing that he wanted to do before they left.

Jimmy always liked to run his bike toward the edge of the cliff and then turn around before he would get too close. He would try to see if he could get just a little bit closer each time. This was not a test of bravery that Michael liked to watch. In fact, he had asked Jimmy many times if he could just stop doing that because he could only push it so long. Jimmy's smile was just a little bit different today, and Michael had a sudden sink in his stomach.

Jimmy gave a wink and then spun his bike around in the mud like a top and headed for the cliffs. Michael started out after him to watch the brave feat as usual, but he could feel that overwhelming sense of fear growing in his stomach. They didn't come up here very often to ride, so when they did, Jimmy wanted to make the most of it. Jimmy was getting closer and closer to the cliff, and he had not turned around yet. Michael never thought of him as suicidal or even reckless. Jimmy had always turned around plenty early before. It was just the concept that thrilled him so much. Closer and closer, and the bike was showing no signs of deceleration or altering course.

"Jimmy, what are you doing?" Michael screamed. "Dump it, for Christ's sake!"

The sound of his own voice echoed repeatedly in his head as he watched his only friend in the world sail off the cliffs.

"JIIIIMMYYYY!" Michael yelled so loud that he thought he ripped his vocal cords.

The bike fell away from Jimmy, and Michael could see him flailing in midair like he was trying to grab for something in a panic. Michael dumped his bike and started running while still leaping off the bike about twenty feet from the edge of the cliff.

He kept telling himself. *Don't watch him land. Don't watch him land. Don't watch him land ...*

Too late. Jimmy's body seemed to bounce in a pink mist, recoil up about ten feet, and then land the second time without any movement. Michael reached the edge of the cliff just in time to see the first landing, but on the second drop, he saw something different. This was to be the first time he would encounter the spiritual side of humanity. He always knew that it was there, but now he saw it.

Michael watched as Jimmy's soul rose up from out of his body and come up to eye level with him while levitating up from the cliff. Jimmy held out a finger as if to say, "Wait just a second." And then he was gone. Michael thought, *What did he mean by that?* Would he ever know? Deep within him, he could feel Jimmy's energy fading out of his connection. He was gone.

All was quiet except for the "NOOOOO!" Michael yelled as he hit his knees on the edge of the cliff and buried his head in his hands, not wanting to look any further. He figured if he hid his eyes long enough, then he would realize that this was all a dream and he would wake up somewhere else. He did not.

Michael let his hands down and stared down the two hundred feet to Jimmy's lifeless body. It was very blurry through all the tears. He wiped his eyes, and he could get a clearer picture. Jimmy's head was sideways on the flat granite rock in a large pool of crimson blood with his mouth closed. His eyes seemed shut. At least they appeared to be at this distance. Jimmy looked like he was peacefully asleep on his stomach. That is the way that Michael would forever remember Jimmy, although it would take years to deal with the night terrors and insomnia that would develop from this incident. He walked back to his brown YZ100 and began the slow ride home to let everyone know and regain his composure along the way. He was in no hurry, Jimmy was dead, and speeding home would not change that.

Michael did not talk to many people during the remaining months before high school graduation. People left him alone and figured that he would come around in his own time. The investigation of the accident had turned up that a small rock that had wedged in between the throttle wire and the housing causing it to stick open. The pebble had most likely come from the mud on the bike. The incident was officially ruled an accident due to mechanical failure.

Why didn't he dump it? He was good on that thing. It just doesn't make sense. Michael would keep up at the constant questioning of the accident for years to come.

About three weeks before high school graduation, the Navy recruiter came to the high school. All the students had already taken the ASVAB military aptitude test, and Michael had received a perfect score. He was actually summoned by the principal's office to meet with him. Michael sat down in front of the recruiter, who was just smiling at him with such great happiness.

"Mr. Stevens, my name is Petty Officer Jennings," the recruiter said. "We see here that you received a perfect score on the ASVAB and your high school records in math and science are exceptional.

You are a perfect candidate for our Nuclear Power Program. Have you ever considered a career in the Navy?"

"No, sir," Michael replied. "This is really the first I am hearing about it. I would wager a guess that my intelligence is valuable to the government for some noble cause." Michael had become skilled in the art of sarcasm. "I do know a few things about nuclear physics, but I am not a big fan of war and conflict."

Michael remembered a report that he had done in middle school about Fat Man and Little Boy, the two bombs that were dropped on Hiroshima and Nagasaki. During his research on that project, he was sickened by what had been done to those unsuspecting people and how an entire nation thought it was just a wonderful act of heroism. Nothing could be further from the truth. What was even more shocking was that he had found out the Japan had already surrendered before the bombs were ever dropped. Truman just wanted to show the world the power possessed by the secret cabal that was now in charge of the world. Deplorable, so much so that the crew of the *Enola Gay* had committed suicide because they could not live with the truth.

"Yes, it is," the recruiter said with a half crooked smile. "Your principal tells us that you are quite the brain but do have a slight problem with authority."

"You might say that," Michael said with a grin. "I have never liked the military much." *I have not applied for any scholarships and could use the GI Bill money*, Michael thought, and then he asked the recruiter, "Anyway, what are my commitments if I sign up?"

"You would have to commit to two years of training and four years of service after, for a total of six years," Petty Officer Jennings rattled off like a policy manual. "The nuclear program does offer substantial reenlistment bonuses that can be as much as $20,000."

Michael was sure that this was a big sales point to get people in the service, but he didn't really care. He just knew that this was the only way he was going to make it to college someday and had no intention of making a career out of the military.

He decided to sign up for the Navy. If anything, he would get away from his father immediately after high school, and he would leave in early July following graduation for basic training. Michael really needed to get out of this town too. There were too many bad memories, but he would manage to make more. His best friend was gone, and his family was no consolation prize. Michael had an overwhelming feeling of fear that would not go away during the final weeks before he was scheduled to leave. He knew that he had some special psychic gifts, but he was not sure what he was supposed to do with them yet or what Jimmy had been trying to tell him in the end. Michael was alienated by his family, as usual, and he spent most of the time between graduation and leaving for the Navy in his room or out driving the back country roads.

He thought about Jimmy and the real friendship that they had. He never judged Michael like his family, and other acquaintances did. Michael would never feel loved by his family unless he was just what they thought he should be. He was getting ready to go out into the world for the first time in his life, and he truly felt alone. There really was no one he could truly talk to anymore, and he hoped to find another friend like Jimmy someday.

Michael boarded the plane while waving back at his family. His father would most likely have not been there in support unless it was something like going away to the military. In a way, Michael was glad to be leaving behind this part of his life. He was sobbing a bit, but he really was not going to miss them all that much. Thoughts of Jimmy were fresh in his mind. They only put him to rest three months ago. The world was all in front of him now, but was it a world that he could be in? As the plane taxied out, he now had no choice but to find out.

SERVING THE MACHINE

I don't want to be involved in their violence, I prefer to live in peace.

—John Lennon

There was nothing quite like the feeling of stepping off an air-conditioned plane onto a jet way in Orlando, Florida, in early July, especially when you are from a northern country town that has four distinct seasons. Michael's body broke the plane of the door and the jet way, and he felt the first rush of over-ninety temperature and humidity, both.

He turned to Butch and said, "If they think I am running and exercising in this shit, then they can kiss my ass."

Butch just shook his head with a smile and replied, "Yeah, they warned us at MEPS Center that we would be shocked by the heat and humidity down here."

Michael had met Butch at the MEPS center in Spokane while going through all the hurry-up and wait involved with joining the military, signing away your freedoms so you could go fight for them. Butch was from a small town in Idaho called Weizer. That name always seemed so funny to Michael, like did the entire town have emphysema or something? Michael usually knew if he would match with someone based on an intuition he would get. He had gained some use of psychic forethought about people by now in his life, but it was only slowly developing over the years.

Michael had just been standing in the same line, waiting for internal processing, when he felt a surge of positive energy from the man in front of him. Michael tapped his shoulder in hopes of making a new friend in this strange environment.

"Hey, my name is Michael," he said with and extended hand and smile, and the man turned to greet him in the same fashion.

"Butch, from Idaho," he replied in kind.

Michael, always wanting to figure out someone's sense of humor from the start, asked him, "Butch, that's not short for anything like Butchathan or Butchibald, is it?" Michael giggled as he asked.

Butch smiled playfully. "No, it's not, smart ass." They liked each other instantly.

Butch was simple, like Michael. He wanted to do something with his life but was never quite sure what. Michael, coming from a family that constantly worried about the future instead of living in the now, was always thinking about a career and making money at that time in his life. But that would change in a drastic way someday. Butch worked hard and valued his freedom as well. Not just the "Ra! Ra! Go, America!" kind of freedom, but the "choose how you want to live for yourself" kind of freedom. Michael felt the same way.

Butch and Michael were in the same company in boot camp. Michael, having the brains, was immediately selected as the education petty officer, or EPO. He was honored with the tasks of helping all the barely educated trustees of modern chemistry that were created in some lab in the middle of a Louisiana swamp somewhere to pass the ASVAB test before the end of boot camp. It was ten weeks to teaching basic education to someone who could not read, write, or think at all, but they could shoot a gun very well and might have some moral flexibility, which was all the military really needed. Michael, having this position that he did, was given a bunk near the common area and was able to request Butch as his bunkmate.

Basic training was a cinch for both of them. They just had to do what you were told and keep their mouth shut. For the simple-minded, boot camp was plain and simple brainwashing, but for the more rationally minded and intelligent, it didn't sink in so well. Michael found some of the drill instructor's tactics to be a bit laughable, but he was always able to contain his smile. Butch, on the other hand, made that mistake once and let out a brief chuckle.

Most people who had been in the military were familiar with what a blanket party was. The only time that it had ever been shown was in the movie *Full Metal Jacket*. It shocked the world with its cruelty. Basically, you singled out the weakest, dumbest, pain in the ass that caused the drill instructor to punish the entire platoon one too many times, and you beat him half to death with a bar of soap wrapped in the bottom of one of your socks while two people hold a blanket down over him so he could not move. This procedure was no longer allowed by the time Michael and Butch entered the service, but it still went on quietly. These were the same men who wrote home to Mom about the family dog and biscuits and gravy while a poor man sobbed in his sleep for the rest of the night due to the unending pain from all the bruises on his body and ribcage, a man who had a heart of gold and really didn't want to hurt anyone but was forced into this world of insanity because he had nowhere else to go.

The chuckle that Butch let out didn't lead to any blanket party; instead the drill instructors decided to make an example of him in what was called a lounge party. Boot camps of yesterday used to allow smoking, and there was still a smoking lounge in all the barracks. This room had the only locking door in the barracks other than the drill instructor's quarters. This lounge now served a new purpose. This was where the DIs would take a singled-out smart ass and personally exercised them for hours with the door shut, but you could hear enough. That was the point. Michael was sure of it. Conformity through the use of pain—it was the oldest control means known to man.

Butch would tell Michael later that he simply couldn't help it. It sort of just slipped out with a temporary loss of reason. But slip it did nonetheless. The DI came right up to Butch just like Lou Gossett in *An Officer and a Gentlemen*. "You got a problem, smart ass?"

"No, sir," Butch cried back without pause.

"You do now," the DI said with a sadistic smile. "Into the lounge, boy. We're gonna see just how much water the body holds."

The end prize for each lucky lounge party contestant was that you would be allowed to leave once the DI was properly satisfied and there was a large enough pool of your sweat on the floor in front of you.

So into the lounge Butch went with the DI. They always pulled the shades after they got in; it seemed to add a little more fear energy to the rest of the group. This was the first time that Michael would realize he had empathic abilities. He suddenly could feel some of Butch's fear. He got a ball in his own stomach like he was about to face the lounge party himself. During the entire time that Butch was in that room, Michael had a sick feeling in his stomach that he almost threw up all the fine Navy ochre that he had consumed in the past week. He had no idea why he felt that way, but he was as relieved when Butch emerged from the lounge.

He had no expression on his face. The skin just seemed to hang from the corners of his mouth with a combination of drool, sweat, and most likely, tears hanging from all over his face in a kind of suspended animation. His hair was a matted sweat-soaked work of art that would make Harry Carey jealous. Butch's eye just moved to meet Michael's without any movement of his face whatsoever. Michael could literally feel the relief that Butch did, that it was finally over.

Butch looked back toward the ground and shuffled to his bunk. Butch had the top bunk, and he just laid his head sideways as if he would sleep standing up. Michael and couple of nearby fellows helped him up to his bunk very gently as the rest of the company looked on in complete silence. Butch let out a sigh of relief and closed his eyes for what would be sixteen hours or so. The DIs left him in his bunk for the rest of the day while the company went about its daily routines. Butch was back in formation at morning muster without much expression on his face at all. One thing was for sure—he was not laughing.

About halfway through basic training, all sailors in training were assigned to a job for the week. It was called work week. There was never too much thought that went into the way the military labelled things. Most everyone was sent to work in the galley since that was where most of the work was needed. The galley crew changed every week as a different company would rotate into their work week.

Michael, being more intelligent and an active participant in the education of other sailors, was given duty in the medical center, which was usually where they sent the smartest trainees. This was a cake walk when compared to having to work in the disgusting, greasy Navy galley—full of okra and mystery meat. His job was to check people in that came in for medical treatment and start a medical file on each one. Things were just dandy for few days; it was a break in the normal basic training routine for Michael up until the third day he was there.

Things were slow at the medical center during the middle of the week. Most sailors who would come to the center were looking for a way out of boot camp, and usually a medical discharge was their best bet. Michael met lots of sailors who were trying to get out during the week. Only about 10 percent of them were genuine cases. The rest were mostly being faked, and Michael could always tell when they were lying, but he wouldn't say anything because no one would believe him anyway.

He had been there for a few hours that day when the shore patrol brought in a sailor and sat him down in a waiting chair directly in front of the check-in window that Michael was stationed at. The SPOs said nothing to Michael. They told the sailor to sit and that he would be attended to shortly, and then they left him there. No one else was around. It was just this kid sitting there with head hung low and Michael looking at him as he sat there.

Michael looked down at the floor, and he could see fresh-blood droplets falling and beginning to pool up on the ground. He then glanced up to this kid's hands, which were dangling between his knees. He had ACE bandages wrapped around both wrists, which were both soaked through with blood. The droplets were falling from the saturated bandages onto the ground in front of him. Michael was shocked as he realized that this was an attempted suicide sitting right in front of him and no one was even paying the kid any mind.

He looked over at this kid, who was just hanging his head, and got the sense that he really did want to die, that this was not just some attempt to get out of boot camp.

"Are you okay?" he asked the kid, but there was no response.

The pool of blood on the floor was growing, and this did not seem like everything was okay. The officers that placed him there couldn't have cared less about him, just more proof to Michael that humanity was truly a compassionless sewer. That was something that he could see his father doing—leaving this kid to die.

Michael left his post to try to find a doctor, which he did in a matter of a few minutes. He got the doctor to come over and tend to this kid. The shore patrol would have just let him sit there and bleed to death, and this kid really would not have had a problem with that. The doctor finally took the kid away, and it was Michael's duty to clean up the bloody floor that he left behind.

The entire incident did not sit well with Michael. He had deep feelings and compassion for the suffering. The complete lack of any kind of feeling from the SPOs just sickened him. The feeling of despair that was emanating from the kid was very overwhelming for him, but he completely understood. Michael had the same feelings of despair throughout most of his life, but he had not contemplated suicide up to this point in his life. But life had more in store for young Michael.

After boot camp, Michael was already preselected to go into the Nuclear Power Program, and he was excited to get there. Butch, not being quite the mathematician, but great with mechanics, was selected for aviation maintenance. Butch and Michael were to be separated after basic training. Butch had school in Pensacola, whereas Michael would be in Orlando. This made it nice, because they would not be too far away to meet at the beach on the weekends or contiguous liberty periods. Their favorite beach was always Daytona. It was a little bit more of a drive for Butch, but it was worth it. For them, everything culminated on the beach. All the bullshit and military rigor would not matter once they got in that ocean.

Daytona Beach was great because it was a wide beach that had a two-lane road, basically running right down the middle of it. Butch and Michael would both meet their first real girlfriends at the same time. It was an interesting experience, being a broke sailor and having to share a hotel room with three other people. They decided to share the room time when they wanted to have sex. Nothing worse than having to accidently see your best friend ball deep in some chick. It was just a matter of making sure the DND sign was on the door. The problem was that they were all in the room at night at the same time, and inevitably sex would be going on. Michael noticed that if they were both having sex at the same time, then they really couldn't hear the other. They were both careful not to be too rude about it, and the girls usually were too, which made it nice, except there was that goddamn screamer that Butch brought back once. But that was a long crazy story to have to relive.

Michael didn't realize it, but during the first year of his military years, he was forming a tight spiritual bond with Butch, like he had with Jimmy. After what happened to him when Jimmy died, he did not want to get too close to anyone, but he was connected to Butch in a way that was stronger than Jimmy. He felt very comfortable around him, and he decided to let him into his spiritual circle. It felt really good to have a close human connection again.

Life was very confusing for an unrealized empath. Depending on your level of recognition of the potential, it could make life in society very challenging. Michael's powers, like most empaths, would continue to grow throughout his life, but so would his ability to control and recognize it. As an empath grew to understand the human condition, they also must realize that society was set up so that they would never realize their true potential. They could even lose it all if they were not careful or have external help.

Michael would notice the psychic connection on the beach one weekend in particular. Butch had broken up with his girlfriend the week before and was in a reckless kind of mood. Michael had separated from his girlfriend months ago, so he understood. Butch took to drinking a little more than usual and decided it was time to swim in the ocean. At certain times of the year, the riptide could be more extreme than at others. The riptide was what drew the waves back into the ocean and could trap you under the water unless you knew how to get out of them. The best way out was to not fight it and let it pull you out while simultaneously swimming sideways to get out of the tidal flow.

Butch might have been a little too inebriated to remember how to escape a riptide, or he might have been trying to end it since his break-up. Who knew? Butch disappeared in the ocean, and Michael didn't pay much attention since Butch was a first-class swimmer—not quite as good as Michael, but close. It wasn't more than a couple of minutes that went by when Michael started to develop a strange feeling of extreme panic. Butch had gotten himself caught in a riptide and was trying to fight it. Panic and drunkenness were a disastrous combination. He looked out over the water and could see no sign of Butch. Michael's panicky feeling deepened, and he started to get a little dizzy and light-headed. Butch was obviously in trouble, and Michael not only knew it; he actually felt like he was there.

Swim parallel to the tide, Michael thought hard in his head.

He thought that maybe he could get through to Butch with his thoughts. Why would he think that? All his life, he was taught to believe nothing like this was possible.

Swim parallel until the regular tide brings you back in.

Was Butch hearing him? Was he going to die? Should Michael go get help? Then Butch's head appeared on the crest of an incoming wave. Relief! Michael could feel how dog tired he was while fighting that current and trying to paddle into shore, but he was managing nonetheless.

Butch finally made it to shore and crawled the remaining twenty feet to be out of the tide path. He collapsed face first in the sand. Butch turned his head sideways to see the sideways view of Michael running toward him, and he could feel the sand in his ear. Oh well.

"You are one sorry sack of shit there, dumb ass," he heard Michael say above him. Michael sat there next to him in the sand for a few minutes and let Butch gain his composure before he said anything else. "Hey, Butch?" he asked.

"Yeah, Mikey." Butch responded while still spitting large wads of water and saliva out of his mouth. He was a little embarrassed to say the least.

"I know this sounds weird"—Michael had to find out—"but could you feel anything when you were out there that helped guide you to safety?"

"What? What are you talking about?" Butch asked, confused, as he sat up a little better to face Michael.

"Just go with me on this," Michael said. "I really need to know if you had a thought as to how to get out of the riptide. Did you feel as if a thought popped in your head to swim away, parallel to the tide?"

"Actually," Butch said, "now that you mention it, I did have a thought as to what to do. I just went with it, and out I came. Why? What does it matter now?"

"It doesn't," Michael said. "I was just curious. I read somewhere that people in life or death situations tend to get intuition as to what may help them if they listen for it."

"Yeah, maybe, I guess," Butch agreed. "Let's go back to the hotel. I could use a nap."

Michael stood up and helped Butch up from the sand, and they started the long walk back to the room. There was really no room in Daytona Beach that was any closer than another to anything. Michael had never let Butch in on the empath powers that he had. He was sure, after this incident, he was honing in on how to use his gift. It was apparent that he had to have some sort of connection to the person and level of concentration for it to work. They arrived back at the room, and Butch wasted no time getting into the bed. He was out in a matter of seconds, and Michael decided to go walk on the beach for a while and do some thinking.

It was quite obvious now that he had a special gift. It was not overpowering, but it was a gift nonetheless. Michael was not sure what it was, but he knew he had what they called psychic abilities. It was only the close-minded and uninspired that had to label things that were actually just unrealized or suppressed human potential. He knew that we must all be tied to it somehow; otherwise, how would he feel his friend's panic and pain? He was sure that we all gave it off but only the developed ones could pick it up.

Michael continued on down the beach until he just felt like turning back, and he realized he had walked probably five miles or so. He thought about everything he had felt while he was younger and still developing, the times when he might have felt someone else's pain and fears. There were many little examples that had the possibility, but other than when he could feel Jimmy, nothing seemed too extreme. Michael got back to the hotel and had been gone for several hours. When he opened the door to the room, Butch stirred out of his sleep. Apparently, he had been asleep the entire time.

After they finished training, they were lucky enough to both get sent to the same city for duty—beautiful San Diego. They had both requested and received the USS *Enterprise*. Michael would be bound to the engine room, while Butch got to be up on the flight deck, where all the action took place. Michael didn't mind it so much; the military consisted of a lot of routine. They didn't want thinkers, only androids. He could turn his mind down and perform the mundane tasks that were required, which did give him time to think when he was alone on watch. Ironic how his ability to use his brain got him noticed by the military, and now he was never encouraged to ask questions or create anything new.

He never felt right in the Navy. Something was really amiss. The feelings he would get were constantly coming in cyclic waves, almost like he was part of an evil machine. He couldn't quite put his finger on it, but it didn't feel like he was on the right path in his life. He didn't belong in the military. He just knew it had been a mistake to join. All warfare of any kind was murder, and he was now serving the very beast in that.

After Michael had been shipboard a while, he was promoted to first-class petty officer and put in charge of the tools that were stored in the equipment room. It was a cushy job, but somewhat boring. There was one thing about having time to think, but it was another to have your mind spin in circles of sheer boredom.

One morning, a shipment of tools arrived at the equipment room, and Michael logged it in as per usual military protocol. It was early during the morning watch, and not many sailors were around. Michael stared at the box and wondered what new tools they received that day. It was usually the senior chief's job to check in the new tools, but Michael was bored and needed something to do. He grabbed a box cutter and proceeded to open the box. There was a large wad of bubble wrap on top, which Michael set aside to have fun with later. He removed the bill of lading on top and set it aside.

In the bottom of the box was a miscellaneous selection of wrenches, screwdrivers, hammers, and pliers. It just seemed like your basic fair of garage sale tools, nothing like he really expected to find.

"Hmmm," he mumbled to himself. "Wonder what they actually ordered?" He grabbed the bill of lading that he had set aside to see what was supposed to be in the shipment.

Michael simply could not believe what he was seeing. "This can't be right," he said with a puzzled look on his face. The bill of lading seemed to list all the items that were in the box, but the prices were enormous. Hammers were $400, and a pipe wrench was over $1,000. Everything else was also about twenty times more cost than it should be.

"What the fu—" Michael started to question but was cut off by a voice behind him.

"What are you doing, Petty Officer Stevens?" Senior Chief Simmons was bellowing behind him as he glared down at Michael kneeling over the box on the ground. "You're not supposed to be in that. I could have you court-martialed for that."

"But, Senior Chief, what is with this packaging list? Have you seen the prices for all the pieces of shit that are actually in the box?" Michael stood up and asked while showing Senior Chief Simmons the sheet of paper.

He snatched the form out of Michael's hand without haste. "Yes, I have, but you never have. Do you understand that?" The senior chief looked at Michael with a concerned look in his eye.

"I think so," Michael said with a grimace. He slowly turned back toward his desk in the equipment room and went back to working on the maintenance logs like nothing had happened. He got the feeling that he did not want to aggravate the situation any more than it already was.

The senior chief bent down and picked up the box and brought it over to Michael's desk, like the conversation the two had a second ago did not occur. "You will need to check these new tools in as well."

They were hardly new tools. They looked like something you would find when cleaning out a barn or an old septic cistern.

Michael started to get one of his feelings. He just knew something was sinister about this box of tools that he had opened by mistake. What was the military up to? What were they accomplishing by doing this? He picked up one of the wrenches in the box, and he had a flash of large groups of Chinese children, guerilla warfare, and widespread drug abuse with loads of money showering down on the fat cat Controllers. He dropped the wrench back in the box and took a fast, deep breath as the visions went away.

"You all right, Michael?" the senior chief asked as he heard the clang from Michael dropping the wrench back in the box.

"Yeah, it's nothing," Michael exaggerated. "I just had a cramp in my arm." He grabbed his arm liked it was hurting and stared down into this box, this box of lies. He just knew, and he could not explain why, but the military must be using this fake tool invoicing as a way to launder money from the smuggling of children, weapons, and drugs for the Controllers running the government. It wasn't just some nutty conspiracy; it was true. Michael just saw some of the most hideous awful visions of human deprivation that he had ever seen in his life and he really did not care to see them again. Michael hid the box of tools by a feed booster pump where no one would find them. There was no way he was about to touch another one of those tools.

Of course, he knew that he couldn't tell anybody about this. People thought he was looney enough already. Truth had a way of driving people away. They would rather stay comfortable, living their lives just the way they were. Mark Twain knew it when he said, "It is easier to fool people than to convince them they have been fooled." Michael would find that to be the case for the rest of his life. He watched an entire nation of fools follow even bigger ones. Continuing to put their faith in evil men that constantly lied over and over and over again and expecting that something would change. But it never ever, ever does. Insanity. He was not crazy, but this world was; and he could find the facts in all facets of society, but he could never find anyone that would listen.

Michael just put this encounter in his memory bank for storage, as he did with all the rest. After he turned twenty-one, while still in the Navy, he began drinking. Something that he never thought he would do, since he had despised his father's alcoholism so much. It just was the thing to do with everyone, and he had a good time, at first. He also noticed that when he would drink, some of his ability to feel others would dissipate, and that was the biggest relief of all. He wanted to keep his abilities to himself and not share it with people, but after he juiced himself up with some liquor, things would occasionally leak out. Since the subject matter was so unbelievable to most people, Michael would gain and lose friends quite frequently.

Even though he started to notice how some people would start to avoid him after a night of tying one on, Michael continued to drink because the relief from feeling others' pain was worth the loss of friends. It was good that there was no drinking allowed while on board ship, but Michael would have plenty of opportunity to start down the wrong path appropriately. His introversion and loneliness started to set in while on board the ship. When he was not on duty, Michael usually kept to himself and read all sorts of different things about many subjects during his isolation. He liked the truth of Thoreau, Emerson, Twain, and Mencken. Intelligent fiction was always mixed with his nonfictional research reading.

Then came that fateful July day in the summer of 1991, during the Desert Storm War. The *Enterprise* was making her preparations to head to the Middle East. They were fifty miles off the coast of Mexico running drills to prepare for the conflict. Between the drills there were always down periods where the crew could go about their normal routines. It was during a twenty-four-hour alert stand down that Butch thought he might be able to get Michael up to the flight deck for his first tour of the active floating airport. Michael had never seen the flight deck while at sea and was so anxious to get up top. Butch got the clearance from the air boss, and Michael would be able to come up during the afternoon while running daily touch-and-go drills, which were always exciting. The planes would come in and touch their wheels to the carrier deck before engaging afterburners and taking off again. Michael had never seen this live, only on video.

Michael arrived at the topside clearance area. No loose items were allowed on the flight deck. The jet intakes could suck almost anything in, tools especially. Every aviation mechanic had to verify all his tools before entering the flight deck to perform repairs and before returning the tools to the tool deck. If you are missing any tools, all flight operations would be suspended until it was found. If the mechanic has any ass left after the air boss chewed it all off, then he could go look for the missing tool. Michael had another acquaintance that had that very thing happen. It was not fun for him to say the least. He left everything that was in his pockets in the basket.

Michael was cleared, and he took the elevator up to the flight deck. When the elevator door opened, there was Butch waiting with all smiles. He handed Michael large Mickey Mouse ear protectors to put on. It had been extremely loud when the door opened, and those ear protectors really worked well. He could hardly hear anything, but he could feel plenty of vibration in his chest. It was such a rush to finally be up there that he just couldn't believe it.

The A6 Intruders would be doing "touch and gos" for the next several hours, so it should be a good show. Michael was, of course, hoping to watch the F14s practice (who wouldn't?), but he always liked the A6s. It was a very fast and maneuverable aircraft, and the refuel nozzle on the front always seemed cool to him. He even like the shitty Hollywood movie that was made about it. Even great actors like Danny Glover make bad script choices from time to time.

Butch gave him some of the lowdown about the flight deck through radio speakers in his ear protection. Michael's set did not have the microphone to speak into to respond. He just had to listen to him with the occasional buddy communication that could be achieved with basic hand signals. The air boss had given Butch special clearance to escort Michael around since Butch had a great fitness report—a squared-away sailor, as the squids said. They had a little saying among their little group: "Only the squared away get to play."

When they walked out onto the open flight deck, the smell of jet fumes sprinkled with ocean air was almost overpowering. Touch and go operations use a lot of fuel and thus quite a bit of exhaust is generated all at once during takeoff. Most air crew on the deck wore a modified version of a gas mask to filter out some of the exhaust fumes, but it was not really life-threatening unless you were breathing nothing but that shit. Michael could also feel the thunderous power of the jet noise in his chest. He thought that it would be a little spooky if he did not have a guide that knew what they were doing.

Simply awesome was the only way to put it. Michael had always wanted to fly, and this fueled the desire even more so. Some emergency planes were kept on the flight deck on standby all the time, but most of the aircraft were stored on the deck immediately below the flight deck. A very large elevator would transport them up and down as needed. A good majority of the steam that was generated in the engine room where Michael worked was used to propel the catapults that flung the craft off the carrier like a giant slingshot. He loved watching that giant puff of steam surround the deck hands as the jets took off.

The flight deck was so enormous that to believe that this all floated on the water became unreal. Michael noticed eyelets all along the deck with hooking points recessed in them. He knew that these were used to secure the planes to the deck when an unexpected storm or high seas came up so they did not go overboard. Seemed like a good idea. The eyelets had to be kept clear at all times and could never be allowed to freeze up in cold climates.

Michael could hear the whine of an A6 coming in. It dropped right down on the deck in front of him. Almost as soon as the wheels touched, the engine came alive with a thunderous roar, and off it went again. Touch and go. Then another came right behind it.

Follow the leader, right? Michael was in heaven. Although every piece of equipment he was looking at was for the purposes of killing another human being, it was something to see.

Butch took Michael closer to the action but far enough away so they weren't in the way of anything. A lot of moving around and pandemonium on deck, but it was all very coordinated. They walked up to one of the A6s awaiting cue into the training pattern. Butch waved at the pilot in the cockpit with some signals that Michael did not know. He imagined that he was letting him know that he was showing a visitor the plane and didn't fire the engines yet. Butch got the signal that he wanted, and they walked up to the plane.

Michael put his hand on the side like he was feeling a special kind of fabric. Wow, he was touching an actual A6, the deliverer of napalm in Vietnam. Why did this tool of death and suffering thrill him so much? Was it the power? Was it the size? Who knew? But it was a thrill for him, nonetheless.

Butch got another signal from the pilot and tapped Michael on the shoulder. He gestured that they needed to get back, that the pilot was coming up in his turn. The sound of the engines firing up was just incredible. The gentle hum that slowly grew and turned to a whine. Then finally a larger popping sound as the turbines fired up, like the loudest propane stove you had ever heard or felt for that matter. The pilot taxied out into the catapult area. Sometimes additional planes were added to the touch-and-go practice as one came in, but it was not a general rule to have a replacement unless there was a problem.

Another plane came in and was exiting the drills. His tail hook caught the oversized rubber band, and to a stop he came. The crew removed the band from the tail hook, and the plane taxied toward the elevator. Butch tapped Michael and pointed toward the elevator. They were walking alongside the incoming A6 as it taxied its way along. The Intruder stopped at a designated line to wait for the elevator, and Michael and Butch were just off to the rear corner of the plane. Michael could feel the heat from the turbines. He stopped, but Butch kept going toward the front of the plane.

The Intruder engines were still running as Butch approached the front. The intake for the engines on an A6 was directly under the nose cone. Michael waved at him, but he couldn't see him, and Michael did not have a microphone to speak to him. He wasn't sure if Butch knew that the pilot had not shut down the engines or had stopped the plane. No one really knew why Butch did what he did, but as he approached the front of the plane, he was leaning in like he wanted to point something out to Michael, and then in an instant, he was gone. If Michael blinked, he would have missed it.

The intake of the A6 drew Butch in as if his body was no thicker than the air. The exhaust cone of the plane seemed to spew like a bloody blender without the lid on, in all directions. The engine coughed and spewed due to the immediate damage it just received from grinding up organs, bone, and teeth. Butch never felt a thing. He had been liquefied. The recessed hooks near the accident were instantly filled with a thick red mixture of blood and little pieces of bone fragments.

Michael was covered with what used to be his best friend. He wiped the blood from his eyes to look at the mess behind the Intruder. Tears began to flow from the bloody haze in his eyelashes. "NO! Not again!" he cried. Everything happened so fast that Michael did not realize that his psychic connection to Butch was just devastated beyond what he was able to handle at this stage in his life. It was more overwhelming than anything he had ever felt with the death of Jimmy. Michael's pupils glazed over, and his eyes rolled into is his head as he fell straight back onto the flight deck and into unconsciousness.

Michael felt as if he were in a dreamlike state, floating in an ether-like substance. A man was walking toward him out of the ether. It was Butch. "Hello, Michael," he said in such a calm and angelic tone. Michael was seeing something similar to what he saw when Jimmy was killed, but this time he was actually in the ether and not just seeing a spirit leave the body.

"Butch, but I just watched you die," Michael said with a wince on his face.

"I know you did, Michael, and this is my opportunity to come and speak with you," Butch said to him. "My soul has the option of visiting someone of my choosing at a critical point in their ascension process, and I chose to see you immediately following my death. You can call me a messenger of sorts," Butch said as he was smiling at Michael. There was a feeling of love and joy emanating from him that Michael had never felt before.

"Enough said. I get the picture," Michael said. "So why are you here, and where is this place, if you don't mind me asking?"

"I am one of your spirit guides, and I incarnated here at this time in your life to help you. We don't get many opportunities to contact souls in the flesh, if you will," the angel told him. "I have come to help you out a bit. You are very special, Michael, and you have trouble ahead. I know that you see the signs that I leave for you, but this one is going to require a little more assistance. I can't tell you what to do or what the troubles are that you will encounter. That is strictly forbidden by my boss. I can tell you that you are going to have some decisions to make, and you will make some mistakes that are going to hurt. You have the ability to know and see things that others cannot. We know that you are already aware of some of the hard truths about humanity, and there will be much more. Some of them are going to be hard to accept, but you must, and you will keep going. We do not know what will happen. Your future will be based on what you choose to do, but the Creator has placed faith in you. You will have to find it by keeping your mind sharp to notice the signs and synchronicities."

This etheric place he was in, must be what the Christians called Eden or the Buddhists called Nirvana. He was in a state of consciousness that he had never felt before. Michael only had to think and things would happen. He was not moving his mouth, but there was definitely a conversation going on here. He sensed no fear, no judgment, no greed, and no sense of the self from the version of Butch that was standing before him. He did not want to leave this overwhelming feel of joy and fear was starting to build in him about having to return to his existence.

"That fear you must get control of, and I sense it deep within you," the angel said without haste. "That is the only thing that is holding you back. Fear comes in many forms: anger, vengeance, and most of all, unforgiveness. If you cannot forgive, you will never make the right decision when that crucial moment comes. Forgiveness is the only path to final destination. Accept what is, but avoid what you must to live without fear. Once you can do that, forgiveness is easy."

"How can I forgive humanity for the cosmic sewer that it is?" Michael asked with a disgust that was only caused by his fear to return to it. "I know what you are saying, and I do agree. I just don't know if I am capable of it."

"Time will tell, Michael," the angel said as he started to fade. "One final thing. Keep your thoughts under control. They will manifest against you." Then he was gone.

Michael's eyes opened, and he was staring up an open blue sky. He turned his head to the side and could see that he was lying on his back on the deck of the ship. Michael tilted his head forward and could see the A6 towering above him with smoke pouring out of the tail. He was spotted with areas of fresh blood, and aircrew workers were running toward him across the flight deck. He had not been unconscious for more than a split second in the time of this world.

As he sat up and got to his feet, Michael leaned over, placed his palms on his knees, and began to cry like he hadn't cried in years. A fellow crewmember got to his side, placing one hand on his shoulder and leaning down to Michael's ear and said, "Come on, buddy, we need to get you out of here."

Michael stood up straight, pulled it together with one deep breath, and followed the sailor off the deck to the tower entrance, where the air boss was located. The tower was off limits to most everyone, but this was as serious of an incident as any, and Michael was going to have to talk to the big man. The air boss was a big burly man that reminded Michael of one of the Gas House Gorillas that Bugs Bunny played in baseball. He smoked a big Cuban cigar under a thick wide black mustache. Some air bosses shared the rank of captain with the CO of the ship, but not many. He was a commander.

"Petty Officer Stevens, is it?" the commander asked as he was squinting at Michael's nametag. "Tell me about what happened out there. I gave special permission for you to be on the flight deck, and now one of my senior crewmen is dead."

"I really don't know, sir," Michael replied nervously. "Butch was showing me around and must have stepped in the wrong place. Nothing makes sense. It just happened out of the blue. It was really no one's fault but Butch's, I think."

"You hurt at all?" the commander asked with partial concern Michael could feel.

"No, not physically," Michael said. "I am a little messed up though. Butch was my best good friend." He didn't think anyone got the joke, but it helped Michael during tough times to make light of the situation.

"I am going to make sure that you have a forty-eight-hour rest period to deal with this," the air boss told him without emotion. "Get yourself squared away, sailor. We all have to deal with a loss at one time or another." He turned back to what he was doing in the tower windows, and Michael was excused to leave.

Michael was a little offended at how the commander treated his loss, but he was used to that sort of heartlessness after growing up with his father. His father could do no wrong, lived the only right way, and his only love in this world was alcohol. Michael hated watching his father slowly poison his mother over his lifetime, mixing her drinks and bringing them to her every night. As long as he kept her drunk, then he could do as he pleased. On more than one occasion, Michael remembered his father saying something to the effect of how long it took to get her to drinking. Wow, a new low in personal selfishness to actually plan to corrupt someone with alcohol. Michael thought there was even a passage in the Bible of woe to those that did just that very thing. His father wasn't necessarily the evil man that Michael thought he was in high school, just a loveless, lost soul in limbo, like Dante described in his *Divine Comedy*.

After a quick trip to the corpsmen to be medically cleared, Michael went back to his bunk and lay down. He was exhausted. No matter how much he thought to himself that he would not be able to sleep, he was out in a few minutes. Michael dreamed about his father. He wanted to love him, but there was just no way to love the loveless. He had a vision of his father's funeral. A large white cloudy haze began to fade, and he could see two large doors to the front of what looked like a church. Not any church that he had seen before. The doors seemed to open for him, and in he walked.

He was dressed to the nines in his best meeting suit and the church was completely full of other fanciful dressed people. All eyes seemed to turn to him as he walked down the aisle toward the idol of the hanging crucified Jesus. A casket lay before it with the viewing hatch opened. As he got closer, he could see that it was not his father that lay inside, but Michael himself. What was this trying to tell him? It was something he had to do regarding his father or he would be dead. As he realized that, the body in the coffin changed to that of his father now.

Michael approached the pulpit and began up the steps. He reached into his jacket pocket and removed a paper bag. He pulled a pint of Early Times from the bag and let the paper drop lazily behind the podium. He stood next to his dead father in the coffin and smiled big. It was a smile of sheer hatred. "Here's one on me, Pop," he said as he tucked the pint into his father's dead fingers. "Didn't want you to leave town without your one true love."

He turned toward the crowd and stared out like he dared someone to speak to him. Then he hung his head partially and began back up the aisle. He glanced over at his mom, and she had no eyes. They were black empty holes. Seated next to her was a demonic vision of his dead father smiling back at Michael. His father was holding up his arm to show him that he was chained to his mother's wrist. The shackle was digging into her arm, and blood was dripping down her bony, wrinkled wrist. She mouthed the words "You can't save me." Michael awoke in a jolt. His shirt was soaked, and he felt hot all over.

Shortly after his powerful dream, pictures from Desert Storm had begun making their way around the ship, and everyone was looking at them in the galley one afternoon. Michael glanced over the shoulder of one of the sailors and caught a glimpse of the horrific pictures. He couldn't even continue to look because the feelings of despair were just so overwhelming. The photos were of many different piles of dead bodies in Iraq, consisting of mostly women and children fused together from being burnt alive. He had never seen anything so sickening. This was definitely not something he had joined up for, and he felt that this happened more frequently than not.

Michael realized something. Up until now, he had done everything that his father thought he should do, and he was miserable. He was not his father, nor did he want to be. His father was the one that was gung ho military, not him. Hell, his father did not even come to his boot camp graduation with his mother. He hated warfare, especially warfare for greed, and needed to do something different with his life. It was time to get out of the Navy.

Although he only had a year and a half left to serve by commitment, getting out a little early was not going to be easy. Michael was smart and knew that with the recent loss of his friend, a medical discharge would be his best bet; he had seen plenty of them during work week in boot camp. He would schedule a psych evaluation and fail miserably. Michael leaped out of his bunk and looked toward the ceiling. "I miss you, Butch, and I don't mean to use your death to my advantage, but you are my ticket out of here. I am sure you would not mind." Michael smiled at the halogen light hanging from the ceiling.

It went just as he had planned. Michael started showing up for his watch shift slightly later and later all week. He moped around and talked to not much of anybody. His supervisors took notice and recommended that he get a psych evaluation. Michael acted like he was in objection, but that was exactly what he was hoping for.

He answered the multiple choice questions like you would need to in order to appear mentally incapable to continue service in the military. When called in for the face-to-face interview with the ship's psychologist, he was all ready to put on the best academy award performance he could come up with. "And the Oscar goes to ... Michael Stevens!"

He was recommended for immediate medical discharge under what was called Section 8. Michael knew that he was not crazy, but very, very tormented. The Navy sent him off the *Enterprise* on a chopper that was going to San Diego, for other reasons, and there was an extra jump seat available. It took a couple weeks to complete the outprocessing back in San Diego, but what a fun town to enjoy while he was waiting.

Michael stayed with a SEAL friend of his in town who was stationed on the 32nd Street Naval Base, where Michael had been prior to his deployment on the *Enterprise*. His friend lived off base in an apartment that had a spare room. He had plenty of time to think about what he really wanted for his future. He was raised by a slave to become a slave himself, so he figured that he needed to go to school to find some career that he would enjoy while he tried to figure out what his real purpose was here. A sedentary existence in a thankless job for life didn't really thrill him much, but that was all he really knew at the time, and he really wanted to find out what college was all about.

Michael thought it would be best to head back toward Washington since he was familiar with the Pacific Northwest. He definitely didn't want to be in a city setting for school, so it would have to be somewhere near the countryside, so he could be close to nature and real freedom when he needed. He figured that college would be stressful to a point, and the only thing that ever really helped him relax was the outdoors and some of the things that grew in it, of course. He left San Diego after his processing was done and headed back north.

Michael had been on a couple hunting trips with his father in Northern Idaho when he was a kid, and he remember a town called Moscow that they stayed in several times during some late fall out of state hunts. He recalled it being really close to all kinds of beautiful areas, and there was a state college there. Michael just seemed to drive there automatically. He took several days to get there, stopping at motels along the way, but he continued each day in the same direction. After a few days, he pulled into the parking lot of the registrar for the University of Idaho in Moscow and registered for his next journey.

THE COLLEGE YEARS

Those who know how to think need no teacher.
—Mahatma Gandhi

College was just what one might expect, a drunken free-for-all.
Michael was starting college about five years after high school, so
he was already well into legal drinking age. Although he was a little
wiser than most recent high school graduates, due to his military
training, he was quite a bit more emotionally damaged. Additionally,
his empathic spiritual psychic abilities were there, but he was trying
to suppress them as much as possible with his growing use of alcohol.
It always started out that way. Things were good for a while, but then
they just seemed to go to shit.

He had chosen the University of Idaho due to its small town
setting and close availability of a wide variety of natural settings. The
town of Moscow in Idaho was pronounced with an *oh* sound rather
than a *ow* sound so as not to be confused with Moscow in Russia.
The U of I had one of the best engineering schools in the country
at that time. Michael didn't have much money, but between part-
time work, the GI Bill, and student loans, it was tolerable. He also
thought that it would be best to stay in the dorm for his first year
until he got used to the town and the college routine.

Michael was given a first floor room in one of the male dorms
and assigned a roommate. Since he arrived on the Friday before
school started, there was plenty of time to check in and get settled
before the craziness began. The room was small with a single bunk
bed adjacent to one wall. The main wall had a large recessed double

desk area with closets on both sides. There was a little window set in the far brick wall that looked out over the rugby field. A single sink and mirror were right by the door and there was a small fridge below the sink. That fridge would definitely get used over the next nine months. It would usually be full of the cheapest and nastiest forty ounce beers that could be purchased just down the street at the Circle K.

He was putting his clothes in the closet, very well organized as usual, when the door opened. There stood a man in his late twenties. He was about the same height as Michael, but a little more muscular. With short dark curly hair and a mustache, he was the spitting image of Tom Skerritt in *Top Gun*, if you were to add about twenty pounds.

"Hey there, guy. Name's Brad Willis. Pleased to know you," the man said as he walked through the door with his right hand extended. Michael really had an overwhelming feeling of positive energy from this man. It was very strong, and he hadn't felt anything this strong since his days with Jimmy and even Butch. When his hand met Brad's in a strong masculine embrace, Michael had a surge of mixed energy that he had never felt before. He had a feeling of great loss combined with great fear. It was a sensation that he did not like. There was no way he wanted to get close to someone again and then lose them.

"Same here, nice to meet you. My name's Michael. Michael Stevens," he replied as he finished the handshake. He glanced into Brad's eyes for a brief moment. Michael was noticing it more these days. He was able to partially connect to someone by looking into their eyes. This had happened a few times before, but he had tried to avoid doing it for too long because he might not like what he saw. On first glance, Brad seemed to have a beautiful spirit.

"Well, Michael, it looks like we're roomies. I suppose we'll have some good partying ahead," Brad said with a big mischievous grin. Michael smiled back. He was getting such a good feeling from him. Something told him that they were very similar, and Michael was anxious to see what time would reveal.

Michael and Brad became inseparable. Just like "peas and carrots," as Forrest would say. They were both engineering students, had a fondness for the outdoors, sported a twisted sense of humor, and enjoyed life. Both of them had the same taste in music, movies, and even women. Brad was Michael's new best friend, the one he had been looking for his entire life, even closer than Jimmy or Butch. Their mental connection began on that very first day, and would continue to grow with each day on. Both of them liked their drinking, most often to excess. Michael had learned about drinking in the Navy, and Brad came from hard knocks in California. Although he didn't drink much in the Navy until after he was twenty-one, Michael's use of booze to suppress some of his unwanted feelings would begin to backfire. It was just the most dangerous and incorrect way to do it, but it worked for quite a while.

Brad had a 1970 full-size Chevy van, and Michael sold his car when he came to school. The van was the greatest thing in the world. They would take weekend trips to the mountains, the reservoir, or some nearby town to party. Then there was the legendary spring break trip of 1992. It was the last week of March, every year, when U of I had their spring break. Michael and Brad were all geared up to take a nine-day road trip through the Panhandle of Idaho. Neither could wait. They packed up the van with all they thought they would needed, which consisted of fifteen cases of beer, four gallons of Evan Williams whiskey, six *Penthouse* magazines, thirty-six assorted cassette tapes, some clothing, and a partridge in a pear tree. Food would be found along the way, as usual.

The first stop was Deary, Idaho, a place they always liked to come on weekends. There was a little campsite a few miles off the main road just east of town. It was near a creek and didn't get many visitors, including the ones with uniforms and badges. Deary was a small country town on State Route 8 that most of the students didn't come to even though it was not too far from Moscow. This was good, because the townsfolk really didn't care much for the college students residing less than an hour away.

Michael and Brad found their favorite spot on the creek and set up their camp. Michael was considerably more of a Boy Scout than Brad, but he seemed to get better as time went on. Shortly after they got settled in, Brad decided that he wanted to hike up the creek a bit and do some fishing. Michael really didn't feel like it that day for some reason. He was just enjoying the silence of the camp along with his twenty-four-ounce whiskey and Cokes.

Brad loaded up his backpack with about a half a case of beers for the "journey" and slung the pack on his back. "See you in a little bit. I'm going to catch the big one, I can just feel it," Brad said with a smile. He grabbed his pole and tackle box and headed on down the creek side trail. Brad was not a graceful hiker by any means. You could hear him bitching and chopping at the brush a good half mile away. When Michael could no longer hear Brad in the bushes, he settled in his chair and grabbed the latest Stephen King novel that he had brought along. He sipped his drink, reading in silence until he drifted off to sleep.

Michael awoke to the sounds of Brad cursing out the bushes. He looked at his watch and couldn't believe that he had been asleep for almost two hours. Good whiskey nap. From the direction of the yelling, Michael could tell that Brad was on the opposite side of the creek now, for some reason. There was also the faint chime of empty beer cans clanging together in the backpack. One thing they always did was make sure that they packed out their trash. Neither one of them could stand the sight of litter in the woods.

Brad emerged on the opposite side of the creek through the thick Idaho underbrush. He was extremely drunk and, from what Michael could see, must have polished off all the beers in the two hours he was gone. Brad saw Michael, gave a drunken wave, and started to stumble his way along the slippery rocks in the creek without looking for the best place to cross, making a beeline for Michael. The creek wasn't that deep or strong, but the rocks were slippery, and Brad was staggering something fierce. Brad was a better drinking pro than Michael was, so amazingly enough, he never went down and made it across completely dry, except for his shoes.

Brad stumbled out of the creek about twenty yards from Michael. As Michael was looking down at Brad's soaked shoes, he noticed blood running down Brad's left leg. At about the midcalf level, Michael could see what appeared to be a fish hook sticking out of Brad's leg. The hook was huge. Just leave it to Brad to use a No.

6 hook to try to fish for ten-inch brook trout. Brad was always very grandiose with everything. If he had a motorcycle, he had to have all the cool matching gear. If he had a stereo, it had to be the loudest on the block. If he had a truck, it had to rally a big rig for towering above the rest of the traffic. And if you were going to fish, grab the biggest goddamn fish hook in your box.

"What the hell happened, you idiot?" Michael choked out through his laughter.

"Ahh, I wish tryin' to gut the shish hook on the bobber, and I shipped on the rotts." He shook his head because even he did not understand what he was saying. "I need a beer," Brad slurred out the words in his drunken glory. Michael was not exactly sober, but Brad was flat shit-housed. Michael did not want to touch the hook, and there was no way they were driving back in to Moscow to go to the emergency room. Michael loaded Brad in the van and headed in to the metropolis of Deary.

Blood flowed much more freely when the body was intoxicated. Brad was keeping a rag on the wound, but he was so hammered that he would drop the pressure off, and it would start to bleed again. At least it was not an artery, or they would have really had trouble. Michael noticed the sign for Fuzzy's Tavern. They had passed by it many times but had never stopped in because they knew that college students were hated in these small town bars.

Brad was acting like he wanted to pass out in the passenger seat as Michael parked the van in front of the tavern. It was the weekend, and nothing was open, but the tavern was, and most likely didn't close too often around these here parts. Michael went around the van and helped Brad out on his feet and walked him into the tavern. There were a couple of local farmers playing pool and a man staring at the jukebox, which was blaring out some twangy sister dating love song that Michael had never heard before. He put Brad in one barstool and sat in the one next to him to help hold him up.

He flagged down the bartender, and she started toward them with a puzzled "What the hell do these frat boys need?" kind of look on her face.

"Hi, ma'am," Michael said. "We have a problem and really need some help." Brad's head was just kind of circling very slowly as he tried to maintain himself in an erect posture on the bar stool. "My friend here had a little too much to drink and got a fish hook stuck, really stuck, in his leg, and we don't know where to go."

The bartender, who appeared to be in her late forties, tapped the bar with her open palm. "Let's have a look. Put your leg up here on the bar," she said.

Michael glanced and smiled at Brad and, in a sloppy drunken motion, tossed his leg up on the bar. The bartender turned and reached up for a bottle of Jack. She poured four shots—one for each of them, including her, and one to dump on Brad's leg.

They all downed the shots, and while Brad was wincing from the shot in distraction, she dumped the other one on his wound. Brad let a drunken "Ouuuuchhh! The hell you do that for?"

"I gotta sterilize it if I'm going to get this out of you," she said as she reached below the bar and grabbed a pair of needle nose pliers and proceeded to perform a half-assed surgery right there on the bar. She poured two more shots for each of them and began. She pushed the hook all the way through his leg and then clipped off the barbs and then backed the fish hook out. Brad was cringing the entire time but not being too loud about it. He knew it would be painful; no need to draw unnecessary attention. She placed a bar rag over the wound to hold the bleeding while she grabbed the first-aid kit from the shelf behind the bar. She sterilized and bandaged the wound as good as any hospital could have done. Michael and Brad both looked at the patch job with amazement. Brad gave a giggle as he dropped his leg back to the bar stool, and they ordered more shots.

When Brad drank enough to numb his leg, they were able to play some "stick," as they liked to call it. It turned out to be a very fun night playing pool with farmer John and his boy. It just so happened that Mr. John was taking his son out for a night on the town after a hard day working the ranch. Michael could feel that they were just real nice, genuine people trying to fit their square life into this round world like everyone else. He would never in his life forget Fuzzy's Tavern.

Next stop was Sandpoint, Idaho. This was one of the most beautiful areas in the entire country. The town bordered on Lake Pend Oreille, which was also one of the deepest lakes in the Western United States, so deep in fact that the Navy had a sonar-testing facility located on a very secure and secluded shore. They would spend the remaining seven days of this spring break traveling around the lake and the mountain panhandle areas to the north.

Michael had heard a classmate of his, who was ex-Army, talk of an abandoned Army training base near the lake, in a heavily wooded area. He actually didn't know how to get there specifically, but he had a rough idea as to about where it should be from the description that his classmate gave him. Michael didn't trust much of anything, but he did trust his memory and especially his intuition. His was just getting spooky.

Brad was not exactly a patient man, and they were driving in the middle of the night. "Where is this god damn place, Magellan?" Brad asked with frustration.

"I know it's around here. Just be patient. What time schedule do we have anyway?" Michael replied.

Just about then, they came upon an old "No Trespassing. US Government Property" sign in the headlight beams that was bent about halfway over and partially hidden by overgrown weeds in the highway shoulder. Just past the sign was a narrow entrance to a dirt road that went off toward nowhere. The road was hard to see and you would have missed it if you weren't actually looking for it.

As they turned into the narrow road approach, Michael got this creepy feeling and looked at Brad. "Do you feel that?" he asked.

"Feel what?" Brad asked. "The hell you talking about?"

"Pain. Fear. Suffering. Not good," Michael said. "Prisoners or something. I'm not quite sure. Keep driving. It's getting stronger."

"What the hell you mean pain? Whose pain?" Brad asked with a confused look on his face.

"Is this part of those psychic feelings that you get, buddy?"

"I think so, but the feelings of agony and suffering are so strong," Michael replied. "This place is so demonic."

They drove further in. The feelings of pain and suffering were growing as they got closer to what appeared to be an abandoned barracks. Michael had learned how to control his feelings and sort them out before they affected him physically. Some were still quite overpowering, like this one could have been before he had learned some skills to deal with them.

They pulled up to the abandoned building. The headlights seemed to cast an eerie glow over the stillness of the place. The building literally felt like a tomb to Michael. "So many children have suffered here. I feel that they are so confused and scared and have no idea where they are or how they got here," Michael said. He was starting to get a hazy vision in his head of what looked like a hospital facility from a *Saw* horror film or something. On the wall he could see the word MKULTRA written in what looked like blood. It faded away quickly. What did it mean? What was this place?

Michael had never heard of the MKULTRA program, but somehow he just knew about it. He could actually see the truth, but of course, no one would ever believe him. Michael couldn't explain how he knew, but he just knew things based on the feelings of the energies around him. Some amount of energy of past human presence always remains, and only the empathic mind could sense it. If he was in a situation, Michael would get a mental vision of what was behind it. Then he would go out and try to find books or other information that people might have published about it. Most of the things that he had visions about throughout his life were contrary to what the schools and governments were telling him. He knew they were lying to him. It was no surprise that information on these so-called controversial subjects was hard to come by, but he was a great researcher and would always find some information somewhere, no matter how scarce.

He instantly became aware of how the CIA and military had been experimenting with mind control for decades. It was quite possible that this base had been used for just exactly that purpose. The location was the perfect cover, being out in the woods of the northern Idaho Panhandle, with very few stray visitors. Michael could not believe the horrific torture and abuse that demented military personnel and psychopathic doctors inflicted on the imprisoned subjects of this program, most of whom were probably under mind control themselves. The CIA and military abducted hundreds of thousands of people, mostly children, worldwide, every year for these programs. Most of the victims that he saw on milk cartons or heard about on Amber Alerts were actually taken into this program. Day cares and foster homes were also sources that are used.

"What does it feel like?" Brad asked. He believed in Michael from the start. It had only been a few months ago when Michael had told him about his "flaw," or "gift," if you will. Instead of calling him crazy, like most of the ignorant, he was curious and inquisitive. He was Michael's only friend at this point in his life, and it was a blessing for Michael to not have to hide and pretend that he was just the same as everyone else. His entire family thought he was nuts, and they were the ones that were supposed to love him. Go figure. Never underestimate the power of ignorance caused by fear of the unfamiliar or unknown. It was stronger than love.

"It feels like a nausea in the stomach without the puking because I am feeling suffering instead of joy. The feelings are weaker when it isn't so horrific," Michael said. "I also get a mental image of the perpetrators, like I am looking through the victim's eyes."

Michael and Brad stared at the building in silence. There was a partially faded writing on the door that must have said "Authorized Military Personnel Only" at one time. "Do you want to go check it out?" Brad asked.

"No way," Michael said without hesitation. "This is the closest that I am getting to that place. You can if you want, but I will wait here. It is bad enough now that I can barely use my skills to contain it without going crazy."

Michael thought of his time in the military and wondered about what he might have been part of that he didn't know about. The overpriced tools and the money laundering—that was probably a source of the money used for programs like this. It made his sick to think about. He was just glad that he got out when he did and was no longer serving the lie.

"No. We can go," Brad replied. "What went on here?"

"I don't think you want to know the details, but near as I can tell people were tortured here by members of our own government," Michael said. "They seem to be government men in lab coats, with empty dead expressions on their faces. I get a sensation of panic like I am in the presence of an evil that is not human. It isn't alien either, just demonic. It's their eyes, they have such cold dead eyes."

"No, you're right," Brad said. "I don't want to know. You seem to be getting better about controlling this thing of yours."

"Yes, I know," Michael said. "That is what scares me the most."

They left the base in silence and drove on down the road a few miles. There was a turn sign that had a tent symbol below it, so they went as directed and came upon a free campsite that was right along a small stream. They had no idea where they were at on the map, and the base was (no surprise) not shown either. The roads they had come in on were not marked.

They just crashed in the van for the night. The next day, they set up camp as usual. Michael had a tent, and Brad would set up his bed in the van. They had a small fold-up card table to set all the food on and rope hammocks that would fit between two trees, provided they were the right distance apart. They always managed to find two that would work within a close proximity of the camp. Nature always provided a good afternoon pass-out spot. The portable gas stove went on the ground in the best spot that was out of the wind. Nothing ate up stove gas like the wind. The beer cooler stayed in the van, as they would take many mini road trips when they were camping out. They decided this would be a good place to relax for the next couple of days.

Drinking commenced once the camp was set. Gunplay seemed like the activity for the day. Brad had packed along his 30/30 and Home Defender shotgun. Nothing went together like liquor and firearms, especially with young men. First they wanted to sight in the 30/30 to make sure it was shooting accurately. People that were seeing double should really not try to verify the accuracy of a deadly weapon. Michael had grown up in the country, and Brad was a city boy. Michael had much more experience with rifles and hunting while Brad had a more extensive knowledge of illegal handguns.

Michael took the reins and laid the rifle over the hood of the van. The hood of a truck made the best bench rest in the world. Pappy had always shown him to sight in a rifle that way. He grabbed the box of rounds and began to slide the shells in the side of the 30/30 one at a time. The Winchester 30/30 was a side load weapon with a lever action, and it held six rounds. Brad's had open sights, which Michael preferred over a scope for accuracy. Michael leaned over the side of the van on the hood and cupped the rifle to his cheek and shoulder. He was a good shot with a rifle, but his vision was a bit hazy today. It might have been the many shots and beers, but that could be left up to interpretation. He laid the back site into the cradle of the front and center it over a log across the river as he held his breath and gently squeezed.

Crack! The rifle went off accompanied by a loud vibration of the hood of the van. Odd, Michael had never heard a hood rattle like that when using one as a bench rest. Just off the tip of the rifle Michael could see the front crest of the hood of the van with a large hole in it.

"Shit!" Michael said to himself quietly. "Ah, Brad. You want to come up here for a minute."

Brad had been a few feet behind Michael to stay out of the way of the hot ejected brass. He was expecting more than one shot. They both had their ears on, so he did not hear. Michael took his off, turned around, and motioned for Brad to do the same. He did, and Michael said, "Come up here right quick." He just knew Brad was going to flip.

"I think I accidently hit your hood," Michael said quite sheepishly. "Sorry, dude. I really didn't mean to."

Brad looked at the hood, and his eyes got a little wider. "What the hell did you do to my hood? No more rifle for you." He went around to the front and looked at the hole, just shaking his head. He reached in and popped the hood to get a better look. The bullet only made one hole, so it did not go straight through. It had ricocheted and gone straight down, just barely missing the radiator by inches. Very lucky. There was an indentation on the ground where the bullet had hit. Brad took out his pocket knife and was able to wedge the bullet out of the ground.

"Well, here's the bullet," he said while holding it up for Michael to see. "You're so lucky it didn't hit the radiator, and you're going to pay for this repair. You can keep this as a lucky charm."

"I know, I know," Michael said in embarrassment as Brad dropped the bullet in his open hand. "When you get the dent fixed on the other side, just have the shop fix this one as well, and they can itemize what it costs." Michael did make good when the time came later, but it took a while for Brad to be able to laugh about it.

They sat drinking by the campfire that night, thinking and talking about the night before. Michael had a tough time dealing with the emotions he would get from a negative reading, which he seemed to experience quite a bit more than joyous ones. This was the turning point in his drinking. Alcohol helped to fog the repeat visions of prior encounters as well as block some new ones from occurring. The absolute horrific visions of the experience the night before were just too much for him to take and there just wasn't enough alcohol to replace it with joy.

Blackouts would soon ensue. There was something very unique about blackouts and memory loss. They were the only memories that you would never get back in this lifetime. No amount of hypnosis, regressive therapy, or biofeedback would bring back those memories; they were lost forever. You would not get to see what you actually did until your life review in front of the Creator, but you could start to repay the karmic debt in this lifetime if you sobered up in time.

Michael had his first alcoholic blackout on the fourth day of the trip. He had been excessively hammered before, but not completely forgotten large chunks of time. Brad and Michael had left the campsite, after two nights, and went back into Sandpoint for a hearty breakfast. They always liked to eat a lot of food early in the day, so they could start drinking early in the afternoon. Not exactly sober in the morning and looking like road bums, they strolled into the Sandpoint IHOP.

Michael had actually started drinking heavily in the morning before they left. He found that it was easy to add hard liquor to a twenty-ounce soda and then just nurse it at his convenience. Brad did most of the driving on the day trip and, although he liked to drink, would never consider starting first thing in the morning. Michael, on the other hand, would find it the easiest way to get through a day in his tormented life. Although Michael never liked to drive when he had been drinking, Brad didn't care. He had two DUIs under his belt in California before he even walked into the dorm room the day he met Michael.

Michael was already starting to carry a good buzz when they got to IHOP. Cheap food, but one of their favorites. It was "Oh, so tasty," but when drinking, it was like it was prepared by the Creator itself. They sat in a booth across from each other, and Brad could tell that Michael was feeling no pain. "You housed already, buddy?" Brad half grinned as he asked.

"No, just tryin' to keep a cool buzz going for the rest of the trip," Michael lied. "I would like to be happy for the rest of it. Think we've seen enough shit on this one." He chuckled a little nervously.

They ordered their meals and scarfed it down in record time. Brad and Michael liked to order an extra meal that they could split, both having ample appetites. Michael would take the extra eggs and hash browns, and Brad would grab up the toast and sausages. Things were always easy between these two since they never really had an altercation, until today.

Back in the van with full bellies, they proceeded out of Sandpoint and headed for the mountains near the town of Pend Oreille, not too far from where the Ruby Ridge murders took place. The trip was not really planned; they just always found a good place to camp eventually. Michael had been sipping away at his concoction all day without Brad really noticing. He was able to freshen it in secret, when Brad had to make any pit stops.

They found another nice camp, with a large fire pit already properly constructed, tucked nicely along the river. After the camp was set up, Brad joined Michael in the beer drinking and shot pounding festivities. Michael had been hours ahead of him and was already far past the 2.0 percent level. At that time, the legal level for DUI was 1.0 in most states that had a drinking and driving law, and in Idaho, you could legally drive with an open container as long as you were not above the legal intoxication limit and not in city limits.

Michael, like the people he knew, was a happy drunk for the most part. He would get stupid occasionally, but he had never heard of any story where someone was drinking and did something noble and intelligent. It was early in the evening when his switch occurred. When the mind went blank and lost control of the body, the soul went to sleep. It was not an out-of-body experience per se but a shutting down of our own consciousness. Michael became an empty vessel that could be entered and guided by whatever spirit chose to do so no matter how malicious and evil. Michael was in the middle of mixing another drinking when he hollered back to Brad.

"Let's get the shotgun out. I feel like blowing off a little steam as well as some chunks of log."

Brad was pretty well oiled by now and confirmed that idea. "Yes. That is what I could use too." Michael grabbed the shotgun from the back of the van and the box of shells. They had bought triple-aught buckshot rounds since they were more fun to shoot. They really explode what you are shooting at since the pellets are so large. Hunting was really not the intent on these outings; it was just fun to drink and shoot.

Michael didn't bother to put his ears on, and he loaded the magazine with five rounds. He barely allowed enough time for Brad to dawn his ears, before unloading on a log across the river. It was a short-barrel pump-action shotgun, and Michael just blazed through all five like Stallone on a good day.

"Wow, Mikey," Brad said as Michael was loading another five in the magazine. "You feeling like Wild Bill today or something?"

"Watch this." Michael grinned back at Brad while he hung the shotgun from one hand, just dangling it toward the ground. He had already cracked one into the chamber ahead of time. As Michael was turning his head from Brad back toward the log, he brought the shotgun up with his right arm and said, "Betcha I can shoot this with one hand."

"No, don't tr—"

Crack!

The gun went off as Brad's words were drowned out by the blast. The shotgun flew backward out of Michael's hand and landed butt first about two feet to the right of Brad. It was aimed straight at Michael's head when it hit the ground. Since it was a pump-action shotgun, the next round had not been loaded. If this had been a semiautomatic, there was a good chance that Michael would be dead.

"That was pretty stupid, Mikey. If there had been a round in the chamber of that gun, it would have discharged when it hit the ground and taken that dumb ass head of yours off."

Michael just looked back at Brad with the most evil possessed smile that Jack Nicholson would be proud of. "I guess we had better get one in there then, huh?" he questioned with a sneer as turned and walked back toward the shotgun on the ground. Michael bent down and swatted it up with his right hand while loading another round into the chamber with his left. He turned the barrel toward himself and began to stare with one eye into the opening like he was looking for a ring that was lost down the drain. "Wonder if I can see the tip of the shell?"

Without pause, Brad ran over and lifted the tip of the barrel, not seeing Michael's thumb on the trigger. The gun went off in the air, and both men hit the ground with the shotgun lying on the ground between them. Brad knew there were still three more rounds in the magazine. He lunged over, swiftly grabbed the gun, and began to eject the shells. He was panting for breath as he looked over at Michael, who was lying sideways, facing away from him.

"What do you think you are doing? What's wrong with you? I have never seen you act this way." Brad managed to get out between big breaths.

In one fluid motion, Michael sat up while still facing away from Brad. He got to his feet and walked toward the stream as Brad stood up behind him, still gripping the shotgun in his left hand. Michael turned to face him, and Brad could not believe what he saw. His face had actually changed. It was still his face, but creases had formed on his cheeks and forehead that were consistent with the way a face would be crumpled up in anger. He had an evil smile on his face; while it looked like he was staring at the ground, his eyes were staring straight out at Brad. His eyes, they were black. The irises had disappeared, and there were only what looked like large black pupils. Then he spoke.

"They know about me," Michael said slowly in a lower voice than usual. "I can feel them, and I know what they're doing to us. I have a power that can hurt them and they're afraid." It seemed to Brad that something was actually speaking through Michael, but in the first person. Michael turned with a jolt and ran off through the stream and disappeared into the bordering woods. Brad gave chase up until the creek, but by then, Michael was already gone out of sight. He was quite a bit faster than Brad.

Brad walked slowly back to the camp hanging his head in wonder. He had never seen this in Michael before and it was very creepy. He sat in the chair and watched the camp fire just waiting for Michael to come back, but he never did. By midnight, Brad gave up waiting and climbed into the van to turn in. If it hadn't been for all the alcohol, he might never have slept a wink that night.

The next morning, Michael awoke in a meadow, lying on his back in the tall field grass. As he opened his eyes, he could see up through the tall grass to the light morning sky. He sat up and could feel his head pound with the hangover. He managed to make it to his feet and look out over a vast meadow. He had no idea where he was or how to get back to the camp, but he could see the path that he made through the grass the night before, but he had no memory of it. He felt like he was the wolf man waking up after a night of the full moon, except he still had on his clothes, though filthy that they were.

He made his way back, trying to see the signs left from where he staggered along the night before. Kicked over rocks, broken branches, and upturned leaves gave good enough signs to lead him back to the stream. When he got to the stream, he did not see their camp on the other side, so he either had to go up or down stream to find it. He remember back in the Navy they had a saying called 50/50/90. This meant that when you were faced with a 50/50 decision to make, there was a 90 percent chance that you would choose wrong. He chose to head upstream.

Michael had chosen wisely, which was nice for once. After about a half a mile of stumbling along the shore of the stream with a four alarm hangover, he could see Brad's van up the creek a little further around the bend. Now it was Michael's turn to stumble back into camp like Brad did in Deary, but this was much more serious. He made his way across the stream and on into camp. Brad was not up, and Michael did not really want to wake him yet. He started brewing some coffee and guzzling water like there was no tomorrow. He didn't know what he would tell Brad when he woke up or what he had done the night before. It was all a complete blackout.

About a half hour after Michael was back in camp, he could hear Brad rumbling about in the van. Time to find out what happened last night, great. Brad popped his head out and saw Michael sitting there with a fresh cup of coffee. He gave a slight chuckle while shaking his hanging head and said, "There you are. I am glad you are all right. I was really worried about you. I see the coffee is done."

"Yeah, I just made it," Michael replied. "Brad, I have no idea what happened last night. I think I had a blackout."

"Well, you had something," Brad said as he jumped from the back of the van. "It was almost like you were possessed or something. I have never seen anything like it, and I have no idea what you were talking about. It was something about knowing who they are, after you pretty much tried to kill yourself with the shotgun."

"I'm sorry, buddy," Michael said sheepishly. "I'm not going to drink like that anymore and please just ignore anything I might have said or done. It wasn't me." He really didn't want to drink like that, and he would control it for a while. Michael did not have another blackout like that while they were in college. He had times when he had too much to drink where the events of the evening were very unclear, but never a full on blackout.

"Okay, buddy," Brad acknowledged. "But if something like that happens again, we're going to get you in to talk to someone. I know you're smarter than almost any psychiatrist out there, but there has got to be someone that you would trust to talk to."

"Not likely, but let's just play it by ear," Michael said as he was standing up to face Brad. "Thanks for caring, though, not many people do."

"No problem, Mikey," Brad said with a loving smile. "You are a very special person, and I feel good for knowing that. We are going to concentrate on having a good time for the remaining half of this adventure. Enough said." The rest of the trip was rather uneventful. They did more of the same and saw some very beautiful country. Not much was said about the Army base or the blackout incident; which was good for Michael, but, the encounters had changed him forever.

Michael felt a sense of aloneness unlike any he could have imagined. Not the kind of loneliness that you feel while sitting in another room at a party, but so much more intense. He felt trapped in a world full of billions of people that he had nothing in common with. He felt the fear of people everywhere and how they were being manipulated through lies creating a wanton need to enslave themselves to a sick system of materialism and conformity. There was goodness in humanity, he could feel it, but it was being overridden by some great force that was creating this illusionary fear. The human potential for love, understanding, compassion, and generosity had been consumed by greed, selfishness, narcissism, lust, and acts of cruelty that would make Charles Manson cringe.

Whatever had happened during that blackout, it had left something behind in Michael. It was part of him now and would only rear its ugly head when he entered a blackout state. One thing though, it gave Michael a heightened sense of awareness about this world and people he would encounter along the way. Maybe that was part of the deal. In order for this dormant evil to reside in him, he was given an even greater gift, partial clairvoyance.

That freshman year of college ended and both Brad and Michael decided to get apartments. They found a complex where they could walk to campus and both ended up moving into the same building. They also found jobs cooking at a local microbrewery and restaurant. The place was called the *Library*. Cool name for a college town hangout. For the remaining years of college, things became fairly routine. Brad worked a little more often than Michael did, since he didn't have as much scholarship money. He also had to study more since the material did not come as easily to him as it did for Michael. They made plenty of time for partying though, and Michael would always be careful not to get the blackout point. It was nice to be able to live, work, play, and go to school with his best friend.

The years clicked by in Groundhog Day fashion. Studying, working, and partying just became the routine college agenda. Michael just could not handle the feelings he would get if he was exposed to human torture and suffering. He didn't even have to be present for it. Descriptions and pictures would be enough to trigger his pain, just like the ones in the Navy did. One thing happened during college that really affected him. It was during the Waco incident. The media was spewing their scripted lies, as usual, and Michael ignored it all. Months after the incident, he stumbled on a documentary called *Waco: The Rules of Engagement*. It completely turned his stomach, as more things did those days. The pictures of infant children chemically and physically fused to their dolls and teddy bears was just too much to take. The entire event was simply government extermination of those that believed differently. The pictures weren't quite as stomach turning as Janet Reno's performance for congress. What a lying pig. Michael knew in his heart that she would see justice someday, even if not on this planet.

Michael had his first experience with psychedelic substances during his junior year of college. Brad and Michael decided it would be a good idea to crash a frat party over the weekend. It was during the summer before his senior year, so most frat boys were lounging around their yuppie family lake cabins, sponging off their trust funds, but the few that had to work during the summer months were still in town. Nice, because Michael could not be around the yuppie ones. They put off an awkward feeling of soulless appreciation of the self. It did not matter that most were away. A frat party was like an AA meeting; it only takes two to start one.

Michael knew a guy from summer classes that lived in the ATO house. He told him about the party and what the code word at the door would be. Michael knew that he was telling the truth, because that was part of his "flaw." With Brad in tow, Michael went up to the door of the house and knocked. The bouncer probably played for the football team because he was just immense. Michael looked at him and said, "Drunk girls." The bouncer smiled and slid aside while motioning the two to come on in.

Neither of them had ever been in a frat house. It just wasn't their crowd. On this particular night, it was a mix of more than just people in the Greek system. Geeks, sluts, jocks, recluses, and drunken super studs were all present. Michael didn't have much in common with any of them as usual. He didn't like labels and groupings. It was part of the illusion of this programmed society. No one wanted to just be who they really were, and they damn sure didn't want to be around the ones that were. It scared them to have to face their own fears by being in the presence of someone who does. Cowards basically.

Michael was learning not to be too forward or share too much with anyone, even ones he had known for a while. Alcohol had a way of overriding this feature though. He needed something that allowed him to drink without getting drunk; psychedelics were it. The two separated for a while at the party. There was a house band downstairs that wasn't too bad, but Michael just wanted to get away from the loud noise for a while. He decided to wander upstairs into the residential parts of the house. The very top loft of bunk beds was for the freshman and sophomores, but the middle floors were for the upper classmen, and they usually had their own rooms, or just a single roommate.

Michael strolled about the hallway of the third floor and came upon a partially opened door with people chatting inside. He was going to move on when the door opened, and there stood a wiry man with medium-length blond hair. He had a Jimi Hendrix shirt on holding a large glass bong. "Come on in." The man, who could have been Kurt Cobain's twin brother, said, "I saw you standing there through the crack and could use the company."

It turned out that there were no other people chatting. The man was listening to what Michael thought was a book tape. The man probably wasn't much into the partying and just up here, trying to avoid it. "I found that if I tape the lectures and then just let them run in the room while I am doing other things, the information seems to lock in my brain better," he said. "I'm Brady, but people call me Tripper. And you?"

"Michael."

"Cool," Tripper replied as he shut the tape off. "I don't dig the parties, but frat house living is very comfortable and accommodating. Here." He passed the bong. "Got some 'cid too if you want."

"'Cid? You mean acid?" Michael asked. He thought about how that was definitely one thing that he did want to experience in college.

"Yep, you ever done it?" Tripper replied as he was digging away on his messy desk to try to find what he was looking for.

"No," Michael said. "I have always wanted to try, and what better time than before I get out of college, I guess. How much does it cost?"

"This one's on me," Tripper said as he handed him what looked like a small version of a postage stamp. It was a single hit of blotter acid, or LSD if you prefer the proper semantics. The government created LSD for the purposes of mind control, and it got widespread recreational use in the 1960s. Recreational use dropped off significantly by the 1980s, but it would always be around.

Michael just placed it on his tongue without much pause. "How long does it take?" he asked Tripper.

"'Bout fifteen minutes, give or take, then it's on for the next eight hours or so," Tripper said with a smile. LSD was a chemical psychedelic, unlike mushrooms. You can't control the effects of LSD like you can with mushrooms. Once it takes over, a bad trip is possible. Actually, for Michael, psychedelics were not overwhelming, considering the way his brain functioned and the visions and feelings he would get. He had been a cannabis user his entire life, but it only served to help regulate his weight, blood pressure, and anxiety throughout his life. It kept him cancer free as well. Michael always got a laugh from the hypo-Christians who strenuously worshipped a God and then denied the very gifts he made for them. The human brain actually had receptors for cannabinoids, which meant that it needed to be used for some reason that only the Creator knew. Just yet another lie in the long string of lies that humans believed in.

Michael was just chatting with Tripper and looking around his room when the 'cid kicked in. "Wow," he said. "This is starting to work. I had better get a move on soon. I don't think that I will want to be in this cozy little room for this."

"No, you don't," Tripper agreed. "Best place will be outside in the night sky in a couple of hours. Come back and visit me some day. I got a couple years left here."

Michael left his new friend and began back down the hall he had come in on. The trippy feeling was coming on strong, and he figured that he better find Brad soon, just in case. Brad was bellied up to the bar downstairs, just yacking away with some slutty gal, as usual. Michael caught his attention, and Brad came over across the room. "I took a hit of acid with some dude upstairs," Michael told Brad while snickering like a child who just watched his dad fall off a ladder.

"Really? You're kidding, right?" Brad looked sideways at him and asked, "You think you can handle that with your thing and all?"

"Yes, I think so. I have already noticed that the drinks don't seem to affect me much on it, which is a good thing," Michael replied.

"No, they won't," Brad said in a low worried voice. "You can drink all you want, but when the shit wears off. You will be drunk as a skunk if that much alcohol is still in your system. You had better not drink during the last four hours of the trip. I'll try to keep an eye on you, but I'm not babysitting you if you get stupid."

"Thanks, buddy." Michael smiled. "I think we had better keep an eye on each other and not stay too long at this party." They didn't. A couple more drinks, and they decided to make their way back through campus in the cool night air. Brad was feeling no pain, but Michael was in another world. He had only been tripping for a couple hours and he needed some space to himself now. "Hey, Bradley, I have an idea. Let's see if we can find our way in the dark in different directions. You're hammered, and I'm tripping balls. It will be fun. We will meet back at the apartments. What do you think?"

Brad didn't care one way or the other. "Sounds good, but I'm not waiting up all night for you. If my door is locked, just go to your own apartment, and I will see you in the morning."

"Great," Michael said as he gazed up at the stars. He had no intention of seeing Brad later. It was a good way to kindly ditch a friend for a while when he needed some alone time. Brad headed off into the dark rugby field near their old dorm, and Michael wandered off toward the golf course. The campus course was up on a big hill that was quite a climb, but Michael was always in great shape and wouldn't notice anyway.

It was a new moon that night, so it was really dark, but LSD made it easy to see in the dark. Michael proceeded to his favorite little par three hole that had an elevated green. He lay down in the middle of the green to star gaze and thought through the rest of his trip. This was one of the best experiences of Michael's entire life, with the exception of the fact that he was afraid that he might not remember it because of the alcohol. That was not the case.

He wasn't sure where his mind ended and the LSD began or the other way around or a combination of the two. Whatever the reason, it was almost other worldly. He contemplated the many things he had experienced up to this point in his life: the loss of Jimmy and then Butch, the troubles he had with his family, the realizations of shocking truths about this world through his so-called gift, his growing problems with alcohol, and mostly, his incredible friendship with Brad.

They would be graduating in less than a year and going their separate ways. For Michael, this was almost like losing again. He wasn't sure how he would take it, having to go back out into another phase of his life on his own. Michael was very self-sufficient, sure, but that didn't mean he didn't need love and friendship in his life. Not easy to find for people like him. He knew that Brad would be there for the rest of his life, but at a distance.

The stars that night were awe-inspiring. With no moonlight and on the dark golf course, he could see for light years into the universe. He swore he could see the ether and faraway galaxies that NASA didn't even know about. It was maybe his real home, the home of the Creator that was shining on him. He loved his family for what it was worth, but he did not feel love himself. Why had he always felt like a stranger here, and everyone else seemed to be getting along just fine?

He knew that Brad probably loved him in some way, but he knew that even he would turn away from him should the wrong thing happen. Maybe that was the vision that Michael had when he first got to college. That sense of fear from the first day in the dorm came back to him. He just knew that something was going to happen between him and Brad someday, but what?

LIFE BEGINS

Do, or do not. There is no try.

—Master Yoda

Michael applied to every company he could think of during the final semester of college. Getting a job, especially in engineering, was tough for a recent college graduate without much practical experience. He knew that there was nothing that he couldn't do, or learn how to do; the problem was getting people to believe in his abilities. He couldn't really blame them. Michael didn't trust most people that he had known his entire life.

Interviews were never a big deal to Michael, but then again, neither was public speaking. Companies were looking for individuals that would fit a certain agenda of profit making. You could be the smartest and most well-spoken individual in the selection group, but that might not be what they were looking for. Most times, he could sense what a potential employer was looking for by feelings he would get from the interviewers and then play along accordingly.

He had no real interest in being a company yes man or gopher. An entry-level position in a career in engineering—that was all they were looking for. Michael received the best feeling from a small construction company in Northern California. He would have to start out working in the field as a construction engineer, but at least it was a start at gaining experience toward getting his engineering license someday.

Michael had a fairly decent alcohol habit before leaving college. He was pretty much a daily drinker now, just like the rest of his family. Being very careful to avoid blackouts through school, that would not be the case as his life progressed from there. He had always been a very functional boozer; at least his parents taught him how to do that right. Drinking was more of a tool to him than it was a pleasure. Oh sure, there were lots of enjoyable times early on, but that always led to the path of destructive alcoholism.

The company sent him to work on the I-15 freeway reconstruction project that was ongoing in Salt Lake City. It was a four-year long project, so he was good for a while as far as job security went. Michael's first reaction was that he hoped booze was not as hard to come by since Salt Lake was the Mormon hub. He was pleasantly shocked that it was not, but boy, was it expensive.

Salt Lake City was only about an hour from the Nevada border and a town called Wendover. It really came as no shock to Michael that the town's nickname was Bendover. To cut down on the costs of liquor, he would make trips to Wendover every month to get it in bulk, and it was a lot cheaper. Liquor was cheap in Nevada because they made their money on gambling. Nothing like a drunk fool with the false hope of striking it rich to finance those elaborate casinos. Oh, how the money poured in. The Jack Mormons of Salt Lake City gave as much or more money to the casinos of Wendover as they did to the church of saints.

Michael kept to himself mostly, but he was not a complete recluse at first. Construction workers liked to party more than college and military combined. Drinking with the crew was fun, but he missed hanging out with Brad. They always stayed in touch on the phone, but Brad had taken a job in Arizona, and they would not see each other for many years to come. He had guys that he liked to hang out with, but not really any close friends that he could really open up to or felt like he could trust completely.

He had been on the job for several months when a new engineer came on board. His name was Sean, and he hailed from the Sacramento area originally. He had just started with the same company as Michael a couple months before, and they decided to send him to the Salt Lake City job as well. Sean came in the job trailer, carrying a box full of personal belongings, and set them on the table that was already completely covered with construction blue prints.

"Hello, anyone here?" he shouted.

Michael poked his head out of the project engineer's office, where he had been going over some revisions to the design plans. He saw Sean scanning a circle around the office, trying to get the lay of the land. "Hi, you can just set up your things in the cubicle over there, and we will get you up to speed shortly. Good to have you aboard." Michael pointed over to the cubicle area. "Sean, right?"

"Yeah, thanks," Sean replied. "Where's the bathroom?"

"That's the crapper down there at the far end of the job shack. I'll be just a minute." He turned and went back into the project engineer's office. The project engineer's name was Joe, and he was born without a sense of humor. Michael wanted to tend to the business at hand before working with the new guy.

He came out of the office after about another half hour of plan revision review and walked up to Sean with hand extended. "Sorry about that. He is not a patient man. My name is Michael."

They shook hands, and Michael had a strong sense of something not quite right. It was a vision of his future self. He was faced down on a cold concrete floor with other people in the room, looking down on him. It was a very hazy vision. Michael could not tell where he was or who the people were, but the feeling of fear was overwhelming. He closed his eyes and began to breathe deep and slow, which always seemed to help. The vision went away. He felt betrayal and isolation, but he could not tell the details like he could with some visions.

"Well, Sean," he said as he released his hand, "let me show you around the shack here and get you up to speed on the project."

Sean learned everything rather quickly and didn't have to ask too many questions. As Michael was showing him the ropes, he saw a little of himself in this guy, but there was just something he didn't quite trust. It wasn't a strong enough feeling for him to avoid Sean, but it was something very uncertain. Michael and Sean began to hang out somewhat after work hours. He was as big of a drinker, if not more so than Michael was at this stage in his life, but he could also handle it so much better, like Brad could. Although Brad would never met Sean face-to-face, he would always tell Michael to be careful because there was something he did not trust as well. Michael always thought that maybe Brad was just jealous that he had a new buddy to hang out with, but in fact, Brad had a connection to Michael that he was not aware of and was just trying to warn him. It seemed that Sean never seemed to try to stop Michael when he was about to do something stupid, while Brad always did. Maybe it was a form of entertainment for him, but a real friend was going to step in when it needed to be done, not laugh at the result. Brad would definitely get a kick out of Michael's antics in college, but he actually cared for him.

After two years on the job site, things seemed fairly routine. There was always a fine line between routine and rut, but Michael wasn't in a rut just yet. He had just purchased a truck, and it was the fat tired four-wheeler that he had always wanted. It was a Mazda B4000, but it was made during the years that the Ford Ranger was basically the same pickup. Everyone called it a Ford Mazda as kind of a joke. It was a beautiful blue color, and the first thing Michael wanted to do was make it muddy.

He drove it to work on the Friday morning of the day of the big company party to celebrate the halfway milestone of the freeway project. Everyone was trying to get their work done early, so they could get ready for the party that night. Michael and Sean were buttoning up things at their office and looking over Michael's new rig.

"We need to get this thing dirty," Sean said with a mischievous grin. "Hey, you know, we could come back here after the party and try it in the dark. The old section of freeway that we just demoed this week has no light plants to run into, and it's full of mud from the rain last night."

"Yes," Michael said as his eyes lit up. "No one will see us, and we can come right back here to clean it off. That section is accessible from the yard here, and we don't have to use the city streets. I definitely don't want to encounter any 'imperial bacon.'"

Sean agreed; it was a plan. They headed off to the party and had a good time as usual. Michael had so much in common with him like he did with Brad, but there was just something missing with the spiritual connection. It would reveal itself soon enough. The two could barely wait to get up to the mud pit in the dark, especially with a good buzz on. They decided to leave the party a little early and they had plenty of beer in the truck. As they approached the mud field with fresh beers in hand, Michael cut the headlights and parked for a quick thought.

He engaged into high-gear four-wheel drive and looked at Sean with a smile. "I hope we don't regret this one later." Then he hit the gas.

They sailed through the mud like a jet ski over water. Of all the times that Michael had been mudding in his life, this was by far the greatest. Around and around, they went in swirls and figure eights. Michael brought the truck to a stop in the middle to engage into low gear, which required that he put it into park to do so. This was the perfect opportunity to grab a fresh beer and change the music. Michael had a Ratt tape along, so "Round and Round" seemed like the perfect choice.

With guitar licks booming in the speakers, Michael shifted into drive, and away they went. Intoxication really did affect the judgment, but more so when you were having a good time. Perhaps it was the overzealousness or the sheer feeling of being totally free at that moment, but Michael hit the gas hard. The truck leaped out of its standstill position, and Michael didn't realize that the steering wheel was still turned hard to the left. When the truck front tires hit the ground, it turned a hard left and tipped on the passenger side, sliding in the mud about fifteen feet. Beer went flying all over and dripped all down on Sean.

"Holy shit!" Sean yelled. "Get your window open and let's climb out of here, quick!"

Michael opened the window, which was power operated, so it was a good thing that the truck was still running. They both climbed out and were not injured. It was not a major accident, just a stupid one.

"Let's leave it running in case we can't start it again," Michael said. "Help me flip this back on its wheels." They both got on either side of the truck, which was not lying over at a hard ninety degrees, more like sixty-five, and managed to flip the truck back on its wheels. It was heavy, but they had plenty of adrenaline running. No one could see them in the dark, and they did not really make any noise. They were clear.

Both of them got back in the truck, covered in mud, but so was everything else. Michael looked at Sean and gave a little chuckle. He put the transmission back in high gear and eased his way out of the hole. He slowly made his way back in the direction of the construction yard. The dark might have been good at hiding their antics, but it was also good about hiding giant sink holes. Salt Lake City was built on top of a giant ancient lake bed, and the ground must be drained of this nasty black oily-looking ooze before anything of significance could be built on it. That was part of the job that Michael and Sean were working on. The sludge was impossible to get out of if you were unfortunate enough to get stuck in it. Michael drove straight into one without even realizing it.

The truck came to an instant stop, and the tires started spinning freely, further coating Michael's new truck with a black highlight. He hit the brake, put it in park, and said, "You can't be serious. Really? Ah, I think we're stuck." That was putting it mildly. They were stuck in the middle of the old freeway, in the middle of the night, with no way to get out before daybreak and no one to call since they were all at the party; they were screwed.

Cell phones were just beginning to become widely used about this time, but neither one of them had one yet, and whom could they call stuck out here anyway? They both climbed out of the truck to assess the situation. The truck wasn't going anywhere, so they just looked at each other and began the walk back to the job shack. There would be a phone and a list to look at there.

Michael was looking though a list of all the equipment operator's phone numbers, and he noticed some that he didn't think would be at the party and should be home. It was about one o'clock in the morning, but they were in a bind and needed to get this addressed right away. Once daylight hit, there would be cops and other similar vermin showing up. Sean managed to pass out in the other cubicle chair while Michael was rummaging through the lists of phone numbers.

Michael called Terry, who was an excavator operator and could operate just about anything. He shouldn't be too upset at the late-night call. Terry had no wife or family to disturb and was not much of a partier. Michael didn't remember seeing him at the party when they were there earlier.

After about three rings, someone answered the phone and spoke in a semisleepy voice, "Hello."

"Terry?" Michael asked. "So sorry to bother you this late, but this is Michael, the engineer from work, and I have sort of a problem."

"Hey, Michael," Terry replied. "It's okay about the hour. What happened?"

"Sean and I decided to try out my new four-wheel rig in the section of freeway that you were just excavating this week, and we got stuck," Michael explained to him. He was still fairly intoxicated, and Sean wasn't even conscious anymore.

"You guys been drinking too, I bet," Terry replied.

"Of course," Michael replied like it was just another college prank or something. "Is there any way that you can come down here and pull me out before morning? I really don't want to lose my job over this."

"Yeah, I'll be right there," Terry replied. "Give me about forty-five minutes or so, but you owe me big for this one."

"Yeah, yeah, I know," Michael said, relieved that someone was coming to his rescue. He hung up the phone and looked over at Sean. Boy, he had not been much help with this. Sean was like that, Michael always had a great time when he was with him, but he would soon find out that he was not the standup guy that Michael had figured him for.

Terry showed up like he had promised and was able to pull Michael's truck out with one of the big CAT loaders that was parked in the yard. Once free, Michael made his way back to the job shack, while Terry followed him in the loader just to make sure that he did not get stuck again. By about three o'clock in the morning, they were back in the office, and Sean was still passed out in the chair.

Terry looked at Sean in the chair and then over to Michael. "You guys really tied one on tonight," he said.

"Yeah, and you really saved my ass," Michael said. "Thanks so much. I should have never let Sean talk me into that."

Terry started to make his way to the door and then stopped and turned to look at Michael. "You know, I hear you guys talk quite a bit when we are out in the field, and it seems that you and Sean really like to hang out and party quite a lot. You have to be about thirty years old, I would imagine. I was just the same way as you two, and now I haven't had a drink in eight years. This may seem like just a small incident of harmless fun, but the antics will get worse if you don't get the drinking under control."

This was the first time that someone Michael didn't know all that well had said something about his drinking. "So that's why I never see you at the company parties," he said as if a light bulb came on in his head.

"Yes, that's right," Terry said. "That is also why I said something to you about it because I see a problem developing in you, even if you don't. I won't say anything to the super about tonight, but I hope you take a hard look at your life and not let something like this happen again."

"I won't," Michael said in denial. "I do appreciate your concern, but I have other issues that you don't know about. Thanks again, and I will take you to lunch next week. I am going to take Sean home and then go to bed for the rest of the weekend."

Terry gave a nod and smile and left the job shack for home. Michael went over to wake Sean and take him home. He was really out cold, and it required a bit of effort to wake him up. He was groggy and made no sense, but Michael was able to get him loaded in the truck, drive him home, and then get him into his apartment safely. After dropping off Sean, Michael went back to his place, had another couple drinks, and then went to bed about the time the sun was coming up.

Crisis alleviated, he was thinking as he drifted off into slumber.

He slept until early Sunday morning and then went down to the spray and wash to clean up his truck. He couldn't leave the evidence and then show up at work on Monday. Michael didn't hear from Sean all day, which was unusual, and there was no answer whenever he tried to call. He figured that Sean was just sleeping it off, as he was quite a bit more housed than Michael was on Friday night.

Monday morning came, and Michael was off to work early. He wanted to get there before anyone else in case there was some leftover damage control to be done. Everything looked shipshape at work, and it was impossible to tell anyone had been out playing in the mud amongst all the large CAT tire tracks from heavy equipment usage. He rested at ease in his cubicle, waiting for the project manager to arrive. Strange, though, that Sean was not in yet.

Joe arrived at seven on the nose as usual, and Michael was just going over some new work plans for sewer pipe installation that he had written up. "I'd like to see you in my office, Michael. Give me fifteen minutes though," Joe said without breaking stride from the front door to his office.

Now, Michael had a bad feeling in his gut that he was in trouble. Someone had talked, and he noticed that Sean was not here yet. Coincidence? He spoke up before Joe got all the way into the office. "Sean is not here yet either." He directed his comment to Joe's back as he entered his office doorway.

Joe paused in the doorway and turned his head to the side. "He called me already and will be out sick today. See you in fifteen." He turned his head back around, went in the office, and shut the door behind him.

Michael waited for what seemed like the longest fifteen minutes of his life. He was just sure that he was going to get fired. He knocked on the office door at quarter past seven, and he could see Joe waving him in through the window. He opened the door, entered, and then closed it behind him.

"Sit down for a second, Michael," Joe said as Michael took a seat in front of his desk. "Terry told me about what happened this weekend, and don't get all mad at him. He had to tell me to cover his own ass and CDL, as I am sure you can understand. This will not go past this office, but I am fairly pissed off about the whole thing." Joe paused, and Michael was just nodding his head.

Joe sat back in his desk chair and continued, "I want you to be clear about a couple things. This is not a frat house playground, nor is it a race track. I know that boys will be boys and you wanted to have fun with Sean in your new truck, but if you were to have been hurt during your little drunken jaunt, the insurance penalties would have been enormous. You would not have been fired. Actually, you might have been arrested and charged with a crime." He paused and leaned up, resting his forearms on the desk. "Now, I like you, Michael. You are one of the best engineers I've ever had working for me, but I know you have a rebel streak in you. Terry will not say anything to anyone else, and neither will you or Sean. This is your one break, but if you ever do anything remotely like that again, then you will be done with this company. Are we clear on that, Michael?"

"Yes," Michael said with his head hanging down a bit. He wanted to interject about how the whole thing was really Sean's idea and he was just going along with it, but he didn't think it mattered at this point. Michael still did the act, but he might not have if Sean wasn't cheering him on.

"Okay then," Joe said. "Get back on those work plans. They are really looking good." Michael got up from his chair and grabbed the doorknob. "By the way," Joe continued, "was it fun?"

Michael gave a smile while opening the door. He looked back at Joe and said, "Oh yeah. It was a phenomenal mudding experience." He left the office and shut the door behind him.

"That was fun," Michael whispered to himself on the way back to his desk. Sean sure missed out on a nice ass chewing. Although Sean would never admit to it, Michael just knew that he had called in sick to miss any chance that they might have been ratted out. There was always something about him that he didn't quite trust, but this just added some certainty to it. He didn't really blame Terry either, and he seemed to go about it the right way so no one was punished to severely. Sometimes the fear of the punishment was more than enough lesson.

Michael and Sean continued their friendship as usual, but Michael would definitely not share too much about himself with him. They drank exceptional amounts of alcohol together over the years. Although Michael would tell him some things when they were drinking, Sean would never remember and neither would Michael. He always feared what things he might have told him when he was drunk. The thing he feared the most was demonic blackouts, but they were due to begin again, and this time there was no stopping them.

Most people who drank excessively would have a blackout at some point. Some said that having a blackout in any form was a sign of alcoholism. Not necessarily true, but in Michael's case, most definitely. He was a fully functional alcoholic before he was thirty, similar to his parents, except much worse. A spiritual psychic with anger issues and a demon inside was something very explosive, and alcohol was the spark. Michael never would do any intentional harm to anything in a sober state of mind. He was a good, kind-hearted, and generous soul—one that was very easy to take advantage of and use for personal gain. He also took it very personally when they did, wishing the most hateful form of vengeance imaginable on them, especially his father. Then he would feel guilty after, but the bottle helped cure that as well.

Sean enabled him better than anyone he had ever known. Brad was kind of like that at first, but toward the end of college, he really didn't like Michael drinking too much and made some comments about it from time to time. Michael knew he had a problem with drinking early on but really didn't care too much. Maybe it was because he hadn't been in serious enough shit yet, or maybe that was what alcoholism was like for most people. All he knew was that the more he drank, the less he felt other people's suffering and the less he was able to visualize it in his mind. It was the one relief that kept him drinking for so long.

People of the world could solve all their problems if they just had the courage, but most do not. One of the main mottos for recovering alcoholics coincidently had to do with courage. What Michael sensed in most people was an overwhelming fear of everything. This fear would spill over into him and lead to anger. His anger would build and need to be vented from time to time. Unfortunately for

Michael, this would usually occur in alcohol blackouts that would be witnessed by many people over the years.

Michael liked to drink down at a local neighborhood bar that was within walking distance of his apartment. He would stop in on the way home most nights, and he liked to walk there on the weekends. The bartender's name was John. He was a tall lanky fellow, with a loud voice that carried like Michael's did. He liked to talk to John about a wide array of intelligent subject matter, and the place was never really that busy here in Mormon town, so he had lot of opportunities for conversation. John seemed very intelligent to him, and he had no reason to think that he was not. He always seemed to know his facts. There was always something kind-hearted and generous about John, and he wanted to get to know him better.

One fall Saturday afternoon, John invited him to come to his house for a barbecue the following day, and Michael definitely accepted. John lived in a small pieced together house at the end of a city alley that doubled as his driveway. He had a girlfriend and a daughter, which Michael never knew at all after knowing John for almost a year. It was his daughter that amazed Michael the most.

Michael showed up with care package in hand and gave it to John. "Here you go. I hope we don't need to run to the store for more later."

John let out one of his loud laughs. "I don't think that will be a problem. There is so much liquor here today. By the way, my daughter over there has been asking me about meeting new friends lately." He pointed at a little infant-sized girl in a wheelchair across the yard. "That's her over there in the chair. She has brittle bone disease, but she is smarter than any other person I have ever met, other than you. Go over and say hi."

Michael made his way over toward the girl. He felt a wonderful peaceful energy surge, growing larger in him as he drew closer. She was thirteen and forever bound to a wheelchair. Her body was the size of a two- or three-year-old since the disease caused her bone structure and muscles to stop growing, but the rest of her still did. He gently reached down and gripped her hand and received an overwhelming sense of contentment.

"Hello there, princess," Michael said to her with a smile. "What is your name?"

"Tisha," she responded with a shy grin and a little slurred due to the problems associated with the disease. "Are you Michael?" she asked.

"Yes, how did you know that?" Michael asked while still somewhat shocked by her knowing that information already, because he didn't think John had told her.

"I just know things about people when I touch them," she said. "I feel something in you that I haven't in any one of the people that Dad has introduced me to."

"Yes, me too," Michael told her. "I felt the same thing. So you have the gift or at least what I call the 'flaw.'"

"It's not a flaw." She looked up at him. "You are using it wrong." She looked down at her wheelchair controls and moved the control knob forward. "Come on, let's go tool around and enjoy the day." She drove that chair better than any of the horrible Salt Lake drivers drove their cars and headed over to her favorite shade tree with Michael in tow. She parked her chair in her favorite spot, which already had indented tire marks since she obviously liked to come out here a lot. Just like Michael, closer to nature was where she felt more comfortable even if it was a single tree stuck in the city landscape. She dumped a little bag out on her lap that had some figures of animals in it and began to amuse herself.

"Tisha dear," Michael said as he put a hand on her head, "I'm going to go over and talk to your dad for a little while, but I will be back to talk to you some more in a little bit, okay?"

"Okay," she replied in the sweetest little voice without breaking stride in the animation of her figurines.

Michael walked over to the cooler and snagged a fresh beer. He could really use one about now. Although he could feel such goodness in this little angel, he briefly felt her pain as well. It was horrid. He walked over to the barbecue pit, where John was demonstrating his best Swedish chef impersonation. Beer in one hand and tongs in the other, John was always a happy-go-lucky kind of a guy.

"Hey, John, how are those steaks coming along?" Michael asked as he polished off his first beer and grabbed a fresh one out of the cooler.

"Just dandy," John cheered. "You got to meet Tisha, I see. She really is special."

"Yes, I know," Michael agreed. "Can you tell me a little more about her illness?"

"Sure," John said. "Brittle bone disease means that her organs grow, but the bone structure around it does not. We have to take her in every few months now to have her chest cavity opened up to relieve the pressure. Basically, her body is constricting itself and slowly dy ... ing." He choked a little on the last word and wiped a tear from his eye with his forearm. "She generates enough natural painkiller to keep her from too much discomfort, but there are no medications that will help her anymore, so we just let it work its course. If any normal person were to feel the pain that her body is able to suppress, they would pass out immediately."

"That's just terrible," Michael replied. "So sad. She is such an amazing spirit."

"Yes, we know," John said as he closed his eyes for a brief moment. He knew how special his daughter was. Turns out the Tisha's mom was killed in a car crash some years ago and John had been there every step of the way for this little girl. He was a good father and, more than that, a genuinely good person.

Michael's thoughts of himself were of no concern to him at that moment. Perhaps it was the first time in his life that he felt love for something other than himself. He turned away from John and looked toward Tisha sitting under the shade tree, laughing and amusing herself. How could she be so happy and so miserable at the same time? Maybe it was just everyone else that thought she was miserable. Good old human assumption and judgment. He started to cry very silently, and he walked casually into the house bathroom to compose himself.

He came out of the house and grabbed another beer and walked back over to the barbeque pit, where John was still cooking away. He had the oysters going now and was really quite the gourmet backyard cook. Michael was a great cook himself after all those years doing it in college and could recognize and appreciate the skills of another.

"So what is going to happen to her?" Michael resumed his conversation with John.

"Can you hand me the spices on the table over there?" John asked, and Michael retrieved them as requested. "Well, she has already lived longer than most doctors have expected. I don't think she will make sixteen, but who knows? Every soul has a purpose, and at least hers was being here long enough to show us what really matters in life. By the way, while you were gone in the house, she told me how much she liked you already, Michael."

Michael gave a little sniffle and said, "Thanks, Johnny. I'm really glad I came over here today. Would it be okay if I came over and visited her from time to time?" he asked.

"You better." Johnny looked at him with wide eyes. "That little girl over there will be so upset if you don't, and not much really upsets her as you can see."

"No, it does not," Michael said as her looked in her direction. Tisha was cruising the food line, now checking out all the goods. She knew that there wasn't much that she could eat, so she had to have the pick of the grill, so to speak. For the first time in Michael's life, he felt exceptional joy in another person and would do anything to feel the same way. She had told him he was using it wrong, and she was right, but he had no idea how to change that yet. Although she would not be here for much longer, at least he was given the gift of her presence in his life, if only for a little while.

Michael came over every weekend to see Tisha for the remainder of his time in town. Her favorite game to play was hangman. She couldn't do many activities that required too much movement, so hangman seemed like the most creative choice. The more he saw her, the more he realized how intelligent and special she really was, and this world would never know. He talked to her about a wide range of subjects during their visits. It was so amazing the level of knowledge in this young girl. To him, she wasn't a young girl at all; she was a teacher. She had read more books than anyone he had ever met and would retain everything. Tough books. She did not read your run-of-the-mill young people's books. Some of them Michael had read, and some he would read later in life. Most of all, they talked of spiritual things and the gifts that they both possessed.

One particular visit, Michael asked her about their first meeting. "Tisha, you said the first time we met that I was using it wrong. What did you mean by that?"

"Oh, lots of things," she said. "I could feel such a great deal of suffering in you, much like you did with me. You have been through much loss and have been treated quite poorly in your life. I also sense that you don't recognize much with modern society. All the same counts for me as well, but I have let it go. You need to do that as well. This power to feel things and maybe change the world someday is quite overwhelming at first and we see the world for what it really is, but we cannot let it take control of our lives. If we do that, then we are no better than the ones who cause suffering. It will not happen overnight, and it is not easy by any means. If you cannot get control of it, you will slowly go mad and be lost forever. Does any of this make sense to you?"

It seemed funny to Michael, but his girl was like Yoda in both size and knowledge. He replied to her insights. "Yes, all too well. You're talking about acceptance. I have a tough time letting go. It is like I am obsessing with payback and vengeance for evil deeds. Then I can feel it turning to obsession from time to time. I just can't let it go that the good are made to suffer while the scum of society rises to the top and lives so comfortably. All the suffering that I feel in people is intentionally caused by other people. The sole source of all human suffering is their ignorance."

"I couldn't agree more," she said. "But you have to let it go. You are never going to change it alone, and you certainly are not going to see people rushing to help you. It is not right, but that is the way it is. The world is full of evil, and you were born inherently good. It is how you choose to use your free will to navigate through the evil that will matter in the end."

"Where do you come up with this?" Michael asked. "Simply amazing. You're not a little girl at all. You're some kind of prophet. Is it possible that you were sent to help me?"

"It's possible," she said as she smiled big at Michael. "Now, can we get on with our game and stop this heavy talk? We aren't going to change the world today."

Michael grinned back at her and began to draw out the hangman board on a blank sheet of paper. Boy, was he glad that he met her, and he knew that their time together would be short. That would be his first test of acceptance. He wasn't sure if he would end up leaving town for his next job before she passed away, but he was quite certain that he was not going to watch another friend die. Either way, he would be at peace with it.

Shortly after the millennium, the Salt Lake City job was starting to wind down and the company was looking to move Sean and Michael to new locations for work. Of course, they were hoping to get sent to the same spot since they were drinking chums. Michael never took Sean to meet John or Tisha. That was something that he kept for himself; besides, he didn't figure that Sean and John would get along too well.

The company was bidding a new job in the Fresno area that would be a two-year long project or more. Sean, being from California, was hoping to get assigned there. Michael didn't care one way or another. The only thing that would bother him was having to say goodbye to Tisha. That was going to happen no matter where they were sent.

Sure enough, the company was the low bidder and awarded the Fresno job. Michael and Sean had both put in requests to go. They were both top performers, so the chances were good. Michael didn't like waiting to hear, and he really didn't want to go and have to make new friends anywhere. He would rather go with Sean, and that was what the company decided as well. Apparently, the company liked the way the two worked together and did not want to split them up. Great. Now he had to break the news to John and Tisha. He never really let on that he might be leaving town someday, sooner than later. Michael decided to stop by the bar after work and see John first.

"Hey, Michael," John said as Michael came through the door. "You know, Tisha just never lets up about you." He could see Michael's long face. "Something wrong, pal?"

"You could say that," Michael said as he sat in the stool in front of the beer taps. "I think about her too. The company is relocating me to another job."

John stopped cleaning the bar glass he was working on and looked up at Michael. "I knew that would be going someday. When do you leave?"

"Next week, so I need to tell Tisha this weekend." Michael looked up at John with a grimace on his face. "To tell you the truth, I knew that it was coming someday too, but I didn't want to think about it. And, John, Tisha probably knows already."

"Yeah, you're right about that," John said as he went back to polishing bar glasses. "You two definitely have a gift that I can't understand, but that doesn't make it any less real. I can see that when I watch you two together. You have been a great friend, Michael, and much more than that to my little girl. I am going to be sad to see you go."

Michael started to get a tear welling in his eye, but he quickly wiped it away. "Well, you might as well pour some cold ones before all the sadness sets in." Michael had never been that drunk around John and Tisha. For some reason, he just didn't need it as much when he was with them.

He went to see Tisha on Saturday afternoon like he did every weekend. He brought her a special gift. It was a leather-bound collection of Emily Dickinson poems that they both enjoyed so much. When he went inside, she was waiting for him in the living room with a smile and pad and pencil in hand, ready for hangman.

"Hi, Tisha," Michael said as he walked into the living room. "You look so cheerful and glowing as usual. I brought you a present."

"Really?" Her eyes seemed to light up more than normal. "What could it be? You know that I am hard to surprise, but I have no idea what it is." She took the package from Michael's extended hand and sat it on her lap. She laid a hand over it and then looked tenderly up at him. "Thank you so much, Michael, but let me open this after you tell me what you came here to tell me."

"You know already?" he asked with a not-so-surprised look on his face.

"I have an idea, but I'm not certain. The future is always in motion as you well know." Tisha gave a fast grin. "Are you leaving here?"

"Yes," he said as a tear rolled down his cheek. "You know I will never forget you." Michael began to sob a little more readily. "You have done more for me than you can possibly know, and I am going to try to make some changes in my life when I get to Fresno."

"Fresno," she said. "That's where your next job is. I wish I could see what your future looks like, and we all know mine is very short." She began to sob. "I will wait for you when I get there. We shall see each other again, but until then, I will miss you very much."

Michael gently wiped the tears out of her eyes with his thumbs and bent down and gave her a soft kiss on the top of her small head. A large tear rolled off his cheek and landed on hers. It was a tear of acceptance that all was well with the design of the universe. "Now open your present, you silly goose," he said as he pulled a chair over and sat beside her.

She tore the paper off with excitement and looked at the dark leather beautifully bound gold-tinted book with its own built-in bookmark. "Oh, Michael," she said, "I love it. We have enjoyed some of her stuff in the past. In a lot of ways she was much like us." She held it to her tiny over-pressurized chest and hugged it as best she could. Michael was afraid that she might be hugging it too tight and break one of her ribs, which had happened before, but not this time.

"I'm glad you like it, princess," he said. "I wrote in the front cover as well. Just something from Emily that I thought you might enjoy. It is part of something in the book that you will have to find when you read it."

She looked up at Michael with a well of fluid in both eyes. "I want to show you something, Michael. You are as special to me as my dad is and my mom was." She set the book over on her little table, where she kept her miscellaneous doodads and picked up the pad they used to play hangman and the pencil and then set them on her lap. She looked down at the pencil and closed her eyes and gave a short low breath that sounded like more of a hum. She then opened her eyes and looked back down at the pencil with a level of concentration that he had never seen on her face before.

The pencil began to shiver and then slowly rose off of the pad on her lap. Michael was just staring in awe. The pencil spun a half circle as it continued to gently rise at a gentle pace.

"See if you can tell what I'm spelling," she said without taking her eyes off the pencil. The pencil began to spell out a phrase, like this was the ultimate form of hangman. It did not leave a mark on the air, of course, but Michael could make out what she was writing with it. It spelled out the phrase "I will miss you, Michael." When she was done, she just guided the pencil back to its original position on the pad on her lap.

Michael's mouth was full open, and he was just staring down at the pencil for a second. "Holy crap! You're like Jesus," he said as he looked from the pencil back to her face.

"We all are, Michael," she said as she set the pad and pencil back on her little table. "Jesus was a man. Religions of the world have been manipulated by evil and have distorted everything that he was. He had the power to fully use the power of the human potential as we all do. The world is so controlled by fear, the most powerful force in the universe, that it can't concentrate on what is necessary to achieve happiness."

"You know, you really are not of this world," Michael said as he gave an approving nod. "I've always known that, and I feel so lucky to have been able to be in your life. I don't see much happiness in this world. I think the Buddha was right to say that all life is suffering."

"Yes, he did. The first noble truth." She looked up at him with one eye shut like she was blocking out a bright light. "Do you know what he meant by that though?"

"Basically, that life sucks and then you die, right?" He chuckled as he uttered such banality almost on purpose.

"Funny, Michael," she said. "He meant that life is never going to be all happy or all suffering, but that we could also concentrate our energy where we choose to. If we concentrate on the suffering, then that is exactly what it will be. Fear and suffering go hand in hand, and that is exactly what evil uses to control man, FEAR. The sole sign of evil is the need to control another. If you haven't noticed everywhere you look, everything is all about fear and suffering and that makes it very difficult for man to find love and joy. Religions, governments, media, and schools all thrive on emphasizing punishment and fear to get society to behave like they want thus controlling them for their own personal gains. If people just stopped concentrating on their controlled fear, then it would cease to exist."

"It's cool enough that you look like a little Buddha, but to talk like him too. You're just too much, Tisha," Michael replied to her expert philosophy. "So who knows that you can levitate things?"

"Just my dad and my mother knew, and now you do," Tisha said. "You have to keep this secret as I promised my dad that I wouldn't show anyone since he didn't want me to end up as some sideshow circus freak on display for entertainment. I am quite certain that he will not mind that I showed you. I did because you have the ability too. Your powers are just so clouded in fear, anger, and alcohol right now that you can't see that."

Michael hung his head. "Yes, I know. I will try though. I really don't have many peers here like you that can help me. You know as well as I do that modern psychology is only a means to keep you behaving as sick society thinks you should."

"Yes, I do, but until you stop concentrating on evil society and revenge, you will never be able to use your gifts," she said quite certainly. "You know, speaking of psychology, did you know that Carl Jung could levitate? I read somewhere along the way that the reason Sigmund Freud stopped associating with Jung is that he levitated in front of him and it freaked him out so much that he did not want to be around him anymore. It really makes sense after reading some of the things that Carl Jung used to write about psychic abilities, which we all really have but just so dormant."

"Yeah, I read that too," Michael replied. "Jung was very antisystem of society, kind of like us. He knew that most of it was based on lies, but Freud was their yes man that they were looking for. By the way, who exactly are they?"

"That is something that you will have to figure out." Tisha looked very seriously at him. "You have a lot left to do, and I know in my heart that you will find it someday, but you have a lot of suffering coming as well. If you are strong enough to see the signs and dangers, then you will succeed."

"The force is strong with this one." He giggled as he pointed at her. "Are we still going to play our regular hangman game?"

"We already did," she replied as she gestured toward the pencil on the table. "I will never see you again while I am alive. I know that, but at least now I have nothing to fear. I feel that I have served my purpose in this life if I have helped you."

Michael leaned down and gave her the softest of hugs. He never really wanted to touch her much since he was always afraid that he might break one of her bones, but they both needed this. She gave a gentle squeeze back, which he could feel took all the strength that she had left in her little body. He broke into hard sobs. "I love you so much and will miss you more than anyone I have ever known, including Jimmy." They had talked at length about the trauma with Jimmy some time before, so she could understand what she really did mean to him.

Michael left that afternoon after they talked a little more about life and things. He really did not want to let her down, but he was afraid she was right. Fear was the strongest thing that enslaved humanity, along with the most destructive. It was so prevalent in this world that Michael was not so sure that earth was not the actual hell that religions spoke of.

BETRAYAL

We have to distrust each other. It is our only
defense against betrayal.

—Tennessee Williams

The San Joaquin Valley was basically a centrally located convection
oven in California, wedged in between Yosemite National Park and
the Los Angeles Grapevine pass. Bakersfield was commonly referred
to as the rectum of this particular valley, but Fresno was definitely the
colon. *Flat, arid, hot,* and *dust covered* were the most commonly used
terms to describe the valley's demographics. The smell of fresh cow
manure in the air was not an uncommon occurrence. Not an easy
place to find work if your business was in tourism.

Sean and Michael decided to rent a house together and arrived
a week before they had to report to work. They didn't want to rush
it and needed enough time to find a decent place that they could
afford. Both took their two-week vacation at this time since they had
to move everything as well. Sean had rented a large moving van in
Salt Lake City, and they offloaded all their stuff into a storage unit in
Fresno while they stayed in a local hotel, spending their days looking
at houses.

They found the perfect place in a cul de sac on the outskirts of
town. This was the beginning of the subdivision growth spurt in the
country. The place had a decent sized backyard with a high board
fence, giving it great privacy. It had three large bedrooms and two
full bathrooms. The floor plan was basically a ranch-style layout with
good open living spaces all surrounding the central kitchen. The

bonuses were the large garage, basketball hoop, and covered back patio. The patio was where most of the partying would take place.

They had already returned the moving van, but it didn't take all that many trips with both pickups to get there stuff moved in. It took a good week and many beer breaks to do it properly though. It was a nice situation with both having their own rooms and bathrooms. The extra bedroom was basically used by Sean's son when he came to stay. It turned out that Sean had been embroiled in a custody battle for a while, and it looked like he might get full custody soon.

Michael never even knew about Sean's son until about their third year on the Salt Lake City freeway job together. His son was from a mistake; basically there was no other way to put it. He got drunk one night at a party and slept with a girl, who already had one child at age seventeen, and of course, he did not wear a condom. Darin was the result. He was around nine years old and a total pain in the ass. He ran around, jumping and yelling all the time, like the Tasmanian devil on acid. There was nothing that this kid didn't play with and break most often. Michael learned early to keep his bedroom door locked and leave nothing of worth out in the rest of the house.

The company had sent them to the Fresno area as there were a lot of state highway contracts in the area that the company was bidding on, and they had already been awarded several. The two of them did not get assigned to the same jobs. Michael was working on a long-term highway reconstruction project in the southern part of the valley, while Sean was working on drainage projects just north of town.

Things were relatively fun for a while. Sean and Michael would have their beers at night during the week, usually just tooling around the house, listening to music or watching the occasional movie. The weekend party would start immediately after work on Fridays and continue until late Sunday night. Michael was fairly controlled and never achieved any serious blackouts until he went to see Brad again.

Brad had met a girl in their final year of college, and she had gone with him when college was over. Michael received the call that Brad was going to get married and wanted Michael to be his best man. Michael had never been asked to do anything of the sort in his whole life, but that was most likely due to his inability to find a genuine friend or really trust anyone.

The wedding was back in Brad's old stomping grounds of Marin County, near the San Francisco bay area. Marin County was such a beautiful area. It was located on the north side of the Golden Gate Bridge in a much more rural setting than the rest of the Bay Area. This was where the big money was, as well as San Quentin prison. Coincidence? One could take the Golden Gate Bridge if they were willing to pay the toll or drive all the way around through the Richmond Bridge, which was the longer way, but you passed right by the prison going that way.

Michael had been down to the area with Brad once during college. They drove down because his mother had passed away, and Michael had decided to go along for moral support. That was the trip where they came back along the beautiful Oregon coast, but Brad was not really in the mood to enjoy it, as one might expect after just losing his mother. His father was some high-up engineer for the Bechtel Corporation, so that was where the money came from. Secret government contracts to build more evil machinery for the purpose of murdering innocent people, resulting in political and financial gain, was a very profitable business.

The bachelor party was the night before the wedding as per tradition. Most people had such gatherings many days before the event to rest up after, but Brad wanted it to be all traditional. The party was actually at his father's house, but his dad was off in some foreign axis power country at the time, working on important projects and could not get away for the wedding.

Shots, beers, doobies, and dancing girls were the highlight of the party, and Michael was having a great time with his old friend. He had not seen Brad since college, but they had talked on the phone many times over the years. Michael was known to imbibe a little more freely when he was at ease or having a good time, and the bachelor party was shaping up to be those exact right conditions for a blackout evening.

The party was fun for all, and Michael just kept drinking at a steady pace. Brad was the brunt of the entertainment for the evening, and Michael had some great stories from college. It was quite possible that he shared more than Brad really wanted everyone to know. Some of the other groomsman were people Brad grew up with and his only brother. Everyone started to clear out after midnight as Michael began to act very strange and was beginning his trip into darkness. Brad could recognize the descent and was trying to get a handle on it, but he was also fairly inebriated himself. Michael decided to get in the hot tub and be alone. Brad didn't think that was such a bad idea while he played host as everyone went home.

Hot tubs and alcohol didn't mix unless your intention was to get really drunk in a hurry and then enter into a blackout state. Brad joined Michael in the tub after everyone was gone. As he slid in, he could see Michael with his head hanging, but he was mumbling out loud, so there was no way that he was passed out.

"Hey, Michael." Brad tried to get his attention. "Are you okay?"

Michael's head slowly rose up, and Brad could see the cold, dead black eyes that he had not seen in a long time. He had a look on his face that was contorted, and his top lip was slightly pursed back, garnering an evil grin. "So you're getting married tomorrow," he said in a rather ominous fashion. "You and I will never be the same. The only man that I trusted, and you are throwing me aside as well. Just like all the rest."

"What are you talking about, Michael?" Brad responded back in a disgusted tone. "You're too drunk again. I never like you when you're too drunk, and it seems to be more often these days. All those late-night drunk calls when you and your roommate, Sean, get too loaded. I still like to hang out with you, but not like we used to. You are the most intelligent and caring man I have ever met, but not when you're drinking."

Michael looked away from Brad and stared off toward the bay. The house had a nice view of the San Francisco Bay since it was positioned high in the hills of Marin County. "You know, I really hate this world. Every time I have someone in my life that I can trust, they leave or die. That is what you are doing with this marriage. She doesn't care about you, just the earning potential that you have. I knew that the first time I met her. All American women really—they never miss an opportunity to disgust me along with most humans." Michael spoke very fluently when he would black out, like a switch went off in his mind. He was no longer acting drunk and actually would make a lot of sense, but it was all being controlled by anger and fear instead of understanding and love.

"I know you feel that way, Michael, but you are not thinking straight right now," Brad responded. "Maybe you should get some sleep. We have a big day tomorrow, and I do thank you for helping with the bachelor party."

"I've been asleep my whole life." Michael looked at him. "What more is another night going to matter? I see things and feel the ones around me. The more I see of this place, the more I want to leave it. I think about it more every day. I really have never belonged here, and I think maybe I should just check out some days."

"That's it," Brad said as he got out of the tub. "You're going to bed." He reached down to try to help Michael out of the tub, and his arm was slapped violently away. This was the first time that he had felt like hitting Michael in some sort of violent altercation.

Michael stood up fast away from Brad's reach and stepped quickly out of the tub. "You don't ever touch me. I will not be man-handled by a scumbag human just using me for his own entertainment." He squared off in front of Brad like they were getting ready to spar. Both of them were standing there, dripping in their swimsuits, and the air blowing off the bay was not exactly warm. Summers in San Francisco were more like winters.

"Come back to me, buddy." Brad tried to reach through the demon that was controlling his mind. He had seen it in the woods during that first spring break trip, but he just ran off. Now this was an actual confrontation. Michael looked like he was going to swing, then something happened. Brad saw his brown pupils come back, and the total blackness disappeared. His eyes rolled back into his head, and he collapsed onto the concrete, unconscious.

Michael awoke the next morning due to Brad shaking him. "Wake up! We got a wedding, remember?" He was leaning over him as he came into view and the initial vision blur that came with a four alarm hangover began to fade. To say that he felt like shit was an understatement. What a party. Brad had carried him to one of the beds in the house after he passed out last night. Of course, Michael did not remember a thing from the blackout at the end of the night, but Brad filled him in. Brad left the room after he was awake and told him to get ready for the wedding.

Brad had bought all the groomsman expensive liquor flasks that were engraved with their names and the date of the wedding. How ironic for Michael that he was going to use that during the wedding to house a little hard liquor to help make it through the day without puking on everyone. This would mark the first time that he had ever continued to drink on the morning after in order to feel better. No one was the wiser.

The wedding came off without a hitch, and Michael did not end up spending too much time at the reception. The liquor in the flask had helped him get through the wedding, but he was still looking forward to getting back to a bed as soon as possible. This hangover was going to take more than a day to sleep off. It was actually the first time that it took three days to wear off, and they would get more frequent as Michael continued his spiral into alcoholism.

Michael was right about one thing. After the wedding, he really didn't talk to Brad that much and did not see him very often. This was due to more than just the fact that Brad was now married and had a different direction in life. He did not like the way that Michael had continued drinking after college and did not want to be around him that much after this recent performance. He wasn't ditching him like everyone else and would be there if he was really needed. Brad just did not want to see his friend get worse, and he knew that it was not something he could change right now.

After almost a year in the Fresno desert, Michael received two pieces of disturbing news. First, Tisha passed away, and John had called to let him know. It was a rough conversation for both, but Michael had said goodbye to his angel before he left Salt Lake City. He knew that he would never see her alive again, that day he told her he was leaving. It was more of a relief than anything. The second was that Sean won his custody battle, and Darin was coming to live with them permanently. Oh for joy!

Things definitely changed after that. Michael definitely had to find more ways to be away from home. Sean was a fun father, but not what you would call a good parent. He got better as time passed, and Michael would drop hints, of course. Darin wasn't all bad. He loved to play sports, and so did Michael, which would give him an edge to be able to bond with the kid. Although Michael was the chubby kid in high school, the military shaved that off, and he always maintained a fairly fit shape through most of his life. His passion was baseball, and so was Darin's. About the time that little league rolled around, Darin could not wait to get on a team. Sean was busy on weekend shift work during the Saturday sign up time, so Michael took him.

Michael didn't play many sports in high school, but he did play little league and loved it. He also played for the restaurant city league team while in college and was one of their best players. Brad played on the team as well, though he was not the natural that Michael was. That was one of the extracurricular college activities they had the most fun doing together. Michael pictured the happiest beer commercial was the best way to describe his college ball years.

As Michael's drinking got worse, he had to find new ways to hide it. Dragging huge coolers full of beer to Little League games was slowly being phased out of this free society. Smoking and drinking was incrementally being outlawed almost everywhere, he was noticing. It was not because governments cared about people. Michael was already sure of that. A need to control other people was strictly an evil quality of all governments. Control involved money, which generated more money, the only god that humans obeyed. Americans loved to sing songs about freedom and bravery, two things that they weren't even close to being. Slaughtering large groups of unarmed civilians in foreign lands so banks and corporations could control more resources was not bravery; it was murder on a genocidal level. He really found his mind wandering into cynicism more and more as his alcohol abuse got worse.

He and Sean would usually go to all the practices and games. Sometimes one of them would have to work, but they scheduled it so that at least one of them would be able to take Darin and be there to watch. Michael was starting to feel like kind of a stepfather at times, and the kid wasn't all that bad once he got through the barriers. Since it was difficult to bring beer to the games and practices, Sean and Michael would mix drinks in water bottles so no one was the wiser. They could easily go back to the car to mix fresh drinks when necessary. It was really no different than the way his father was when growing up. Michael's dad would always drive everywhere with a beer and frequently had Michael grab him one when he was too busy driving. His mother never said anything, but she would never drink until the evenings usually.

Michael would try not to call home during their evening happy hour times, but sometimes it was inevitable. No matter how little understanding he would receive from his family, his mother was one of the only people he had to talk to, which would frustrate him even more. Most calls ended with yelling to one another, and his mother would hang up sometimes. All, of course, due to his father's influence on everyone. It did not matter what he wanted to talk about. His father just had to try to prove him wrong for some reason. He tried never to talk to his father much over the phone because he did not need any more "tough love" solutions, which weren't solutions at all. Tough love was no love.

Michael didn't need more trouble. He needed someone who would understand him like Tisha used to. He really did miss her, but he still had the gift of the knowledge that she did share with him. He knew that he was blaming everyone for his problems, but then again, they did help to create some of them. It was his choice to let people into his life in the first place, and the more he did, the more he realized that he really didn't want to let anyone in anymore. They were not to be trusted.

It was during the second year of little league that Michael's direction in life began to change. As years of drinking had decreased his psychic abilities, which was why Michael started drinking in the first place, his severe alcoholism was starting to affect his life. He had almost no intuition about people he would meet anymore, so he had no more defense mechanism against the ones that would use him for their own gain. He would also not receive future visions like he had up until a few years ago.

Sean didn't seem to care how sloppy drunk Michael would get. He almost seemed to encourage it, because no one really wanted to drink alone. They did have fun, but Michael would black out more frequently and make scenes when he would get too drunk. Sean did seem to always intervene before things got too bad, but that was a trait of a true enabler. Michael never did tell Sean much about his past or his psychic abilities, but he was losing them anyways. Butch and Tisha had both warned him about his future, but he just didn't listen. Alcohol was the most powerful removing tool in the world. It removed compassion, common sense, bank accounts, and any chance at a loving relationship. Ironic that Michael was trying to find love in the world while doing things to ensure that he never would. Then came the day that he thought he did. Boy was he wrong.

Michael was extremely hung over at a Saturday morning Little League game. He had tripped and fell on the sidewalk walking home from the bar on the previous night and had a giant cut on his lip that he was trying to hide. He had a mixed drink with him to try to feel better while sitting in the stands, watching Darin play. Sean was not there that day, so he just sat quietly and nursed his medicine.

He felt a tap on is shoulder and turned around to see this petite little woman. She had medium-length dark hair, big puppy dog eyes, and the cutest little crooked smile he had ever seen. She was so beautiful and kind of reminded him of Holly Hunter in her midthirties.

"Is your son one of the players?" she asked.

"No, my roommate's son is playing," Michael said as he tried to cover up his cut lower lip with his fingers. "He is at work, and I am here for support. Plus I love baseball."

She slid down next to him and asked, "You mind if I sit with you since I am here alone too?"

"No, not at all," Michael replied with a smile that hurt his lip a little more. "I kind of had a rough night as you might be able to tell." He pointed to his cut lip. He quickly put a cough drop in his mouth to cover the alcohol smell. It always worked like a charm and even got him out of field sobriety test once.

The lovely little gal sitting next to him looked tenderly up at him. "My name is Rina," she said and didn't even say anything about his lip.

"Michael," he said as he shook her hand while turning slightly sideways. Wow, he was thinking. The first live one in years. He had a few short-term relationships over the years, but nothing too serious since he always got lied to and left alone. "Quite a game," he interjected after the short awkward pause that always followed introductions.

"I have seen you here before," she said while looking out over the field. "My son is on the team. He is the right fielder." She pointed out to the child in deep right field as she said it.

There was no way he was going to tell her that the players they put in right field were usually the worst players on the team. "My roommate's son is the second baseman," he said as he looked her way. She was looking at him and gave a smile. She was just so petite and cute, the kind he liked. Michael used to tell people that he liked his women like he liked his coffee—hot, strong, and bitter—but that was just for laughs.

"So what did happen to your lip?" she finally asked. Eventually people would have to talk about the elephant in the room.

"Well," he began, "my roommate and I closed down a local bar last night, and we walked home. I tripped on the curb and fell and cut my lip on the sidewalk." Michael didn't lie but did not want to elaborate too much and lose his chance at getting to know this girl better, and he knew that he had a drinking problem that could get in the way of that. Most alcoholics knew they had a problem, but until real disaster happened, they didn't even think about confronting it. Why would you change something that made you feel good and got you through this life and hadn't caused you any real problems yet?

One thing was bothering him though. He did not get any of his normal intuitions when he shook her hand. What was happening? Had he finally lost the "flaw"? Michael would live to regret not seeing the truth on this one, and it was the many years of hard drinking that had diminished his abilities. Technically, he had succeeded. They hit it off very nicely. She was so sweet and easy to talk to. It turned out she was a schoolteacher and was really interested in the fact that he was an engineer. They didn't see much of the rest of the game and talked about what people talked about when they first met, like romantic interests, movies, music, food, and general superficial stuff.

When the game was over, they made plans to get together for lunch the next day. Lunch was always a safe first date. There were no hidden agendas or expectations, just good food and conversation. That was just what it was; they had a wonderful lunch. Plans for date number 2 were made, and Michael was definitely hooked on Rina, but for the first time in a long while, he had an overwhelming sense of fear when they parted ways after lunch. Ah, there it was again. The feelings. He felt trapped and alone for some reason and was worried about the risks of his drinking and what a blackout could do to him. He didn't want to quit, but he knew that he would have to do something.

Things started improving for Michael in general. He started to feel good about things even though he was really living a lie. Darin was calming down at home and starting to act more normal, if there was such a thing. Their bonding through Little League most likely had a lot to do with it. Even Michael and his father had fun at Little League together. He also got along with Rina's son on and off the field, which made things easier on the relationship.

It was actually some time before Michael would introduce Sean to Rina. It was the last Little League game of the season, and Sean had to work for the awards banquet that followed, so Rina, Michael, and the kids all went together. Michael never would drink that much in front of her, but he would find ways to sneak it here and there. He even had a flask for extreme situations, which he made sure to pack along. He was sure that she could tell he was drinking, but she never said anything about it.

Michael started to spend more time over at Rina's house, which was in a small middle-class suburb north of town. He still managed to spend time at the house with the boys, though. Rina was a good Catholic girl, or so she claimed, so she wouldn't allow penetrating sex before marriage. They did manage to do everything but that, so it was really not the biggest deal to Michael. Rina had also been married and divorced several times before, which was also against the ways of the Catholics so he never quite understood about the "no sex" thing. Why couldn't they have sex if she was already in bad graces with the church?

Although extremely naive, Rina was a very gentle, kind person as near as Michael could tell. Years of alcohol abuse had really stumped his intuitive abilities about people, but things would come to light in time. Her family was very Italian and devout to the Catholic faith. Michael was already familiar with how brainwashing organized religions were, and Catholicism was the leader in mind control.

Sean finally met Rina when picking up Darin one day. Michael was basically staying at Rina's house most of the time, and sometimes he would take Darin so he could play with Rina's son, Nick. Sean rang the bell, and Michael answered to let him in. He came in the house and around the corner and saw Rina for the first time. Michael did not really like the wide-eyed look on his face, which made it quite obvious that Sean was attracted to her. Who wouldn't be really? She was very beautiful. Sean was supposed to be his best friend, so he shouldn't mess around in that area or even indicate it.

Sean seemed to change after that. He was upset that they did not spend as much time partying at the house as they used to, and he would always try to get Michael to stick around as long as possible to delay him from going to Rina's. He could still drink at her house since she was fairly naive to most of it anyways. She did not seem to like Sean from the start and did not encourage him to spend that much time over at his other house. There was more than one occasion when Michael would come back from spending time with Sean that he was fairly intoxicated but still somewhat in control. Rena did not like that.

The time came to meet Rina's parents. They had been together for a little over a month when they went to visit. Her parents lived in a town about a half hour away, and they were of pure Italian descent. Her mother was a typical Italian mother, not obese or even heavy but a very good cook. It was her father that stood out the most when he first met him. His name was Albert Mann, and he was a very warm and compassionate man, completely the opposite of his own father.

Michael was quite certain that he was falling in love with Rina after the trip to meet the parents.

When he first shook Al's hand, Michael received a surge of positive energy like he did when he met Brad a long time ago. This was a good-hearted person, and he knew it. He didn't receive any visions, but there was no fooling the feelings he had since they didn't lie. "Hello there, Michael," Al said as they were shaking hands in the doorway. "Won't you guys come on in? I am so glad we finally meet. Rina's told us some good things about you."

Michael felt so at ease with Al almost instantly. That was not a common occurrence for him in this world, so it was always refreshing to come upon a genuine soul for once. He seemed to have that with Rina, but nothing like the readings he was getting off Al. He was a shorter man than Michael and was a bit stockier, mainly in the stomach area, but nothing like his father's enormous gut. He had a full head of hair, though slightly thinning, and had a very gentle voice to go along with his calm demeanor. He wore glasses, which seemed to run in the family, but Rina only wore her glasses when she wasn't wearing her contact lenses.

They all went into the massive living room and sat down to talk like people who were getting acquainted usually did. Rina's father liked his drinks too, so Michael fit right in. One thing about Italians, they enjoyed Michael's two favorite things in the world, drinking and eating well. There was an interesting trait of Italian culture. Wine and other alcohol were enjoyed on a regular basis with all meals, gatherings, and the like, yet they had the lowest rate of clinical alcoholism of most cultures. It just went to show that the more you restricted something, the more trouble you tended to have with it.

"So, Michael, Rina tells us you're an engineer," Al stated as he sat back in his easy chair, sipping his drink. Bushmill's scotch was the liquor of choice in this house. Good stuff.

"Yes, I do mainly highway and drainage system design, but I also do some concrete design work as well," Michael replied in the most respectful manner possible.

"Great." He held his glass up like he was making a toast. "My daughter sure seems quite taken by you. She's had some dandies in the past." He gulped his drink and dropped his glass back to resting on his leg, making the ice cubes tingle. "But enough of that."

"Dinner sure smells good," Michael told him as he drew in another nostril full of that wonderful aroma. "Rina's not too bad in the kitchen herself. She must have learned from her mother."

"Oh yes. Those two are very compatible in the kitchen." Al smiled as he got up to mix another drink. "How's your drink?" He looked over and asked Michael before going all the way to the bar.

"Mine's fine for now." Michael knew that he was not going to drink too much around them, as he tried not to around Rina's house. He always had the house to go to if he wanted to get his load on with Sean, and he always kept the flask that he received at Brad's wedding in the console of his truck for emergencies. Full, of course. Dinner was, of course, just incredible. Comparable to fine, expensive Italian dining. Everything about her family seemed quite normal to Michael, but something just seemed so incredibly hidden from him that he couldn't quite place his finger on. Rina had been married to other men. Did her family treat them the same as they were treating Michael? Obviously, the other men did not work out with Rina, so why did they think that she had found the one this time?

Al was so much more of a father than Michael's own, or at least they did things that he wished his own father would do. They would go golfing and play cribbage or maybe just meet somewhere for a couple and shoot the breeze. Monthly poker night with the other Italian uncles and brothers became an enjoyable activity as well. He always felt like he was in a scene out of *Goodfellas* when they would gather to play. Michael was digging his time with Rina and her father so much that he actually finally wanted to ask her to marry him.

He took her back to the same place that they had their first lunch and popped the question. They had only been together for a few months, but he just was so in love that it seemed like the right thing to do. She bloomed like a spring tulip when he finally got around to asking, and it was a done deal. She accepted the soon-to-be a family, but booze was coming along too. They thought that it would be a good idea to get married in Vegas, just between the two of them. He really didn't want to have his family come down and visit or stick their noses where it didn't belong. They might not approve, and if it wasn't something they would do, then Michael shouldn't either.

Michael realized that most of his life had been spent trying to be the son that his parents thought he should be. It was so sad how well they were programmed to be slaves to the system and not have dreams or goals that were contrary. He really didn't want to have some long career and then just retire somewhere to wither and die away slowly. His parents had no dreams left, and that was one of the many things that alcohol removed from a person. The system loved alcohol, the exact reason why it was advertised everywhere you looked. A person would never be able to make changes in this world if they were drunk and enslaved. The very thing that almost every American was. The Controllers absolutely needed liquor to be able to control the masses.

The time the towers fell was an awakening period for Michael. He and Sean were both at work when the news came in about the attacks in New York. Two planes had apparently crashed into the upper levels of both World Trade Center towers. Everyone was sent home from work since all government offices were closed, including the contractors that were just working for and not in the government. When they got home and started watching the events on the news just like the rest of the country was doing at the time, something didn't seem quite right.

When the first tower fell, Michael looked at Sean and said, "What was that? That building looked like it was just blown up. That was no different than how demolition crews bring down the old casinos in Nevada, don't you think?" He instantly felt the pain and suffering of thousands of people, with an overwhelming sense almost as powerful as the day Butch had his accident right in front of him. He was nowhere near these people that were being attacked, but his could feel the reaction from those around him. It was devastating.

"Definitely," Sean replied back without taking his eyes off the TV. Sean had a better background in structural engineering design than Michael did, but they both had enough experience to know that they had just witnessed a controlled demolition. Then the second tower came down the same way, and there was no doubt in his mind; this country was under attack from something inside their own government because these two demolitions had to have been planned far ahead of the time to be brought down so perfectly.

Rina was still at work when the events happened, and Sean and Michael had gone to what was now basically Sean's bachelor pad. They watched the coverage repeat itself until it got old, and then Michael went home to wait for Rina. It wasn't until a few days later when the news reports started rolling in about the attacks, and to no big surprise, he noticed there were many inconsistencies. Michael would later find out that WTC7 building fell the same way later in the day, and it wasn't even hit by a plane. He could not believe that the government stance was that the jet fuel in the planes was what brought the buildings down and that the people were eating it up. There was no way in the history of engineering that this was the case. If it was, then demolition companies would not waste all that calculation time and money to bring old buildings down in the first place. In fact a B-25 bomber crashed into the Empire State Building a long time ago, and although it suffered damage, it was in no at risk of collapsing. This was yet another lie in the long string of mainstream lies that Michael continued to find out over the years.

The conclusions came out so fast that it was quite obvious that our own government had been involved with it in some fashion; otherwise, why would they be putting out unintelligible conclusions so quickly? It was no different than the magic bullet or the atom bomb lies. What was really shocking is that the sheepish people keep on believing this bullshit. This was the turning point in Michael's spiral into loss of sanity. He knew that he was not where he belonged, and he wanted out, just like he did when he found evidence of money laundering in the military.

He started to spend more time in the garage at Rina's, alone, working on odd projects all the time. He had a fridge in the garage and plenty of other liquor to keep most of his drinking hidden from the rest of the family, but the results tend to eventually be apparent to everyone else. The family started to take notice about a month after the New York attacks happened. Sean was no angel in all this.

It turned out he had a thing for Rina and was not the least bit happy about spending more time alone at his house since Michael had gone and taken the plunge. He would try to get Michael over to the house whenever he could. Once Michael had a few drinks in him, he was definitely easier to influence. Time would slip by, and then he would realize that he had killed more time than he wanted to over at Sean's. He was aware of Michael's potential to slip into a blackout and start talking and acting crazy. Maybe he thought that he would look better in Rina's eyes if he could appear to be the concerned friend after Michael screwed up. Who knew? But he was definitely trying to help put a strain on Michael's marriage.

Michael was drowning all his pain and anger in a vat of alcohol. He could no longer function in the capacity he used to. Michael would stumble about the house and constantly be slurring what he was saying, which didn't make sense to anyone in the first place. He spent most of his time alone, and the family was drifting away from him. One Friday afternoon, Michael came home to a weird feeling in his gut. He sensed a presence that he had not felt in some time. His father was here for some reason, and he did not know why. Michael walked into the house and around the corner, where he saw Sean sitting in the main room and heard the voices of other people. This was an intervention; he knew right away. Why would Sean be here, though, he was just as big of a drunk?

Rina walked into the kitchen, where Michael was hiding from the others in the living room. "You know that they are all here for you. I knew you would not like this very much, but I called your parents and they recommended this."

"I don't doubt that." Michael looked at her in disgust. "They are the drunks. This is just their way of hiding their own problems by switching the attention to mine. You know that. I have told you many times about my childhood. I didn't realize that my drinking was getting this bad, or are you just so naive that you just think it is bad?"

"Don't insult me, Michael." She pointed at him in anger. "I can't watch you drown yourself anymore, and your parents was all I knew to call. Sean has been very helpful too, actually."

Michael didn't say anything because he didn't want to bury himself any further than he was already. If they had problems like this early on, then any future divorce would definitely go in her favor. He could somewhat sense that she was actually thinking that. It was the same case with Sean being here. Now there was a joke. He was acting like some angel in all this when he was actually one of the ones that was contributing to the problem. Michael also knew that Sean thought Rina was cute, so he had additional motivation to make him look bad as he played the role of the caring friend.

There was no way that he was about to listen to his father and Sean talk about his drinking problem. Yes, he knew that he had one, but so did they. Michael walked into the room with all the people seated in a circle. There were, of course, his parents and Sean along with Rina's parents and some other coworkers.

Michael said, "Thank you all for coming to this, but this will be unnecessary as I already agree to dry out. I will meet with Rina and the intervention counselor, but you can all go home. Thank you for caring." Michael walked down the hall and went into the bedroom and closed the door.

He felt so betrayed by everyone, and he did not want to go into the "treatment" system that was set up so that you would fail and generate more repeat funds for the drug-and-alcohol industry, which did include all the treatment centers. Prosecutors and judges went home at night and enjoyed all the cocaine and heroin that they were paid to help smuggle into their counties, while people that had smoked a joint rotted away in a jail cell. It was a pretty sick society where Martha Stewart could share a cell with someone doing time for marijuana possession while both watch OJ play golf on TV.

Michael convinced Rina to let him stay at the house while he went to an outpatient treatment center. This enabled him to still be able to work for part of the day and be home at night. The system of greed was so in bed with most treatment centers anymore that the failure rate in all of them was astronomical. He knew that he was really not ready to be sober in this life, but he did want to get everyone off his back. They didn't understand him, and he was starting to believe that he would never meet anyone like Tisha again.

He thought he could stay sober for a while, but then plans didn't always work out the way we would like them to. The longer he was sober, the more he started to have his empathic feelings again. Michael started to feel that something wasn't right about his wife. Rina was hiding something, and he was starting to see it. She had been married more times than he had thought.

Michael went down to the county courthouse one day to look up marriage records. Boy, was he surprised when he found that Rina had five previous marriages, not the two that he was led to believe by her. They were all men with decent careers and incomes. This really came as no shock to Michael since he knew that a lot of women, and men, were just fueled by greed and they would do anything to achieve the almighty dollar. She would basically find a man who had money and/or potential to make money that had a problem, like alcoholism, that she could exploit. She would then divorce them and get large sums of money out of the deal. She was so cute, sweet, and innocent, which was the perfect front.

Sean was also not the genuine friend that he appeared to be. Michael had felt that for a while, but with the show he put on for the intervention along with his obvious attraction to Rina, he did not trust what might be going on behind his back. He had not had a drink in months, but now he was really not liking the betrayal feelings he was getting. He was starting to think about drinking more and more every day.

He figured that it was time to have a talk with Rina and time to get Sean out of his life. Over the next twenty-four hours, he would manage to do both of those, but not how he thought it would go. When Rina got home from her errands that evening, Michael asked her about her other marriages that she had not told them about. The conversation did not go as he expected.

Rina was so upset by his newfound facts. "Where did you find that out, and why did you even check in the first place?" The Catholics took a lot of offense to discussions about divorce and other things, or maybe she was just upset that he had found out her secret.

"I just had a feeling, Rina," Michael said. "I went down to the courthouse and found it. Look, I am not trying to cause an argument, but since I quit drinking, some things have just not felt right to me, and that was one of them. I just want to know the truth, and we can deal with it from there."

She became so enraged, like she had just been caught in the biggest lie and now had to come clean. "Maybe you should go stay somewhere else for a while if you don't trust me anymore."

"It isn't that I don't trust you, but everyone wants to point out what is wrong with me, and there is plenty wrong with the ones that accuse me of shit," Michael said. "I don't want to fight over this. It is really no big deal to me, but it seems to be to you. I am going to stay with a friend, not Sean, for a few nights until you calm down and are ready to talk. When can we meet to talk about everything?"

She was quiet for a few minutes while Michael just stared at her, looking away occasionally. "Well," she said, "come by at six on Wednesday, and we can talk then."

He had another coworker that would let him crash if he needed. Wednesday was only a couple days away so that shouldn't be any big deal. He spent most of the time thinking about getting drunk again. He didn't sense noble qualities in anyone. It seemed like everyone wanted to lie to and deceive him for some selfish gain. Now, his best friend seemed to be after his wife. Michael didn't suspect that Rina would have anything to do with Sean since he did not sense an attraction to him by her, but then the weak mind could be influenced to do almost anything. Then came the worst night of his entire life.

Michael showed up, as scheduled, on Wednesday except there was no Rina. Her car was not there, and he knew that there was no room to park in the garage right now. He went to the front door and tried his key. It did not work.

What is going on? he thought. He went back to the truck and used the garage door opener, and the large door began to creep up. She must have been running late is all he was thinking. Michael stood in the open garage staring at the large pile of everything he owned that was stacked up in the garage like it was just waiting for him.

"Deceptive bitch," Michael said out loud. He knew that she was not coming, and this was how she told him that he needs to move out. No discussion. She just left and took all her shit while she kept the money that Michael had sunk into the house that was in her name. He tried the door from the garage to the house, and his key did not work there either. "Damn, she changed the locks." Michael became enraged and he sure as hell was not going to pick up and leave like this. The first thing that he could think of though was that he needed to get a drink.

Michael drove down to the corner store and bought a couple of bottles of Bushmills with some snacks and came back to the house. He didn't even bother with mixing the drinks when he got back, just straight out of the bottle. Oh, what a relief it was! Next, he had to get into the house, so he drilled a hole next to the lock on the door leading from the garage to the house and then used a reciprocation saw to cut the brand new lock out of place. He was in.

He tried to call everyone he knew, but no one was answering. They must all be in on this, especially Sean. Who else moved all that stuff into the garage for her? Sean had been around more often than Michael had liked since he quit drinking. It didn't bother him much before since he didn't think that anything might be going between him and Rina, but it did bother him now. He got a mental image of Rina with Sean and let out a demonic scream as he tugged away on the bottle.

Michael continued until the first pint was gone and then started into the next one. He was on his way to the worst blackout episode of his life. Things became very hazy in his memory as the evening went on. He started to move his stuff back into the house as he continued to drink straight whiskey. A shitload of his money went into home improvements on this house, and he was damned certain he was not leaving it.

He went into total blackness before finishing moving his stuff around and remembered nothing else from the rest of the night. Michael was well into a demonic episode when his father called him. Wrong time for that. His father had told him that Rina had called him and told him what she had done and that he just needed to find a place for his things until the divorce could be finalized. Divorce? That had not even come into the discussion several days ago. She had been a lying bitch, and Michael was sure in his mind that she had told some more lies to his family.

Michael completely lost it on the phone with his father. "Now you listen, you drunken, loveless excuse for a father. I am going to find Sean and Rina wherever they might be and kill them both. Then I am going to come home and do the same to you. I hate you so much, and you helped this happen with your deception." Michael slammed the phone down and laid down on the couch. There was no way that he was serious, but he was extremely hurt, extremely drunk, and extremely fed up with all the people in his life. He slipped into an intoxicated slumber for the remainder of the night.

The next morning, Michael continued on the liquor that he did not quite finish the night before. He wasn't really sober long enough to feel hungover, as he was most likely still drunk from the night before when he continued drinking. He went into the garage and hit the door opener on the wall. His pile of stuff was gone, so he figured that he must have moved most of it back in the house. What had he done last night? He did not know. He woke up in the house, so at least he did not leave and drive around looking for trouble.

With the garage opened, Michael went back to straightening up the garage and organizing his tools. He heard a car pull up behind him in the driveway. It must be the missing Rina come to talk finally. He turned around to see a local police car parked in the driveway. Michael's stomach sank because he knew they were here for him, but he had not left the house to do anything wrong.

"Are you Michael Stevens?" one of the cops asked him from outside the garage. They had to try to get him to come out of the garage to arrest him, but Michael did not know that at the time or he would have gone back in the house.

"Yes, that's me," Michael replied in his revived drunken stupor. "Why are you guys here?"

"We received a complaint, and we just need you to come talk to us for a minute," the cop lied as they always did. If anyone was dumb enough to trust a cop, then they got what they asked for. As soon as Michael stepped out of the garage, one cop came up behind him and pushed him into the hood of the car. "You are under arrest for making terrorist threats." The other cop went to the back of the car to open the door while the other cop shoved him in the back seat. He was very intoxicated still, so he shot his mouth off all the way to jail as one would expect.

Michael was booked into Fresno County Jail and placed in a small cold dark concrete holding cell. It was most likely the drunk tank for his first night. He was going ballistic since the idea of being locked up did not sit well with him, as it didn't with most empaths. Michael kept seeing the faces of Sean, Rina, his father, and a host of other faces of people that he blamed for all that was happening. He began to hit his head severely with both and hands and slammed himself into the concrete walls; he had completely lost it. On the second slam against the wall, Michael hit his head on the concrete with enough force to end his fit of rage, and he fell back on the floor, unconscious. Michael would remember none of it.

JAILED

If the machine of government is of such a nature
that it requires you to be the agent of injustice to
another, then, I say, break the law.
—Henry David Thoreau

Michael opened one eye and could see that he was looking parallel
to a concrete floor that he was apparently lying on. He raised his
head to open both eyes and allow his vision to clear. His head was
pounding, and his guts were killing him. He glanced around while
still lying on the ground, and he could see the shoes of people standing around him. This was exactly the vision that he had when he met
Sean. It was a premonition of this future event, a sign that he did not
heed, a warning that he did not listen to. Maybe it was time to start.

He was lying in what appeared to be a jail holding cell, but
he could not remember how he got here or even how long he had
been here. It actually still felt a little drunk mixed with the extreme
hangover and a gut ache like he had never had before. He faintly
remembered being arrested but could not remember why. The last
thing that he really remembered was drinking whiskey in the house
by himself.

The people standing around him were jail officers. One of them
dropped a bag full of clothes by his feet as he was trying to sit up and
then stand up. He was the biggest cop that Michael had ever seen.
There were two other officers in the room, and all three were just
staring down at him like he was human garbage. Michael climbed
to his feet, as the human mountain spoke. "You need to change into

those jail clothes and check the bag to make sure all your clothes are there."

Michael knew that he was no criminal, and he could not have possibly done anything wrong since he was just at home last night, unless he went out again. "Wait a minute. I haven't done anything wrong. Is there someone I can call? Don't I get to call someone?"

"You will change, or we will change you," the giant said. "Besides after your performance last night, I don't think you have anyone to call."

"No," Michael said with an overwhelming feeling of fear coming over him. What performance last night? "I can't go into jail. I don't belong here."

The two cops that hadn't spoken a word came up behind Michael. He could feel a solid wood baton in the nape of his neck as he was shoved into the concrete wall, and the officers began to undress him. It became apparent to Michael that things would go easier if he just did as he was told, and he could figure out this mess later. It didn't matter much now. He was going into the system whether he liked it or not.

"Okay, okay," Michael said as his lips were touching sideways to the wall. "I will do exactly as you say. Just don't hurt me anymore." The two cops backed off, and Michael was allowed to get into his clothing bag. He kneeled on the concrete floor and opened the bag that was dropped in front of him. The contents were four pairs of grey socks that were all different sizes, three pairs of off-white boxer shorts, two T-shirts, two jailhouse jumpsuits with Fresno County Jail stamped on the backside, one pair of shower shoes, two towels, three sheets, two grey wool blankets, a laundry bag, and one destroyed future.

Michael grabbed one of the jail jumpsuits and a pair of boxer shorts and proceeded to change out of his own clothes and into his new attire. As instructed, he placed his clothes in the bag and then gave them to the officers. His other belongings must have been taken when he was booked, but he did not remember that.

Michael was left alone in the cold cell. He was so scared and confused. He went over and sat on the steel bench that was chained to the concrete wall next to the wide-open steel toilet that was attached to the same. He stared out at the steel door to the cell and gazed at the little locked opening that was used to pass things into the inmates he imagined. For the first time in his life, he was all alone. He knew that no one was coming to save him this time. He buried his face in his hands and started to cry, the kind of cry that was years in the making. Tears poured into his hands, running down his forearms. Michael cried for what seemed like an eternity until he had no more liquid left in his tear ducts. All cried out, he became sleepy and lay down sideways on the cold steel bench and fell into a deep sleep, the type of sleep that only an honest cry like that could bring.

Bang! Michael awoke as the door slammed open, and two jail cops entered. "Rise and shine, Michael," one of the officers said.

Michael's vision was so blurry from all the crying and the hangover, of course. "Please, give me a second for my eyes to adjust?" Michael asked as he sat up on the bench.

"No problem," the other cop responded. These guys weren't as bad as Michael thought they would be, most likely due to the fact that he had decided to cooperate.

Each deputy stood on either side of Michael as he rubbed his eyes, and his vision came back in to view. God, how his guts were hurting though, but he sure didn't want to say anything about that in here. *Just deal with it*, he thought. He stood up carrying his laundry bag and new wardrobe and followed one deputy out the door as the other one followed.

Michael was led into a room down the hall where he was instructed to drop his jumpsuit. It was strip search time. His naked body was inspected thoroughly by the two deputies who were now wearing latex gloves, but there was no cavity search of which he was extremely relieved. He was instructed to pull his jumpsuit back up and face the officer.

"Open up," the officer instructed him to do, so Michael opened his mouth so it too could be searched with a flashlight. Michael thought to himself that it was practically impossible to sneak contraband into jail, so it had to get there some other way. Knowing how corrupt the system was, he had his ideas as to how it was done.

Money was all it took to get anything done; it just mattered how much you were willing to pay.

After the search, one deputy took Michael back out into the hall, and they went through another new doorway. On the other side of the door was yet another hallway with a solid green line painted on the floor, obviously a line he would soon be following.

"Follow the green line," the officer told him.

Michael looked ahead and began walking. He felt like a rat in a maze with all the cameras looking down and the task of going where instructed. The hallway made a few corners and ended with an open elevator that he entered. There were no buttons in the elevator.

Express elevator to hell, Michael thought. The door closed and up it went, faster than any express elevator he had ever been on, only in the wrong direction.

The door opened, and Michael was greeted by a new deputy standing his post in front of a computer. He motioned down at Michael's wrist, and he noticed that there was a wristband that must have been attached during booking. He hadn't even really noticed it until now. The band had his name and birthday on it. His jail identification number, or JID, and the booking number were also on the wristband. It also indicated the fact that he was right-handed. He showed it to the officer, and he typed away at the computer for a few moments.

The large steel door in front of the deputy clicked, and he looked at Michael and said, "Go on ahead."

Michael walked toward the door, stopped before opening it, looked back at the deputy, and jokingly questioned, "Do I have to?"

The deputy shook his head with a slight grin that indicated he knew Michael was joking. He did get a good feeling from this officer as if his grin was telling him not to worry and that things would be all right. He was worried about his guts though; they felt like they were on fire.

He walked through the door, and it slammed shut behind him with an authority he had never felt before. Laid out before him was a tall open horseshoe-shaped hallway with doors about every ten feet. There were five doors total labeled Pods A through E. Each pod door was surrounded by a large window about twenty feet by twenty feet square with the door kind of centered at the bottom of it. In the middle of the horseshoe was looked like a mini air control tower, which could see down into the windows of all five pods. Ironically, this was called the Tower.

"Go into Pod B." Michael heard over the loudspeaker in the hall, so he walked over and stood in front of the correct door as instructed. The door clicked as all the others had and he walked in. The door shut with even more authority than the one before. This was his new home for a while, and he was not getting any feelings as to how long. He was uncertain of the future to say the least.

The pods were more of a modern-day barracks kind of setting. There were no individual cells with bars. Everything was made of concrete, plasticized glass, and metal. There was an upstairs and downstairs bunk area with stairs running along the left side of the pod. At the top of the stairs was the wide-open bathroom area, kind of like you would find in the gym and very similar to military boot camp. The upstairs had thirty bunks, and the downstairs had forty-two. Each rack had three sets of bunks on them instead of two. Just packing them in, each filled bunk was more money for the state. Plenty of unconstitutional laws to keep them full.

A TV was attached to the wall both upstairs and downstairs. Steel tables with four seats each were bolted to the floors for TV viewing, card playing, etc. Some of the tables had checkerboards that were glued down in the middle of the table. A solid steel railing ran along the top floor and down the stairs. The bathroom area had three open shower stalls in the back with six steel toilets on the right wall and six steel sinks on the left. The mirrors above the sinks were even made of shiny metal not glass.

Michael could literally feel the seventy-one pairs of eyes on him as he made his way to an open bunk on the first floor. The only open one was on the very bottom of a rack of three. His guts and head were still killing him, and he could not wait to get some sleep. He was also picking up on all the negative energy. Although he was not in great shape to get any clear visions, the feelings of anger and fear were overwhelming. He pulled the blankets out of the laundry bag and spread one on the bed while rolling the other into a makeshift pillow. That was something that was not issued. He stuffed the rest of his newly received items in the opening below the bunk and laid down. It was just a matter of minutes, and Michael was off into jailhouse slumber.

He wasn't asleep very long when he could feel himself shaking and awoke to another white inmate trying to wake him up.

"What's up?" Michael asked.

"You need to come with me upstairs with the English speakers," he said. "The bottom floor is for the border brothers and paisas." Michael was being slowly educated on the rules of the system of incarceration. Gangs and ethnic groups kept with their own kind, and this guy waking him up was actually trying to help him. "We were waiting for a rack to open up to come and get you, dog." He gathered his stuff up and followed the man upstairs.

There was an open top bunk, so they must have rolled someone out when Michael was coming in. The top bunk was better as you could sit up in bed without hitting your head and could watch the TV from there. Michael was not much for television, but it was a good time killer. He was getting a better feeling by being on the top floor than the bottom, although there was still such an overwhelming sense of evil in this place, there was good as well. He remade his bed and climbed back in to go back to sleep. He was still very sick and did not feel well at all.

Michael was suffering from severe alcohol withdrawals as well as a mild case of pancreatitis from the night of the heaviest binge-drinking that he had ever done. He poured sweat while he slept and was having minor convulsions. He was dreaming such awful things about Sean and his wife. All speculation, but hard visions for him to take nonetheless. There was a mixed energy in this place that was confusing him, but he would find out soon.

Michael awoke at four in the morning to the yelling and hollering of all the inmates. It was chow time as well as count time. He got up and just followed everyone else down the stairs. They were showing the guards their wristbands and then would receive a paper bag with the daily food in it and a pint of milk. Michael did the same and then went back to his rack. He put the milk in the bag and the bag in the storage area below the bunk and then crawled back up to get some more sleep.

While sleeping, Michael was having more awful dreams about the future and the present. He was still not quite sure why he was here, but he knew that he had to get himself feeling better. He started to have detox nightmares, and the pancreatitis pains were slightly stabilizing. Michael had been told over the years that he talked in his sleep and had even been sleepwalking a couple times in his life.

Suddenly he screamed out in his sleep, "Why don't we take it outside to the tree in front, and we can settle it there." He was dreaming about Sean and the tree in the front yard at Rina's house for some reason. The scream woke everyone up, especially Tank, who was in the top bunk next to him.

Tank was the unofficial leader of the pod. He was large and in charge as the cliché went. If anyone had a problem, you went to Tank. He was not a vicious person, but he was a stern one, and no one dared to try to take him. "Hey, buddy, you are waking everyone up with your yelling." It was daytime, but there were always people asleep in jail.

Michael was not even awake when he responded, "Yeah, well, you guys do it every night, so what's the difference if I do?"

Everyone in the pod who was listening laughed at that. Tank respected it as well. "You're all right. I like you. We will have to play some cards later." Michael did not hear or remember any of it since he was still asleep the whole time.

Evening chow time came at five in the evening. He awoke again to get his food and provide the evening count to the guards. At least the night meals were hot. The only other food that you received all day was in the bag that you acquired in the morning. Michael had not even looked into the bag he still had from that morning. He hoped the milk would last as well, probably a safe bet that the milk they gave to the inmates was on the verge of spoiling to begin with.

Michael did need to get some food in him. The only thing he was doing is drinking a lot of water when he would head to the bathroom from time to time. He took the tray to his bunk and ate it all. He was hungry, but this food was just a step up from dumpster diving. People were staring at him. He was sure they were wondering what was wrong with him or who he was, but Michael did not feel like talking to the other pod mates just yet. After dinner, he took his tray down with the others and then went back to bed again.

It was just after midnight of his second day that Michael woke up and felt a lot better. He still had a minor gut ache and the water helped that out. He just could not sleep anymore, so it was time to mingle with the others. He jumped out of his rack and headed over to the game tables in front of the TV. There were two Mexican chaps playing dominoes. One of the Mexican guys looked up at him standing over the game table. "It's about time you stopped hard-timing it, bunkee." He was rather scrawny, smiley, and very young looking, probably barely eighteen years old. He had a few scattered hairs about his chin like he was trying to grow a goatee but didn't have the testosterone levels to be able to do it. "You can only sleep so much before you start to lose it," he continued.

"Yes, but I have been very sick as well. I think my liver or pancreas is inflamed from all the alcohol," Michael replied. "What is your name, and did you call me bunkee?"

"That's right." He looked up at Michael with a smile. "My name is Daniel, and I am on the bottom bunk below you. We could all tell that you are not well. I think everyone in here is curious to find out your situation. You don't seem like someone we would encounter in here."

"My name is Michael, and I'll fill you all in later," Michael said with a sarcastic, joking tone. "Glad to be the latest soap opera for everyone, but at least no one is trying to hurt me or mess with me too bad." He was looking down at the domino game they were playing.

"I think they all kind of respect you now, especially since you stood up to Tank yesterday." Daniel looked up at him. "You play?"

"Yeah, years ago," Michael said as he took a seat next to his new friend. "I'm sure it won't take me long to learn again. I do pick things up rather quickly." He just smiled as he was sure they would not get the joke. "What do mean stood up to Tank?"

"You told him that they make so much noise all the time that what did it matter if you did." Daniel looked sideways at him. "You were probably having some nightmare and just don't remember. I thought it was hilarious. Way to go, man." He held his hand up so Michael could clasp it in the usual "dude" way for a couple of seconds. Daniel pointed down at the domino maze. "Jump in the game. Grab seven out of the pile."

"Yes, you're right. I don't remember." Michael looked down at the pile of dominos and began to select his seven. "I'm glad I did that early though. I guess it won't be so bad in here, but at least I met someone to kill time with." He smiled over at Daniel. "So what do I do here?"

"We will spot you a hundred points so you can catch up," Daniel told him while showing him the score sheet. "If you have a double domino, you can lay it in either direction ..." He went on and explained all the house rules, and they had lots of time to discuss some of the written and unwritten rules of jail that Michael was not familiar with. It would be safe to say that Daniel was his first friend here, and he thanked the Lord for the valuable information.

Michael and his friends played until the four o'clock chow call and count. It was also Monday morning, so he should be getting a call later to see a public defender and find out what the hell this was all about. He and Daniel sat at the back wall by their bunk and had breakfast together, which would begin to be a regular occurrence. Michael still had his food from the day before, so he shared with his friend, and they had a little feast of sorts. Their bunk was in the far back corner, so it was a little quieter as far as jail went.

Eight o'clock rolled around, and Michael was summoned over the loudspeaker that he had a visitor, which was most likely the public defender so he could talk before the arraignment. What he would find out next would send him into a sickness like he had never felt before. Michael was directed to a room outside the pods where the lawyers would meet with clients that were incarcerated. He walked into the room and was surprised to find an attractive young woman sitting at the table, waiting for him. She stood up as he walked in the door. "Hello, Mr. Stevens. My name is Monica, and I have been assigned by the public defender's office to your case as you requested during booking. Won't you please sit down?" Michael sat down at the desk across from her. She had a file in front of her that he could see his name clearly marked on. "Well," she began, "you're being charged with three counts of domestic terrorist threats. Each carry a prison sentence of two to five years."

Michael's eyes got wide, and his jaw dropped for a brief moment as he looked hard at her. "You're joking, right? I don't even know what this is all about. I was in a blackout state of drunkenness and don't remember much of anything between being home last night and waking up in that cold concrete tomb of a room a couple days ago."

"Oh," she said rather sheepishly. "Apparently, your father called you last night at the request of your wife to let you know that she was not going to meet with you and that you needed to move your stuff. She was going to stay with a friend for a few days to let you move. You then, allegedly, became uncontrollably enraged and threatened to kill her, your friend Sean, and your father. Your father could not reach you again on the phone and knew that you were in a risky state of drunkenness, so he phoned down to the local police department to check on you and told them the same story. The police came by the same night, but you did not answer the door, and they had no cause at the time to force entry. They returned in the morning, and you were detained outside your garage. That is the big picture for the most part."

Michael was overwhelmed with a barrage or feelings that were so intense that he might have lost consciousness right in front of this pretty lady, except he was getting better about controlling that. His father had put him here, simply astonishing. If he ever despised his father before, Michael now crossed over into a level of hatred that could only be described as severe. Of all the things to do to your own child, put him in jail, which might lead to prison. Even if he did say those things, there was no genuine threat. He had no idea where his wife was, and his father was fifteen hundred miles away. Plus, the fact that there couldn't possibly be a legal recording of it for evidence.

He stood up and walked to the back wall of the room. "Well, life seems to be pretty much over for me at this point. I am beyond screwed." He turned around and sat back in front of Monica. "How is this even possible? It is all hearsay, and they didn't even detain me when the complaint was made. And my father, of all people, should know that it was just a rant in anger. I have never physically assaulted anyone in my life."

"Things are different now after the Patriot Act," she responded back at Michael. "Any threat of violence results in an arrest whether recorded or not."

"Wow." He looked at her with drawn eyebrows. "That is not even legal according to our constitution. They should call it the Treason Act." He knew there were lies surrounding 9-11, and it was painfully obvious that the government was using it to invoke more tyranny and control over the people. He did not think that was a good point of discussion right now, as he was enough shit as it was. He was sure of one thing though. When this mess was all over, he was going to do a little research of his own on the Patriot Act and what the government was really up to. If anyone was an ace researcher, it was Michael. If the information was out there, he would find it.

"Regardless of what it is," she said, "we have some work to do. I assume that we will plead not guilty in the arraignment today?"

"You're damn tootin'," Michael replied. "I just can't go to prison. I don't know what I'd do. How long do I have to stay in jail?"

"That could be the not-so-good news," she said with a little empathy in her voice. "The judge will set bail today, which could be quite high considering there are three felony charges. I don't know if you know someone who would be willing or even financially able to come up with the money. The longer we delay and talk with the DA to reach an agreement, the longer you will most likely be here and the system is very slow. It could be weeks between court dates."

"Are you saying I could be here for months?" Michael was becoming exponentially terrified as he asked her the question.

"Yes, Mr. Stevens. That is exactly what I am saying." She looked at him in a very professional manner.

Michael was just dumbfounded. His life, career, and marriage had been wiped out in a matter of a few minutes on a telephone which he could not remember. The arraignment went just as his lawyer expected. The judge set bail at $20,000 for each charge which totaled $60,000. Most bail bonds required a 10 percent investment of the total bail amount, which would be $6,000, and he knew no one would be doing that for him now. He might have been able to get Brad to do it, but he did not remember his phone number, and Brad was not aware of what had happened to Michael yet. There was one other problem as well. He was not allowed to contact anyone involved in the case, including his wife's family. They could contact or visit him, but he could not make the move. That made it rather difficult to find help with the situation.

Michael was in a daze as he made his way back to the pod after court. He had strong feelings of aloneness and started to think of suicide. He was hanging his head as he walked back into the pod. He walked slowly over to the stairs and headed up to get in bed again. Daniel stopped him at the top of the stairs. "How did it go in court, Michael?"

"I think I need to lie down, Daniel." Michael felt sick to his stomach like he may puke, which was just inevitable. He ran over to the nearest toilet by the top of the stairs, and started heaving like there was a National vomiting competition; and he was the front runner. Michael felt betrayed by everyone he had ever known, with the exception of Brad. It would be nice to be able to talk to him right now. When he was done puking, he just stood up and went toward the back corner by his bunk with a curious Daniel right behind him.

Michael leaned against the corner and slid down until he was seated on the floor and buried his face into his hands. No crying though, Michael figured out early that was not a good idea in jail. Daniel sat Indian style in front of him, waiting, and asked him. "So what happened? It had to have been bad if you're still this messed up."

He slid his face up out of his hands and looked at Daniel. "It is." Then he filled him in on all that was going on. Daniel was just in awe of all of it. Michael realized early that people in jail were not all bad; they just didn't obey the system of control in this not-so-free country. He did get a lot of negative feelings from some, but he had some genuine ones as well. Daniel, of course, was a genuinely good person. He even offered Michael a place to stay when he did get out of jail, whenever that might be, so he could get back on his feet.

It turned out, Daniel had a wife and baby boy waiting on the outside, and he really wanted to stop breaking the law, no matter how much the laws should not be the way they were. That was the problem with a system that created poverty and destitution on purpose. Sooner or later, you would have to do whatever it took to feed yourself and your family and the system would make even more money off you. Stealing and drug dealing become a means of survival; most of them didn't want to have to resort to those things at all. It was a sick cycle that was only about profits and nothing else.

There was a very large black man that slept in the bottom rack about two bunks over from Michael and Daniel. His name was Ben, who ran about 6 feet, 5 inches tall and 260 pounds, but he was very gentle and soft-spoken. He had heard Daniel refer to him as Gentle Ben from the story about a bear just the other day. Ben was lying in his rack, facing Michael as he was telling the story to Daniel and decided that it was a good time to get better acquainted.

Ben walked over to where the two were sitting in the corner and spoke. "Hey there, Michael, couldn't help but overhear all you were talking about. So horrible. This really doesn't seem at all right for someone as good-natured as you seem to be. I have been watching you and how sick you have been, but I wanted you to get to feeling better before I could really talk to you."

"Thanks, Ben." Michael looked up at his huge frame. He had met Ben briefly already but had never talked to many people except for Daniel. "Do you have some suggestions for me?"

"Maybe, maybe not," Ben replied as he sat down on the floor next to the two. "I will make sure that everyone here knows that you are my friend. I could be here for a while as well, and trust me, I know the system." That was the thing about jail, though. Everyone was in there for some reason, but they didn't talk about it too much, and you never wanted to ask people outright what they had done to get in here. It just wasn't proper jail etiquette. Things Gloria Vanderbilt never told us.

Although Daniel was his first friend here, he would be rolling out soon as his case was almost settled. Ben took Michael under his wing and introduced him to other good people. They would all play spades together, and with Michael's extreme intelligence, they would rarely lose. Michael was not his bitch. He was his friend. There was definitely something very genuine and spiritual about Ben. Michael could feel it more each day as his intuition began to return the more he was away from alcohol, kind of like situational sobriety since the only bars in jail were the ones keeping you away from booze.

The next morning, Ben joined Michael and Daniel in their morning breakfast routine. This was to be followed by some dominos and then maybe a nap or Bible study. This was quite popular in jail. Michael had been raised Lutheran, and he had to attend confirmation classes when he was a teenager before he was allowed to take communion. During the two years of these classes, he had read and studied the entire Bible, but the interpretation was deemed by the church, not himself. By now, in his life, he was fairly opposed to organized religions as he never felt right in a church. The energy was all wrong. It had nothing to do with spirituality, but more like money generation and control of the way people thought. Control was the first sign of evil, and that was the feeling he would get in church. It was very ironic, given the next person that would come to his rescue.

He was again summoned by the loudspeaker that he had a visitor as had occurred the previous morning. He went down the stairs, but his time the visitor was in the pod. It was the jail chaplain. There were a couple of inmates standing around the chaplain, asking him some questions, when Michael walked up to the group. "Did you ask to see me, Father? My name is Michael Stevens."

"Oh yes, Michael." The chaplain looked at him over his crowd of followers. "I spoke to your dad this morning. Give me a minute, and I'll get to you." He went back to talking to his other groupies, and when he was done, he walked up to where Michael was standing just out of the way of everything. "My name is Chaplain Davies. Your dad wanted me to come see you personally. Do you have time to sit down and chat?" He somewhat smiled at the dark humor. He was definitely Michael's kind of guy. He was in his late sixties or maybe early seventies and a medium thin-framed man. He had a full head of silver hair and wore round glasses.

"Well, it just so happens that my schedule is clear," Michael said with a hearty laugh. "Let's go sit at the table." He was not too thrilled with most so-called men of the cloth, but he got a good feeling from this one. It was the same feeling that he had when he was around Tisha all those years ago—a kind of genuine spirituality that was not religious, just true.

They walked over and sat down as the entire pod of inmates was watching them. Michael filled the chaplain in on his side of all things, and he seemed to listen very intently. He was not sure how many people were locked in this facility, but Michael was sure it was in the thousands, and this man was here to see him specifically, which was most likely what made the other inmates so curious. Michael shared a little of the rocky history that he had with his father and how he really felt about religions and churches.

"Your dad tells me that you're from up in the Pacific Northwest." The chaplain seemed to make a statement and a question at the same time.

"Yes." Michael was just not in the best of moods. "Does that apply to something in my present situation?"

"No, not really." The chaplain smiled at him quite genuinely. "I just used to live up that way. I was a pastor at the Old Rock Church near the town of Chelan. Do you know the place?"

Michael thought about it for a moment, and he did recall the place. There was an old abandoned church on the outskirts of the town of Chelan not too far from where he grew up. He had passed by it many times as a kid when heading up to the lake for fishing weekends and the like, with the version of his father that was rare. It always reminded him of some old Scottish church built from uncarved stones and miscellaneous sized bricks, all sealed together with mortar and mud. Sections of the walls and ceiling were missing. The place just looked desolated as it loomed far off the highway.

"Yes, I know the place," he responded.

The chaplain could tell that he was distressed, so he returned to the point. "It was nothing. I just wanted to let you know that I used to live up that way. So now to the business at hand. I think your father didn't realize what this would turn into when he made the call," Chaplain Davies told him in the most sincere manner. "I think that he was genuinely scared for you and did not know what to do."

"How about call a friend to check on me or have my wife call one, not the cops?" Michael said rather defensively. "Tough love is no love at all, and that is what I grew up with. You know what this is? It is me having to pay for the sins of my father. That's what it is. He has never tried to understand what is different about me because it is outside the realm of what he will allow to be his comprehension. He is so brainwashed by the system like most people in this God-forsaken country. Sorry, I know you're just trying to help, but this really sucks."

"I know, Michael," he said. "I know what you are. I can feel the good in you and the power you have to feel deeply. I have that too. Yes, I agree it is not something that I could talk about in a church, and I don't like what religions have done to destroy true spirituality. That is why I left the church long ago and decided to work in the jail where my help could really be appreciated."

"Really?" Michael was pleasantly surprised. "All right, you have gained my trust. Now where do we go from here?"

The chaplain took out a book that he had in his pocket. It was a printed version of the New Testament only. "I want you to start reading this. Ask God for your ability to understand what you are about to read before each time that you begin reading. Pay heed to the things that Jesus had to say and really think on it with that powerful mind of yours. Go ahead and underline the things that mean the most to you, and we will discuss them the next time we meet. You don't have to read it all in a week. I am going to make it a special duty of mine to show you what you can do if you can get your heart right. What is in your heart must also be in your mind. A man cannot truly do the good that is in his heart until he rids himself of the evil thoughts that are in his mind."

"I couldn't agree more, Chap," Michael said as he took the book from his hand. "I will do it, and thank you for taking the time to come see me. I imagine that you are a very sought-after man around here."

"That is putting it mildly." He smiled as they both got up from the table. "I will be back next week sometime. God bless you, Michael, and you know, you are only the second person to ever thank me in the twenty-five years I have been here." They shook hands. Then the chaplain turned and waved to the guard in the tower, and he was let out of the door.

Michael went back to his corner rack and leaned up against the wall. He looked at the book in his hand that the chaplain had just given him. Ben walked up and looked down. "Chap give you a Bible?"

"Yeah, imagine that," Michael said while holding it up for Ben to see. "It is a sign, I guess. For some reason, this man was intended to come into my life, and I am glad that he did. I already feel a little better." Just then Michael was being summoned for another visitor over the loudspeaker. "Wonder who this is now?" He got up again and went back downstairs.

The pod door clicked, and he walked out into the horseshoe hallway. A man in a suit was standing with a deputy, waiting for Michael. He got a very evil, soulless feeling from this man, and his intuition was correct as usual.

"Are you Michael Stevens?" the man asked.

"Yes," Michael said. "You just called for me in the pod." The man handed him a packet of papers.

"What's all this now?" Michael asked while looking down at the inch-thick sheets of official-looking crap.

"You are being served," the piece of sewage spoke. "Those are divorce papers and a restraining order." The man turned and walked away, leaving a slimy trail behind him, Michael thought.

Michael was frozen in place while holding the forms like he was still being handed them. "Just what the hell am I supposed to do now? It has been less than a week since everything happened, and she has all this done already. How much worse can this get? I am a good man, goddammit."

He felt a soft hand on his shoulder, and it was that of the deputy. "Come on, son. You need to go back to the pod. I guess I would try to find a good lawyer if I was you."

Michael could feel that the deputy was genuinely sympathetic to his situation, and it just didn't help matters all that much.

He really wasn't sure how much more of this he could take, but he just didn't think it could get much worse. All was silent as he made his way back through the pod. He got back to his little corner, and Ben and Daniel were there waiting for him.

"What was it?" Ben asked.

"She served me divorce papers in jail," Michael said while shaking his head. "Can you believe this shit? She's definitely good at it, being married as many times as she has. What a bitch. Got a restraining order too as a little extra bonus." Michael shoved the stack of papers into the storage box below his rack. He did not even want to read them.

"Wow, you must have done something really wrong in another life to deserve all this," Daniel said like he truly believed that to be true. "Whatever it is, I feel for you, man."

"Listen, guys," Michael sighed, "I'm just going to go back to bed for a little bit. I need to sleep for a while and deal with this. By the way, thanks for the earplugs, Ben."

Ben just nodded in generosity, and Michael climbed up in his bunk. He looked at both of them standing next to the bunk. "Thanks for being here, guys. I couldn't do this without true souls of the spirit like you both are. I know that in my heart, and my intuition is rarely wrong. See you in a little bit." He rolled over and faced the wall, covered his head, and tried to sleep. He cried silently so no one could hear and eventually fell asleep.

Michael's heart ached liked it never had before. No death or loss had ever affected him in such a way. He was so alone and unloved. The dreams and nightmares began that night. He could not remember all of them, but whenever he woke up, it felt like a dagger was sticking in his heart. For an empath that feels things differently, he might as well have been dead. This was not a world for him, and his birth here among humanity was a mistake. He didn't understand how you could just stop loving someone. How could you just turn it off? What if there was no love to begin with? He started to believe that unconditional love did not exist in humanity. To even call it unconditional was totally redundant. This was simply because the human ego, the root of all evil, would not allow for it. If you harmed anyone's ego bad enough, they would abandon you. That had been the case here, and Michael was more disgusted with humanity than anything else.

He never had the chance to even talk to his wife before the incident, and he wanted to make things right. It was all just an act to secure another money generator as a husband. She could not face him because she knew that she would be making up lies about him to ensure her success in the divorce. Rina had an evil soul, and now he knew what she had done to her other husbands. Just another demon, and the world was full of them. He knew that was true now.

Michael awoke the next morning, feeling like he had barely slept. The dreams were taking a lot out of him, and his most recent revelations about humanity hurt his heart so much. He sat up on his bunk for a minute and just glanced around the pod. It was about three in the morning, so that was why he had not heard the chow call yet. He reached down under the bed to his storage area and pulled out the Bible that Chap had given him.

He was not much of a Bible thumper, but that was because he had never really read it objectively. The church was always interpreting things for him, and that would not happen again. Michael opened it to the book of Romans like the chaplain had told him to and began to read while underlining the things that he wanted to discuss with Chap.

Chow time came, and Ben and Daniel joined in for the breakfast sit-in as usual. Ben looked at Michael. "Saw you reading the Bible that Chap gave you."

"Yeah," Michael said with a partial mouthful of cereal. "I figure that I have lots of time ahead of me to study this thing the right way, so might as well get to it."

"It changed my life," Daniel chimed in. "I don't like churches either, but Jesus I like. He was actually an anarchist, which is not what people think it is. Just a world without evil control structures and people living free and happy."

"Everything that was built can be built again." A new voice from the left side of the bunk came through. It was Trent, another very large black man that Michael had seen with Ben quite often. He had a tall afro and always kept his hair pick sticking out of it. Michael had seen him walking around and picking his 'fro from time to time. There was a good energy coming from him. "I have been watching you, Michael. You are a decent person, and everyone in here knows it. To tell you the truth, you are doing better in here than I thought you would. Once you start to get honest with yourself and reading the Word, trust me, you will need someone to talk to. If these two jokers"—he pointed down at Ben and Daniel—"ever get tired of listening, then you can come see me."

"Thanks a bunch, Trent." Michael put down his cereal and stood up to shake this man's hand. So far, he had encountered a better group of souls in jail than he ever did out in the world. What a shock. But not for Michael, the higher your status was in this world, the more dishonest and corrupt you were. If a person could not see that, then they had no brain at all. When his hand gripped Trent's, Michael got an energy surge like the first time he met Brad. He felt so relieved all at once, and his fear was melting away. This man would be his next good friend. Ben and Daniel were friends as well, but he was sensing something benevolently different about Trent.

Jail was rather surreal for Michael. Other than your legal case, there was really no outside interference, although isolation was not for everybody. He existed in a not quite asleep, not quite awake state of consciousness. There was no cause to be phony or fake. He was just able to be his true self almost like a dream.

It was the morning of his sixth day, and he had another visitor. *Who could it be?* Michael thought. *More papers, more lawyers, or Chap maybe?* This time, Michael was directed into a different room where outside visitors came that weren't part of the court system. An actual visitor from the outside, he was excited and terrified at the same time. He did not know how much more pain he could take though. It was Al, Rina's father. Michael felt so relieved and not so alone to see a familiar face. He had the kind of smile that seemed to let Michael know that he was sorry this had all turned out so terrible. They both picked up the phones in the booths.

"Hello there, Michael," Al said very sincerely. "Are you okay?"

"Yes. I'm fine," Michael replied. "So good to see you, Al. I won't waste time with the specifics, but you know I'm not the monster they are making me out to be."

"I truly know that." Al smiled then switched to questioning look. "Rina, however, is out for blood again, it seems. I am aware of her marriage history and not proud of it, but she has always been so naive and vindictive as well."

"Is there any way that you can talk to her?" Michael asked. "I will play nice and divorce or whatever. Just work on getting the charges reduced or something. Tell her I don't want any payback for the money I put into her house. I just want out of this shitty mess, and then I will leave town forever."

"I will try, Michael, but she doesn't listen to me like she does her mother, and she is the queen of all vindictive bitches." Al seemed to chuckle at that one. "Did they set bail?"

"Yes," Michael said with an angry look. "Sixty thousand, which means someone would have to come up with six. Maybe you could talk to someone for me because they won't let me call anyone since everyone I know seems to be involved."

"I can definitely do that," Al said without hesitation. "If no one will do that, then I think I may be able to. I do have an account of my own that has enough, and I know you would pay it back someday."

Michael's eyes lit up like he just opened a buried treasure. "Yes, great. I would owe you more than you can possibly imagine if you can get me out of here. I've made some friends that are helping me in here, but I need to get out to try to put my life back together."

"Will do, Michael." He smiled. "Just hold on for a little longer, and things will be okay. I have to go, but I wanted to see what I could do to help. You take care in there."

"Thank you so much, Al." Michael placed his hand on the glass, and Al responded in kind. "I knew you had a great spirit about you the first time I met you." They both hung up the phones, and Michael left feeling very relieved, like a weight had been lifted.

Back to the pod and the crew was waiting for his news. Michael practically ran up the stairs, gleaming with joy that he shouldn't be here too much longer. The first person he saw was Trent, who was playing dominoes with some other guys that he didn't know very well.

He tapped Trent on the shoulder. "When you get a minute, I need to talk with you."

Trent gave him the signal that he would be just a minute as he was concentrating on the domino play he was about to make. You never left a game in jail once it had started; other business could be taken care of after the game. Michael went back to his corner, and Ben and Daniel were both sitting on their bunks, talking about whatever would kill the time the best.

"So"—Daniel looked up at Michael as he approached—"tell us what it was."

"Not yet." Michael pointed back over his shoulder. "Wait until Trent gets done with his game and joins us." They both gave an approving nod. They only had to wait about fifteen minutes until Trent was done, and then he joined them in the corner.

Michael told them about the visit and how it looked like he might be getting rolled out soon. He was so excited but at the same time would kind of miss his new friends. They might have even got along on the outside, but society would never allow it.

"Wow, great news, buddy," Ben said as he stood up from his bunk. "We need to make sure that we exchange our outside information so we can see each other again." Michael, Trent, and Daniel all nodded in agreement.

Michael enjoyed the rest of the day with his friends in the usual way, a couple hours of spades with Trent, dominos with Daniel, an atrocious dinner, and some good spiritual talks with Ben. He thought that it was kind of funny, but when Daniel was not around, the other three together looked like one of those big vanilla sandwich cookies.

Sleep came easy to Michael that night, but this night would forever change the next course of events in his life. He started to see a faint white light, and it began to grow until it was much brighter than the sun. It did not hurt his eyes, though. He felt totally at ease and full of joy as the ether clouds began to surround his body. He felt as if he was just floating without a worry in the world.

Off in the distance, he could see a small dark figure. He tried to squint so he could see it better, but it was coming closer and getting larger. Soon it looked as if a man was walking in his direction across the ether and getting larger still, but he could not make out the face quite yet. Michael kept squinting to try to see the face. Then the figure emerged full and the face was obvious. It was Albert Mann.

"Al?" Michael questioned the figure. "I just saw you today. What is this?"

"Just listen to me, Michael, as I don't have that much time," Al said to him. He was glowing all around like a spirit; only he did not look like he was floating, but more like standing. "I am not going to be able to fulfill the promises that I made to you today, but you have another way out of this. You need to listen to Chaplain Davies. He has been placed here for you and will help you through this. This will not happen fast, but you must stay positive. I know all the truth now, and you do not deserve any of this. You cannot return to your old ways after this, and you are almost out of chances. The Creator has a purpose for you, and you must fulfill it if you want to ascend someday. When the time comes, the signs will be in place. Anger has always been your problem, and it will continue to be until you start to realize that you can't save everyone, but you can save yourself." Al turned and walked back into the ether cloud that he had emerged from and was gone as quick as he came.

"Wait!" Michael shouted out. "Come back, Al. I need to know what this is all about." There was no reply, only the calm, misty glow. The ether cloud began to withdraw, and then the light faded until it was gone. Michael awoke, while slightly hyperventilating. He was soaked down to his groin like he had just sat up out of a bathtub. Had he been screaming? He looked around the pod, and everyone was asleep, so he did not wake anyone. He looked over at the clock, and it was about twenty minutes after two in the morning. Michael grabbed his towel and began to dry himself off a bit and then leaped out of the bunk to head to the water fountain for a drink. After the amount he had sweated out, he was borderline dehydrated.

It was all dark in the pod, except for the lights that were on all the time, and no one was up. That was very strange. There was always someone up at all hours, but not tonight. He just shrugged his shoulder and went back to his rack and climbed up to go back to sleep until morning chow call. He was going to keep this to himself as he didn't really feel like explaining it to everyone. Michael was confused about how Al was able to visit him. Had something happened to him? Was he more powerful than Michael had thought? He was not sure, but something wasn't sitting right in the pit of his stomach. Slumber found him rather quickly and the rest of the night was uneventful.

Chow came and went, and the crew all went back to sleep after breakfast, which was also unusual, but sometimes everyone was just tired. Morning visitation came, and Michael was called again. Who now? He was really tired of having to leave the pod for more legal system crap, but he was in the game now and had no choice but to play, just like any other game in jail. That was kind of funny to him.

He came down the stairs and could see Chap was there, standing in front of the pod door. His visits were always allowed inside the pod unlike everyone else. He had a sad look in his eyes, and Michael slowed his walk down the steps. He already knew. He went to one of the tables and waved the Chap his way, and they both sat down.

"Michael," he said, "I have some bad news for you. How well did you know Albert Mann?"

"He's dead, isn't he?" Michael asked right back. Now he knew how he was able to visit him in the previous night's vision.

"Yes." Chap looked up at him with a questioning, pursed look on his face. "How did you know?"

"I just did." Michael knew that Chap would understand, but he wanted to keep last night's events to himself. It was meant for him and no one else. "How did it happen?"

"Well …" The chaplain looked down at his folded hands. "Apparently, he stopped along the freeway to help a lady that was stranded, changed a flat tire. Someone came along who was not paying attention and basically ran him over. No other easy way to put it. Were you two close?"

"You could say that." Michael hung his head and shook it like he just couldn't believe it. Al was going to help him get out of here soon, and that information never reached anyone. He was almost upset with himself as to how selfish that really was. No matter how much he was starting to hate his wife, he had a sympathetic feeling for what she must be going through right at that moment. "My wife has got to be a mess," Michael said while still staring down at the table. The chaplain placed an open palm on the top of his head without saying a word, and they remained in that position for a few quiet moments.

"He came to see me yesterday, you know." Michael looked back at the chaplain. "Said he was going to try to get me bailed out of here. That's not going to happen now, obviously. I know that I cannot be that selfish about it, but I am devastated to say the least. Thanks for letting me know. I am doing the readings, and some guys in here are even joining with me."

"That's good, Michael." Chaplain Davies kind of straightened up a bit. "You will need it now more than ever. I sense a great conflict in you and a great gift as well. It is very powerful, and you don't even fully realize it yet. You could be dangerous if we don't get you on the right path." He winked at Michael with a playful grin on his face.

"Thanks, Chap," Michael said with an expressionless face. He stood up while the chaplain remained seated. There was already a small line waiting to talk to him. Redemption through salvation. "I'm all yours now. You are about the only person that I trust right now, and I will get my mind set for the long haul in here." He turned and walked back up the stairs very slowly.

"This really sucks," Michael said as approached the crew, who were busy watching some morning TV about then.

"What happened now?" Trent looked up at him from his seat at the table with his hair pick in a different spot as usual.

"Just when you think it can't get any worse." Michael looked at Trent. "My father-in-law was killed yesterday on the way home from here. Remember, the one who was going to bail me out?"

"Ouch, man." Ben turned around from the table in front of them. He had been listening in as well. Daniel was gone to court, where he thought he would be getting the jump today. Trent was just shaking his head with a look on his face like, "What else could possibly happen to this man?"

"You seem to be taking it well," Ben continued.

"I need to request a meeting with my public defender." Michael explained like he was actually trying to talk to himself. "I need to convince the DA or the judge or whomever that I need to be cut a break of some sort. I will see you guys in a bit. I have some reading and things to do."

He went back to his bunk and filled out a request to see his attorney, but things moved slowly around here, so he did not expect any response. His next court date was a week away still. It seemed like all court dates were two weeks apart in this place. Michael knew that he had to keep it together in all this. Al told him that Chap would be there for him, and he could already feel that from the man, to say the least. He knew that Al was telling the truth because he came to him just like Butch had so many years ago. There were no lies in that place, only truth and joy.

The chaplain came to see him the day before his next court date. He was sure that Chap was keeping tabs on Michael's court schedules since he always came the day before any scheduled hearing as well as many other times. Michael discussed the readings with him and decided to actually listen to the things that Chap had to say. This was no normal preacher man; he was another prophet in Michael's life.

His public defender came to see him about an hour before court the next day just like the last time they had met. "I have been working with the DA, and he is not altogether comfortable with destroying the life of a citizen with a promising career and future that might be saved," Monica told him. "He said that he is willing to drop charges to a kind of misdemeanor assault with some conditions."

"Conditions?" Michael looked at her, somewhat puzzled. "What conditions? Am I screwed for life or not?"

"That really depends on you." She looked back at him with raised eyebrows. "You will have to undergo a psychiatric evaluation, during which there is a sixty-day hold. After that we will go back to the court with the results and recommendations. The judge will most likely honor this and then proceed with the recommendations of the psych official when it is done."

"Actually"—Michael smiled at her—"that doesn't sound that bad, except for the fact that I am going to be in here for months. Is the DA going to recommend that in court today?"

"Yes, he is," she responded. "Can you make it in here that long?" She was actually concerned for him; he could feel it. She seemed so cold and professional at times, but as much as she tried, she could not hide the empathetic energies that Michael could pick up on.

"I can make it that long," Michael said with a confident sigh of relief. "With the knowledge that I will not have to go to prison, I could make it as long as it takes. I have some good friends in here already, and that helps. Let's go to court, I guess." He got up and went back to the hallway to await court with the other inmates that were scheduled that day. One thing he did not like about court was that all inmates were required to wear shackles and their hands were handcuffed to a chain around the waist. It was very demeaning and rather unnecessary with all the guards that were watching them.

Inmates sat in a special section in court that was like a jury box, except it was located on the left side of the judge. The jury box was across the room from them. Inmates were brought in a special door attached to the courtroom. The jail was located across the street, and they had to travel down a corridor that was actually located under the street between the courthouse and the jail.

All went as Monica had indicated, and the DA recommended a psych holdover. The judge scheduled his psych evaluation for two weeks out. What a shocker. His next court date was set at two and a half months away, which included the sixty-day holdover period as well as another two weeks on top of that. Simply predictable.

Back in the pod and he went to find the crew. He found Ben and Trent, but no Daniel. "Where's Daniel?" Michael asked Ben after he made several loops of the upper level of the pod and couldn't find him.

"Rolled out," Ben said. "They settled his case the other day and sent him home. He never said anything after court the other day, but he did want us to tell you goodbye. You have his information that he gave you when we thought you were getting bailed out."

"Damn." Michael slammed his fist on the bed. "I really wanted to say goodbye to him." He did too. Daniel had been the first friend that he met in here almost two weeks ago, and he just knew that he would never see him again.

Trent came up behind Ben and looked at Michael. "They may move you too now. They send most of the long-term prisoners over to the old section of the jail. Most of the inmates in the pods are only here for a few weeks at the most. This is the newer section of the jail closer to the courthouse. They don't build jails with bars anymore."

This was the worst news Michael could have received at this point. He needed Ben and Trent if he was going to get through this. They were good guys and real friends. There was nothing that they needed from him; they were just offering friendship. The old jail didn't sound very promising. That was where they kept the more hardcore inmates, and Michael became scared once again. He had to be able to control his fear if he was going to be able to work on his anger, and the more negative the environment, the harder that was going to be.

Trent was right. The next morning came, and Michael's name came over the loudspeaker. "Michael Stevens, get your stuff together. You are being rolled out." Michael had already made his peace with it yesterday, so he got all his belongings, ready to go, and went over to see Ben and Trent for the last time.

"I will try get word to you guys where they are putting me," Michael told them. "I am sure the chaplain will find me, and he can probably let you know. He is a good man."

"You have a good heart and soul, Michael." Trent looked at him as he shook his hand the old school way, no jailhouse slaps this time.

"Keep on the path of spirituality, and things will go fine. There is a chance that one or both of us may roll out of here soon. Our cases are long and have federal involvement, so they should be moving us soon too. Maybe they will send us to the same wing that you're in. If you think hard enough about it, it will come true."

"Thanks, Trent. I really hope so," Michael said as he turned to Ben and extended his hand again. "Been a pleasure knowing you, Ben. I hope all the best for you in your spiritual quest. Thanks for the times we read together. Both of you are good men, in my opinion."

"Well, we love you, brother," Ben said as Michael thought for a brief moment that he might shed a tear. He just sniffed it away. "I think we will all see each other again soon. Take care, my brother." Just like that, Michael walked to the pod door and was gone.

He was taken through several hallways, elevators, and locked doors like a maze until he arrived at the old section of the jail. This place was like Alcatraz with all the bars and dirty walls and floors. It definitely more closely resembled a prison than where he just came from. Michael came to a locked door full of bars and heard the door mechanism click. The voice over the loudspeaker instructed him to go down the hall and into the first cell on the right.

Michael entered the hallway, and he could hear someone yell "Fresh booty!" from down the hall a ways from one of the other cells. The hallway was long and narrow with barred cells on the right and window like bricks in the walls on the left to let light in during the day, but you could not see through them. He stood in front of the cell door full of bars, and the door opened, so in he went. The door slid shut behind him, but it did not slam with any kind of ominous authority.

The cell housed twelve inmates, and his presence would make it a full cell. The area was split in half by bars with a door between that could be shut and locked if necessary. Most likely for a lockdown scenario. The left half was the sleeping area with two levels of bunks three deep on each side and a toilet on the far wall that was clean and only used during lockdown. These were solid metal bunks that can-tilevered out from the walls unlike the standup barrack-type bunks in the pod. The right half had the TV, phone, and tables kind of like a jailhouse living room. The toilet and sink were on the back wall of the "living room" just below the camera that was watching them all. There was no camera in the sleeping area, however.

Michael walked to the sleeping side and placed his stuff on the only open bunk without saying much to anyone. The bunks had a pecking order, so the new guy got the bunk that no one in the cell wanted. He figured that he better be social right away if he was going to make any friends at all. He came back out to the door between the two rooms and glanced out at everyone's chests. Michael didn't like to look people in the eye much until he got to know them better.

"My name's Michael. Guess I'm going to be bunking here for a while."

There wasn't much of a response, and the energies were pouring in quite a bit more negative than in the pod. Good people were in here, though; he could sense it. He just had to figure out which ones they were. He had grown so comfortable with Ben and Trent's great spiritual energy that he had become spoiled. Now it was so messed up and confused, and with so much time without alcohol, his feelings were getting stronger, so he needed to get control of it and fast. Might as well try out the shitter with everyone looking on and get that out of the way.

After a good movement, he went and sat at an open seat to watch the TV and let someone approach him. No one said a word, so he just sat in one spot for a while. Michael got up and went and leaned against the bars on the divider wall and continued to watch the tube. He heard a Mexican-accented voice speak just below him at the table. "Come on, sit here and play with us, *amigo*." Michael looked down and saw an older-looking Mexican fellow about his father's age looking up at him with a half grin. So Michael sat down.

"Juan," the gentle-looking fellow told him. "They like to call me old Juan around here, but it don't bother me so much." He was kind of plain looking and well kept, so he didn't look like he would belong in here as well. Juan had been married for thirty years, and his wife was out there, waiting for him. If he was in jail and she was waiting, there must be some form of love there. Michael could not say the same.

Dominos was the game. Michael had never played so much dominos, spades, and checkers in his life until now, and there were lots more to come. Juan filled him in on the new rules. This was a completely different world than the pod. They split the TV time between half Spanish and half English to avoid conflict; of course, they had to be fair with the prime times. Switching times was allowed if all agreed. TV was the main source of killing time in here. They all shared in the cleaning of the cell at scheduled times, and there were inspections once a week. The commissary came around once a week, where you could get candy and treat food if you had money on your account that someone from the outside would have to put in for you. Michael did not have that luxury.

Chaplain Davies had come to visit him just two days after he relocated. Michael knew that he wouldn't abandon him. They continued their study and discussion on Michael's readings once a week, sometimes on different days of the week but every week. He was not like any pastor Michael had ever met. The chaplain would encourage him to express what he interpreted and felt from the readings and never once did he tell him that he was wrong. Michael did not feel controlled, and he was encouraged to think out of the box. It was an absolutely wonderful experience in the middle of the worst experience of his life.

After about a week in the new digs, something would happen that would forever scar Michael in the worst way. A new inmate was brought in, and everyone watched him walk by the cell down the hallway to a cell a few doors down. He was a tall skinny skater pretty boy–looking dude, the kind that make good bitches for the wrong cell mate. Apparently, he was put in with a few of those wrong cell mates.

Nighttime came, and Michael could hear a skirmish building up down the way since he was the only one still awake in his cell. It was coming from the cell that the pretty boy went into. It wasn't overtly loud, but Michael had a keen sense of hearing as well as other things. It sounded like the new guy was being harassed although somewhat muffled. Michael could pick up on this poor kid's fear since it was so strong, and for the first time, he was able to see what another person was seeing just as clearly as if he were there. He could not control this vision, and it came whether he wanted it or not. He was locked into the energy field of the contact and could not get out. The kid was being raped.

Two large skinhead-looking fellows were holding this kid down, while a third was muffling his voice with a sock shoved in his mouth and a hand over it to boot. They were out of the view of any cameras. A fourth man tore down the kid's jumpsuit and began to brutally rape him. Michael began to cringe and tried to get the vision out of his head. He could hear the kid moan and whimper with each thrust of forcible entry. The men holding him down would hit the kid in the ribs or side of the head just for added kicks from time to time. Once one was done, then they would switch places and start all over.

Michael began to beat the side of his head like he did when he was a kid, and he could not get through to his parents. "Get this out of my head," he said aloud in a deep whisper. Michael did not even make it through the second scumbag's turn at pounding this kid before he passed out at the table.

He awoke several hours later sometime in the middle of the night. All was quiet in the hallway and the cell. Michael did not get the sense that the boy had been killed or anything. He could vividly remember the experience, and it was just horrible. It was almost like he was the one being raped. If this was what his spiritual teachings were doing to his powers, then he wanted no part of that. Maybe it was just a fluke and wouldn't happen again. Whatever it was, that was not something that he ever cared to experience twice. Michael did not share his experience with anyone else, but he was sure that he could not have been the only one who heard it. You just didn't rat on somebody like that around here.

Michael went to bed after morning chow and tried to put the event past him. He awoke about midmorning to the sounds of heckling someone. He glanced up from his bunk in time to see the kid that came in yesterday shuffling back up the hallway with his jail-issued belongings. Apparently, he was being relocated by request. Who could really blame him after being raped on his first night? Michael could feel this kid's anger and rage from what had happened the night before. He was very good at picking up on that since he had such a high level of it himself.

The one thing that bothered him the most was that he knew that he was not the only one who had heard the events from last night. There was just no way. Someone was always listening in jail. Hell, the guards might have even known about it, but some of them were more twisted than the inmates themselves. The thugs would get away with it, and there was really nothing that this poor kid could do. Humanity really never missed another opportunity to disgust Michael.

A couple days after the gang rape excitement, Michael was called for his divorce hearing, which was separate from his other legal issues. When an inmate had other court hearings, they made sure that they were brought there on time; that was for sure. He was taken into court just like usual with the shackles and waist cuffs and seated in the inmate box by a deputy. This would be the first time that he had seen Rina since before his blow-up almost a month ago.

She came in behind her lawyer and was hanging on to her mother. Rina did not even look attractive to Michael anymore. He felt like standing up and saying, "Ready to destroy number six, are you?" He knew that would not be a good idea. Michael had dealt with so many awful things in here that he didn't feel he needed to make it any worse. The three sat on their side of the court, and of course, there was no attorney present on Michael's side since he had no access to money to get one. Monica was just there for his state charges. They did not handle the divorce too; that was a civil issue that was not covered by the Miranda.

Michael glanced over at her for brief moment. She would not look at him, and he could feel the dishonesty in her. She looked like she had been crying most likely to put on a good show, but he had to consider that she had just lost her father as well. She had a tissue in her hand, but there was no mascara on it. Just a prop for the show. Not long into the proceedings, her attorney began to report that his client was in fear for her life and that Michael was not stable and had even talked of blowing up the office at work since they teased him so much. He indicated that he felt that it was a viable concern since Michael had nuclear experience in the Navy.

It was at this point that Michael could not take any more lies and torment in this place, and he really didn't care what the judge would do, so he spoke up out of turn. Inmates were not allowed to speak. He was already standing as required by all inmates during their cases. He turned and looked at her attorney. "Now wait a minute. I have been accused of some real crap in here, and I can't allow these lies to be admitted. There is no truth to any of this. I am a good man, but—" Michael was cut off by the judge.

"Hold on a second, Mr. Stevens." The judge looked at him with a half grin, letting Michael know that he could also tell that the lies were going too far now. "Please refrain from speaking out of turn." He turned back to her lawyer. "We will not allow any hearsay in this case, and Mr. Stevens is currently no threat to anyone as he is incarcerated. I am willing to grant the three-year restraining order that Mrs. Stevens is requesting and begin the divorce proceedings. Mr. Stevens is not able to access an attorney at this time, so I will allow him to appeal the restraining order when his legal matters are settled. You may all be seated while I review the case material for a moment."

Michael sat back down and never once looked back in her direction. He was so disgusted with this whole thing over a goddamn drunken phone call. He hung his head and began to cry very silently. Not making much noise, but the tears were just dripping off his face onto the floor. At one point, the judge looked over. Michael did not see him, but he could feel him. He was actually emphatic to his predicament, and even the judge did not think this was right.

The entire thing was over in about ten minutes. The divorce would be finalized in six months provided Michael did not have some appeal to be heard by the judge. He had no intention of appealing anything. He just wanted out of this whole mess and knew that any fight that he put up would just cost him more money in attorney fees that he would not be able to recover. With the fiasco that this whole thing was, there was no way that any judge would pay him any consideration in divorce proceedings. That would be the last time that he would ever see Rina in his life.

The bailiff escorted Michael out of the court after the proceedings. He did not even raise his head the entire time and kept it so as he left the courtroom. The bailiff gave him an understanding pat on the shoulder as he headed out of the court and back to the jail. He cleaned himself up a bit on the walk back through the tunnel under the street. Michael definitely did not want to look like he had been crying. Nearing his cell, he started to shake his head, wondering what could possibly be next in the destruction of his life. He was getting a funny feeling though, as though the energy in the cell had changed.

As he got to the door to the cell, he looked through the bars and there, big as life, was Trent with his signature hair pick sticking in his 'fro. This was the best thing that could have happened right now. Here was his spiritual brother, now in the same place once again. "Oh thank God, Trent." He didn't quite yell out, but everyone could hear him. As the door opened, Michael did not care what others would think; he hugged his friend. "So good to see you again."

Trent gave him a squeeze back and then separated from the hug. "You too, Michael. The pod wasn't quite the same after you left. I have never seen jail inmates take to anyone like they did with you."

"Ben too? Is he coming over?" Michael asked with some excitement rather ignoring what Trent just told him.

"No, brother, they rolled him out to prison," Trent said with some disappointment. "They rolled me over to the old section since I have been placed on a three-month hold while they try to put a federal case together."

Michael just shook his head, and he knew that Ben would be fine no matter where he was. "Just the two of us then. It will be nice to have my spades partner back." He and Trent were the unbeatable pair when it came to spades there was no question about that. "You know this has to be Chap's handiwork for them to roll you in with me."

"Chap or his boss." Trent looked at Michael, and they both had a hearty laugh. Michael felt so at ease again to have his confident back. Trent was big and intimidating to most people, but not to Michael. Trent never had to defend him as Michael could take care of himself and most people just left him alone anyway. There was no special way to put it, he was Michael's friend. Everyone else in the pod was just a little confused by this most unlikely of friendships. They did not have the spiritual capacity to understand.

It was from here on that things got very routine for Michael. Inmate conversations very loud in the daytime, so he took to sleeping mostly during the day with earplugs; sometimes staying up all night, until morning chow time. The conditions were better for reading and writing at night when he could actually concentrate. No one was coming and going, and the majority were all asleep, thus quiet. The chaplain wanted him to really concentrate on what he was reading and ask God for assistance. Once he got used to the adjustment, it made time pass a lot easier as well.

Michael started to gain weight as well as grow a beard. With all the carbs that they fed in jail, it was almost impossible not to pork up a bit. They were allowed yard time only once a week, so it was not conducive to burning the carbs back off. As far as shaving went, it was a pain. The razors that you were given were so shitty that you might as well shave with a broken shard of glass; it might be smoother. So to hell with that; let it grow. There was no one to impress for a while; he knew that.

Now that Trent was here, Michael started going up to the yard with him as there was a basketball court up there, and they could both use the exercise. The yard was located on the roof of the jail surrounded by a chain link and barbed-wire fencing. Not like you could really go anywhere, if the fall from the roof didn't kill you. It was great to be able to see the sun and outside world at least. He wondered, who were the bigger prisoners? The ones in here or the ones out there?

Michael's psychiatric evaluation came as scheduled. He had been in jail for over a month already, and he definitely wanted to start the sixty-day waiting period after the evaluation was done so he could get that time over with. He handled it very similar to the evaluation that got him out of the Navy after Butch was killed. He was sober now, and the years had tuned his psychic intuition more than when he was in the service. The evaluation went just as he had expected. Psychologists were the easiest people for him to read. He knew what they were looking for and what they wanted to hear. The profession of psychiatry was a joke to him. Their only purpose in this world was to get people who had fallen out of line back to acting and conforming like the sick system wanted them to so the government and corporations could continue to profit from their obedience.

Since Michael didn't have anyone that was putting money on his account for commissary, he had to find other ways to get candy and the goodies. With Trent back as his spades partner, that was easy. They cleaned house so much that eventually it was harder to get the other cell mates to play, but they still would eventually.

For the next month, not much changed. He and Trent would have their weekly yard time and every week the chaplain would come to see him to discuss his Bible knowledge. Michael's gut and beard continued to grow, as well as the fact that he was just so tired of being in the cell all day with not much in the way of variation. The deputies had been keeping an eye on him, and they could tell that he was honest and reliable, so Michael was offered a job.

He was pulled from the cell and asked by the lead floor guard if he would like to clean the jail on a daily basis. The guy that was doing it had rolled out, and they wanted Michael to replace him. Of course, he jumped at the opportunity. He would be able to leave the cell every morning for a few hours to clean all the jail hallways and areas on the floor as well as A block, which was the county jail's version of the hole. This would sure help to break the daily monotony and give him something to look forward to each day for his remaining time here. He would also be more respected in his own cell because he had a special position now.

Michael's first morning out cleaning was a trying one. All the inmates could see you out working. Some were just jealous that you had the opportunity to leave the cell and others viewed you as a kiss ass that got the job in the first place. A few would make comments, but with all the Michael had been through already, it was easy to block out. He was out here, and they were in there. Inmates would always try to get him to pass things for them as well, and Michael would just ignore them and move by. He knew not to trust anyone he didn't know. It was when he had to clean A block for the first time that he was devastated.

When the guard opened the solid steel door to the hole, Michael was hit with an overwhelming sense of evil and wickedness that he almost did not want to go in. There was something in there that he could sense, and it was a powerful negative energy like he had never felt before. He looked at the guard with a questioning glance and went in.

The place was an open area with individual barred cells in a horseshoe-type configuration. The center of the room had game tables like the other cells in the jail, but they never got used and must have been put in before the area was designated to be used for isolation. The shower stalls were just to the right of door. These inmates were kept in their cells all day except they were let out individually each day to shower if they wanted. Each cell had its own toilet and sink as well. The place felt like something that would house Hannibal Lecter, and the current residents were not too far off.

The filthy comments and language that came from out of the cells was phenomenal. Michael would not look into the cells to see what they looked like. He would have no choice but to just listen. They never threw anything at him since the cameras were watching, but they sure tried to intimidate him. This was the slime of society, most just waiting to go back to prison. They would use the shower stalls to masturbate in each day, and Michael had to clean that up as well. He figured it couldn't be much worse than having to clean up one of those peep show booths. They never let up either. It was the same experience every day he went in to clean that horrible place.

It was about the same time that his new job came along that Chaplain Davies introduced him to a Bible story that really hit home for Michael. The chaplain was sitting at the table across from him and asked him a question. "Have you ever read the story of Joseph?"

"Sure," Michael said. "Everyone kind of knows the story of Jesus's stepdad."

"No, not that one." The chaplain giggled a bit. "Joseph in the Old Testament. It is in Genesis." He opened the Bible and pointed to Genesis 37. "Start hear and read to the end of the book of Genesis."

"Okay." Michael looked down at the starting point that he was showing him. "Thanks, Chap. I will have it ready to discuss for next time."

Michael did not haste and went right to reading after the chaplain left the cell. It was just an amazing similarity to his own life. Joseph was criticized and used by jealous family and friends, where Michael was really no different. Thrown aside and forgotten by ones that were supposed to love and care for you. Odd, how humanity has not changed in all that time. Michael was really not sure what the point of humans actually was. They not only destroy themselves, but everything else around them. It was an encouraging story in the end, as God provided all to Joseph and he ended up living a very happy existence. His family was not so lucky.

The weather was getting warmer and basketball was in full swing. Michael and Trent enjoyed watching the Laker games on Sunday afternoons, but sometimes it would interfere with the Spanish TV times. For the most part, it was never really a problem. The Mexicans did not like to watch the sports that the Americans did and they really did not care for basketball in any form. Trent was always having issues with them letting us watch the games on Sunday, well one day, Trent had just had enough of it.

Michael always let Trent deal with the Paisas, jail slang for the Mexicans. He was bigger and took a lot less crap from anyone. The game was still on when Trent had to make a phone call. While on the phone, one of the paisa's changed the channel to the Spanish station, and Michael just sat there, waiting for the fireworks to ensue when Trent got off the phone. Trent did have a short temper at times, which was why most of them were in there in the first place.

A guard was in the process of making his rounds when the battle ensued. Trent came over from the phone and turned the TV back to the Laker game. He turned and grabbed the TV schedule off the wall, balled it up, and threw it out into the hallway in front of the guard. "If someone touches that TV again, I am going to break their jaw." This behavior was not allowed. The guards viewed this as trying to incite a riot and you would get sent to A block.

The guard signaled the monitor for the cell door be opened, and another guard joined him. Trent was handcuffed by one guard, and his stuff was gathered up by the other. All at once, Michael's friend was gone again. Most often when you got sent to the county hole, you remained there until you got out of jail to go to prison or go home. It was another setback for Michael, but he figured that he did not have that much time left in here if all went like he thought it would.

Morning came, and Michael was called for his morning duties as usual. He sauntered out and was just still a little upset at losing Trent again. Why could he not have just let it go and not cause a skirmish? He went to the cleaning closet to get his gear together and started work on all the hallways and general areas, always saving A block for last. Today, A block had a new feel about it when the guard let him in.

The teasing, cursing, and foul comments began as usual, and Michael just ignored them all. About the time he came to the fifth cell, he heard a familiar voice. "Hey, ass kisser. How did you get this job anyway?"

Michael turned and looked at one of the inmates for the first time ever. It was Trent with a big grin on his face most likely due to his amusement at the comment he just made. They had brought him over to A block after the skirmish yesterday. Michael was not sure where they were going to send him. He thought that it was just another cell, but they put him in A block. "Well, here you are again, my good friend." Michael stood up from mopping and stood in front of the bars of Trent's new home. "Why did you have to go off like that? We could have done it some other way."

Trent was lying in his bunk, facing out, looking very somber, and Michael could tell that he wished he hadn't done what he did. "I don't know, Michael. Why did you go off on your father?" Trent dropped his head and paused and then looked back up at Michael. "Sorry, Mikey. That wasn't fair."

"Touché," Michael said with a smile. "I understand. Anything I can do for you? They don't watch me too closely anymore, and I could bring you some commissary. Plus, I can see you every day, and

I know you're not going anywhere for a while." Both Michael and Trent laughed at that one.

Michael continued to clean the cell while talking to Trent, and the other inmates were a little quieter now. Trent was a fairly well-known guy in the underworld, Michael was sure of that. He always garnered respect whether it was in the yard, pod, or whatever. He never asked him what his charges were, and he never did care; but it was evident that he was respected for something. All Michael knew was that he had a spiritual connection to this man with the hair pick in his 'fro. That kind of bond could not be explained by words; it needed to be shown through the forces of energy.

Most people would not be able to handle the feelings that Michael would live with on a daily basis, just like most people would not be able to handle the pain that his friend Tisha was under for her entire life. People got so sedentary in their day-to-day slave-like routines that they didn't have the capacity to understand how things were different for others. It took Michael going to jail for him to see that. His entire life was thrown into a blender and set on "destroy," and he definitely was forced to break routine. For as much routine as jail was, it sure changed a lot.

The next day when he came back to A block, Michael snuck in a couple of Snickers bars for his friend, and things felt different in there now. For one thing, Trent must have said something to the others about flipping Michael any shit since there was not a noise to be heard except for the daily conversations he had with Trent. Michael would continue to bring in commissary for Trent, which he would share with the others in A block. Michael went from scumbag to hero almost overnight. That was truly something to behold. He would not fear going to hole after that. In a strange kind of way, Trent came to his rescue again by ending up in there in the first place. Some people had to take one for the team when you were running with the spirit.

The sixty-day wait was over for Michael, and he had been in jail for over three months. He was expecting news anytime about another court date and his possible options. He had completed all of Chaplain Davies's Bible courses and was reading the scripture on his own. The chaplain would not come until every two weeks these days since Michael was doing well and getting stronger, albeit fatter and hairier.

Chap came to see him one Friday morning about a week after Michael was supposed to have gone back to court. It was odd timing as he had just been there two days earlier. He came in wearing the usual cheerful, holy grin, and they sat down at the table. "What's up, Chap?" They both gave a little snicker at the sound of the way it came out.

"Well, Michael"—the chaplain folded his fingers together on the table—"I just wanted to let you know that you have really proven yourself to me and you are going to be just fine. As you probably have been aware of for some time, I've been keeping track of your case, and now I'm going to help you out a bit."

"What do you mean?" Michael looked at him, a little puzzled.

"The judge on your case has been a friend of mine for twenty-plus years, and I do get allowed a favor from time to time—part of the perks of being the only chaplain in a jail this size and being here for as long as I have." The chaplain looked at Michael, a little serious. "Regardless of your psych evaluation results, I think he is going to let you go with some conditions, and you may be able to go home."

Michael's jaw just dropped and froze. He looked at the chaplain for a few seconds. "Are you serious?" He smiled big. "That is the best thing I've heard since Elvis. You are the greatest man that I have ever met. Do you know that?"

"There will be others, Michael." The chaplain extended his hand, and they shook hands for a few moments. "I also have a men's home ready that will take you in when you get out so you will have a place to stay to get everything buttoned up before you go home."

He just could not believe his ears. After three and a half months, there was a light at the end of this miserable tunnel. "Chap, I really do not know what to say. I will remember you for the rest of my life. You put your faith in me, and I will not fail you. I promise."

"I know that, Michael." The chaplain nodded repeatedly. "I truly do. I feel that you have some more stumbling to do, but you should be done falling for now." He smiled rather lovingly like a father should for a son. "When you go, I want you to never look back. Go find that place to help you learn and be who you were destined to be. You have something that I have never felt from an inmate in here in twenty-five years. It is remarkable. I will never forget you as well, but you have a little more time left in here because I think that your psych evaluation review is next week, after which it will be two more weeks for the final hearing and the judge's decision, and then you should be out. I just wanted to set your mind at ease for what the outcome will be so your time left is easier."

"I'd say thank you three times, and it still wouldn't be enough." Michael thought he might float away for as much weight was just lifted off of him. They both stood up, shook hands again, and the chaplain waited for the door to buzz then walked out the door.

The very next morning in A block, Michael broke the good news to Trent and all about the special visit from the chaplain. He could barely contain himself at the thought of being out of here in a few weeks.

"I'm happy for you, Michael." Trent told him from the shitter in the back of his cell, just bad timing that day, but Michael had been so used to that kind of thing by now that it didn't even register. "Let me finish up here, and we'll chat."

Michael went to cleaning the block while Trent finished up. When he heard the toilet flush, he went back to the front of Trent's cell. "That Chaplain Davies is really something else. I never told you this before, but the night after my father-in-law died, he came to me in a dream and told me to listen to the chaplain. You may not believe in that sort of thing, but that is what happened months ago."

"No, Michael, I believe it." Trent came to the other side of the bars while fixing his jumpsuit. "You are special. We all knew it back then too. How else does a 260-pound streetwise black man become friends with a clean-cut, average white guy? It is spiritual, my brother." They clasped hands between the bars in honor of the victory. They both chuckled at how odd their friendship really would seem to others, but it was that, spiritual.

At the next hearing, the psych evaluation was presented to the judge, and they set a final hearing date for the so-uncommon two weeks away. They did not read the evaluation in court. It was simply another formality in the legal system to admit the report into the official file and then give the judge the two weeks to review it and make a decision. If the decision at the next hearing was as the chaplain had indicated, then he could be out that very same day.

He had faith in what the chaplain had told him, but he could not help but be worried a little bit. Nothing was over until it was over. His intuition was telling him not to worry, but it was the damn mind that was the problem. Michael knew that the chaplain really cared, and that was a new experience in his life. Jail was not what he expected, and he had received more compassion in this place of lockdown than he ever did from his own family.

The morning of the final hearing arrived, and Michael was performing his morning cleaning of the jail as usual. He saved A block for last that day as it might be the last time he would see Trent. Michael was not looking forward to saying his final goodbyes. He was definitely in a chipper mood due to the possibility of getting out today after being trapped here for over four months. He would never trade the growth that he had made spiritually, and maybe the Creator deemed it necessary for him to be in jail to do that.

He was just lying on his stomach in his bunk, reading a book, when Michael came to his cell door. Of course, he had brought a final gift of more candy bars from the commissary. "So my hearing is today," Michael said to Trent, who just remained lying in bed, reading the book. He could tell that the isolation of A block had really taken its toll on Trent.

Trent put down the book and got out of his bunk to come to the cell door. "So you may go home today?" Trent looked down at him like he himself was about to cry, but that would never happen.

"Yes." Michael smiled. "If all goes well, I may get out this afternoon. I need to thank you for all you have done. I don't really have the words, and I wish I could do more to help you out. Friendship doesn't really come easy for me. Most people cannot get past their human judgment of me long enough to actually be my friend, but you didn't do that. You are a good man, Trent. Is there anything that I can do for you if I get out of here?"

"No," Trent said as he hung his head a bit. "Nothing much you can do to help me. I have messed up my life for good, and only the Creator can help me now. You are the most decent and genuine person that I have ever met in my life, and I don't see how you have been abandoned like you have. I don't like most people much, and I know you don't either. Forgiveness is the key to salvation though, no matter how difficult it is. Thanks for all the commissary though. I won't get that after you leave."

Michael extended his hand through the bars, and they shook hands. "Well, if I don't see you tomorrow. This is goodbye, my friend." They looked at each other and understood the bond that they had made. Even though they would part ways, they would forever be together in the spiritual world." It was a happy moment, not a sad one.

He finished his morning duties and headed back for his cell. It was still rather early in the morning, but the chaplain was waiting for him when he got back to the cell. "Hey, Chap, come to see me off?"

"Something like that." The chaplain smiled at him. He had a Bible in his hand, and he brought it up and extended it out to Michael. "This is for you. It is a special Bible that I wanted you to have for the remainder of your journey in this life. I have written a little something inside the front cover. I wanted to get it to you today just in case you get to leave."

Michael looked down at the Bible, and a tear ran down his cheek. He wished for a brief moment that this man was his father and not the drunken fool that he would have to face again someday. "I really appreciate this, Gene." Michael doesn't ever really remember calling him by his first name before today.

Chap handed him a piece of paper with a phone number on it. "This is the number to the men's home that I had told you about a few weeks ago. If you get out, call this number, and they will come and get you from the front of the jail. They already know about you and have a bed waiting. I have faith in you, and there is definitely an uphill battle ahead."

"You are a prophet. I know that with all of my being. Thank you for all you have done. You have saved my life in more ways than you can possibly imagine," Michael told him, but there was so much more he wanted to say but just couldn't put together the words. The chaplain left, and Michael sat down to kill the hours before court. The hearing went just as the chaplain had indicated some weeks ago. The judge decided to waive the felony charges and put him on probation. He would be allowed to return to his home state and undergo counseling, anger management, and alcohol treatment.

When Michael returned to his cell, he waited while watching TV, with butterflies in his stomach, hoping to hear his name on the loudspeaker, and it finally came just before noon. "Michael Stevens, get your stuff together and roll out." He had never heard such beautiful words in his life. He gathered up all his gear and waited by the cell door. The door opened, and out he went.

He went through the long process of signing for his things and waiting in several different rooms before he actually got to the end of the line, where he could actually see the civilian entrance to the jail. When he changed back into his street clothes, he noticed that the pants would not button anymore. He had gained over twenty-five pounds in jail, and they did not fit like they did four months ago. Michael just zipped the pants up as far as they would go, left the top button undone, and hung his shirt over to hide the belly.

Then he was out. He made the call to the number that the chaplain gave him and then exited the building. After 130 days, 12 hours, and 57 minutes since the day he did not remember coming to this place, he was free again. He did not have that many belongings, but there was still a cigarette lighter that worked but no cigarettes. He looked down at the ashtray outside the jail and filtered through the remains. The only cigarette long enough to smoke had lipstick stains on the butt, but he did not care at all after all this time without one.

Michael sat down on the front steps of the jail, leaning with his elbows on his knees to wait for his ride. His pants were cutting into the underside of his new belly, and he could really give less of a shit what someone walking by might have thought of him just then. He smoked that nasty used cigarette with the lipstick stain like it was the best thing he had ever tasted. Everything that had occurred over the past four months just seemed so surreal. This had to all be a dream, because it was just so ridiculous. Child molesters spent less time in jail than he just did. He just shook his head in absolute disbelief, looking out over all the people going up and down the stairs and chuckled as he said aloud, "What the hell just happened?"

REALITY

The individual is handicapped by coming face to face with a conspiracy so monstrous he cannot believe it exists.

—J. Edgar Hoover

Michael walked through the chain link gate of what looked to be an old apartment complex. It was the entrance of the men's home that he would be staying in for a while. The owners, who picked him up in front of the jail, were really nice Christian people—real ones and not one of the deceived. They had purchased the run-down, abandoned property, fixed it up, and turned it into a nice shelter for homeless men to come and get back on their feet. It was a very hard place to get into, but Chaplain Davies had pulled some strings. He had helped Michael with so much already—a true man of the Spirit.

He was assigned to one of the many two-bedroom apartments with another roommate, who had already been there for a while. The living quarters consisted of five or six two-story buildings with a grass-covered central common area of picnic tables and barbecues. There were some conditions that the residents had to follow: no drugs or drinking, which really should go without saying. They had to attend AA meetings on a regular basis, be in their room by ten at night, and were required to work, if physically capable, when the opportunity came around. Residents did not have to pay to live there, but if you wanted to stay, then you had to follow the rules very strictly. Michael had no problem complying with rules that were based on the consideration of others and not the control of his own free will.

Every morning, local people who needed to hire laborers for the day would park on the street and wait in the common area. Any current residents that wanted to work would mingle about and find work for the day. Landscapers, contractors, and maintenance companies were always present and looking to hire temporary laborers. They didn't pay much, but at least it was work. Some residents even ended up in full-time work or a career path as a result of starting out here. Michael did not have any pride left, so he just sucked it up and worked the odd jobs every day that he was available. There was never a day where someone wasn't looking for work or workers, including the weekend, and the owners were good about getting the word out to the businesses.

The positive energy of the shelter was overwhelming. The owners gave off a benevolent feeling, just like the chaplain did, which was probably why they were such good friends. They worked round the clock to help the residents with legal and personal matters, spiritual growth, and even counseling when necessary. Michael had a lot of time to grow here—mentally, physically, and especially spiritually. He used the time to try to dig deeper within himself and figure out why he was really here. With still so much deep hatred for those that he thought had wronged him, that task would prove to be quite difficult. Thoughts of his father would still enrage him so much. He knew that time would have to show him the answers, and he was not going to solve it all during his short stay with these good people.

These were the outcasts, the misfits, and all the ones that society had turned their back on. Michael always resonated better with the underdogs, as most empaths did. He was finally figuring that out. Even in jail, he felt more comfortable than he did around any kind of corporate scum. He always thought that how one walked with the broken said more about a person than how they sat with the fortunate. People struggling to get through life were more genuine and real than the ones that harnessed ways to manipulate life around them. Michael was always very intuitive and could see right through the thin veil of those who weren't genuine. Now, especially, he could feel everything again since he was sober.

Food at the shelter was accepted by donation only, and it was always coming in. That seemed to give Michael hope, an odd feeling for him. There were more good souls out there than he had noticed before due to the dark cloud of all his anger. People would pull up all day long, and the residents that were around the common areas at the time of the delivery helped to bring the boxes into the kitchen. Everyone was required to help out with food delivery and preparation, and Michael would volunteer to cook since he spent all those years in college doing it. He would be thankful that he had that skill to fall back on when he wasn't able to work in engineering. At least he had a small sense of worth in this low period of his life. Sometimes it just feels good to be able to do something right for a change.

Residents sat around the outside common area, smoking and shooting the breeze during the idle times, which were heaviest in the evenings. Some of them played instruments, like the guitar or a harmonica, and would frequently be practicing. Michael even obtained his own harmonica and would join in. Happiness was more important than talent, and no one judged you. Bible studies and AA discussions could always be found if you needed one. People would sing and dance from time to time, and the general feel of the place was one of joy. There was no ownership and attachment to clutter up their lives and distract them from what really mattered the most—happiness.

Since no one had any transportation, residents used the city buses to get where they were going, although the owners would take people some places personally if it was necessary. Using a bus for transportation was a new thing for Michael. His truck had been repossessed while he was in jail since the payments were not being made for months. It was the very truck that got him in trouble in Salt Lake City with Sean, and now his life's devastation had been assisted by Sean's deception as well. He was not the friend that Michael thought he was; his judgment had been so clouded with alcohol at the time that he couldn't feel the warnings.

Chaplain Davies came by to visit him after he had been there a couple of weeks. It was refreshing to finally be able to see each other without bars around. Chap was thrilled to see how well Michael was doing adjusting to the home. For the first time since he had known this dear man, he was able to finally hug him after one of their talks. In jail he could never do that; it was not allowed even if bars weren't separating you. Michael could truly feel the deep spirit in him. He was a genuine gift in his life. When he finally left here, Michael would never look back just like he promised the chaplain over a month ago when he was still in jail. That was one man he did not want to break a promise to; it would be as bad as breaking a promise to himself. He would never forget him though. Chap would always hold a dear place in his heart.

Michael did not venture out much because he did not want to run the risk of running into anyone that he knew, especially Rina and Sean. If he actually saw them together after all he had been through, he could not honestly say what he might be tempted to do, and there was no way that he was going back into that hellhole over something stupid. After a few weeks, he thought that it was time to get in touch with Brad, who had no idea as to what had happened to him yet. Michael knew that he should still be living in the Spokane area, but he had not spoken to him much since the wedding in 'Frisco. Brad was the only one that could really help him out now. He didn't dare contact anyone else, and he really didn't want to reach out to his family after their role in the mess he had just experienced. Michael's mother would be willing to help him, but his father would never allow it. That man was dead to him now anyway, and he was not sure if he would ever be able to forgive him.

Through a directory look up, he was able to find Brad's phone number. Sure enough, Brad was still in the Pacific Northwest in a remote area south of Spokane. Michael thought that he should call at about seven o'clock in the evening to have the best chance of reaching him. He was not going to believe all that had happened in the last six months. Brad had his own bouts with the law when he was younger, so he was no stranger to jail; but not four months of it and certainly not for such ridiculous shit. He tried to call him about seven thirty that night, and for the first time in ages, he would finally be able to talk to his best friend in this world. He could feel the overwhelming anticipation of hearing a familiar friendly voice.

The phone rang about four times before he heard Brad's wonderful deep voice. "Hello."

"Brad, it's Michael," he blurted it out so fast in all his excitement. "So glad you are home. It's been a while."

"Jesus, Michael," Brad said with a tone of relief. "I have been so worried about you and didn't know whom to call to try to find out where you went. I tried to call you several times in the last few months to let you know where I was living now, but no answer and no return calls. What the hell?"

"It is a real long story, but to sum it up, my dad had me thrown in jail after I got drunk and apparently made some threats on the phone about my father and several other people. I don't remember doing it because I was blacked out. The court made several counts out of it, and the bail was so high that no one could get me out. I had no way of getting ahold of you in there and didn't know your new number, or I would have. With the antiquated speed of the system, I ended up spending four months in Fresno County Jail."

There was a long pause for about six seconds. Then Brad spoke in a concerned tone Michael had never heard before. "You're shitting me. Are you all right? Did they hurt you in there? I have been in a few jails, buddy, but none as scary as that one."

"No, no. I'm fine," Michael assured him. "My life, however, is destroyed. I have nothing left and nowhere to go. The chaplain in the jail helped me get out of the mess and into a temporary men's group home, but I can't stay here forever."

"Say no more, my old friend," Brad said very encouragingly. "You get your ass up here when you can, and we'll get you back on your feet. You can fill me in on the details when you get here. We have a lot of things to catch up on." For the first time in almost five months, Michael did not feel homeless and abandoned. He wrote down the address that Brad gave him. They shot the breeze for a few minutes longer. Then the conversation was over. Neither of them had ever been long phone talkers. Now all he had to do was make enough money to get there and finish all the legal business.

It took Michael about a month to finish the court formalities and work enough odd jobs to save money for a moving van, gas, food, etc. for the trip to Brad's. Rina had someone put his stuff in storage while he was locked up. He would find out later that his mother had been paying the bill, unbeknownst to his father, who didn't have the compassion to help out in any manner. He could almost see the smug, egotistical look on his father's face as if to say, "I did no wrong and good thing that kid learned his lesson." Asshole! Finally, he was out of that awful desert oven. When he finally got out on the open road, Michael was completely free of every burden that he had in his life even if it was only for a little while. The long drive gave him all kinds of time to clear his head and try to make sense out of everything. He felt like a big piece of him died in Fresno while at the same time gave birth to something new. He knew it was there, but wasn't sure what it was yet. Michael's spirit was unwavering, and there was no reason to ever look back. Chap would be proud.

He had called Brad, previously, to let him know the day and approximate time that he thought he would arrive. It was an emotional reunion like no other. Brad was waiting on the front porch with a big smile when he pulled in. Michael might have missed putting the moving van in park if he didn't think twice about it since he was so excited. Jumping from the van in a frantic hurry, he met Brad halfway and bear-hugged his long-lost friend. It was true that some men didn't cry, and that was truly a bad thing since their egos made them believe it was a sign of weakness. Michael, however, cried almost daily at this point in his life. He sobbed uncontrollably on his friend's shoulder and didn't want to let go. Brad finally settled him down, and they went on inside to do nothing else but talk the rest of the day.

Michael told Brad about all the events that led up to his disaster. Brad had a much better picture about what his life was like, and he was right about his uncertain feelings about Sean. He had warned him about Sean so many years ago. Michael told him about how the chaplain had saved him from probably going to prison for a long time and how it renewed his faith that there were some people involved with religion that were still spiritual. They talked till early in the morning. Brad had asked his wife beforehand if she would just leave them undisturbed for the night so they could have lots of time to talk about everything, and she graciously did.

The next morning, while sitting at breakfast, Michael felt more relaxed and safe than he had in years, literally. He looked up at Brad. "Thanks for all this." He paused to chew some of the delicious breakfast. "I really mean it, no shit. I don't have anywhere else to go right now."

Brad was just setting down his coffee cup and smiled over at Michael. "I know. You think nothing of it, buddy. I can't turn my back on a brother." That was what they were, brothers—not biological, but spiritual.

"There is just one other problem." Michael grimaced. "When I return the moving van, I will have no way to get around to job interviews and other appointments, and I need to put my belonging somewhere."

Brad chuckled before taking a sip of his coffee. "We will come up with something, but after breakfast, there is something I need to show you. There is room in the barn for you to store your stuff. We'll go out there after we get cleaned up for the day." He smiled again, and Michael knew he had something up his sleeve.

After the wonderful home-cooked meal, a shower, and a good shit, they headed out to the barn together. Brad's place had an old dilapidated barn that wasn't really being used anymore since he was no farmer and didn't really have use for it other than storage. It was about a hundred yards away from back porch of the house along the back fence line. Brad lived in a nice pine tree–blanketed lot, with just the right amount of outbuildings, shade, and open space.

They got to the door of the barn and Michael looked at Brad. "You know, that is the first home-cooked meal that I have had in over six months, not counting the tolerable meals that I cooked at the men's home. It might be the best breakfast I've ever had actually."

"If you liked that, then you'll like this a whole lot better." Brad smiled as he unhinged the door and swung it open. Michael turned his head to see a beautiful sight. He felt like a doorway to the past just opened up in front of him. Here it was, all dusty and spider web–covered, Brad's van from college, the one that they went everywhere together in for years. More memories were surrounding that van than anything Michael could think of.

"You're kidding," Michael said, with goose bumps, on his way over to touch it and see if it was actually real. He ran his hand down the side, leaving a clean line in the layer of dust. "You still have it. Does it run?"

"Yes. It still does." Brad was pleased to see the surprise in Michael's face. "I take it out every few months or so and start it from time to time to keep the battery charged. I keep the tabs up, but just store it back here. I am going to loan it to you so you have transportation to get back on your feet while you're here. You will just have to clean it all up."

Michael just couldn't believe it. Things were starting to look up in his life. "No problem at all. This is just great. Thanks, buddy. I will get it all cleaned up and do some maintenance on it for you as well. I still have some of my own money left to pay for gas." He shook Brad's hand and went back to looking over the blast from the past. Brad went back in the house to leave Michael alone in his reminiscing.

He opened up the back doors of the van and looked at all the remaining garbage still strung about. Miscellaneous potato chip bags, beer cans, and whiskey bottles were scattered about. It didn't seem that Brad had spent much time cleaning it out. Just under the back seat, he noticed what looked like a metal rod poking out from some wrappers and fast food bags. Michael crawled up in the van on his knees and reached under the seat. To his amazement, it was the Winchester Defender shotgun that the two of them had always liked to shoot out in the woods.

Michael reached out for the weapon and grabbed ahold of the barrel. He jumped to a flashback of that day in the woods during his first blackout. He was looking down on himself like he was out of body. He could see that the shotgun was in his hand, and he was pointing it out into the night. Brad was there too, almost like watching a live rerun. He instantly came back to the present with a little jerk of his head. Michael dusted off the wood stock of the ancient relic to reveal their initials that they had carved in it so many years ago.

M.S. B.W.

While holding the gun, Michael got another feeling, but this was one of despair and death. Something evil was present, and it was inside him. Shit! He must have picked something up during that first blackout, and it had been growing ever since. Not sure what it was, he shook it off as paranoia and placed the gun back under the seat.

Over the next few days, Michael cleaned up the van as nice as it could be and now he had some wheels. Even though it cleaned up nicely, it still looked like an old hippy van. He did not need it much, but it sure made things nice to not have to worry about transportation. He knew why he felt such a strong positive energy when he met Brad more than a decade ago. He had helped to save what was left of Michael's life and turned into a better friend that he had ever expected he would be.

Brad worked for a manufacturing company in Spokane, and was making a great living by now. He lived about a half hour away from town. Michael was able to use the internet during the day to find a good counselor to finish his legal stuff as well as start looking for work. He had gained enough experience to take the engineer licensing exam, so he also signed up for that. Michael had plenty of time to prepare for the exam since finding work would be a near impossibility with the economy in the shitter; not to mention having to explain his most recent disaster in California to any potential employer. There would be no way to hide that; besides, Michael did not lie anyway.

Life at Brad's was great. The duo got along better than they ever did. Brad was a social drinker and not the whiskey slammer that he was in college, and Michael had not had a drink since the night that put him in the slammer. Brad never talked about those big issues much; they were just moving on with different phases of life. Even though Michael had grown leaps and bounds spiritually and learned so much from the chaplain and the men's home, he had a lot of anger and a hidden rage that he was not aware of yet, and it would continue to grow for years. He did not want to admit it, but he didn't think he would ever forgive his father no matter what he said on that damn phone. It did not require the level of punishment that he had received. It cost him his job, marriage, friends, and somewhere in the neighborhood of $75,000 lost. Michael figured he paid for everything he had done wrong and everything he would do wrong for the rest of this life, and then some.

Michael passed his engineering exam the first time out, and suddenly he was a licensed professional engineer able to stamp design plans for construction. It was one of the hardest exams in the country to pass, including the bar exam, since there was such a comprehensive amount of material that you needed to be ready to answer. Getting a job, however, was still not developing into much, but having the license under his belt would certainly help out a bit. He had applied to many companies in the local area, but he was never called for an interview, most likely due to the recent bout with the law that he had to answer on the applications.

Finally, a small irrigation district in northern Idaho called him for an interview. He was excited as he really did not want to work for the large corporate firms that he was applying to, but he had to apply to everything if he was even to have a chance. All totaled, Michael probably applied to over sixty firms before this opportunity came. This was the one, though, he could feel it, and his intuition was rarely wrong when he wasn't drinking.

The drive up for the interview was only about an hour and half, but it gave Michael some time to think. The area was such a beautiful country setting, and he felt so at home. Nature was the only thing that made him feel like he belonged in this world. The trees and fresh air just seemed to prove the existence of some external higher force that created all these good things. He waited outside the interview room with butterflies in his stomach. What would he tell them about the things that happened in California? He decided that honesty would be best since he had nothing else to lose in the first place. Michael was called into the interview room and sat in front of the board of directors, just as nervous as a small boy at a Catholic priest convention. After all the initial routine questions, the board did not waste any time in getting to the point of the interview. "Mr. Stevens, we see that you have recently passed the engineer's exam. That is definitely a plus as far as we are concerned, but we do want to talk to you about this arrest last year that you have on your application."

Michael paused and looked down at his hands briefly then back up at the board members with a shy smile. "I would imagine that you do. Well, the whole thing was a bit ridiculous. My wife and I were separated, and I was led to believe that we could work things out. That turned out to be a lie, and she was having an affair with my best friend. I made a bad decision." He started to sniffle a bit, forcing back tears. "I got drunk and made threatening comments to my father on the phone, which I don't remember doing. I did not mean it, but my father called the police to complain." Michael could not hold back the tears anymore. "I had my life destroyed over it and have never been in any trouble before." He wiped his eyes a bit. "I satisfied all the requirements, and I am now ready to get back into the engineering workforce. I just need the chance." He looked at the men in the room with teary eyes.

The president of the board seemed to believe him. He looked at the rest of the board members and slid the tissue box over to Michael as he leaned on the table and looked at everyone. "Well, I have heard enough." Michael was just sure they were going to tell him thanks and goodbye. "When can you start?"

He could not believe his ears. "Well, I am staying with a friend just south of Spokane for right now, so I will need some time to get a place to live. I would think that I would need a couple of weeks to a month to get settled. Thank you so much for the opportunity." He stood up and shook the hands of all the board members and left the room. He held his head high as he went back to the van. He climbed in and buried his head in his hands to finish the crying that he started in the interview room. Michael didn't cry quite as hard and long as he did when he woke up in jail, but it was a close second. His life was getting back on track, and he had managed to save his career. These were tears of joy.

Michael found a little townhouse to rent and had just enough money left to get in and cover monthly expenses before he would get his first paycheck. He stayed with Brad for a few more weeks before he moved up to north Idaho. They had a heartfelt parting but would stay in touch for quite a while. Since they did not live too far away from each other anymore, it would be easy to get together on a regular basis. All possibilities were laying out in front of him.

Brad let him keep the van until he was able to get his own car. It only took a few months. Michael was due to take the van back to Brad and visit for the weekend, but before he left, he decided to take the shotgun out from under the back seat and keep it. There were a lot of memories there, and he was pretty sure that Brad never realized that it was still in the van all these years so he wouldn't miss it. He reached under the back seat and grabbed the old Defender, and something happened. Michael got another vision, but this was much more vivid. He saw himself lying in a coffin with Brad looking down on him. Tears were running out of his eyes, falling onto Michael's dead body, and he could feel the overwhelming sense of loss in the air. Suddenly, he was propelled back into the van, holding the shotgun, and the vision was gone. He had no idea what it meant, but he took the Defender into the townhouse and put it under his bed for the time being.

Springtime came the following year, and things were going without a hitch for both Brad and Michael. Brad was doing even better financially as he had not been through hurricane Rina like Michael had, and he decided to buy a boat. Michael had been saving well and had enough to buy a jet ski to go along with it. The boys were back in town. Brad was not quite the water lover, like his buddy Butch had been, but he did love that boat. Michael loved the time in the water and would be able to work on his waterskiing, which he had not done since he was in the Navy. They had their sights on a little lake just north of Spokane called Deer Lake. A few times they had gone there just for the drive and a swim and noticed that there were cabins available to rent or buy. The lake was small and not too crowded at the end of a dead end road. Good location.

The two decided to go in together on renting a cabin for a while. Brad would eventually buy it outright, since he always had more money than Michael. It was just perfect for all the weekend outings, and it gave Brad a place to put his boat so he didn't have to haul it back and forth all the time. They had such hopes and dreams of years of fun in the woods. The place was not directly on the lake, so it kind of gave off the "cabin in the woods" feeling.

On the second trip to the cabin that summer, the two were sitting around the cabin after a day out playing on the water. Brad was sipping on a beer and for the first time in almost a year and a half, Michael wanted to have a drink. His life was back in order, and he was feeling a lot better these days. His psychic forethought did not seem to be as active lately, and he really didn't know why. Most likely that he restricted his company to those that he was used to, and did not allow anyone new into his life. Maybe he was not thinking about it that much, so it didn't rear its ugly head like it used to. Who knows?

Michael went and grabbed a beer out of the cooler and went to sit by Brad in the lawn chairs. Brad looked over at him with the beer in his hand. "You think you will be okay with that? It has been a while since you had anything to drink."

He twisted the cap off and looked confidently back at Brad. "Yep, it's about time, really. I have been through everything now, and I don't feel tormented like I used to. I just wanted to be away from it for a while to see if I could do it. I can take it or leave it anymore."

Brad took a sip and just looked back into the trees. "Well, if you say so. Just be careful. I have seen the blackout side of you a couple times, and I really don't care to see it again. I definitely don't want my family to see it."

Michael took a big gulp, and he could swear that nothing has ever tasted so good. For an alcoholic, it is only a matter of time before things return to the way they used to be. It could take months, or it could take years, but it was inevitable. He really did not have much contact with his own family after he had been jailed and abandoned in California. They were no family at all to him anymore, except maybe for his mother. Brad's family was becoming his new family, and he felt so much more at ease and comfortable around them. They did not judge or try to control him. They actually seemed to listen and care, unlike the majority of society.

He did not visit home at all after the disaster. Michael could not avoid talking to them on the phone from time to time, but he did not return messages and sometimes would not answer if he noticed the caller ID. Excuses why he had to miss the holiday gatherings got more difficult as the years went on, but he managed. What did they really have to talk about anyway? He always figured that his mom would just check on him from time to time to make sure he had not committed suicide yet because deep down she knew what a shitty deal he had been dealt in his life. Maybe that was her way of saying that she understood.

His life at home was growing rather stale, and Michael really needed something else in his life. The rural life could get a little boring, especially without another life around to talk to. He was standing outside his little townhouse rental one night, just looking up at the sky, wondering where his home really was. With the exception of a few people, earth never really felt like home to him. He closed his eyes and prayed for some sign that he was not forgotten, and the answer came.

Michael heard a little bark off in the bushes, and he went over to investigate. It was a little puppy that looked so cold and hungry and shaking to beat hell, something like an Australian shepherd, but he was not sure. He bent down and picked up the puppy, and it was like instant true love. She started to lick his face with excitement while he took her inside to get some food and water.

She had an hourglass-shaped white section of fur centered between her large brown eyes with tiny black irises. On her forehead, the white color merged to gray, making it almost look like she had a human head of hair between her large isosceles triangle–shaped ears. The far-reaching tips of her ears only poked up about an inch above the top of her head, giving her a relaxed unalarmed look about her. Soft brown hair ran down her cheeks and neck to meet the fluffy white tuft of her chest. The only really noticeably dark black color was her nose, but she had small occasional patches of black fur mixed in with the other fur. He decided to keep her and named her Rikki. They went everywhere together. She became his best friend, even better than Brad. Where there was one, there was always the other. Although he even got some discouragement from the board of directors at work, he was finally able to bring her to work with him gradually, and then it became every day.

He finally had time to begin his research into this whole Patriot Act business that he first heard about while in jail. Patriotism was the virtue of the vicious according to Oscar Wilde, so he didn't image he was going to find anything encouraging. He was great at digging up information that was hard to find, and the internet became second nature to him. It led him to dozens of books that he would read and many documentaries that were quite compelling. Then he stumbled on the movie that was called *Loose Change*.

He must have watched that movie three times in a row before he stopped and couldn't believe the information that he was seeing. Michael did not take the information in the documentary at face value, of course. An educated man would never make conclusions based on one source of information. So he did some more research on the supporting facts that were provided in the film. There was no question about the facts; they didn't lie. The truth about the disaster in New York was not being told by the government. He and Sean had even been talking about this on the day it happened, shortly before Michael went away. A light went off in his head. That was why the damn Patriot Act was enacted by congress within a month; it was already prepared before the events even unfolded. Something that behemoth would take years to prepare, review, and edit before it could ever be approved. This meant that the entire US government had been infiltrated by the Controllers.

The Buddha said that there were only two mistakes that one could make on the search for truth; one was not starting, and the other was not finishing. Michael would eventually regret finishing. The rabbit hole of truth was bottomless, and the deeper you went, the more truly stomach turning it became. It was simply astonishing; demonic was more like it. For the next five years, nothing much changed in Michael's routine. He and Brad would spend joyous summers at the lake, where they would discuss their college fun times while creating new ones to talk about. Drinking was restricted to beer, and Michael did not really take anything too far. Finally being around a family that seemed to care about him, he did not feel the need to get drunk every day, but that would change soon enough.

Michael continued his research into the truth and was slowly finding out that almost everything that he was ever taught was a lie just like he had touched on in high school. He always knew that something didn't feel right, and now the confirmations were rolling in on a daily basis. As with other budding truth seekers, they started to be labeled as conspiracy theorists and nutjobs. It was another brainwashing tool that society was programmed to believe that anyone who had information that was counter to what the government was telling them must be a kook of some kind, which helped to further discredit the truth. The CIA actually created the term *conspiracy theorists* to deal with those investigating the truth of the JFK assignation. Actually, the very word *government* means "to control the mind."

After his revelations about the tower destruction, he started poking into a little more unknown true history of the Bush family. The family was very evil. It turned out that not only was granddaddy arrested for financially backing the Nazis in WWII with his bank but Daddy was in the CIA when Kennedy was killed, and there was even a picture of him in Dallas at the time of the shooting. This was a picture that he had never seen before, and it sure did not look altered in any way. Barbara appeared to be the daughter of Allister Crowley, a hardcore Satanist that was very influential with the government behind closed doors. Her mother had an affair with Crowley, and Barbara was the result. As Michael looked at a picture of her when placed next to Crowley's, he was sure of it. They could be brother and sister, but they were father and daughter. A more sinister family he had never heard of.

The list of evil atrocities just went on and on, and he was so amazed that people had not been talking about these things. How could they pull the wool over so many people's eyes and no one be the wiser about it? Then he began to figure out how because people hadn't changed that much since the era of the magic bullet. Americans believed what they were told in the mainstream media, and that was the number one tool that the Controllers used to deceive. All the wealthy people in the world were involved. There was no specific government behind it, but all of them were infiltrated by them.

Michael couldn't believe the information that he was stumbling on. It was so big and so evil that no one would believe it. He could see the way that all media seemed to support the lies since the wealthy owners of these companies were all part of the plan. He had to take a break from the research from time to time, as it would become quite overwhelming. Over the course of a few years, Michael would become reclusive and angry again. His life had been destroyed by an evil system of a lies and a grand fool who supported that. He could feel the rage grow as he progressed further down the rabbit hole. The further he got, the more hatred he felt, and the beer was just not going to cut it anymore.

After all his years of research into the truth, Michael was able to conclude what the three biggest lies were, the ones that were enslaving humanity and keeping it from being free. The first was the lies about the knowledge of free energy. The club knew that if free energy were to be released, then there would be no more need of a monetary system, the very system that kept the sheep enslaved and the wealthy very comfortable. If people were to be able to generate their own power without having to pay for it, then they would be completely self-sufficient, and Satan's government would be no more. He had pages of documented cases of hundreds of scientists that were working with free energy and achieving it. They were all dead.

The second lie was the ongoing cover-up of the beneficial uses of cannabis. This plant alone would generate all the products, medicines, and food that humanity needed to survive. Henry Ford made his first cars out of this plant as well as generated the fuel to run it. The club made sure that he was not allowed to do that. Combined with free energy, the people could produce everything they needed with cannabis. The Creator knew this when he created everything; it was Satan that was keeping it from the people to control them.

That was the third and biggest lie of all. Humanity was being controlled by demonic entities that have infiltrated all governments, corporations, and religions of the entire world. It was amazing how easy that was to see when a person woke up to the truth. Michael could see all the lies that were placed in movies, television, schools, and churches. All of it was coordinated very well to keep humanity segregated and fighting amongst itself, so they could not see what was really going on and who the real enemies were.

The best tool that the Controllers used was the spreading of disinformation and distraction. They controlled all the media that was provided, and anything contrary to that must be looked for. Some of it was not that easy to find, but Michael managed. He would research different websites and read the comments that people would leave at the end. That was where the truth was found, in the comments, before they are taken down by the government trolls that constantly patrolled the internet to obliterate the truth. He would learn about books and documentaries that he had never heard of before due to the control of the mainstream media, and then he would search those sources.

It was one conversation that he had with his mother that really told him a lot about this society. He could see how people had been manipulated now and how masterful the agenda really was. Being so dumbed down by everything, they could not even think anymore. Michael had dug up more undeniable proof of these truths, but he could never get anyone to look at it. For his highly intelligent mind, the facts didn't lie, but only a coward would not look at it. His mother had called to chat shortly before five one evening, so she had not been too oiled on gin by then. Michael decided to share some information with her regarding the truth and the lies we have really been fed. He explained how he was starting to see now and the world made sense no matter how sick and twisted, and he was not crazy. Her response was "I can't change anything, and I don't want to talk about it." He really couldn't believe what he was noticing. That was truly what people had been programmed to believe. They would conform to whatever law came about and question nothing. They submitted to just about anything while calling themselves patriots, even though most of it violated every freedom that the country was based on.

The more he heard this very thing on a regular basis from other people, the more he grew angrier. The angrier he grew, the more reclusive he got. Then it was time to start turning to something more than beer. Michael thought he would give wine a try. He found that a five-liter box of cheap wine would last a while in the fridge. It was easy to pour and mix with juice while at home alone at night. After some time, wine was not enough and he started to move to hard liquor.

The negative energy and mindless herd mentality that he felt in crowds of people was just becoming too much. Willfully ignorant and narcissistic, the general population had the power to solve all their problems, but they refused to do anything about it or stand up to anything. They were drowning in fear and lies—that was, of course, unless someone was making fun of their favorite pop star. His hatred of the world at large was amassing with every day his awareness of the truth was growing, and he had to make a change.

Michael had built up enough funds to finally put a down payment on a small home out in the woods. It was actually closer to work than the town house was, and there was so much more room for Rikki to play. The location changed, but not much else did. Evenings were for drinking, internet research, and reading. His thirst for new knowledge was only outdone by his thirst for alcohol. At first, he did a good job of just drinking enough each night, so he did not have bad hangovers or blackouts of any kind. As any drunk knew, that didn't stay that way for long.

Although he did not see Brad that often after the move to north Idaho, they still would have summer trips to the lake. Michael would go to less and less of them with each passing year. His solitude and drinking were taking more of a hold on him. After a couple years, he could tell that Brad would stop inviting him. The more his rage about the world grew, the less he would feel anything. His empathy was failing and his ability to be calm and rational was decreasing. Michael continued to spiral into isolationism. He had no real friends, and it had been ages since he had been with a good woman.

Things continued on like that for a while and then he decided to call Brad one night. Michael figured that Brad would be the only person left that might be able to understand him.

The phone rang a few times, and Michael figured that no one was home. He was getting ready to hang up when Brad answered. "Hello."

"Brad." Michael was relieved to hear his friend. "It's Michael."

"Hey, Mikey." Brad actually seemed glad to hear from him. "It's been a while. Is everything okay?"

"Well"—Michael paused for a few seconds—"not really. Actually, I was wondering if you wouldn't mind coming up to see me for the weekend."

There was no response for a moment. "I can't this weekend, but I may be able to next week. It is kind of out of the blue since you seemed to have dropped off the grid a bit. I will come up by myself if you can wait until next weekend."

That brought a little sigh from Michael since he wasn't really the most patient man, or maybe it was the evil ego working over-time. "Yes, that would work fine. It just that I seem to be starting to lose it, and I need someone I trust to talk to. How is the family doing?"

"Oh, we're doing great." Brad had really turned into the good family man. "You do sound distressed. Will you be okay until I get there?"

"I'll be better now that I know that you are coming." Michael set his mixed drink down on the coffee table. "Call me when you are on your way."

"Will do." Brad hung up the phone. Michael started to get another one of his bad feelings, but it was so overshadowed with alcohol and bitterness. The days until the following weekend couldn't pass quick enough.

The fateful Friday finally arrived. Michael got home from work and started into his nightly drinking routine. He figured that it would be a few hours before Brad arrived, so he had plenty of time to get his load on. He had seen his good friend in person in quite a while, so there was some level of anxiety. Maybe he had grown somewhat paranoid in all this time of seclusion, but that was really not the point at this juncture.

It was about eight o'clock when the doorbell rang, and Michael leaped from the couch to meet his old friend. He practically jerked the door open with excitement, and there was Brad, not having changed very much at all—the same haircut, open-ended smile, and still in fairly good shape. Married life had been treating him well.

"Hello, Brad, please come in and make yourself at home."

Brad shook his hand and came in and glanced over the place. "Nice and organized as I would have expected. You got a beer or something?"

"Yeah, sure. There is plenty in the fridge around the corner there." Michael went back over to his couch and tended to his drink as well. Maybe he hid it well, but he was already fairly intoxicated by then. Brad could always see through him, so he would have been able to notice without much additional confirmation. He heard the beer bottle open with a swish sound in the kitchen, and the bottle cap hit the trash can. He came back out of the kitchen, and Michael offered up his favorite chair. "You can have the captain's seat. That is a real comfortable easy chair."

Brad took a seat in the big chair, and he seemed pleased with its comfort level. He took another tug on his beer and looked at Michael. "So, buddy, what's all the fuss about?"

Not really knowing where to start, Michael just stared down at the drink in his hand. "I just feel so alone in this world and needed some company. You are about the only one left that I trust to talk to." Brad just took the occasional sip on his beer and listened for a few minutes. "I have always felt like you are a brother to me, something that neither one of us has really had before. Both of us have been essentially fatherless for most of our lives, and I was always so sad that you lost yours at such a young age. I have always had such deep feeling for other people's problems."

Brad decided to interject for moment. "Yeah, that one still bothers me to this day. I wished that you could have had a better one with yours too. I always accepted your, flaw as you call it, but I never did understand it. I never figured that I had some of it too, only that we were just good friends."

"Actually, we all have it a little. Most just don't know how to harness it." Michael continued on with his diatribe. "Well, over the past several years, I have been doing a lot of research into this world and the lies that we have all been fed. Most people are just so scared that I can't seem to get through to most of them. I know that I should not be drinking as much as I am again, but it is the only thing that seems to drown out the truths and emotions that this knowledge has caused me. That is why I have been so distant and haven't seen you in so long." He paused for a moment, and Brad did not say anything. "It is not what you see on the news or any one political figure that is behind it all. All I can say is that it is some kind of demonic dark energy that controls everything. The Bible even talks about it."

Brad sipped on his beer and stared at Michael like he was crazy then slowly set the bottle on the end table and leaned up on his knees. "So what you are saying is that this is something that is not human?"

Michael got up to mix another drink and get Brad another beer without responding. He came back and handed Brad the beer and sat back on the couch, looking back at his friend. "Yes, buddy, that is exactly what I am saying. Before you get out the straightjacket, just listen some more. When I started looking into the Patriot Act, which is the unconstitutional piece of shit document that basically put me in jail. I just couldn't stop with that. It is too big for me to explain it all, but all the wars, murder, pedophilia, mind control programs, scandals, laws, lies, and everything about the entire system is only to serve one single purpose. It keeps us all in a negative mind-set that creates an energy that these demons need to survive on. They are in every level of our government, and most of them are in on news every day. The more fear that they create, the more that they can feed. Some time ago, I use to think I was just becoming some kind of nutjob, but that is not the case. I am not like the majority of the sheep in this world since I know the truth when I read it or see it. I also know the bullshit. The other problem that I have is that I cannot deal with injustice at all. That is why I have been drinking more and more since I cannot get anyone to see it." Michael got up and fixed another drink. He was really rolling through them now and starting to get rather intoxicated.

Brad came in the kitchen and sat at the counter. "I hate to see you do this to yourself, Michael. You were never really one who could handle their alcohol very well. I know that I have always trusted you and your abilities, and what you are saying might be true. Some of things that you told me back in college seemed rather fantastic, but I didn't really take it to heart. What do you really want from me? Why did you call me up here this weekend? I cannot just sit here and watch you drink yourself into a stupor and hate the world."

Michael stood in the kitchen, leaning on the counter opposite Brad. "I don't know. It is not my intention to do that, but I can feel my rage growing exponentially every day, and you were the only one who was ever able to calm me down. I want to hurt the people involved. It's like I have these visions of killing them all, which basically means killing just about everyone in the federal government. I need to see justice served, and they are all part of the Controllers. Have you ever seen any of them go to jail over the scandals and leaks that seem to come out from time to time when a whistleblower comes forward? Blackmail is how they do it." Michael was getting angrier with each word. "They find the sickest and most depraved pedophile sons of bitches so they can blackmail them into serving the agenda of the Controllers.

Brad shook his head and thought about that for a moment. "No, I can't say that I have. You haven't gone psychotic on me, have you, Michael?"

"Maybe." Michael closed his eyes and started to tap his forehead viciously with his thumb. "People have just become so apathetic. As long as they have their fast food, sports, and television, then they just don't seem to care. Entertainment and other distractions is the number one tool that these bastards use to keep people in the dark to their agendas."

Brad leaned his head back and sighed and then looked back at Michael. "What do you think any of us can do about it?"

This set Michael off. He was so tired of hearing that from everyone and started to get angry. "I want people to wake up and do something, goddammit! This isn't the home of the brave. It is a sewer that is home to enslaved ignorant cowards." He uncorked his bottle of whiskey and took a big draw.

Brad was now starting to become a little uneasy, and what he did not realize was that Michael was starting to slip into one of his blackouts. "Easy there, buddy. I think that we need to get you some help. I know that you are smarter than anyone I have ever met, but you need to do something before you hurt yourself or someone else." He stood up and came over a put his hand on Michael's shoulder.

Michael came unglued. He had gone black. "Get your hand off of ME." His voice had changed to that old familiar demonic tone that Brad had not heard since college. Michael turned away and then disappeared into the back room and went into his closet. He grabbed their old shotgun out of the corner of the closet.

Brad stood idly in the kitchen, wondering what his friend was up to, but he had no idea what was about to happen. He wasn't sure if he should leave or not, but something seemed very strange now. Michael was not the person he used to be, and he was afraid that his friend was too far gone to help. He was about to be proven correct.

Michael came around the corner and cocked a round into the chamber of the shotgun. He pointed it at the best friend that he had ever known. His eyes were completely black, and his face was contorted.

Brad had seen this before, but never this bad. "Eeeeaaasy there, Michael. Don't do anything stupid now." He just froze in place, not knowing what to expect.

"I'm sorry, but Michael is no longer with us now." The demon had completed its transformation. "I think that he might have told you too much about us."

Brad tried not to make any sudden moves. "What is it that you want? You need to release my friend."

Michael let out a chilling laugh accompanied by the most evil smile. "I don't have to do anything, and what I want is very simple. We want to destroy you humans. Your race is so pathetically easy to manipulate, but now it is time for us to take control of this planet and just keep a few of you around to serve our dark lord when he comes."

In desperation, Brad tried to reach out to Michael. He knew that he had to be in there somewhere. "Let go of him. Michael, if you can hear me, I need you to try to fight this. You have to come back to reality. I loved you like the brother I never had, and you can't do this. Remember what you are and what you can do for this world."

Michael felt a pain surge in his head just like what had happened in jail in California. He let out a terrifying scream and dropped the gun on the ground while holding his hands over his ears. The sound was absolutely bloodcurdling. He fell to his knees and continued to wail like he was bursting open at the seams. Brad saw his opportunity and ran past him for the door. He hurried outside, got in his car, and sped away without looking back.

The battle in Michael continued to rage until his eyes returned to normal and his face came back into shape. He fell over unconscious, and his face slammed into the kitchen floor. No police came, and no one came for help. Michael had lost the last friend that he had in the world, and he would never remember what happened. The demon had won this round, and it could quite possibly be the last round.

NO MORE

Insanity: Doing the same thing over and over again and expecting different results.
—Albert Einstein

Michael awoke in severe pain, lying face down on his kitchen floor. He felt like someone was delivering a series of right and left hooks to his upper abdomen. He recalled the pains that he had when he had been thrown in jail; this was the same but much more intense. His head was pounding like never before, and he started to heave uncontrollably, dribbling foamy swirls of blood from his mouth onto the floor.

Michael said aloud with a half-puked foamy load in his throat, "Oh no, what did I do?"

He had blacked out. Michael was overwhelmed with fear as to what he could have possibly done. He looked around and saw the shotgun lying on the floor next to him. Brad was nowhere to be found, so he knew that he must have done something shocking enough to make him run off. He wasn't in jail, so that was good, but it still didn't help him figure out what had happened. He had to get some composure before he tried to get ahold of anyone and then brace himself for the news of whatever horrible act he had committed this time.

Michael crawled to his feet, partially buckled over from the pains in his abdomen. He shuffled ever so slowly to his bathroom and knelt in front of the toilet. He continued to puke as much as he could, but he had obviously not eaten too much during the events from yesterday and was basically dry except for the occasional bloody foam. After he felt like he could stand up, he went back to the kitchen to get some water. He had a full-blown pancreatic attack going and did not know what he should really do.

Pancreatitis was quite serious, and a person could easily die from it. Michael had done his share of research on the subject after he got released from jail and knew what needed to be done. A hospital was probably a good idea, but who could he really call right now to help him? He was pretty sure that he had pissed off everyone he knew and didn't want to try to call anyone for help. He would not be able to eat or drink anything for a few days, and the pain would be immense. Most doctors claimed the pain was the closest that a man could come to feeling what it was like to give birth. It was also one of the top three pains a human could have—some say the worst one.

The initial shot of water did not stay down for more than a couple of seconds. It was very difficult to survive a pancreatic attack without outside medical attention, but Michael, being the self-sufficient man that he was, would do it himself. He lay down on the bed, and Rikki jumped up next to him and laid her head on his leg. Dogs could always tell when someone was injured and in large amounts of pain. They seemed to have a special connection with their owner, but Michael had a much better ability to bond with animals than most common people did. He remembered how Brad had always called him the dog whisperer due to the way his dog freaked out every time he would see Michael.

He reached over for his phone and saw that there was a waiting text message. There was just no way that the text was going to be good news, so he wanted to wait and then read about tropical storm Michael. It looked to be daytime through the dark curtains, and the clock was reading ten thirty in the morning. He knew that the message had to be from Brad, so he did not put it off any longer, and just read it.

> Hello, Michael. I know that you are not going to feel very well when you get this, and you probably don't remember what you did. You pulled a

gun on me last night before I managed to make it out of there. I decided not to call the cops, but you have to get yourself straight. We were such good friends for a long time, but I can no longer be your friend. I wish the best for you, but don't ever contact me again. Brad.

Tears were already in his eyes from the overwhelming burning in his stomach, and for a brief moment he was considering just finishing the job with the same shotgun on himself. Looking down at Rikki wagging her tail at him seemed to change his mind. Michael knew that he had to do something. He dug around for the home phone numbers of the board members for the irrigation district and found the number for the president of the board and decided to call him.

There was no one home, so Michael just decided to leave a message. "Hello, Richard, this is Michael Stevens. I don't really know how to explain this, but I will not be in Monday morning. I have decided to check myself into an alcohol-treatment facility." He started to blubber a bit while continuing. "It seems that over the past several years, I have developed a problem, and I need to do something about it. Please call me if you get this, and I hope that the board will understand. Thanks again." He hung up the phone and called Rikki up to his arms to have a big hug. He knew that life was going to get better from here, but he had never been so scared.

Michael took Rikki outside for a while to get some fresh air and hoped that it would help with the massive amount of pain in his abdomen. The wind was blowing hard, and he glanced up and saw a bald eagle just floating on the wind like a kite. He wondered how great that must feel to live a life with no problems, no control, no judgment, and no pain. It was just true freedom. When Rikki had her fill of running around, they went back in the house. He had to get busy finding a place to go dry out.

There was a message on his phone, and it looked as if Richard had called back and left a message while they were outside. He listened to the response, not knowing what to expect. "Hello, Michael, it's Richard. To tell you the truth, we were all kind of wondering if something was going on with you lately. Don't worry about a thing. We will take care of things around here while you are gone, and your job will be waiting for you. Just go and get yourself better and call and let me know what is going on when you know more. At least you are doing the right thing. Take care." What a big relief that was for him. God knew that he didn't need to lose his job right after losing his best friend.

Michael knew that he would not fit well in a hospital type of setting, so he searched the internet for all other possibilities. He found a place called the Ranch, which seemed to be a nationally recognized place. It was affordable and located in a rural setting in eastern Washington. It sounded perfect, and they even had a place for pets to stay so he did not have to worry about what to do with Rikki. The Ranch had a philosophy that pets as well as family members needed to be present in the healing. He called the place on the phone right away, and by chance, they had a spot available for the following week. It would be about three or four days, but he figured that would give him enough time to detox and get though the pancreatitis. Michael was very strong when he wanted to be and could get through almost anything. This would prove to be no different.

The synchronistic signs at the treatment center were just over-whelming. One of the counselors had the exact same painting on the wall of his office that Michael had at home. The chaplain had the same spiritual book on his coffee table that Michael's mother had given him years ago. The feelings of déjà vu were coming in on a regular basis. He was supposed to be here on his correct path in life, and the signs were telling him so. These smaller signs paled in com-parison to the one that he saw on his very first day, though.

After checking in to the facility and settling into his new room for the next month, Michael had decided to take a stroll around the beautiful rural facility to find his way around. The place had a separate section for the nonadults. They all shared the facilities at different times but had separate living areas so as not to mix. The odd thing was the gym. He came around the front side of the gym and quite simply could not believe the sign that he was seeing. The large sign above the gym door said Brad Wallis Memorial Gym.

Michael had to sit down and catch his breath. He backed up to one of the picnic tables, sat down, and just stared up at the sign. It was only one letter off from the name of his best friend that he had lost with this final drinking episode. If this was not a sign from the spirits, then he did not know what was. It was if the spirits were telling him that he was finally on the right path in life and that he should keep going.

Alcohol rehab was overwhelming, both emotionally and physically. The counselors encouraged you to reveal all that was wrong with you and tore you down to your essence. You became born again sober. Michael approached it with an open mind and just let the programs work. He didn't judge the information that he was being told, even though he did not like the lies they spewed about cannabis based on the government's agenda against it. He was all too familiar with that old song. Once the evil system got ahold of any program, the government vultures took over to generate as much as they could for their corporate butt buddies. Profits before people.

The group therapy sessions were where the real healing occurred. Facing people that you barely knew and talking about the worst things that you had ever done was quite an experience. Maybe it was because their judgment didn't matter as much as it would from someone you knew fairly well. The powerful thing about it was that once you admitted to your wrongs openly, you really did feel better even though some of the things that people had done while in a drunken stupor were very shocking, to say the least.

Step work was absolutely necessary but became somewhat regimented for Michael. He did not cut any corners, but in the end, he had to find what really worked for him. After facing all that he had done, there was really no desire left in him to ever take a drink again. He cried a lot when he was away, and he was ashamed of the things he had done. There was the thirteenth step, forgiveness. He had to forgive himself before he could forgive others. That would be the real challenge for Michael. Knowing was half the battle—one of the best clichés, albeit rather true. He knew that it would take time, but he did have his doubts. Would his regret and resentment ever be able to be healed? He did not know. Time would have to tell on that one.

Michael left rehab a changed man, with a month of not drinking already out of the way, and returned back to his previous life. He resumed working at the irrigation dam within a few days of getting home. The board of directors had their eyes on him for quite some time, but he really had to expect that. All conspiracy research was thrown out the window. He deleted websites, burned files, and even got rid of related documentaries. This all didn't change the fact that he still knew the truth and was fully aware of what was being done to humanity by its rulers, but he no longer thought about it or shared it with anyone. Michael saw their agenda in everything all around him every day, but he would process it and then let it go.

He started to research what being an empath was all about and topics that had to do with spirituality. As usual, he left no stone unturned and tackled all kinds of far out things. Michael studied all about metaphysics, dimensional consciousness, astral projection, spiritual awakening, psychic abilities, chakra meditations, aliens, demonic possession, near-death experiences, Jesus and other messengers, and empathy. No topic was out of reach of his fully opened mind.

The vibrational sensitivity and intuitions that he had fought all his life were getting stronger. He started to view them as more of a gift than a hindrance. Michael had spent so much time dwelling on what was wrong and evil about this world that he had overlooked the most important thing—how to start trying to fix it. He would begin a semiregular meditation habit and even tried to learn tai chi. Life was going well. Then he met her.

Michael had really learned to eat healthy when he was away at dry-out camp, and he loved to go to the Saturday morning famer's market to get organic foods. While turning away from one of the bakery booths, he found himself face-to-face with this beautiful woman. He smiled at her and excused himself as she passed by him to look at the fresh breads. When she brushed against him, he got a strange feeling, one that he never had before. Her energy was very strong, and he sensed a large amount of pain in her. She had a wonderfully pure heart with a severely damaged spirit. He watched her for a few moments as she sampled some different breads and talked with the vendor. She was so very beautiful with midlength auburn hair and perfectly sculpted body about five and a half feet tall—a simple stunner by anybody's standards. And she looked to be a little older than him. He glanced at her left hand and did not see any ring. It had been a long time since Michael had a girlfriend, but he just knew that he had to take his shot with this woman.

He walked over and tapped her on the shoulder, and she turned around, looked at him, and gently smiled. "Yes?"

Michael was just in awe at how beautiful she was. "Ahh." He tried to get words to come out of his mouth. "My name is Michael, and I have this overwhelming feeling to find out who you are. I just think you are so beautiful." He just swung for the fence.

She laughed for a brief moment, and he wasn't sure if she was flattered or slightly on the vain side since she didn't thank him for the compliment. "Now that's pretty original." Then she extended her arm to shake hands. "My name is Caroline, and I'd be happy to talk to you. Do you want to walk around the market together?"

He could not believe she responded in kind. "Sure. Yes, that would be great. I guess it would be after the fact to ask you if you come here often." They both laughed out loud.

The two walked around the local park for a couple hours, checking out all the booths while engaged in introductory conversation. They decided to meet later that night for dinner at a local bar. It had been a long time since Michael had been in a bar, but he was sure that it would not be a problem after all the triggers he had been through. He really didn't care if she drank at all. There was some attraction that was deeper than a physical one, and that was all he had to go on at this point.

Dinner went fabulously. Although it turned out that she was a lot more social than Michael and did like to drink on occasion, they had quite a bit in common. Even though nothing too detailed about their pasts was discussed on the first date, he knew that she had a lot of past damage, much like he did. As far as his reasons for not drinking, he just told her that he had a medical condition where he couldn't consume alcohol. Technically, that was the truth, but he knew that he would have to come clean with her at some point if this developed into any kind of honest relationship.

They continued to date regularly after that. He was starting to form feelings for her very quickly. Most of his past girlfriends had not made him feel as comfortable as Caroline did. There were issues though. She had a deep secret that he could overwhelmingly pick up on, and she was a little narcissistic. Empaths seemed to be attracted to more self-centered people for some reason, and Michael could definitely recognize that the trend in his past relationships. Empaths and narcissists both had deep feelings—only one was directed inward, and the other was direct outward.

Michael fell hard for Caroline. Maybe it was the fact that he hadn't been without a woman for quite a while or that he was just tired of being alone, but he knew that it was much more real than that. He began to call her his little Blue Dove since he was able to catch a glimpse of her beautiful indigo aura from time to time. It was not even a month that they had been dating when she moved into his house. She was not originally from the area and really did not have that much stuff to move in. He knew that it was way too soon to be living together, but she really needed a place since she had been living in a friend's basement since she came into town. They were going to have to find out a little more about each other before things just got swept under the rug like they usually did.

He refrained from talking much about his research into conspiracies, which had not worked out with many people from his past. Having done a lot of research on satanic ritual abuse and mind control, Michael could not help but to notice some things about Caroline that seemed odd. He figured that as many as 5 percent of the population had been victims of torture and sexual abuse either from wealthy secret cults, shadow government black operations programs, or generally deranged sociopaths. There was a real chance that she could be one of them, but which one?

She sometimes talked in her sleep about wanting people to stop hurting her, and Michael would just try to ignore it when it happened. Some words that he would mention seemed to trigger small changes in her personality. If they had a disagreement, she would almost become someone different and then not remember it after it was over. The signs of multiple personality were all over the place, but Michael knew enough about that to not bring it up until the appropriate time. If this was the case, then he thought maybe he would be able to help her.

After about six months of the off and on odd behaviors, Michael decided to bring it up to her one night. He prepared a nice meal, and they engaged in nice dinner conversation. After the dishes were put up, they relaxed in the living room. Michael put on some easy listening seventies music and lightly began to delve into some deeper dialogue. He knew that he would have to air some of his own dirty laundry first if he was to have any luck in opening up her own closet. If his suspicions were correct, then he would have to approach her with the utmost gentle caution as to not trigger anything that might put her at risk.

"You know I just think the world of you," Michael said gently while looking at Caroline with a tender smile. She returned a similar but almost puzzled smile. "I figure that we have been together long enough to share some deeper things with each other." He continued on while fidgeting a little nervously. "I told you when we first met that I had a condition that didn't allow me to drink alcohol. Well, that is not entirely the whole story. I am actually an alcoholic. There are some things about my past that I am not exactly proud of, but I thought it was time that you knew a few more details."

She looked at him with wide eyes. "You're not going to tell me that you're a serial killer or something like Ted Bundy, are you?"

"No, no, nothing like that," he responded with a chuckle that developed into a couple of loud quick laughs. "My story is a little different, so you will need to keep an open mind. I know you have one of those."

"Yes, I definitely have one of those." She chuckled along with him. "So lay it on me, Michael. What did you want to tell me?"

"Well, it actually goes back all the way to my childhood. You see, I have this little problem …" Michael talked for quite a while as she just listened. He told her about his abilities that he first realized when he was an adolescent and how the death of Jimmy had triggered something in him. He talked about the things he saw when in the military and in college and the loss of many more friends, leading to more drunken periods of his life and his decades-long struggle with it all. Although very difficult to bring up, he talked of the disaster that his marriage was and the time he had spent in jail. He especially illustrated the long history he had with his father and what that had really done to him, how he could never really forgive him for putting him in jail all those years ago. Although not going into too much detail since the subject was too vast, he told her how he had spent over a decade researching global corruption and did not like what was at the bottom of the rabbit hole. Michael left no stone unturned. He treated it as if was confessing his soul to a representative of God.

When he was done, he just looked at Caroline for some sort of sign. He was so afraid that she might not want to be with him after all he just unloaded, but that was not to be the case. She just looked at him with an empathetic smile and came over, pulled him out of the chair, and gave him a long, deep hug while gently rubbing his back. There was no crying, just a compassionate understanding between two people. Michael hadn't had that kind of understanding in a long time.

She sat back down and looked at him without much expression. "Wow. That is quite a story. I can understand how it is to hate your family. Why did you feel the need to tell me this now, and all at once?"

"Well, many reasons actually." Michael scratched his head and looked at the ground. "I had some questions to ask you about, and I thought that I might share my past with you first."

"Oh." Caroline shifted a little like she was uncomfortable all of a sudden. "Questions about what?"

Michael explained to her about all the little signs that he was noticing, and she would not look at him while he was explaining. "I have some knowledge of what these signs seem to point to."

"What, that I was abused in some way?" She looked at him sarcastically. "I've heard that same line my whole life, and it really means nothing to me."

"Maybe there is a reason that you have heard that your whole life." Michael nodded at her a few times. "People tried to get me to drop the liquor for decades, but I didn't think there was that big of a problem. I am not going to pry, if it is something that you don't want to talk about right now."

Caroline stood up and looked around while putting her hands on her hips. She looked down at Michael sitting in the chair. "Well, it is not a problem that we will ever need to talk about since there isn't one." She stormed off into the bathroom, and that was to be the end of this getting-to-know-one-another session.

Michael knew that there was something else there, but he decided to drop it until she was ready. She might never feel the need to talk about it, and unless it started to affect their relationship, then there was really no point in discussing it. Things were good between them, but that could change since he brought the subject up. There could be a mental backlash from him now having an idea into her dark secrets. He knew that he could just wait it out and see what happened from there and how she might react.

He spent a lot of time in the outdoors at work, and he started to notice something strange one day. The skies were being filled with multiple long streams of what appeared to be aerosol coming out of airplanes. They were persistently covering the sky with an entire haze by the end of the day. Something sinister was going on, and he could feel it. He would start to get headaches and feel slightly nauseated on the heaviest days. He just knew that something was amiss, so he started digging into the truth realm once again.

As he dug further and further, Michael found out that there was something called geoengineering that was going on, and it all seemed to be tied to what was referred to as Agenda 21. Apparently, the Controllers didn't think too highly of the general population and needed a better way to neutralize the masses. The population was simply too high, and the overlords were worried that the internet was awakening more people up, and that would be a threat to the illusions that they had worked so hard to create. So they needed a way to chemically lobotomize the people.

It had been a long time since the Controllers evil agenda had upset Michael as much as this did. He just couldn't believe the disregard that these vermin had for the people's lives and well-being. As he dug a little deeper into how this incremental control was implemented, he found that it also involved controlling the water supply, which would lead to controlling the agriculture and eventually putting local farmers out of business and transferring ownership to the Controllers. That was how all enslavement came to fruition, by small increments of control that was continually accepted until there was nothing left.

Michael managed a rural irrigation dam. He knew that eventually the Controllers would be coming for the irrigation water rights by using migratory fish habitat as an excuse. How right he was. It was always under the guise of environmental protection, under which new federal regulations seemed to be born on a regular basis. Incremental agenda, anyone? If they cared so much about the environment, then why were they spraying chemicals and metal particulates into the air? There was really no point in asking why since the answer was always the same—power and control.

The small rivers and streams that fed the irrigation reservoir were reclassified as a steelhead habitat, which placed them under new federal requirements for water releases that would allow for the annual migration. The government would now require that water be released from irrigation storage during the migratory periods. There were two problems with this. One, it would take away from the storage that would be used for irrigation of local agriculture crops during drought seasons. This storage is entirely dependent on mountain snowfall, so crops would suffer during low snow years. Two, the steelhead habitat has never existed in these particular waterways according to local historical records. It was another case of an unchallenged lie leading to more regulations. The government would pay for the water that was released for the migration, but there was no way to opt out. It was complete voluntary servitude, where liberty ended. Michael received the agreements that had to be signed by the board of directors and the manager. The problem was that this manager was not going to sign it under any circumstances.

A thought popped into Michael's mind about the Controllers using the aerosols in conjunction with other technologies to control the weather patterns. Experiments with this had been going on since the 1940s, and he briefly flashed back to one particular time while he was still stationed in Florida in the Navy. It was mid-Autumn in 1989, Hurricane Hugo had just come through Florida and continued far inland to the Midwest. No other hurricane in history had behaved in such a fashion. Michael and some classmates had just received their security badges and were heading down to the Cape to tour the USS *Tennessee*, which was in port just for the weekend. One of his classmates had a friend that was stationed on the *Tennessee*, so they had a guided tour of the ship and base. While walking along the mooring docks, Michael noticed a submarine that didn't look like anything he had seen before. It appeared to be taxiing into the harbor. There were very strange wires, coils, and shapes all over it. It looked like something Willy Wonka would have. He flagged down their guide and asked him if he knew what it was. He did.

"That's one of those storm drivers. I think it is just getting back from work on Hugo." The sailor just went back to talking to his friend after he responded to Michael. It didn't appear that what he said had even registered in his mind since he just said that the military was contributing to weather control against its own people.

When he flashed back to the present, he realized that the Controllers had indeed achieved their agenda of weather control. No longer did they have to use ships and mobile devices. As long as the aerosol was in the sky, it could all be done with land-based electromagnetic stations that would manipulate the ionosphere. How ironic it seemed to him that suppressed Nikola Tesla discoveries that could be used to generate free energy for the world were instead weaponized and used to control them. Sadly, it didn't shock Michael any.

Things were just getting worse for Michael. He was back to reading articles and books on the fringe subjects of conspiracy. Even though he didn't ever want to start drinking again, he was slowly losing his mind. It began to drive his relationship with Caroline to a distance, and he could sense something was wrong with her. Ever since he had brought up his concerns about her past to her, things had begun to change slowly, and now they were getting worse. One day after work, he found out everything that he needed to know.

When Michael came in the door, Caroline was sitting cross-legged, rocking in the easy chair, sipping on some wine. Soft music was playing in the background, and it looked like she had been crying some. Michael kicked his shoes off and came over to sit on the edge of the sofa next to her.

He put his hand on her knee and looked at her watery eyes. "You okay? What happened to you today?"

Caroline looked over at him with a half-painful smile. "I need to talk to you about some things, but I didn't want to have to relive some painful memories." She set her wineglass on the end table and used both hands to wipe her eyes out. Michael didn't say anything as she took a deep breath and let it out with a sigh. "I have been listening to you talk lately about conspiracies, cover-ups, and many other things."

Michael interjected as he shook his head in acknowledgment. "I know. I know. I am sorry about that. I really shouldn't have got back into the research, but I just couldn't help it after finding out about the Agenda 21 stuff and having to watch the sky spraying every day. This stuff is so complex and monstrous that it just unbelievable."

"Michael, I want you to let me talk for a minute." She held up her palm as if to put a stop to any excuses. "I am not mad about you doing research or even the things that you dig up, but I can't talk about it all the time. You have to find something in life that makes you happy and stop worrying about the way the world has become. I can tell you one thing though. You are right about it more than you know."

Michael raised his head up a bit and locked eyes with her. "About what? Do you know something about these things?"

"Well, yes, I do." She reached up and itched at her eyes to keep from crying. "You know when you told me about your past a while back and had asked about mine?"

"Yes," Michael said a little surprised at where this conversation seemed to be going.

Caroline grabbed her glass and polished off the rest of the wine. "You were on to something. I didn't want to ever talk about it with you, but something is nagging on me lately, and I need to release it. It is because of some of the things that you have been talking about lately that has triggered some bad memories in me, especially with regards to mind control and the secret society stuff. I was part of that when I was young. More of a victim really."

He couldn't believe his ears, but the feeling about her was definitely right on the money. More curious than anything, he just remained silent and let her continue. "I was raised in a very evil family." She continued her story. "We weren't skinhead racists, but much worse. We were Satanists. We owned a big piece of forested land near Lake Pend Oreille, but it was very secluded. There was only one way in and out through a locked gate that was also closely watched. I was actually born at the house and not in a hospital, and I have no birth certificate or social security number. We maintained an elaborated satanic ritual grounds located out in the forest, and they participated in the rituals. I was also forced to participate, but I will not get into the details. I don't think I can take those memories again, and I am sure that you know enough from all the research you have already done to know what I had to endure."

She paused for a moment to breathe and keep her composure and then continued on with Michael looking at her in wonderment. "My parents ran the facility for high-level rituals comprised of some of the most prominent members of business and politics. These people have a lot of money and may dress well, but they are world-class filth. Rituals occurred on the sacred secret holidays and monthly full moons. There were other occasions as well, and they seemed to go on quite regularly. I witnessed some of the most horrific acts to women and children than I ever could have imagined. Most of the participants were masked, so I never really saw who they were. It took me years to figure out what was really going on and who was involved."

Caroline paused for an uncomfortable silence to gather her thoughts, and Michael just had to say something. "Oh, wow. I knew it was something, but not this big. I feel so terrible for what you must have gone through, if it is anything like what I have read about.

You're obviously out of it now, so how did you get away? Please continue. I will listen."

She continued on reluctantly. "I have to tell you something incredibly shocking. No soul alive has ever heard me talk about this, but I need you to understand, because of what you are, how severe it really was." She paused for a moment, licked her lips, gently cleared her throat, took a quick deep breath, and continued on. "I began to be ritually sexually abused at about age four. Most sexual abuse done for ritual reasons ends when a child is seven. After that, the children continue on to other services in the organization, but the important ages are between four and seven. These are the ages when the energy of the soul is most susceptible to intrusion. Satanists need this energy to survive. It is best extracted through the chakra system at the tailbone during anal sex. The fear of the child generated by being raped is also tapped into like a delicacy. There is absolutely nothing sexual about it." Caroline paused again while tapping the side of her forehead with her forefinger and managed to continue. "In order for young children in the organization to be able to accept an adult-size penis, they must be trained, much like you would a leather product, only in the most sinister of ways." She looked up at Michael, deep in his eyes. "They placed me on a satanic phallus to stretch my rectum and vagina when I was three years old. It was a large statue of the Baphomet with a large ceramic penis. My father would slide me on it, place me and the statue into a dark closet in the basement, lock it, and leave me there for days on end without ever opening the door—that was, unless I made a sound. Then the door would fly open, and I would be knocked unconscious. This went on for about six months until I was ready for the ceremonies." She could say no more and began sobbing uncontrollably.

Caroline wiped her eyes gently once more and resumed the story. "Details aside, I was abused in order to try to control my mind to serve the organization. The abuse is so traumatic that it splits your mind into other alters that can be used for specific purposes. Victims are used for government espionage, sexual blackmail, and assassination. Basically anything that they want to program alters to be used for. I was very resistant to the programming and was scheduled for termination in a ritual sacrifice, but I escaped before they could get me. I was only thirteen when I left that place, and I have never been back since. They will always be looking for me, and I thought they had found me once a few years ago, but I disappeared again. I know too many of their secrets, and they don't like loose ends. Family has no meaning with these people other than the bloodline alone."

She seemed to be maintaining her composure quite well with all that she was revealing to him, but Michael guessed she had dealt with this for so long that she was used to it. He leaned back on the couch to relax a little bit. "So how did you get away, and when did you realize all that had happened to you?"

Caroline relaxed a little bit as well. "Well, I just left one night. I knew the woods very well and made my way to the main highway, where I caught a ride. I finally made it all the way to Seattle, where I got into a foster home under an assumed name. My foster parents died in a car crash when I was seventeen, and I have been traveling around ever since. I have always had bad dreams of the things that had happened to me, but it wasn't until I did a hypnotic regression that I started to remember everything. It was in my midtwenties that I met a lady that specialized in my kind of history and helped me to deal with the memories through hypnosis. The only downside is that I still remember everything—that will never go away—but I have made my peace with it."

Michael's mind was full of questions. "You said something about high level people. I have always read that the people who run this country are all involved. I call them the Controllers. Business owners and politicians at every level devise their power from these secret societies and rituals. Is that really true?"

Caroline lowered her head a bit and nodded. "Yes, it's true. It wasn't everybody involved with the management of business and politics back then, but it was getting there. I imagine by now it is all of them, including media icons as well. It includes all law enforcement too, that is how they maintain the fear in society. Cops, lawyers, and judges are all bought like a new car. It is more prevalent than you can possibly imagine."

"I knew it. Trust me, it is not beyond my imagination." Michael grimaced and nodded his head. "There are some real psychopaths running the show on this planet. Why did you decide to tell me now? You could have waited or never told me at all. Why now?"

She took a few moments to respond. "Because you have a gift, I can feel it. You knew about me from the start. If you can truly figure out your true potential, then you would be a threat to people like these. They don't fear much, but they do worry about psychically powerful people that could seek to expose their network and awaken the general population."

Michael thought for a minute about his trip back in college with Brad to the northern Idaho panhandle. He thought that this must be connected to Caroline somehow. "Okay, follow me on this Caroline. When I was in college, I went on a spring break trip to north Idaho, and we were traveling around the forest around Lake Pend Oreille. One night we stumbled unto this abandoned Army base, and I got some very weird visions while at that place. In my mind, I saw the word MKULTRA written on the wall in blood and had an overwhelming sense of pain from that place. Do you know about that base?"

Caroline's eyes became wide, and she looked at Michael like she just saw a ghost. "I know the base. So weird that you have been there. That is where my parents used to take me for mind control programming. There are many facilities around the country that are used for this. Most are military, but some are churches, universities, and hospitals. I can't believe that you brought that up. That is a place that I have truly done a good job of forgetting." It wasn't too much longer, and Caroline began to cry.

Michael just sat quiet while she worked through the pain. She quickly got control of herself and went over to the couch and sat and hugged him for what seemed like the better part of half an hour. She cried a little more, and then they slowly separated. They sat holding hands looking deep into each other's eyes for what seemed like hours. Caroline continued talking. "You know, Michael, I have never felt as close to anyone as I do you. I would comfortably say that I love you. It scares me though, all these things that you know, and most of it is true. Some of it I have even seen with my own eyes making the rest of it much easier to believe."

Michael interjected as she paused. "I love you too. No one has made me feel so worthy in all my life. I am not so sure what my future holds, but I do hope that you are in it."

She shyly smiled at him. "I appreciate that, but there is one problem. If you draw attention to yourself by talking about fringe subjects; then you might get noticed by people that you don't want to be noticed by and so will I. Being on the run for a long time, I have been able to stay safely hidden. There is no way that I will ever let them find me even … even if it means I have to disappear again."

Michael hung his head a bit and let out a deep breath as he reluctantly nodded his head. "I know what you are saying, but I hope it never comes to that. There isn't much more loss that I can tolerate in my life." He thought about something puzzling. "One thing though. We aren't living too far away from where you grew up right now. How come you chose to live so close?"

She smiled wide and chuckled a bit. "I know it doesn't seem safe, but there really is no difference between a hundred miles and a thousand miles if they don't know where to look. I really like this part of the country and seem to keep ending up back here from time to time. You know, sometimes things are hidden better when in plain sight."

He grinned at that and really could not disagree. The two of them continued to talk until the late hours of the evening. Michael wanted to bring up the troubles he was having at work with the new agenda that would soon be implemented. He decided not to. Things at home were better than ever after they had their little talk. Caroline seemed much more at ease and less worried about herself. She was having dinner ready when Michael got home from work and was even out looking for work herself. It seemed like she was trying to get out into the world a bit more, and maybe a little less concerned that she might run into people from her past.

In three weeks, Michael was going to have to sign the water release agreement at work. He knew that he could not do it and would not sell out the local farmers who were barely able to keep up with ever increasing amount of inspections and requirements as it was. The new agreement would require farmers to meter their water and prove beneficial use. Farmers were always looking for more efficient means of irrigating, but to have to prove it all to the government was simply tyranny.

It could be very difficult to be awake to how this world really was and also be able to make an honest living that generated enough income. Michael could really see how gradually all positions of employment were being made to serve an agenda. The morning of the fateful board meeting arrived. He was not going to sign the agreement, but he was not sure how the board would react. They had approved his leave of absence when he went to the Ranch, so they might be understanding to his reasoning for noncompliance here. It was a crap shot, but he had to do what was morally right. Even though it could cost him his job, he just couldn't do it.

When the time came, the water release agreement came around the board table for signing and finally ended up in Michael's hands. "I can't in good conscience sign this agreement." He could feel the stare of the five board members. "This is just another incremental step by the government to control the water and eventually control agriculture itself. Power always corrupts, and if a government can control the nation's food supply, then it can control everything."

Discussion ensued, and Michael did his best to try to explain his position. It was not worth the effort, as it usually is with most people in denial. Apathy was so destructive. The funny thing was that all the board members owned crops that would eventually be affected by this agenda. It made no sense to him how they were so afraid to challenge the issue, even at the cost of losing their own livelihoods.

After all the discussion, which seemed to go on forever, the board decided to go into executive session, which meant Michael would have to leave the boardroom while they talked. The last time he remembered an executive session was when he had come clean about his drinking problem and requested approval to get treatment for it and save his job. He already knew what was going on in the room and feared that this time his job would not be saved. The meeting went on for almost a half an hour when they called him back in the room.

Michael looked around at each of them and already knew that he was fired. All that was left was for them to tell him. The reason that they gave was that he was violating the district's economic policies that would cost the district hundreds of thousands of dollars in annual government funds. Money means more than morals in this world. Although he was upset, he could feel that some of them almost agreed with him and maybe even respected him a little bit. The fear of standing up to government overreach was simply too powerful.

After years of faithful service and conversion to sobriety, Michael packed up his things. It was hard to feel anything about anything. He wasn't sure what he was going to do with his life. This was supposed to be the retirement gig. All he really wanted to do was find a shoulder to cry on, and he needed to get home to Caroline to help him with that, but that gave him another bad feeling in the pit of his stomach. Something else was wrong, and he really was not needing any other surprises that day.

When he pulled into his driveway, Michael had a terrible feeling that this wonderful day was far from over. He heard Rikki inside whining as he put the key to the lock. She always knew when he was coming up the steps, and couldn't wait to see him. He opened the door, knelt down, and let Rikki get her fill of cleaning his face. He glanced around for Caroline, but there was no sight of her. Michael made his way around the house listening for sounds, and looking for any sign of her. She wasn't home. Thinking she might be out in the yard or elsewhere, he continued his search outside for a while. Nothing. He came in the back door to the kitchen, and then noticed a letter hanging from a magnet on the fridge. Slowly he approached the front of the fridge and stared at the hanging letter. He was afraid to grab it. After standing and staring for a couple minutes, he took the letter and went into the living room.

He sat in his favorite chair and unfolded the letter. Tears were welling in his eyes before he even began to read it. After just losing a job that had so much promise, this would be the lid on the coffin of his life.

Dear Michael,

By now you have figured out than I am not there and have found this letter. I didn't know the best way to do this, so I just did it the only way that I know how. First, I have to tell you that you really did nothing wrong and that I do love you. I was more comfortable with you than I have ever been up to this point in my life. The way you could always read me so well was kind of disturbing, but I was learning to live with it. You remember when I told you that I have to be ready to disappear if I ever think that they found me? Well, I think they found me. It was last weekend at the farmer's market that I spotted someone I recognized, and he noticed me. I got out of there before he had time to follow me through the crowd. I never did tell you why I would have to leave. When I went through hypnosis, they did not unlock everything in my memory. I have seen things that could be discovered under hypnosis that would be very damaging to some of the most wealthy and influential people in this country. I know you can understand what that can be like to live with. Maybe we will see each other again someday, and I will keep a special place in my heart for you. Keep your thoughts positive. You need to find your purpose and fulfill what you were put here to do. I know that our paths crossed for a reason and our time together was not in vain. I will always love you, Michael, and I wish the situation could be different.

Caroline

As he finished the letter, Michael simply could not believe that this was all happening now. He read the letter through a couple more times and placed it gently on the coffee table. He leaned back and closed his eyes and didn't even have the will to cry. Rikki, sensing something was very wrong, jumped up in his lap and licked the top of his hand very gently. He sat in the chair, did not move at all, and eventually fell asleep.

Michael awoke to the sun coming in through the living room window. He quickly recalled losing his job and girlfriend in the same day. Maybe it was all a dream. He jolted Rikki off his lap and got out of the chair. He was still wearing all his clothes, so maybe he really did fall asleep and dream the whole thing. The house felt cold, and he went into the bedroom to check the closet. Caroline's things were all gone, so he knew that it wasn't a dream. A good man's life was coming apart once again, and he felt completely alone again. Michael did not know what to do or who to call, and he was sure that he did not want to drink again; instead he went down familiar territory and became reclusive.

Time moved by very slowly when you were alone and didn't have much to do. The ego had a lot of time to blame everything on other people rather than to take personal responsibility. Michael had not held on to his spiritual teachings and was filling once again with negative feelings. He had lost big before and didn't think he would recover, but this time was much worse. When you broke something and glued it back together, sometimes it would hold just as well; but if you broke the glue, there was little chance it would glue again very well. Losing big this time was just too much for him to take.

Days turned into weeks and weeks into months. Going out only once a week for supplies, Michael kept to himself at home. Periodically, he would wander around the house or out in the yard with Rikki. Reading, movie watching, and dwelling on his failures became the ways he passed the time. He had no real friends left to talk to since he lost Brad and would find himself talking to shadows on the wall with greater frequency.

Michael was used to solitude, so the alone time did not bother him so much at first, but with all the time for his powerful mind to think about everything and wonder what he was supposed to achieve in this life. People had always told him that there was some greatness that he was supposed to achieve. There was no greatness left in his life, only regret.

His funds were growing short, and he knew that he would have to sell the house soon. There were no other jobs available for engineers in this rural area, so his chances at gainful employment were almost nil. After several months of the same old stale isolation routine, he decided that he really did not want to be in this world anymore. In a fairly short period of time, he had lost his job, girlfriend, house, mind, and will to live. In a desperate attempt to talk to someone, Michael decided to call his mother.

"Hello, Mom, it's Michael." He was glad that his mother answered since he had no intention of discussing anything with his father even thought his mother shared everything with him anyway. At least Mom had compassion for Michael's difficulties in life, and he really had no one else to talk to at this point. She had been supportive when he was sobering up and always had kind things to say. His father would only make things worse.

"Hello, Michael. So good to hear your voice. It has been a long time, honey. How are you doing?" She genuinely seemed happy to hear from him.

"Well"—he sniffled a bit—"things have not been going too well lately." Michael filled her in on everything that had had happened some months ago and about all the time he had just been home alone and feeling gradually worse. "I am really at my end here, Mom, and I don't know what to do. I hate to tell you this, but I have had feelings of ending it all. Please, I beg of you, do not let Dad know that you are talking to me."

There was a silence on the other end, and then he could hear a faint sobbing. "Michael, why are you talking like this? My heart just can't take any more problems."

Michael was choking back the tears as best as he could. "I know that, Mom. I have never wanted to hurt you, but I was just born at the wrong time. It sickens me that this reality is not what it seems. I have tried to explain it to you before, but you never listen. Forget about even trying to talk to Dad. His mind is so polluted by alcohol that you can't discuss anything with him, and he has too much influence over you. I just feel so utterly alone. I see and feel more than most all people do. This 'flaw' that I was born with. It is not your fault."

His mother was crying so hard by now that he was afraid that his father would hear and soon be getting on the line. She gained her composure rather quickly. "All right, Michael. I want to help you, but you have to promise me that you are not going to do anything rash until you can talk to someone. Can you do that for me?"

Michael wiped the tears out of his eyes and tried to clear his head. "Yes. I can do that. I was thinking of coming home for a while because I really don't have anywhere else to go."

"Yes," she said without any hesitation. "Come home. We can work things out from here. I am so sorry that your life has been so rough, and I do love you very much. Maybe we didn't do things quite right and didn't try to understand you. I hope you can forgive me for that. Please just come home, and we can talk about it then. Just don't do anything."

Michael felt a little more at ease. "Okay, Mom. I promise and will be home tomorrow." He hung up the phone and decided to pack for the trip home.

Several hours went by, and Michael had finished packing and was sitting on the couch, watching some television with Rikki's head on his lap. The phone rang and he could see from the caller ID that it was mom again. Thinking that she was calling to check to see if he was okay, he picked up the phone. "Hello, Mom." Only it wasn't his mother this time.

"Son, this is your father." Michael could tell that he was already well into nightly stupor from the word slurring. "Your mother told me about the conversation that you had earlier today."

"She wasn't supposed to tell you." Michael got an overwhelming sense of fear and anger like he knew something bad was about to happen again. "What do you want?"

"We really can't take any more of your antics, and it took me several hours to calm your mother down. I just got her to bed." Michael could hear the ice cubes in his drink as he was sipping while talking to him. "You should just go ahead and kill yourself and quit talking about it, because you have been nothing but a disappointment to your mother and me."

Michael could not believe what he had just heard. His father had just crossed every line that he could possible imagine. "Are you serious? What kind of father are you? If anyone is the disappointment, it is you. All you love is alcohol, you sick son of a bitch!" He slammed the phone down and let out a scream that scared Rikki so bad that she ran into bedroom and hid under the bed. She hadn't done that since he used to throw fits when he was still drinking.

Something took control of Michael at that very moment, and he seemed to enter a blackout state of rage without any alcohol at all. He went into the closet in his room and saw the shotgun that he and Brad had so much fun with back in college. The same gun that he had found in the van. The same gun that he had almost killed himself with in college. The same gun that he had almost killed his best friend with. The same gun that he was now going to use to finish the job. If his father wanted him dead, then that was what he was going to be.

MONTANA

You are never rich enough to buy back your own past.
—Source Unknown

Click.

Michael opened his eyes at the sound of the dud shell. He lowered the weapon and looked down the barrel, wondering what had happened. When he pumped the action to load a new shell, he grabbed the spent one off the ground. There was a dent in the primer pin, but it hadn't gone off. He was dedicated though, so he tried it again, putting the barrel back in his mouth, but this time he just jerked the trigger.

Click.

Michael lowered the barrel out of his mouth again and cocked the shell out. "Again! You have got to be shitting me!" he yelled with frustration as Rikki looked up at him from the couch. He grabbed up the other shell, and it had the same dent as the first one. What were the odds on two dud shell in a row? Very low, he imagined.

All at once a small white light began to form about groin height off the floor across the room from Michael. The light began to grow larger and brighter and gradually took on a human outline. The light began to fade into what looked like person. Michael rubbed his eyes like they were blurry because he could swear that he was looking at Jimmy.

"Jimmy." Michael looked at the spirit in front of him, all wide-eyed with awe. "Holy shit! It really is you. I have missed you beyond belief." Michael always had this feeling that Jimmy would come back some day, and his intuition was rarely wrong.

"In the flesh." Jimmy gave a little chuckle. "Okay, so maybe not the flesh, but I have been waiting for you to get here. There are no accidents in the universe, Mikey. That is why I told you that I would be back later. After I passed, I instantly knew that I had a future purpose to help you. There was nothing that I needed to say to you at that moment because I knew that this one was coming."

"So that is what you meant." It was like a light came on over Michael's head. "Right after you left your body, you were trying to tell me to hold on that you would be back. Now I understand. Only took a couple decades. Have you been waiting for me that long?"

"Time has no meaning here. My death seems like yesterday, and I can go to any moment in time to see anything that I could possibly want to," Jimmy said as Michael listened intently, still a little freaked out that he was actually talking to Jimmy. "I stopped this suicide nonsense and am here to deliver you a final warning. Your nine lives are up. You quit drinking, and that is commendable, but you will fall again, permanently, if you do not confront the demon inside you. I am sure you know what I am talking about, but you have never seen him. Only others have when you have been blacked out. It is not a pretty sight, Michael. I have been watching you all these years."

"Yes, I know." Michael shook his head in embarrassment. "People have described it to me, and it does sound a little disturbing. It has ruined my life, and I just don't want to do this anymore. This world is such a shithole, and I don't want to be a part of it, drunk or sober. With no one to love, what point is there?"

"You must love yourself first, Michael." Jimmy held up his index finger at him. "That may sound so cliché, but it is true. Suicide is the ultimate cowardly act. You complain so much that the country is full of cowards, and now look what you are doing. You must become what you were meant to be and help this place heal. The Creator has a job for you, and he will not let you leave until it is done. You have to understand that."

"What job? And no more with the esoteric beating around the bush." Michael came right back at him. "If I am supposed to be this special person, then what the hell is it, and what exactly is this demon inside of me?"

"As smart as you are, I can't believe that you have not figured it out by now." Jimmy closed his eyes and shook his head. "You are an empath. You channel the energies around you, and you already know all that." Michael nodded in agreement. "What you did not realize is that when you drink, your grounded connection to the natural world declines, and you are more susceptible to picking up energies from the unseen entities around you. When you black out, you have lost all contact with reality and open the door to channel dark energies—the demons. And believe me they are everywhere. As you channel them, they steal a little of your empathetic power and leave a little dark behind inside your subconscious. The result of your many blackouts has actually created a demon that resides in you; and your powers of empathy, intuition, and second sight have dimmed to the point that you don't think you have them anymore."

"I can see that, I guess." Michael pursed his lips and squinted. "I thought that I had really lost my powers, and when I sobered up, they did not come back. This demon that you speak of must be blocking my potential. What do I need to do to kill it?"

"Indeed it is." Jimmy paused for a few moments. "Rid yourself of all debt and ownership and head for the continental divide in Montana." Jimmy pointed toward the east. "You will see the signs along the way and you will need to figure out what they mean to lead you to your final destination. When you get there, you must kill the demon." Jimmy raised his hand as if to signal stop. "Don't ask me how. You will have to figure that out for yourself. I have only been allowed to give you a push in the right direction. I can tell you that you are in for quite a ride, and your ultimate quest will begin after you succeed."

"What happens if I succeed?" Michael giggled. "Do I become like a warlock or something?"

Jimmy smiled back at the joke and continued on. "You will be able to connect to people and sense what will really make them happy and know how to provide it for them. You will be able to change the course of human history by changing the energies around you. I know that you have an idea as to what I am talking about. Every prophet that the Creator has sent to warn and guide humanity has suffered the same fate. They could not get enough people to listen to what they were saying to actually make a difference, and the leaders of the time had them killed or worse."

"Okay, that does all make sense to me, but what if I fail?" Michael squinted a little back at Jimmy.

"You will not fail." Jimmy looked at Michael almost like he was looking through him. He could see that this looked like his childhood friend, but there was an immensely powerful energy emanating from him that human words just couldn't describe. As Michael was looking closely at him, Jimmy faded away just as he had come. All at once, he was gone.

Michael kept looking off in the distance like he was trying to catch one last glimpse of his long-lost friend. He shook off the stare, came back to reality, and began to ponder the information that was just exchanged with what he was pretty sure was a higher dimensional being. Not to mention the fact that Jimmy, or whatever it was, just stopped bullets and saved his life, a life that he was now going to get on with. Jimmy told him what to do, and that is exactly what he was going to do. No more excuses this time.

He went to the garage and started going through his camping gear and pulled out everything that he thought he would need to live in the wild for an extended period. He actually didn't know how long the journey would take since Jimmy did not tell him, so he had to wing it the best he could. Michael did not get overly paranoid as to what he needed to pack for, but his vast history of camping experience sure came in handy. It all managed to fit in his rig while not being overly stuffed, with room in the front for Rikki.

Back in the house, Michael began to go through everything he owned. He did not even sleep the first night as he was too excited to finally feel that he was striving for something real. He packed everything into the garage for a yard sale that would be coming shortly. Almost everything was to go, except for keepsakes that had some special meaning. After the entire purge was over, he could fit all he would continue to own in the bed of a pickup truck. The cleanout and yard sale preparations only took a few days.

He decided that it would be a good idea to camp for a couple weeks before leaving. This gave Michael the opportunity to make sure that he had all the gear he would need for the trip as well as work on the sale of his household goods and getting the house ready and on the market. He placed his tent camp at a local lake that was not too far from town so as to be similar to what he would be doing on the trip. Tent living could get old, but it really depended on how much you liked it as to how long it was before it got old. Michael loved camping, so he knew he could do months of it. Years would be another thing all together.

It was almost two weeks to the day that he had been visited by Jimmy that Michael was finally ready to hit the road. The house was all cleaned up and listed with a local realtor. He managed to sell or donate all his possessions and would leave town with a couple of grand to help on the trip with food and the occasional hotel to regroup from time to time. He would not be off the grid completely, and then again, he really didn't know. Jimmy said he had to follow the signs as they came up, so where was he supposed to go first?

Michael sat outside of his tent door on the fold-up chair and looked back inside the tent. His portable alarm clock was sitting on a can of pork and beans. The clock showed the time 11:11. He remembered reading some spiritual books on the synchronicities and spiritual signs that people frequently talk about. These were the signs that Jimmy told him to look for, and this was definitely one of them. He looked down at the can that the clock was sitting on. It was Libby's Pork 'n Beans. That was it, his first major stop would be Libby, Montana. Michael wasted no time and was off for Libby the next morning.

Michael took a few days to get to Libby staying at a couple campsites along Lake Pend Oreille that he remembered from college during the good times with Brad. Those would never be back, but he had grown to accept that fact over the last couple years. He was careful to be watchful for signs. It was 11:11 that he recognized the easiest, but there would be others. The signs must have been there

239

his entire life, but he just didn't take the time to process them. Even with the gifts that he had, the signs could go unnoticed due to the amount of fear emanating from life's distractions and illusions and how powerful that truly was.

He decided to stay in a hotel for the stop in Libby as he had already been sleeping in the tent for almost three weeks. Michael was just going with his gut instinct. The sign said Libby and that was all he knew. As he pulled into town, he noticed a little hotel off the side of the road called the Sleepy Time Motel. That sounded just great to him, so he checked in for a few nights to get the best rates along with the pet fee. It was great that most hotels allowed dogs, but some of them sure charged some outrageous pet fees. Pet friendly could sometimes mean no more than fee friendly, but this place was reasonable.

Not much happened the first night other than it was great to sleep in a bed again. Rikki didn't mind it so much either. There was a nice little pet area out in back of the motel, and Michael would go down there several times a day. During his second day there, while on the way back from the afternoon poop session, Michael noticed a pair of women checking into the room next to his. It looked to be a younger girl traveling with her mother or aunt or something.

Still being a smoker, Michael would sit outside of his room several times a day to have his nicotine fix. That night, he came out, and the younger girl next door was out doing the same.

She was not shy and introduced herself right away. "Hi there." She looked over at Michael from her chair. "My name is Tiffany. I had to get outside away from my mother. She is driving me nuts."

"I'm Michael," he replied. "So you are traveling with your mother. I know that has to be tough. Where are you heading?"

"She is traveling with me to East Glacier National Park." She slid her chair closer to be able to talk to him better. "I am a seasonal employee and start next week for the summer. She has never been there, so she is going to do some sightseeing and then fly home."

Michael just shook his head in approval. "That sounds fun. Maybe you will have some good bonding time with your mother. I sure wish I had more of a connection with mine."

She nodded with a slight grimace. "Yeah, I guess. So where are you headed?"

"Not sure. It's complicated." Michael smiled at her like he didn't want to look stupid. "Call it a vision quest, if you will. I can't explain it, but my life was in shambles, and I had this sudden urge to head for Montana."

"Really?" She smiled back in approval, and Michael knew this was another free spirit like himself without regard for society's judgments. "If you have never been to Montana before, then I may have some suggestions."

"That would be great." Michael was so happy to meet a new friend. "I have a map and great traveling skills, but I am just letting the spiritual signs guide the way, if you believe in that sort of thing."

"In that case," she said, "you would probably be interested in the Buddha garden."

"Buddha garden would be right up my alley." Michael looked at her rather inquisitively. "In Montana though? I never heard of anything like that."

"They don't really look for visitors that are just stumbling on the place while traveling." She replied. "Although they do have a website, only the ones that really want to find it actually do, but I will tell you where it is." She grabbed a piece of paper and began to explain it to him. "It was started by a monk who came over from India. He too was following a sign that led him to Montana, of all places, to build his Garden of a Thousand Buddhas. It is a few miles north of a town called Arlee on Highway 93. Arlee lies about forty-five minutes north of Missoula on the way to Kalispell, or vice versa." She drew a little map on the paper. "It is on White Coyote Road, which only goes to the east from the highway. There is no sign for the garden on the highway, but when you get about a half mile up the dirt road, you will see the signs then." She handed the map to Michael.

He looked at her with much appreciation. "Thank you so much. This is my next sign. I am sure of it. I was supposed to meet you and get these instructions." Tiffany just smiled back at him, and they continued to talk until late in the night. It had been a long time since he had connected to anyone, and it felt good to be talking with a like-minded spiritual individual. It turned out that she would be leaving the next morning with her mother. Michael was booked in for one more night.

Michael said goodbye to Tiffany as they were leaving in the morning. He gave her a hug and could feel a connection to her like he had not felt in some time. It was like his power to feel was coming back, but then it quickly went away. The demon in him was preventing it; that was just too strong. He really could not wait to get this thing out of him, and he knew that would be coming soon.

He and Rikki relaxed for one more day, and then it was on the road time again. Michael had noticed a town on the map that was only a couple of hours away called Marion. It bore the same name as his grandmother, so he thought that maybe that was his next destination. Some interesting things that he was beginning to notice about Montana.

The speed limits were seventy miles an hour on most highways, and it seemed as if the drivers seemed to think that they needed to always go that fast. Most two lane highways were not designed for those kinds of speeds, and the result was many white crosses lining the sides of the highways. These were locations where people had died, and most often there was a multitude of crosses at most locations that were usually near dangerous curves. Consequently, there were many road signs reminding people not to tailgate, but not many heeded the advice.

When Michael got near Marion, he noticed a little RV park called Elk Crossing, and he was getting one of his feelings, so he drove on in. He rented a tent site for a few days and proceeded to set up his new temporary home. There were a lot of campers that actually lived in the park all year due to the economy and the damage associated with that. More and more people were living this way in the country. That good old American dream was more like a nightmare for some, but you could be happy anywhere. That was it, really. Happiness was just a choice that was reflective of your level of acceptance of what you consider to be reality. Nothing could be truer of the soul he was about to encounter.

Michael finished setting up his tent site and began relaxing in his lawn chair. He was reading some Carl Jung book on dreams when a truck pulled into the trailer site across the road from him. The trailer looked like it had been there a while, and the truck looked like it had seen its better days. Out of the old truck came a long-bearded, wiry-framed old hillbilly. He walked around the other side of his truck and opened the door to gather up his dog. It was the cutest thing that Michael had ever seen. The dog's face looked just like the owner with a long beard and overgrown eyebrows.

The man set the dog on the ground to go about its business as he grabbed a thirty pack of beer from the bed of the truck. He headed over to the old metal cooler positioned to the side of the stairs leading into his small early eighties model trailer. The hinges creaked when he opened it just like old metal coolers usually did, and after he had filled it up, it creaked when he shut it too. There would be no mistaking when this man went into the cooler for another beer. Michael just didn't realize how often it would be.

The man came up with a fresh beer after loading the cooler and noticed Michael sitting in his fold-up chair across the way, looking in his direction. "Hello there," the man said while walking in Michael's direction. His dog seemed curious to get to know Rikki as well.

Michael stood up out of his chair as the man approached and extended his hand in greeting. "My name is Michael. I'm just going to be camping here for a few days."

The man shook his hand firmly. "I am Willie, and this little mop is Waylon," he said as he gestured down at the dog who was acting a bit skittish. "He is a purebred wire hair. I rescued him from neglect about five years ago, so he's still a little bit unsure about people." The two were quite a pair to draw to. Willie had a laugh that reminded Michael of Gabby Hayes. When combined with the creaking beer cooler, it made for an interesting first evening at Elk Crossing.

The two talked only briefly the first night. Michael explaining to Willie that he was almost two years sober and didn't socialize too much at night with the drinking crowd. Willie seemed to respect that, but through the thin walls of the tent, he could hear that creaking cooler until the late hours of the evening.

Michael heard him leave the next morning to head to work in his truck that really sounded like it needed a lot of maintenance, especially on the muffler and exhaust system. Willie had told him the night before that he lived here in the park in his trailer and had a job working with a local construction company. He knew there was something about this man, and it could possibly be the next sign that he was supposed to see, but he wasn't sure what that was. He would just have to stay in the park until he figured out what that was.

Willie returned that night about the same time as the night before with his faithful dog and a fresh load of beer. Michael thought that he wanted to get to know them a little better, so he wandered over when Willie fired up his barbeque. "Hey there, Willie. How are you and Waylon doing tonight?"

"We're doing great," Willie said as he started his burger on the grill. "Waylon has sure taken to you quickly. He doesn't trust anyone, but he seems to trust you. I guess that makes you okay in my book. What is your story anyway?"

"Well," Michael began, "I am on a vision quest of sorts. I have come to Montana to find something, but I am not sure what it is yet. I don't even know where I am going until I actually go. Man, does that sound nuts, but I don't know any better way to explain it."

"No, it's not nuts." Willie looked at him and smiled. "We all have to figure out what we need in this life, and it is quite commendable that you are making the effort. You should go to Swan Lake. That is where I am from. It is such a beautiful place."

Swan Lake—that was his next sign. Michael was sure of it. "Where is that at?" he asked anxiously and knew that he would be heading there soon.

"It is southeast of Bigfork which is on the east side of Flathead Lake." Willie sort of pointed toward the east. "If you go to Bigfork, you will see the signs for Swan Lake. It is up in the high mountains just on the west side of the continental divide." Now he was sure that this was his next sign as Jimmy had mentioned the continental divide as being the location that he would have to battle the demon.

Michael headed into Kalispell to find a hotel for a few days and regroup a bit. The remainder of the journey was starting to take shape, and something in Kalispell would help him to figure the rest out. The tourists were starting to flock into the Flathead Lake for the summer, so the hotels were starting to fill up and raise their rates. He really couldn't afford to stay too long, but he needed another sign to be able to put this all together.

On the second night in Kalispell, Michael walked across the street from the motel to have a good meal at the Montana Club. These restaurants were all over Montana, so he figured it was time to eat at one, not to mention this would provide the final key to the puzzle of his journey. Although he did not drink anymore, he still liked to sit in the bar area to have dinner. He ordered a sesame chicken salad and began to think while paying close attention to his surroundings. Michael had always been very observant, but the next sign was a little more difficult to see.

He pondered what he needed to do next. Michael needed to go to the Buddha garden and Swan Lake according to the signs, but which would come first and why? For some reason, he knew that the final destination would be the Swan Lake area, so he needed to go to the Buddha garden first. There was something else that he needed before he could confront the demon, and that was at the Buddha garden. Just as Michael was thinking that very same thing, he looked up at the TV. The Stanley Cup finals were on, and a timeout had been called, but what was really interesting was the time left in the period. It was 11:11 left to go on the clock of the third and final period. There it was, the final sign.

Michael looked at the map when he got back to his room. He figured that he could head south to Arlee and come back to the hotel in the same day then head to Swan Lake the following day. He wasn't sure what it was that he needed to find in Arlee, but he was not about to question the signs. They were obviously leading him somewhere.

The next morning, Michael filled himself with a big breakfast and headed out with Rikki for the long day ahead to Arlee and back. He was anxious to see what he might find at the garden. Michael could feel his intuition coming back again, that he would meet someone having further instructions for him; but no idea as to what it could be.

Arlee lay at the bottom of a long hill that led the traveler out of the Flathead Valley into the Missoula area. Michael actually missed the sign for White Coyote Road on the way into town. He was able to get directions at a local café in town and managed to find it during his backtrack up the hill. Rikki didn't care much either way, she mainly slept on the passenger seat when they were travelling.

The area along the dirt road looked like any other small-town farming grotto. He was not sure if he was on the right road or not. The place was definitely not that well marked. About a mile up the road away from the highway, he finally saw the sign to the left and the parking lot, which had ample parking and a small porta-shitter-type restroom.

Michael's was the only car in the parking lot, and it was about the midmorning part of the day. He could see the Buddha Garden off in the distance. There was a dirt trail that led off into the weeds in the direction of the garden. He headed down the trail, which was partially overgrown and a little unmaintained. He wasn't sure if that was the way it normally looked or that he was here before the annual tourist season. The trail was a good quarter of a mile long, and then there was daylight out into the garden area entrance.

To say that it was the most beautiful spiritual retreat he had ever seen might not even do it justice. In the middle of the high desert of Montana was the most amazing sight. A large rock sat at the entrance with a very powerful quote from the Buddha engraved in the side of the rock. It read, "You can search throughout the entire universe for someone who is more deserving of your love and affection than you are yourself, and that person is not to be found anywhere. You yourself, as much as anybody in the entire universe, deserve your love and affection." Michael knew that this was yet another sign letting him now that he was in the right place since Jimmy had basically told him that very same thing before he even started on this quest.

The garden contained a thousand smaller Buddha statues laid out in one large circle and along six spokes that led to the central point. In the central point, there was a large two-story ornate statue of Shiva. The entire garden had small trees and pristine landscaping of flowers from all over the world, including opium, which had a large beautiful red flower. Beautifully maintained grass and evenly graveled walkways blanketed the area, all set in the middle of rolling hills and Montana scrub brush. Around the central statue were plaques at each station with the heart sutra written in every language that practiced Buddhism around the world. As much as Michael did not like organized religions, they were all initially based on the correct premise, and he was here for some reason.

He sat down with his legs crossed in the middle of the lawn in front of Shiva. He laid his hands open on his knees, closed his eyes, relaxed, and began a period of deep meditation. Michael could see the trees and mountains from where he would have his final encounter on this quest. It was a place high in the Rockies and not too far away. There was a dark feel about the place, though not the place itself since there was no evil in nature. No, it was something else. Something evil waited for him there. He felt like he was getting a clear glimpse of the future, a power that he never was able to master that well before. Michael's mind was becoming clearer and stronger.

He thought that he should be feeling fear, but he was not. The evil feeling was so overpowering like he had never felt before, yet Michael was not scared. He continued his meditation and was trying to get a good idea what the place looked like in his head so he would know it better when he stumbled upon it. Somehow, he knew that he would feel it when the time came, but a little visualization wouldn't hurt. His meditation was thrown off a bit as he began to hear footsteps coming in his direction slowly growing louder.

Michael backed out of his vision and opened his eyes out of the most successful meditation that he ever had. A man was walking in his direction from the far side of the garden, like he had materialized from the circle of Buddhas. It was quite strange. Maybe he just didn't see him there when he had arrived. There were no other visitor's cars in the parking lot, so this must be someone that lived there. Whoever it was, he would be finding out shortly.

As the man got closer, he appeared to be some kind of monk. He had pale skin, chrome dome, robe, and sandals just like he came from a monastery. Michael climbed to his feet and waited for the gentle-looking man to approach. He was about average height and just shy of the scrawny side.

He walked up to face Michael with a smile and gave a slight bow. "Are you Michael?"

Michael's eyes got wide as he replied. "Yes, as a matter of fact, I am. How in the world did you know that?"

"This may seem a bit far out," the monk said. "Please bear with me as I explain, but I get the feeling that you will understand." He smiled as he continued. "My name is Has Nam. I am originally from India. I came to this country about ten years ago and dedicated my new life in America to help spread true spirituality and awakening to the truth. I readily have visions and dreams that help to guide my life and reveal future paths, but I had one recently that was the most powerful I have ever had. About a week ago, I was visited by a spirit in my sleep that told me I was to be here now and meet a man named Michael."

The man paused for a brief moment, and Michael just kept looking at him in amazement. He did not want to speak at all, for any chance that it might change this man's train of thought.

The man continued on. "I was told to bring a special item for you as well." The man pulled a closed hand from under his robe and opened it to reveal an odd-looking metallic amber crystal of some kind that was shaped like a half-flattened marble about two inches in diameter. "This is an Orgonite crystal. There are lots of these kinds of crystals in existence, but this one is extremely exceptional. It is said to have been held by Jesus Christ himself. I have carried it for a long time, and it has guided me through a most glorious life. I was not told why or what for, but I am to give this to you." The man stretched out his hand so Michael could retrieve the crystal. "You must take it. I cannot give it to you."

Michael reached out and slowly grabbed the crystal from the man's open hand. Once the crystal was free of the man's palm, Michael got an incredible surge of energy and emotions from all directions. He felt like he was in some sort of *Matrix* or something and opening his eyes to a whole other world. There was no fear, only love. He felt at ease with the world that things were truly the way they were for a reason. He knew that he could not change everything for the better, but he could help to even the stakes a little bit. Michael knew that he had a purpose, but he was not sure what yet. The flashes ended, and he was pulled back into reality, looking at the smiling monk in front of him.

"It's quite a rush, isn't it?" he said.

"Yeah, no kidding," Michael said as he stared at the crystal in his hand. "What did you say this was again?"

"It's called Orgonite," the monk explained. "It is an ancient crystal made by spiritual humans to ward off evil spirits and possibly more than that. It is made from copper, quartz, resin, and other things. This one contains exceptional power has been around for thousands of years. No one really knows its origin. Wilhelm Reich learned about the secrets of Orgone, and the Controllers jailed him for it. I received it from my grandfather with some stories that captivated my attention. He also gave me special instructions that someday I would have to pass it on for another purpose. This is that purpose."

Michael never looked up from staring at the crystal the entire time the monk was explaining, but he heard everything. "This is what I need to kill the demon."

"Demon?" the monk questioned. "What demon?"

Michael looked away from the crystal and at the monk with a half grin. "It's a long story, but I really do appreciate this. I need this for something I must do along my quest in this life. Is there anything that you need from me?"

The monk shook his head. "No, not at all. You have already given me that by being here like I was told you would be." He folded his hands back under his robe and turned to walk away.

Michael paused for a moment and then called after the kind monk, "Hey, wait. One more thing. What was the spirit that visited you?"

The monk paused and turned his head to the side rather than turning back around. "It was a beautiful young girl. I think her name was Tisha." He turned his head back and continued walking about the garden as Michael watched in amazement of the news he just heard.

Michael was simply floored. His old friend had come out to help him just like Jimmy had. He wished he could talk to Tisha again and felt that maybe he would someday, but this was all the conversation that he needed. She was always right, and now he understood what she had been telling him. He was using it wrong, she had told him. He knew what he must do to kill the demon. When he could bring himself to love and forgive all those that he felt had wronged him, then he would be able to achieve powers that were beyond this world. He would be able to use it right and help those that could not do otherwise. He clasped his hand around the crystal, hit his knees, and began to cry.

He wiped his eyes after a good long, deep cry, and the beautiful garden was coming back into focus. Michael looked around the garden, and the monk that he had just spoken to was nowhere to be found. He stood up and placed a hand above his eyes to block the sun and looked all around. There was no sight of him. It was another gift from the Creator and definitely the final sign in this quest. The only other place he needed to go was Swan Lake. He had all the tools he needed; now all he needed was the right place. It was out there, and he would find it.

Michael went back to his truck, where Rikki was waiting anxiously for his return. She was overjoyed as usual, and he wasn't gone all that long. They headed back into Kalispell to get ready for the remaining leg of the journey to Swan Lake. He spent the next day making sure that he had all the food and essentials that he thought he might need for the trip into the Rockies. One thing was for sure—the special crystal never left his person, and he checked for its presence continually.

Michael and Rikki headed out early the next morning for Swan Lake. It wasn't very far away, but he knew there would be a nice place to camp. He was not wrong. As he pulled into the small resort town of Swan Lake, he noticed the local trading post and store had a small campground that would work out perfectly. He reserved a tent spot for a week to begin with as he did not know how long he would be there. His destination lay further east into the continental divide, but this would be his base camp for now.

The park was not too full yet as the summer tourist season was due to begin soon. The owners of the establishment were very personable people and they both shared the same name which Michael had never encountered before. They were a man a wife and both named Chris. That would get very confusing at Christmas time, but Michael would soon find out that the wife spelled her name with a *k* instead of a *ch*.

Michael kept to himself mostly, but he would manage to have one meal each day at the restaurant at the trading post. It was really good food, and the cook's name was Charlene. She also served as the store attendant. He felt a strong connection to her and knew that he needed to get to know her a little better. On the second day there, he finally was able to open up to her a little more and find out his final destination.

For some reason, he felt comfortable sharing things with her and, during lunch, had told her that he was on a vision quest and had been destined to travel to this location. When he told her that he had been sober a while and was looking for his purpose in this life; that was when Charlene really came alive.

She was a very soft-spoken and gentle person and told him that she had been sober for twenty-nine years and had come here years ago for similar reasons. She never left. Her home was here in the mountains, and she never regretted her choice to move there although the winters could be a bit extreme at times.

"I am not sure where it is that I am supposed to go to complete my quest." Michael nibbled on the delicious sandwich. "All I know is that it is near here somewhere, and I will stay here in Swan Lake until I find it," he said with one cheek full of food, but he did not do it rudely.

Charlene looked at him a little puzzled. "Perhaps I know a place that you might like to go. I am not sure if it is the location that you are looking for, but it sure can't hurt." She grabbed a pen and small notepad from under the bar counter and began to draw and explain directions to him. "It is a place called Serenity Falls and doesn't get hardly any tourist traffic at all. Most people don't know about it, not even some of the locals."

Serenity Falls—what a perfect name for a recently sobered up alcoholic, Michael thought. His interest was definitely piqued, and that little voice inside of him that was quite a bit more than little these days told him that this was definitely the place that he was looking for. He thanked her for the information and tucked the homemade map in his pocket for use soon. He was not sure if he would be ready tomorrow or the next day, but Michael knew that was where his final destiny was, and it was time to get up all the courage.

He spent the next day thinking about the task ahead. Could he really kill a demon? He could still feel it inside of him, but it was so very dormant. Just add alcohol, and that would change. It was still holding his true potential hostage, and he was definitely ready to get rid of it. Life weighed so heavy on Michael from carrying the extra load for so many years. He reflected on the damage that he had caused in his life. No matter what anyone else might have done, it was his reactions and perceptions that he was accountable for, and he could finally accept that. A vision of his father popped into his head and Michael could feel the anger swell. That one was not so easy. Forgive the one that he had blamed for most of what went wrong with his life. He knew that he must forgive or he would not succeed in his quest.

Michael thought about everyone and everything that he had encountered in his life. He thought about all the unresolved pain from the losses and failures. Tomorrow would be the day that he would let them go. He would exchange his resentments and anger for the demons life, and he was not quite sure that it would be that easy to do.

As the night fell on that final day, Michael found it very hard to sleep. He dug deep in his soul and began to really pray—not to the false gods of religion, but more like a communion with the Christ mind. "Jesus, come unto me. Let my heart be free of the burdens that have hindered my true potential. Give me the strength to face the beast inside me and let go of my pain. I will use my gifts to help mankind find its way again to help them become what was intended. Release me of all fear of the unknown and the known. I admit that I was wrong in my actions that led me astray in this life and ask for genuine forgiveness. I will forever place myself in service wherever it is needed to assist my fellow man."

The night was so quiet outside of the tent. Most of the unruly wildlife did not wander into the camp areas unless you were dumb enough to leave food out. Michael could feel his heart beating gently in his chest, and he felt at ease. He reached down on the comforter and gave Rikki some loving strokes and finally drifted off to a restful sleep that he had not felt since he could even remember.

Michael awoke in the morning to a piercing light on his eyelids that seemed to be the crux of a dream that he was having. Then his eyes opened, welcoming in the morning sun. He sat up on his elbows and could see the beam of sunlight coming in like it was revealing the location of the Ark of the Covenant. Rikki was still laying down at the bottom of the comforter just looking up at him with eyes wide open wagging her tail as if to say, "I'm ready for the day when you are."

Michael wiggled down and gave her an enveloping hug and kiss on the top of the head. "Today's a big day, old girl," he said as he scratched the skin between her ears. She really did love that. He wasted no time getting dressed and out of the tent to get Rikki fed and the coffee going.

Michael sat in his chair and stared out over the pond while sipping his coffee. The sun was making its way up through the trees, and all was eerily quiet. He finished off his gourmet dehydrated breakfast meal and packed up a day pack of food, water, and snacks. Rikki had backup food and water in the truck at all times. He coaxed Rikki up into the truck and headed out for Serenity Falls.

The map that he had acquired from Charlene turned out to be quite accurate. The trailhead to the falls was a good ten miles or more off the main road, and the final section of the trip was an eight-foot-wide weed-covered road that looked like it maybe had eleven vehicles per year that drove on it. Michael was not too worried about encountering a vehicle coming in the opposite direction.

The road came to an end in a narrow rocky makeshift vehicle turn around just like Charlene had described in her map. Michael parked and got out the truck. Rikki was all anxious to jump out as well, but he held her back. "No, I know, girl. You can't go with me this time. I have to do this one alone." She jumped back over to her perch in the passenger seat, acting somewhat dejected. Michael felt bad, but he knew she would get over it. He made sure that he had the monk's crystal in his pocket and reached for his pistol belt. He picked up the gun, looked at it, and then placed it back in the seat. He knew that he did not need it. There was nothing out there that would hurt him today.

Michael walked over to the gate in the barbed wire fence. The top of the gate had been hanging over, where someone had only replaced the bottom wire. Quite typical of most gates in the middle of nowhere. The gap in the gate was large enough for him to step through. He turned around to the trail, and the first thing that he noticed was a pair of birch trees that were essentially two trees grown from one trunk. At about eye level, there were what appeared to be bear claw marks on both trees that were side by side and straight down forming the number 11:11 (without the colon). Now he was sure that he was in the right spot and smiled with a little chuckle of this synchronistic confirmation as he started down the trail.

Although not that well used, the trail was well defined. Michael walked down and up rocky faces that were not for the squeamish due to the extreme steepness in parts. He could hear the sound of what seemed like rushing water growing louder and louder, indicating an increasing proximity to what he knew was Serenity Falls. The scenery and backdrop really reminded him of the beginning of *Raiders of the Lost Ark*. Down the last long steep rocky face, and he finally arrived at the river.

He first came upon a wide pond, where the water was wonderfully serene, moving rather slowly along the narrow river. There was a campsite near the pond where someone had built a teeter totter out of a split tree trunk. Michael followed the pond around to where the river began flowing faster out toward the falls with the increasing sound of mountain water dropping off below.

When he came to the edge of the falls, Michael could see that they were not very wide, maybe twelve feet across, but went down for hundreds of feet. There was a trailhead off to his left, and he went over and looked down the steep trail. It was more of a spiral rock staircase than a mountain trail, but he knew that he had to go down to the bottom. Something else was guiding him now, and he no longer needed the map or the synchronicities for direction; the rest was all up to him.

Michael closed his eyes for a minute and felt the crystal in his pocket to ease his fears. He was still feeling some fear, and he knew that he had to let that go. He would have to let everything go soon and that would be the key to expelling the demon out of him. He kept reaffirming to himself that he could do this, and then, when Michael felt ready, he opened his eyes and started down the path.

It was a long trip down, and he had to actually scale some of the larger rocks on the way down. After about a half hour, he finally made it all the way to the bottom. There was a large beautiful pool at the bottom that the falls fell into. The place was surrounded by large granite walls and a small open meadow adjacent to the water with low-lying grass sprinkled with the many rocks of Montana. If Michael ever felt like an adventuring archaeologist, it was at this very moment.

He walked over to the middle of the meadow, and there was a large boulder that just seemed like it was out of place. He approached the rock and placed his hand on it as if to get permission for his presence. Michael pulled the monk's crystal out of his pocket with his other hand. It was very warm, not just from his body heat; it was almost hot, and he could swear the he had felt it heating up in his pocket the entire time he was climbing down the trail. He placed the crystal on the rock, stepped back a few paces, and then knelt down in front of the rock like he was getting ready to pray.

Michael closed his eyes and began to concentrate. Thoughts of his pain and resentment in life began to swell in him. He thought of the loss of Jimmy, Butch, and Tisha, but he especially thought of the loss of Brad. That was so much more painful since he was still alive and within reach. He could feel the empathy for Brad and how much pain Michael had caused him. His selfish thoughts about his own feelings began to fade, and he could see what he had actually done and how much Brad was actually hurting out there somewhere as well.

He thought of the betrayal of his wife and Sean and how much that had angered him. The pain that he had suffered began to combine with his feelings of loss, and then he had a vision of his father. The anger raged within him. His own father, whose ego had put him in jail and had told him to kill himself. Michael blamed everything that was wrong in his life on his father and had been willing to end his own life because of it. He combined all these feelings of resentment, loss, and anger into the well of his stomach, and he could feel it beginning to grow. The rage within him was like nothing he had ever felt before. A purple aura formed around Michael like an opening in space and time, and an astral light form stepped out of his body as he remained kneeling in front of the boulder. Michael could now see the world for the illusionary existence that it was. A red ball of light began to glow in the distance in front of him. It continued to grow and approach his astral body.

He could see the large glowing red orb in front of him and felt totally at ease. The feelings of forgiveness and acceptance were overwhelming. All his fear and anger were contained in this light form. Michael felt so powerful and stood strong. He spoke at the light form authoritatively but not in anger, "Show yourself."

The light form began to morph into many changing human shapes like it was trying to find the right one. Michael noticed that, for a few seconds, he was seeing the form of each person that he had ever felt had wronged him in his life, and then it would switch to the next one. Eventually, it shaped into that of his father and remained that way as it finally spoke to him. "Just what is it that you intend to accomplish here, Michael?" The voice was that of his father's, but it was much more ominous.

"I'm going to kill you," Michael replied. "You are not my father. I have manifested you through years of anger, resentment, and alcohol and it is time that you were out of my life for good. You are simply taking the shape of the one that I blamed the most. I know now that nothing in my life is anyone's fault but my own. You have failed, and I no longer want this pain that you represent." The being leaned its head back and let out a cry of rage. When it tilted its head back forward, it had now taken the shape of Michael. In surprise, he took a few steps backward.

The being just stared at Michael with black empty holes where the eyes would be. "You can't get rid of me that easy," the evil Michael said. "You don't have the power in you to forgive. Who do you think you are? Jesus?"

Michael slowly closed his eyes and opened his palms to the sky. He began to breathe slowly and deeply. With all of the will that he could muster, he spoke. "I release all my anger and resentment to the Creator. I accept the Creator's will as my own. The past no longer has any meaning for me, the future does not exist, and the present is where I now reside."

The crystal on the boulder began to glow with an immense white light as Michael kept his eyes shut in concentration. The white light became intolerable and painful as Michael began to cry out in agony. He continued to concentrate on forgiveness and acceptance as the positive energies flowed into his body from all around him in nature. The trees and rocks seemed to resonate with him and refuel his energy. He could feel the perfect energy of all creation and all that had ever been. The purple aura, now surrounding Michael's astral body, grew more intense until the crystal turned color and shot a purple beam at the demonic figure in front of him. The entity exploded into a thousand pieces and disappeared into the darkness.

Michael opened his eyes. The demon was gone, and the crystal just sat lifeless on the boulder in front of him. He felt overwhelmed with joy, a feeling that he had never felt before. It was as if everything was right with the world, that it was as it should be. He could see the beautiful glow of nature around him as if everything was surrounded by a bright, pure white light, but it did not hurt the eyes. The unconditional love of the light of source was emanating from all nature around him. Michael knew that grounding himself to this would become necessary for the rest of his life if he were to survive in this world. With his new powers would come a weakness; if he were to absorb too much energy of suffering without being able to ground in a reasonable enough time, he could die. This would take some time to adjust to.

The full extent of what had just happened to him would be revealed in time, but he was sure that he was more powerful than he could have possibly imagined. There was no more remorse and fear in him as he had truly become a spiritual warrior. He retrieved the crystal from the boulder and placed it back in his pocket. It may come in handy someday, but it had definitely served its purpose for now. For some reason, he did not feel alone anymore. It was as if there was a presence around him that he could not explain, but it was comforting.

Michael heard a noise coming from a small distance away. It was like no noise he had ever heard before, one so pleasant and calming. There was no pain or suffering in the sound, only joy and compassion. He slowly made his way through the tall dry meadow grass in the direction of the noise. He chuckled to himself as he was reminded of the tall grass where the raptors lived in *Jurassic Park* because this sound definitely did not invoke fear like that. The sound grew more pronounced as he reached the middle of the meadow.

He became lost in thought as he continued toward the source of the sound. The demon was dead, so what was left? Michael did feel different, but something was still missing. Why couldn't he wrap his mind around it? Jimmy had told him to come all the way out here to the continental divide to get rid of this demon, but he still didn't feel all that different. Michael knew that it must be something that he must still figure out, but what?

As he was pondering that, Michael came upon a clearing in the grass, revealing what appeared to be a small brook meandering through the middle of the meadow. It had called to him. The stream was only about six feet wide and crystal clear. There was not a pollutant in it. He knelt down next the creek and scooped up a handful of the pristine water and touched it to his lips. Michael could taste the purity of the essence of the water. He could sense the feeling of being alive.

Michael sat down next to the running water in his typical Indian-style position to begin a meditative session. He knew that he must ground himself right here to complete the journey. First he began to bring himself into a calming meditative trance; he then spread the fingers out on both hands in front of him and jammed them down into the dirt in front of his shins. Michael was instantly hit with a blast of source energy from this grounded connection with the great mother, Gaia. He had never felt this kind of surge before. He synchronized his breathing with the rhythm of the stream. Michael had found the breath of life, but he was overcome with sadness.

He was completely immersed in the loving embrace of the ether and began to glow as he left his body. Michael saw the earth being destroyed by evil, and it did not have much longer to survive. Humanity was in a Fibonacci spiral to destruction. His thoughts were instantly taken to a field of view positioned above the earth. The earth seemed to glow blood red in distress. It was so bright. As he focused his concentration in further, he could see that the red glow was actually made up of smaller brighter individual glowing red dots. Michael just seemed to know what those were, and he couldn't explain how. Each light represented a separate human in suffering or distress. Holy shit! It all just seemed to make sense now. He knew he had the power to help them.

For the first time in his life, he knew what his soul's purpose was. It is a very cruel joke to be sent back here for life after life with amnesia. Soul growth would be so much easier if we were able to retain the previous lessons. Michael knew that there was an omnipresent evil that kept us in this third-dimensional soul trap called earth. Humans would never be able to ascend to better dimensions if they did not learn to get out of this one. He saw how the source spirit loved humanity so much that it sent empaths like him to help. Humanity was at a point that it would not survive without intervention. This was a world overrun with fear, and the only destroyer of fear was love. Michael's purpose here was simply "to be in love." Upon realizing this ultimate purpose, he was instantly thrown back into his body sitting in front of that stream.

Michael was not any more special than the rest of humanity. He was simply more awake at this point in his ascension that he had volunteered to come here to help. All that suffering and agony that he had to go through to get here was necessary. A tear began to form in his eye, which quickly developed into an uncontrollable cry. More of a laughter really. It was as if he was simultaneously experiencing all joy and suffering at the same time. He finally got it. Love was the acceptance of all that is, and all that ever will be without any fear. It did not mean to remain quiet in apathy and let evil succeed. That was nowhere to be found in the definition of love.

He sat there next to that stream, crying until he had no tears left. It must have been for over an hour. After they finally ceased, he wiped his eyes and sat next to the brook for few minutes longer. As he thought about all that had happened that day, Michael knew that he had a new journey to begin—a journey that could possibly be a bit more challenging than his life thus far. He laughed as he thought that "a bit" might become an understatement. He brought himself to his feet and slapped his right leg, which had fallen asleep. Michael looked out over the vast meadow with complete peace in his heart. He smiled, sighed, then turned around, and began walking back the way he had come in.

It was to be a short hike back to the waterfall, and Michael had time to think about his new journey some more, but with a clarity he had never possessed before. He began to think about what it meant to be in love. Michael knew that he had to break that down further since the basis of his purpose would take the rest of his life to understand. He smiled as he realized why he had to kill that demon first. Michael had to conquer his final fear in order to even understand what love was. Jimmy was right! He turned his head sideways to the sky with a half-cocked smile. "Thanks, Jimmy. I miss you, buddy."

He first started by thinking about what it meant "to be." Shakespeare talked about "to be or not to be" being the grand question, and Descartes believed he thought so therefore he was. That seemed to be nothing more than horseshit to Michael now. He knew that it simply meant exactly what it said. No matter where you were, you were. There was no past or future, only the now. Humanity spent countless hours and fortunes searching for the meaning of life when it was right in front of them all along. The meaning of life was simply life itself. That was it! Michael grimaced as he thought at how many civilizations have come and gone in the history of humanity only to be wiped out by the their own ignorance. The Atlanteans, Sumerians, Mayans, Incas—the list went on. It had happened time and time again, and for a brief moment, Michael wondered if humanity was could even be saved or was worth saving. He shook his head as he quickly removed that thought from his consciousness.

Michael laughed out loud as he thought about the "in love" part of his purpose. That was not going to be as easy to define as "to be." Not by a damn sight. Since he knew that there were only two forces in the universe: love and fear. He was pretty sure that it meant to conquer all fears with the use of love. He frowned again as he thought again about the history of humanity and how they never learned. The source spirit had sent many teachers throughout time, but the world was riddled with fear as usual, and they never learned a thing. How many teachers, really? Krishna, Buddha, Jesus, Mohammed, Gandhi, MLK, JFK, and the list goes on and on and on. Sad, but Michael was not about to let that stop him.

He thought back about all the lights of distress that the universe had showed him. The world had become lost in misery because it refused to wake up and see that it had become bathed in fear. Michael was already well aware as to how the Luciferian Controllers of the world had accomplished this with the constant streaming of fear-based programming. From birth to death during all our waking hours, humans were bombarded with lies and distractions to keep them from seeing the truth that they were all enslaved. Slaves to the fear and nothing else. It became like a drug, some sort of addiction. Fear was the only thing necessary to control a society for the insatiable gain of the few. The only thing that would kill it was love.

Michael knew now that both love and fear must always exist. No one would ever be able to eradicate all fear in this third-dimensional prison of duality. Without the other, there would be no definition of itself. In other words, in order to know what love was, you must first experience fear. To him it was like trying to place a definition on words like *normal* and *weird*. Who would be the ones to define these? Society, government, religions? Only in an enslaved world would words like that even exist. Even though he knew that fear must exist, the world was WAY out of balance with this duality.

The problem with the two opposing forces was that they were all encompassing. No one could live any part of their life partially in love or fear. If fear existed in any form in one's life, then they were living their entire lives in fear. The same could be said for love. Humans liked to throw around the term *unconditional love* at will with no realization that it was redundant. The word *unconditional* did not belong. As Michael had found out only moments ago, love had no condition and applied to all that was.

He thought about this a little deeper since one could be on the path of growing in love and breaking fears without living in complete enslavement. Michael had no fears left, but it was going to be very difficult to show others how to accomplish this. Nothing was impossible, albeit improbable; but difficult didn't quite describe the uphill battle he had ahead of him. Society was programmed to fear everything. We had a fight-or-flight kind of mentality, and everything we were shown or led to believe seemed to feed one of the two. Fight and flight were both actions based on fear. Love would never engage in battle or flee in any way.

His abilities would help to make the task easier, but he knew that he would not be able to alter a person's freewill. The universe did not allow for that. All must make their own choices, even if those choices had been manipulated with manufactured fear. That was the only way the Controllers could get away with what they had for most of the history of humanity. Even though humans had been mind-controlled, they still had made the choices to obey, follow, conform, consume, and deny. It was a harsh loophole in the universal law of free will, but a loophole nonetheless.

Michael looked up ahead and could see the base of the waterfall getting larger in his view. He thought about all that had just happened and how miraculous it was. The years of suffering, hatred, and fear that he had to go through to get here now—it all seemed worth it. The past no longer mattered other than the lessons he had taken with him. The future was uncertain, but not hopeless. The time was now; however, and that was where he would spend the rest of his life. Depression set in from holding on to the past. Anxiety developed from worrying about the future. Peace was a result of living in the now.

There was something new now. Michael could recall those lights of distress at will. If he concentrated on a certain one, then he instantly knew who was hurting, why, and where they were located. Each one of them had one thing in common—they were all in fear of being happy. Misery had become so common that it was uncomfortable for people to feel good. They simply weren't used to it, and that scared people shitless. The only way that anyone would be able to change was to exit their comfort zones, and that took courage, as did acceptance of the truth. Courage was nonexistent if fear was allowing society to be controlled.

As Michael got to the waterfall, he could feel that something wasn't right. He pulled up the distress lights in his mind, and there was one blinking. As he zeroed in, he could see that it was blinking over his own hometown. It was his father. Something had happened, and he could feel that the life force was weakening. With all that had happened and all the forgiveness and love in his heart now, there was still one more hurdle. He had to help his father. Although he wasn't sure how yet, Michael knew that he must go and should hurry.

DILEMMAS

Happiness is the spiritual experience of living
every minute with love, grace, and gratitude.
—Denis Waitley

When Michael arrived back at the truck, Rikki was about to eat her
way through the passenger window. He could tell that she knew
something big was going on. When he opened the door, she jumped
in his arms and licked his face uncontrollably, like she hadn't seen
him in a month. "Calm down, girl!" Michael laughed. He managed
to get her back in the seat, but something was different about her.
She seemed to be glowing.

He stepped back a few paces and could see this beautiful green
glow surrounding Rikki about two feet out from the edge of her
entire body. Michael knew that he was seeing her aura. He had seen
these before throughout his life, but he had to concentrate very hard
to do it, and it didn't always work. Now it seemed he could just see
them at will. This was just another power that he now possessed due
to the events down by the waterfall. Michael shook his head and
smiled as he imagined he would find out a bunch of new talents
revealing themselves in time.

Green, he thought, *is the color of the heart chakra.* Each of the
seven chakras in the body had a color association. One chakra might
be controlling more than the others, which would reveal in the aura
color. The aura told the spiritual state of being of a person, and it
changed periodically due to one's condition of wellness. The heart
chakra, controlling love and compassion, should be more active in

dogs; so the green color around Rikki made sense to him. With the ability to see auras, Michael could decipher the truth about people and where their consciousness resided. Each chakra placed a role in one's complete spiritual health and had individual purposes. The bulk of humanity had very few active chakra points, or they were way out of balance. Michael had already learned most of this, and he could sense that he was in a perfect state of balanced chakra energies, known as *kundalini* activation.

Michael looked back at the floppy broken gate crossing the trailhead. This journey had changed his life forever. He gently shook his head up and down as he realized that he was truly ready to fulfill his life's purpose without any fear at all. He closed the passenger door while smiling at Rikki on the opposite side of the window, walked around to the driver's side, opened the door without haste, and planted down beside her. As he was petting the top of her head, he closed his eyes since there was so much to think about before he made his way out. Michael was quite a bit more powerful now but found himself wondering what was still waiting to be activated.

"Patience," he told himself. It would be necessary, but that didn't mean that he couldn't feel excited. He opened his eyes, started the truck, and left the same way he had come in, but with a whole lot less baggage.

The negativity in his life was gone. Michael saw everything in a positive light because love was acceptance of all that was, including the truth. Truth was not negative; ignorance was. It was what a person did with their knowledge that could be deemed positive or negative. He pulled out his copy of Khalil Gibran's *The Prophet* on his journey home. It seemed to call to him in that little used book section of a local quick mart that he had stopped in a couple weeks ago. Michael didn't even remember the name of the town. It was so small that the quick mart was most likely the local grocery store as well. He had heard about the book before but never read it. It was the book that June Carter gave Johnny Cash to help him out. What a wonderful read it was.

He had become a very powerful empath—that much was certain. But being an empath did not always mean empathy. Michael did legitimately have concern for those that were willing to hear his message of love and truth. He would not, however, waste his time on the ones that wanted to remain willfully ignorant. The people that killed the messenger and attacked the ones trying to help, he would not go out of his way for them, but there is always the possibility that one of them could see the light. The fact that this possibility existed was the reason he would continue to try to help even if it was not being well received.

While making his way through small town America, Michael started to take more notice of some social trends. The exponential increase in the presence of banners in support for athletic teams, American flags, and landscaping doodads in people's yards was staggering. He couldn't recall this level of symbol worship during his childhood at all. The Controllers used many symbols to manipulate humanity, but these days, more and more people seemed to be willingly displaying things for them. People drove their cars around in complete paranoia that they were breaking a traffic law, slamming on their breaks because someone was approaching a crosswalk, not pulling past the edge point of an intersection to wait for a left turn, making sure to not go one mile per hour over the speed limit, stopping ten feet back from a crosswalk and making sure the metal sensor for the traffic light didn't trigger, texting to remain even more distracted from reality, and so on. It seemed painfully clear to Michael that the more obvious the tactics of the Controllers were becoming, because of the information age, the more that the denial tactics of the population became obvious as well. It was basically psychology, really. These were just symptoms of an ever-expanding Orwellian police state, or control.

The weirdest part of the trip home came when he made his first official pit stop. Michael had already seen Rikki's aura and the beautiful light energies given off by nature. To Michael, nature was literally like poetry from the Creator. He exited into a little Snack and Shit (otherwise known as a quick mart) along Route 93 when he had the urge to go to the bathroom and get a bite to eat. As he pulled into the parking spot in front of the store, Michael noticed that some of the people milling about had glowing auras similar to the one he had seen around Rikki. He was amazed that this new skill worked on people and not just animals and nature. He put the truck in park, by rote, as he continued to stare at them all.

"Stay here, Rikki. I've got to see this," Michael uttered as he opened the door and climbed out of the truck. He shut the door, almost hitting Rikki's nose on the window since he could not stop looking at all the auras around the people. The colors were so varied and not everybody had them. He noticed that no one had a white aura, which would indicate awareness and a balanced chakra system that he now possessed. The lower chakra colors of reds and oranges were present, but not so much the higher ones of blues and purples. The majority of the auras were not chakra colors at all; they were brown and black. Of the ones that did have auras at all, Michael thought that about 75 percent or more were this way.

Michael didn't know how he knew, but the brown and the black auras were the bad ones. These were the hopelessly enslaved and evil ones that retained them. Brown indicated the ones living lives of willful ignorance and voluntary servitude. These people would be dangerous to help, because not only did they not want to wake up—they will almost fight you to the death to remain in familiar bondage. Black, on the other hand, was a completely different set of conditions.

Evil knew no color, only black; it was the absence of all color, just as evil was the absence of all empathy. Michael knew that these people were in service to the group that he called the Controllers. The Abysmals, as he called them, were the humans that had willfully cooperated with the Controllers in order to further their agenda of worldwide enslavement. They did all this in exchange for higher standards of living and wealth while they lived in this brief third-dimensional existence with the rest of us. Basically these people had sold their eternal souls in one lifetime and would receive the ultimate punishment for their crimes against humanity. Anyone with a black aura should be avoided at all costs, but not for Michael, since these were the ones that he was here to help neutralize.

As he walked through the store entrance, Michael noticed that a small percentage of the people had no auras at all. He walked past one of them in the snack isle and glanced, with a quickness where time seemed to stand still, deep in his eyes and was literally sickened by what he saw and felt. This person was not human, and he was sure of it. Knowledge was just coming to him as he needed it, another powerful gift to be certain. Although he knew that much, Michael wasn't certain if they were aliens, interdimensional beings, demonic entities, or a combination of all three; most likely the latter, he suspected. Whatever the case might be, these were what compromised the Controllers.

The rush of these different energies was starting to exhaust him, so he put on his isolation bubble. Wow! He had never been able to shield himself so efficiently and so quick. Michael was even getting the sensation that he was able to borrow other people's auras and bubbles, provided they were human. He continued around the store, mingling, now comfortably, with the people. Something else seemed odd. (Boy, these just seemed to keep coming, and he was loving it!) He almost felt invisible to them. Michael could actually feel that they really didn't notice him meandering about. It was much like that of the hive mind of the Borg in *Star Trek*, where unless he was sensed as being a threat, they had no interest in him. It really was not an encouraging feeling for Michael, to say the least.

He decided to tune them out for a while, use the bathroom, and get some snacks for himself and Rikki. Michael shook his head and chuckled all the way back to the truck. His journey was not going to be that hard with all these skills, Michael thought. Little did he know that was to be the exact opposite of the way things would be. He started the truck and continued his way home, nonstop.

Michael randomly accessed the human distress map in his head as he made his way home. His father's signal was like a GPS map in his mind, so he just followed it home so to speak. He pulled into his little hometown hospital parking lot just shortly before one in the morning. He left Rikki in the truck and went in to see his father for the first time in almost ten years. He had mixed feelings about the coming encounter, as he had let go of his anger in the mountains and forgiven his father for what he had done. Michael felt a little uncertain about his resolve. He was no angel. Michael had definitely done some very bad things in the past. Ultimately, his entire life had been his choice, albeit a train wreck. The auras and vibrations that he was seeing as a result of the encounter in the mountains were telling him all that he needed to know about our lives here. We manifest our own lives with the perceptions that we have about our experiences here, but this was one experience that was a lifetime in the making.

It appeared that Michael's mother had already gone home for the night, so no one even knew that he was in town yet. He walked to the nurse's station and told him who he was and that he wanted to see his father. Michael did not care that visiting hours were over and that it was so late. He had driven all night to get here, and who knew how long his father might still be alive. The nurses did not have any objection to it, and he proceeded down the hall. Michael stood in front of the door to the ICU and took a few deep breaths. He was recalling all he had learned about forgiveness and the gift that he had received because of it. The demon was dead, and the man behind this door was key in Michael's manifestation of it in the first place. He kept trying to tell himself that he had forgiven his father and it should be easy to see him again. He let out his final deep breath and entered the room.

He approached the side of the half upright bed and looked down at the frail body in front of him. Decades of alcohol abuse had aged his father's body and face so much that he almost didn't recognize him, but it was definitely the man that he was here to see. He was in his late sixties, about the same as grandpa when Michael saw him in that coffin so long ago. There was a very faint red aura about him as he lay there. It was fading in and out. Michael knew that the red aura was common in people of very low vibrations due to their ignorance, love of the self, and problems with ego.

His father was hooked up to a life support monitor. His eyes looked to be open, but he wasn't able to speak. Michael stood there, looking at his father's teary eyes staring up at him. He had the power to save his father, but would it be a life worth saving? Was it even his position to judge? Michael thought of his mother and how much he loved her. She had really been the victim in all this. He began to think about all the shitty things his father had done, and some resentment began to well within him. His father had never said the word *sorry* to

Michael, or anyone for that matter, in his entire life. Michael began to tap into what was left of his father's ego. Even though Michael had killed his own ego, his father's was beginning to creep into him like a virus. It was difficult to fight. A demon was beginning to form inside him once again as the hatred for his father welled within him. Without even thinking about it, he went over and disconnected the nurse's station monitoring of the life support system and turned off his father's life support.

Pain began to shoot through Michael's head as he thought about what he was doing. Everything he had just gained would be lost in the blink of an eye. This was the first dilemma of his ascension, a test of forgiveness. He had to truly let go and heal the one that had caused him so much pain and suffering.

Michael harnessed the same strength that he used to kill the first demon and let out a scream. "Nooooooooooooo! Not today."

Michael swung around to face his father in bed and placed his hand about two inches above the top of his father's hand, careful not to bump the IV needle sticking out of the top of his veiny hand. A white light began to glow between the two hands until it became blinding. Michael connected with his father's life force and could feel that it was very week. He could see how beautiful a human's life force really was, and it appeared to be uniquely shaped rather than symmetrical. Michael gave his father a piece of his own life force that had been rejuvenated in the mountain. He began to recharge his father's life force with empathy, love, and understanding.

The EKG blinked a faint vertical white line. His father's heart jumped back to life as he sat up sharply, took in a deep breath like he had just come out of drowning in water, and fell back into the bed. His father's eyes opened like he could sense an outside presence was hovering over him. He turned his head slightly toward his son and tried to give a small smile through the plastic breathing tube. A tear gently dropped from the corner of his father's eye onto the pillow.

"Hello, Pop," Michael said. "I came as soon as I knew. Don't bother trying to speak. I can hear you just fine." He could too. It was as if he could hear his thoughts, as if they were connected somehow. It was what Michael always wanted to be able to do—to connect to people in such a way that they might be able to understand him. And now he had it, and he could control it. It was wonderful. This was the final gift he was waiting for—to see the thoughts of others. Just by touching someone's aura, he knew their regrets, fears, and dreams, if they had any left.

"I am not about to make you feel bad about things you have done to me or blame you for anything that has gone wrong in my life. I can feel that you already regret what you have done." Michael placed his hand over the top of his father's hand again. The white light began glowing between their hands, and his father closed his eyes and began to twitch ever so slightly as the information was transferred.

"Now, I am going to show you what I am and what being this way has done to me. I apologize ahead of time because this is going to hurt, a lot. It won't be physical pain, but it will be necessary pain." Michael closed his eyes and began to think deeply about all the things, good and bad, that his father had done to him in his life. He showed him how all the years of drunkenness resulted in no compassion or understanding for what he was and how it made him feel. He showed him how he had slowly poisoned his mother intentionally. He showed him the feelings of helplessness and aloneness that Michael felt as a result of these things and all the things that he missed out on. He showed him all the evil truth of the world that he had been too ignorant to realize. He showed him what it felt like to want to kill yourself because you had no hope left. Most of all, he showed him what it was like for an empath to have to live in a world like this one, with the father that he had to grow up with. He showed him enough to break his heart, but this also caused Michael immense emotional pain. He felt the regrets of his father and had true empathy for this man that he had hated so much.

He could tell from the sweat and racing heartbeat that his father had enough, so Michael moved his hand away from his father's and let him settle down. He looked down at his father and leaned down to talk closer to him. "I forgive you for what you have been in my life, and I have no regrets. In a way, you helped to make me see my true potential, and I thank you for that."

His father opened his eyes wide just like he was coming out of a bad nightmare and, without turning his head, aimed his eyes up at his son. All the pain that he had caused had been revealed to him in the blink of an eye, and the feeling was overwhelming. A leaking of tears began to gather around the outskirts of his eyes, slowing filling the well of the socket until he began to sob uncontrollably. Tears ran down his face and congregated around his mouth on the breathing tube.

Michael looked down on his father with a smile. "I have given you this gift for a reason." He paused for moment. "Love." He paused for a few more moments. "Life is going to be quite a bit different for you for a while, but you will adjust just fine. I need you to make me a promise, and all I want is for you to blink your eyes once for yes and twice for no. Can you do that?" His father blinked once. "Good. You need to tell me if you want this new gift or not. I imagine you are already feeling the wonderful changes beginning inside you, and you will probably go home tomorrow. I can take it all back, and you will most likely die. Do you want it?" His father blinked once.

Looking down at his father, Michael closed his eyes and reached deep into his subconscious to see his father's life force again. It was no problem this time, and he did not have to put his hand over his father's. He simply had to touch his aura. Michael could feel that his father's essence had really changed, and he would have a good remainder of life with his mother. This set him at ease, and he opened his eyes. While looking at his father, he could see that his aura had gone from a red color to a light greenish blue, which was definitely a good sign.

He spoke gently down at his father, who had managed to get a handle on the sobbing. "I am going to go see Mom for a couple days, and then I have to leave for a while, but I will be back soon. When you get out of the hospital, it is only uphill from there. Mom will know how to get ahold of me. I love you, Pop. I think that much is self-evident now." Michael gave his hand a little squeeze as his father smiled the best he could with the breathing tube in. He turned around to leave the room.

Michael noticed that one of the nurses that had been at the station when he came in the hospital was now standing behind him by the door in the room. He rolled his eyes up a bit and knew that the nurse must have heard him scream a few moments ago and came to investigate, so he must have been standing there quietly in awe for most of it. Michael just walked up and stood an arm's length away from him and waited for him to speak.

The man was an average-height blond-haired man with perfectly round glasses, wearing blue scrubs. He had a bluish-green aura, so he seemed to be a good-enough soul. While reaching his hand out to shake Michael's, he spoke to him. "I have heard of people like you. In the medical profession, you hear a lot of things. Most doctors and nurses disregard the natural and even the supernatural. It would put a large dent in the industry profits to say the least. I wanted to let you know that your secret is safe with me. Man, God sure gave you a gift. I hope you can put it to good use." He smiled, finished shaking Michael's hand, and then left the room. All was quiet once again.

Michael looked back and smiled as the man was leaving and then went back over to his father's bedside. His father was looking up at him with an even more intense state of fear than he had before he died. He had been given a second chance by the son that he had never really had a spiritual connection to before. All the feelings that Michael had shown him were just hard to deal with for the first time ever. His father would have to live for a while with the pains in his head until he too learned how to deal with it. Michael finally turned away and exited the room.

He leaned against the outside of the door for a brief moment and just reflected a little on what just happened. He couldn't believe how powerful he had become, and he was sure that this was not the end of surprises or tests. Superman couldn't even save his own father. He reached down and felt a lump in his pocket. It was the monk's crystal, which he would always keep with him for the rest of his life. It was warm again, like it had been when he was on the mountain. He pulled it out and was amazed when he looked at it. Now he knew where he had seen that shape before. His father's life force was in the same shape as the monk's crystal. Given any other day, that would have seemed odd, but not today.

Michael heard the sound of footsteps growing in volume and coming in his general direction. He glanced down the hallway and saw what appeared to be one of the night staff doctors coming his way. He was wearing a long white doctor's trench coat over a really nice shirt and tie, very expensive suit pants, and ridiculously nice Italian leather shoes. The doctor was about six feet tall, had dark-brown hair that was slightly receding, and looked to be in his midthirties. He had a black aura and did not look pleased. The nurse that he had talked to, he was sure, didn't say anything. Michael figured that someone must have caught wind of his after-hours presence because he thought he had disabled the monitor, which they were probably on to by now. He casually slid the crystal back in his pocket, pushed himself off the hospital room door, and turned to face the approaching figure.

As the doctor with the black aura reached him, he stopped in front of Michael and began to speak. "The nurses told me that you are the son here, visiting his father, but it is way past visiting hours. We also noticed something wrong with his monitor after you were in there. We have to make sure that our patients are properly cared for, and your presence has disrupted the healing pro—"

"Save it!" Michael just cut the doctor off in midsentence. He raised his hand to touch the black aura around the doctor, who retracted slightly in fear as to what Michael was doing. Michael could see the true dark nature of the soul in front on him. Just another doctor in the business to get rich of the suffering of others. He could sense this doctor's lack of empathy and his greed for wealth. He saw that this doctor even knew about holistic and natural cures for diseases that had been suppressed by the governments for decades so the Controllers could make fortunes off insurance and pharmaceutical drugs. He was an evil man who had betrayed his kind in exchange for easy living.

The doctor looked as if he was going to say something, but Michael started in first. "I know what you are. You're vermin. I don't mean that as an insult. That is what you are. You feed your selfish ego by allowing and even causing the suffering of others, all while giving off the facade that you are some kind of humanitarian. I believe we would call someone like you a vampire, almost literally. Now"—Michael paused for brief moment—"you're going to move out of my way, and I'm going to leave the hospital."

Michael felt as though the doctor was about to retort when something just short of incredible happened. He was able to connect with the doctor's mind directly with ease. The black-aura people were at such a low vibration that it was no effort at all. As he concentrated, Michael was able to get the doctor to step out of his way so he could get by. This was some Jedi-level shit, he was thinking now. Michael began to feel as though he would like to kill this man for his crimes against humanity. Why was he feeling this way? He also knew that he had the power to do it. This was the second dilemma, a test of judgment. It was not his position to judge and carry out sentence. That duty was restricted to source only. Yes, this man was a piece of shit, but that was simply an assessment of what he was able to tap into from his aura. An empath could not kill, and he never would. That would be put to the test one day.

He left the hospital and headed for his childhood home. It was still the middle of the night, so he would be sure to be quiet. No one knew that he was back except his father, and he was sure that his mother would be fast asleep. He let himself and Rikki in using the hidden key that was always outside, in the same place under the planter box. Michael was always good at sneaking around places quietly, and tonight was no exception. He and Rikki silently went inside.

Michael walked through the house and found that his mother was fast asleep, snoring in alcohol coma, as per normal. She was most likely worse than usual, considering the events that had taken place with his father. Sure enough, there was still a bottle of gin and some tonic left on the counter from the night before, along with a partially finished dinner plate that had crusted over. He walked back to his old room with Rikki and decided to get some rest until morning, when he would surprise his mother with his presence. He hadn't really slept much since the encounter with the demon, so his sleep was filled with new lucid dreams. Michael's abilities in the conscious world were not the only powers that had improved. He was able to use the dream world like never before. You could call it astral projection of sorts, but it was like second nature to him now. The first thought that came to his mind was Brad. Michael really missed his best friend and would love to repair that damage. His mind zoomed in on Brad's location fast asleep in his bed. He could see what Brad's major problem was. It was also that of his father. Wow, that made so much sense. No wonder they were so well connected after having unresolved paternal issues.

Brad's father had died from colon cancer while he was in high school. Michael remembered when he had first told him about it back in college. Brad had never had the chance to say much of a goodbye before his death, and he still carried that empty hole to this day in life. Apparently, his father had only told his mother about his sickness, and they both promised to keep it a secret until it became so apparent that they would have to let others in the family know. The problem was that they never got the chance. His father hemorrhaged one night, and it was too late to say anything to anyone. Brad had never been able to live with that, and Michael could now sense all of it remotely. He could also tell Brad was missing Michael as well, but pride and resentment were keeping him from doing anything about it.

Michael phased back out of his astral world view and slowly opened his eyes. A smile came over his face as he realized what his next journey was. He needed to leave society and seek out these lights to help humanity a little at a time, beginning with Brad. With his new level of power, he knew that he could help his dear friend and mend a terrible wound of his own in the process. His smile slowly faded as he drifted off to peaceful dreamless sleep, which was just what he needed about now. Michael was exhausted.

He awakened to the sound of Rikki whining very softly next to him. She was careful not to be too loud about it; she was smart that way. Michael's eyes crept open, and he could hear why she was whining. His mother was up in the other room and rummaging around a little. She still had no idea that he was there. He got up and threw some sweats on while Rikki waited anxiously by the bedroom door.

There were other people to smell and greet, and she just couldn't wait. After a few quick breaths to relax, he opened the door and headed down the hall for what would most likely be an emotional reunion with his mother after all these years.

When Michael came around the corner to enter the kitchen, his mother was looking away from him while sipping on her coffee. He could see that she had a dark green aura around her, which was encouraging. Rikki came around the corner in a seizure of excitement. Startled, she dropped the coffee cup on the floor, put her hand over her chest, and gave a little gasp.

She looked over to see him standing there while she tried to keep Rikki from mauling her in the broken glass and coffee. "Michael, is that really you? My son, my wonderful son."

She came around the kitchen counter to embrace him with a hug—a hug like he had never felt since he could really feel her distressing vibrations as he touched her. She was sobbing uncontrollably, and Michael could not help but do the same. She pulled back while still holding the sides of his arms, looking up at his water-soaked eyes through her own.

"I didn't know if I would ever see you again, but I am so happy. I am so glad you are home and safe."

Michael smiled as she dropped her arms from his and went to work cleaning up the coffee spill while still sniffling quite a bit. He knelt down to help her pick up some of the glass pieces and looked at her face. He could feel how much she had been through emotionally going back her entire life.

"It's good to see you again too, Mother. I have missed you. I went to see Dad last night when I got in. The nurses let me in to see him."

"He was stable when I left there last night," she said as she threw the soiled paper towels in the trash and began pouring herself a fresh cup of coffee. "How did he seem when you saw him? I know that must have been hard for you."

Michael smiled at her. What happened at the hospital would always be between him and his father only. "He seemed fine. We talked a bit, and I think he will make a full recovery. In fact, I think he wants to change his lifestyle a bit, with you included." He smiled inside of himself at his loving hand in that alteration.

"What does that mean exactly?" She sipped at her fresh cup of coffee.

He pulled up a stool at the counter, let out a quick sigh, and explained, "It means that you have fault in this too, as I did. I shared that with Dad last night." He could tell by her face that she was becoming defensive and it was only going to get worse. "You guys are going to stop all this boozing and deal with life on a new level. I know why you can't see what is really going on, and you have some choices to make. I have felt the internal struggle in you my whole life, and now it is really overwhelming. I need to give you something special so you will understand and show you things from my perspective, but we can wait until after breakfast. It is just really good to see you."

She hung her head almost in embarrassment. "I know, Michael. It is time we make some changes, but we may need help. We were proud of the fact that you did it and didn't even realize the extent to which our own problems had an effect on that. I have been doing some of my own reading on all this while you have been away."

"Good." He went over and gave her another big hug. "I will help with whatever I can. Do whatever it takes, for some it is easier than others. It is expectations that you must also avoid. They cause nothing but resentments that lead to hate, where hope conflicts with reality. I have no time for hope or hate, Mom, only action and love. Now let me make you a nice breakfast, and we can have a talk in a while. Then you can go visit Dad. I think that we have made our peace, and you can't begin to understand what a load off it was—or maybe you can."

After they were pleasantly fed and relaxing in the living room, Michael began to explain everything as best as he thought he could convey. "I can't even begin to tell you what I have learned and how much there is that we really don't know. All I can say is that something incredible happened to me when I was away. We are all eternal beings with nothing to lose but fear. Love and truth are the solution, with true freedom being the prize. Things like luck and karma are just words for the ways that the Creator will let you know whether you are on your correct path or not. We must always show gratitude for the positive things in our lives and concentrate on the little periods of joy that occur from time to time. This is the only way that a soul can maintain connection to the light of source while they are here. Star seeds like me have been sent here to help. I will try not to get too deep into all that now. In time, you may be able to understand, but just the fact that I can feel you are willing now is more than a gift to me."

His mother smiled, like the smile that one had before they began to cry, but there were no tears. "We always knew that you were different than the rest of the kids, but I never knew how special. The fear of not fitting in with the rest must have been too much to take."

"Wow." Michael smiled big. "You are on the right track. Now all you have to do is be open to new things and forget about the judgment of others. It will help you to stop judging as well. The booze makes it very easy to deal with for a while, trust me, but it is nothing more than a symptom of underlying problems dealing with fear. We live in a society that thrives on fear because it makes it easy for people to be controlled for the benefit of a few sociopaths. In fact, humans seem to be designed to make very efficient slaves. The fact that we need shelter, food, and water to survive is the very thing that makes us controllable. Advanced beings adapt to their environment and receive their energy directly from zero-point source. That is way too big for us to discuss today." He paused for a moment and scratched his head. "Now, I need you to do something with me."

She looked at Michael with the all familiar face of fear. "What?" She pondered for a moment. "You aren't going to melt my brain or something."

"No, no, nothing like that." He chuckled. "You remember how all my life I have wanted to be able to connect to others so they could understand what was going on in my head?" She nodded. "Well, now I have that ability. I just need you to sit in that chair while I stand behind you and place my hands on you." Michael got up from the couch and walked around to stand behind his seated mother.

She was very nervous, and he could feel it very strongly. "I really don't like this, Michael, but I suppose these are the fears that you are talking about." He could feel his mother trying to relax a bit. "Okay, son, I am ready when you are."

Michael stood calmly behind her and let out several deep long breaths and then placed his hands on either side of her head. He was a little worried himself as this would be the first time he had ever done this, not counting what he had just done with his father and the doctor last night. "Just keep relaxing, Mom. I will not give you more than you can handle. Shut your eyes and just breathe normally. You will see a faint white light in the distance, and I just want you to concentrate on it. I will take care of the rest." Michael shut his own eyes. He could sense that his mother's consciousness was also present, and he was able to easily synchronize with it. Then he began.

He showed her a summary of the highlights of his life and the essence of what he was, but he did not show her all that he was now after his awakening. Michael showed her the misunderstanding that he felt and the way she acted when drinking all those years. He showed her the compassion that he had for those in need and the empathic feeling that he had and how the world treated him because of it. He showed her the truth about the dark entities controlling the human race, but he did not go too deep as she would not have been able to handle how stomach turning the whole truth really was. He showed her the deep sorrow that he had for all the bad things that he had done. And most of all, he showed her the forgiveness that he now had for all that. He did not blame anyone, but she needed to see it for herself.

After he was finished, he opened his eyes and removed his hands from his mother's head and went back over to the couch to sit back down. She still had her eyes closed for a few moments and then slowly raised her lids. Michael fully expected her to be very emotional and upset, but this was not the case. She seemed almost relieved, most likely from all the energies of forgiveness that he had shown her. Most times people were set at ease just from knowing and not necessarily fixing the problem, just like how Buddhism taught to be mindful of your thoughts, even though you can't change them.

The past and the future did not exist, and the only thing that mattered was our time in the present.

She let out a breath of relief, looked over at Michael, and smiled a genuine smile like he had not seen on her face before. "I see now." She shook her head in utter amazement. "I really wished I had listened to you before, but I am not sad. It is hard to describe, but I feel ashamed and relieved at the same time. I felt your forgiveness, and I forgive myself as well. You have never been the person that I, wrongly, thought you were, and now you are so much more. What happened to you? How are you able to do this?"

He smiled at her and gave a chuckle. "That, we will have to save for another time. I am just glad that you can see now, and I know in my heart that you will do what is right with it. You have nothing but joy ahead if you choose the right path, and I will never be more than a phone call or e-mail away, if you need help."

"Away?" He could sense the fear in her voice. "How long are you going to stay? We really have a lot of catching up to do."

"I will be here until Dad gets out of the hospital so you are not alone." Michael looked down at Rikki, who could sense the high vibrations in the room, and gave her a scratch behind the ears, which she loved so much. "I have one other person that I need to help before I can head out on my mission."

"Who?" she asked. "And what mission are you talking about?"

"Brad." Michael closed his eyes for a brief moment. "I need to apologize to him for what I have done, and there is something that I need to help him with. I owe him that much at least. As far as the mission, well, call it a life purpose, if you will. I'm going to cash everything in, get out of all debt, and hit the road. There are a lot of people out there that can be helped, and I am tired of slaving away in this world of lies to acquire more possessions in this life. The only thing that I need is that which I possess inside of me. You may not understand this yet, but I think you can see that I am finally happy."

"Yes, you're right." She nodded in agreement. "I don't fully understand yet, but after what you just did with me, I can see that you have a gift. It should be shared with the world. I can see some of the truth that you shared, but there is still so much that I need to learn. I am just glad that you are here right now. I haven't felt this good in quite a while."

Michael scratched his head and grinned. "Well, you still have a challenge ahead of you, much like I did, but I instilled some tools in you that will help you along the way. You aren't consciously aware of them yet, but they are there. I love you and Dad both very much, but it took me a long time to realize that. There was so much hatred and anger in me for so long, but once my perception changed, that all seemed to melt away."

His mother was hanging her head a bit in the chair, like she was holding a deep secret that had always bothered her. "Michael, there is something that I need to tell you. It has always been something that has bothered me about your birth. Actually, it is a couple things. After you have shown me these things that you have, I think that it all kind of makes sense now. I never really told you about the complications that occurred with my pregnancy with you." Michael just sat and looked at her while she talked. "The first thing that was strange was that something happened almost immediately after you were conceived, and I could also feel the exact moment that you were conceived. Immediately after conception, I started to feel severe abdominal pains, much worse than what childbirth should. When I went to the doctor, I told him that I already knew that I was pregnant, but he told me that I had a tumor." Michael smiled at that thought while reminiscing about the Nobel Prize winner that he just ran into at the hospital a couple of days ago. "It didn't matter much what he told me since I already knew what it was. The pains went on for six months. It was almost unbearable. At the time, no one could figure out why, but now I think I might know. I think your soul was actually trying to get me to abort your existence. The thought never crossed my mind at the time, but I think that you were hoping that the pain might force me to the abortion. That's the first thing. The second is that I was in full labor for over thirty hours. It almost killed me for real. The doctors had never seen anything like it and had approached your father to decide which one would live. He never had to make the decision because you decided to come out right then, and it was over. It never really made much sense until now. It was like your soul really did not want to come here, like you already knew how evil this place was and was resisting being born into it. Your soul just couldn't allow me to continue to be in pain when your methods weren't working. I can actually feel that now. You put up a good fight, but in the end, destiny seems to have won." She paused and thought for a moment when a slight grin came on her face. "Ever since then you have definitely been a challenge." Through moist eyes, they both laughed heartily at that.

His mother was tearing up again. "I knew it too, that this world was really shitty. Something was making me feel guilty for bringing a child into this world, but I just knew in my heart that this child will make a difference. He will eventually become very powerful and be able to battle the evil that has overshadowed humanity. That is when you decided to be born. Now I can see that I wasn't wrong, Michael. You are a real life miracle."

He had a big smile on his face. "That means more to me than you could possibly know. I love you, Mom, and you won't ever have to worry about me again."

"I love you too, sweetheart." She got out of her chair to give him another hug, and Michael responded in kind. "You make yourself at home, and I am going in to see your father." She wiped tears away with the sides of her palms.

The hospital was going to keep his father for observation for a few more days, so Michael had some quiet time to do some soul-searching and thinking. He still didn't feel completely confident like he imagined he would be. There was still something else. A final dilemma of sorts. He would have been lying to himself if he did not admit that he was a little worried about that one.

There was a heartfelt parting between Michael and his mother, quite similar to when he left for the Navy so long ago, before he knew all the things that he did now. Tears were flowing, but the feeling of love was overwhelming. She knew that he would be back someday, and everything seemed to make sense. Her son was going to do some good for the world, and everything had come full circle. She watched as he loaded Rikki in the truck and waved goodbye as they drove off into the early morning sun.

Michael arrived at Brad's house about noon that day, and it looked like people were home. This surprise reunion could go a lot of ways, but he was at ease and could sense that all would be fine. He walked quietly up the walk, rang the doorbell, and waited. The door opened, and Brad stood there, just staring at Michael for a few moments.

His face seemed to crumple a bit and then he spoke. "Well, well, well, if it isn't the drunken avenger. I knew that I might see you again someday, but I didn't think that you would ever have the nerve to come around here. I should slam the door in your face, but I am curious." Brad paused for a moment. "What do you want, Michael?"

"Hello, Brad." Michael spoke with a relief that the initial confrontation was over. "I don't expect you to let me in, but I really need to talk to you. I know that you never wanted to speak to me again, but if you can find it in your heart to at least give me a few minutes, I think that it will be beneficial to both of us. I can't begin to tell you how sorry I am for what I have done, and I am not looking for forgiveness. Please just give me a few moments." He began to sob a bit, but he was not looking for any pity, so Michael just put off any emotion for a while.

Brad just stood there for a few more moments, staring at Michael. "Okay, I will meet you out on the back porch. You know the way." He then shut the door gently, and Michael went around the house to the back. He sat down at the table at the back and waited for Brad to emerge from the house. He knew the family was home as well, and he could see them looking out the window in amazement at the fact that he was actually there. He had spent a lot of time with Brad's family and had missed all of them immensely.

Brad came out on the porch with a couple Mountain Dews in hand and sat opposite Michael at the table. "Here is a soda if you want." He handed it to Michael. "Okay, it's your show. Tell me what you need to say."

After opening the can and taking a sip, Michael clasped his hands together and rocked back and forth a bit. "Once again, I am truly sorry for my behavior and the danger that I had posed to you. You were the only friend that I had left alive in this world, and I really messed that up. I haven't had a drink in over two years, and I actually went to rehab to do it."

Brad shook his head in approving acknowledgment of that fact, and Michael continued on. "This may come as a shock to you, but I had an attempt at suicide recently, and I took a trip that changed my life forever. I know you remember how I have always been able to feel and read places, people, and situations, but I have never been as strong as I am now."

Brad held up his hand as he was coughing a bit on his soda. "Suicide? Oh man, Michael. I had a feeling that might be the case based on the way you were headed. What happened exactly?"

Michael filled Brad in on the past couple years and all the shit that had happened but still managing to stay sober. Then he got to the rehab story and the name on the gymnasium. "When I saw your name on the gym, I knew that was a spiritual sign that I was on the right path. It was actually the first sign that I have ever really been conscious of, and I have been seeing a pile of them ever since. It is quite possible that my suicide attempt was even predestined no matter how morbid that may sound."

"Who knows, really? Truth is definitely stranger than fiction." Brad looked out over the lawn for a brief moment. "So tell me about this magical trip of yours."

"That would be the word for it." Michael laughed a little at that. "This may stretch your imagination a bit, but you have always had somewhat of an open mind, so here goes." Michael told him about the suicide attempt and Jimmy's intervention. He laid out the entire story of his journey, the signs he had seen along the way, the final awakening, and what had happened with his parents as best that he could remember.

The look on Brad's face was about like that of an executive who had just been approached by the FBI for embezzlement. He held that pose for what seemed like an eternity. "Michael, do you know how fantastic that all sounds?"

"Yes, Brad, I do." Michael leaned forward a bit while looking in his eyes. "I can prove it too you though." He slid his chair around the table next to Brad's and leaned close to him. "You know how much you would like to see your father again and actually say goodbye? Well, I think I may be able to give you that gift."

Brad looked at him in complete anxiousness. "Are you serious? You know, you'd better not be showing up here after all this time after what you pulled just to be shitting me."

Michael shook his head. "I'm not shitting you. I think I owe this to you at the very least. If you are willing to give it a try, we can do it right here and now. I warn you, though, it can be a very powerful experience."

"What do you mean powerful?" Brad looked at him with raised eyebrows. "My head is not going to blow up like in *Scanners*, is it?" Both of them laughed out loud together for the first time in years.

Michael put his hand on Brad's shoulder and continued to giggle a bit. "No, no, nothing like that. My mom was worried too. It won't hurt, physically, and it won't cause any fear, but it may cause an emotional response that you have never experienced before."

Brad pursed up his lips a bit while nodding his head in deep thought for a few moments. "Okay, let's do it. What do you need me to do?"

"First, we need to be seated with me behind you. These lawn chairs will be fine." Michael and Brad both got up so they could position the chairs one behind the other. They then sat back down with Michael positioned behind Brad, very similar to what he had done with his mother. He could sense the fear vibrations coming from Brad also very similar to his mother. "Are you ready?"

Brad fidgeted a bit back and forth in the chair and then shook his hands out like he was trying to dry them. "I think so. We need to do it before I change my mind."

"Okay, I am going to cradle your head in my hands very gently." Michael placed his hands on either side of the back of his head, just like he had done with his mother. "You need to rest your hands in your lap, close your eyes, and try to relax. This is your journey. I will not know what happens. All I am going to do is transfer some of my power to you. Take a deep breath and let it out slow." He did. "Now just breathe normally and place all your concentration on your father, what he looked like, and how much you loved him. Think of what you would tell him if you could see him again." Michael could feel his energy being shared with Brad, so he knew that something was beginning. He was very careful not to share too much, which could literally drive Brad insane.

Brad began to twitch and shake a little bit, but nothing overly extreme. Michael could feel that he was concentrating very deeply, and he sensed that Brad was making some kind of contact with something. He could see what was going on if he wanted too, but he wanted to leave the memory to Brad alone. It was not for him to see, so he kept his conscious awareness away. The connection went on for several minutes. He assumed that Brad would have a lot to say, but he only had so much time. Then the energy transfer began to decrease, and Michael could feel an overwhelming sense of relief in his friend. When he could feel no more vibrations, Michael dropped his hands back into his lap and simply waited.

Before his eyes could completely open, Brad was already sobbing. He seemed to be laughing a little as well. He got up and turned to face Michael with open arms. They hugged each other in deep embrace, and Brad sobbed on his friend's shoulder for as long as it took to release years of pain and loss. Michael could not help but to cry as well, but for a different reason. For an empath to be able to help anyone was like a gift from God himself. It was one less miserable soul that lowered the spiritual vibrations of this world. They broke their embrace, and Brad wiped his face a bit and tried to compose himself. They looked at each other with a deep understanding, and neither one spoke; then they rearranged the chairs and sat back down to talk more about everything.

Brad was looking down at the ground in utter disbelief. Then he locked eyes with Michael. "Thank you so much, buddy. I don't really know what to say. I do forgive you, you know. I actually did when I opened the door, but I never expected this. It was simply surreal. You have a gift. I always knew that, but this is something much greater."

The two of them talked for hours after that. Brad told Michael about the reunion with his father's spirit that had just happened. He had seen his father step out of the ether cloud and walk toward him just like fog in a dream, but he knew it was all too real. His father looked to be a healthy version of the way he had looked before he had become ill with cancer. He exchanged conversation with his father and had the closure that he had always longed for. They talked about all the memories of the good and wild times of their past and even made mention of some of the not-so-pleasant ones. A powerful broken friendship was mended.

"So what now?" Brad asked Michael, still amazed at all that had just occurred. "You sure have the opportunity to live a different life now."

Michael stood up, rather tired of sitting, and leaned against the deck railing, looking out over the yard and the suburbs beyond. "There are a lot of troubled people out there, Bradley, and I think I can help change this world." He turned back around and faced Brad again. "I'm getting rid of everything, and I am leaving for a while. The house and yard sale should provide me enough to get a little motor home and hit the road with a little cash and no debt or bills left behind. I will cease to exist and fly as far under the radar as possible. I have a few advantages over the bastards now." Michael laughed at that.

Brad joined him by the deck railing and reached his hand out for a shake. "I hope that you will not be a stranger, and I wish you all the luck." They shook hands and embraced for a final hug. "I know that you will do something good, and I really thank you again for what you just did for me. Don't burn your bridges, and don't forget the little people."

"Don't worry, buddy, I won't." Michael left the porch and walked around the outside of the house to the truck in the front yard. He had a sense that he would be back here in the near future, but he wasn't sure what it meant. The future was cloudy and uncertain. He reached over and gave Rikki a pat on the head and then turned back for one last look. Brad was waving by the side of the house, and Michael just waved back with a smile. Then he drove off.

It didn't take but a couple months to finish selling the house and all his belongings. He found a nice used motor home in the classified ads, and he was also able to trade his truck to the owner, who was looking for a used car for his son that was about to get his driver's license. Everything worked out just fine. Michael figured that things moved along easier when destiny was aligned with purpose. Usually if things weren't going your way, then you were probably going the wrong way. As he left his old life behind, Michael started to think about Caroline, his little Blue Dove. She was out there somewhere and still needed to heal. He would find her someday—of that he was sure. Nothing happened by accident, and they had met for some special reason. Perhaps it was so that he could feel what true love really was, or maybe she was just the catalyst for his transformation. He wasn't sure, but he was sure that they would meet again.

The more he thought about Caroline and all the horrific things she had been through, Michael would hurt deeply just for knowing about them. He could feel her life force out there somewhere, but it was so full of fear and suffering. Even if he did find her, would he be able to help her find love? Would it even be worth the effort? Humans did not have a good history of awakening.

Michael was really having a problem with his soul's purpose of aiding human ascension. He just didn't see how humans were worth the effort of trying to save them. They were so self-deprecating, self-enslaving, and self-mutilating, like no other species on the planet or the known universe for that matter. He thought how James Joyce was really on to something when he said, "History is a nightmare from which I am trying to awaken." That was exactly how Michael was feeling right then.

Was the world even worth staying a part of, even with his new powers and awakening to the truth? The world had always been the nightmare for him as well as it had for most throughout human history, so was it even possible to fix it? The world was just so hermetically sealed in hate.

He closed his eyes and asked for direction on this final dilemma. Michael's mind was filled with thoughts of the Old Rock Church near Chelan when he was a child. Why was he thinking of that right now? What did it have to do with anything? A church? Then a vision of Chap started to overlap the vision of the church. Now he knew what was going on. Chap used to preach there. He told him that when he was in jail. Michael never forgot that. That was where he was headed next.

As he pulled up to the old run-down place of worship, Michael had a good feeling in his gut. The place seemed to be glowing a light blue with no feeling of any evil presence, probably because Chap was here once and had left his beautiful energy behind. Rikki was asleep on the passenger seat, so Michael was careful to not disturb her when he exited.

Michael walked gingerly up to the entrance of the church. There was an old wooden door hanging from two rusty screws in the top hinge. The other hinges were nowhere to be found, and the bottom of the door was just leaning on the brick lined door jam. He could make out the faded wood outline of an ornate cross that once hung on the door. The church was probably built sometime during the mid-1800s. He gently swung the door open as to not compromise the final hinge, laid the door gently over on the rock wall, and entered the church.

The place smelled of old bibles and the lingering scent of liniment. Two rows of rotten wooden pews lined most of the one-room church, with the pulpit area taking up about one-third of the area. The door opened into the isle way of the pews. This was the same church Michael had seen in the dream about his mother, only it was not dilapidated in his dream. Things were really starting to make sense with that for him now.

Michael looked at the pulpit in the front. It was elevated by one step. There was a cobweb-covered podium on the left with a large wooden statue of Jesus in robes hanging over the middle next to a clutter covered table on the right. As he approached the pulpit, Michael could see some interesting object on the table next to Jesus. He stepped up on the pulpit and looked at the wooden statue of Jesus. It was still in fairly good shape after all these years. He glanced down at the items on the table. There was a dusty old conch shell and a tarnished bronze eagle. These were very important symbols for Michael. Both were glowing white like the light of the source. The eagle was symbolic of energy renewal and resurrection, just like Jesus was to his followers, and the shell was even more significant. Shells grew in the shape of the Fibonacci sequence, the basic code of all life, including human DNA. Leonardo of Pisa, who found this living sequence, saw it as the pattern of the ascension path as did many who had awakened since.

"Stop with the signs already," Michael said aloud as he smiled to himself.

He looked down at Jesus's right hand, and it was pointing over to a podium on the far left of the pulpit area. He walked over to the podium and noticed a Bible was lying face up and open. The Bible was open to a page in Philippians. The page was filthy, and Michael just seemed to zoom in on a clean section of the page, which was section 22 of chapter 1. He read the passage out loud to himself: "If I am to go on living in the body, this will mean fruitful labor for me. Yet what shall I choose? I do not know! I am torn between the two: I desire to depart and be with Christ, which is better by far; but it is more necessary for you that I remain in the body."

Michael was truly beside himself. This was what he was looking for all along. All the trials and situations that he had faced to get here had all came down to one final question, one final dilemma. Could he remain in this world? YES! He could. No matter what the world would deal him from now or forever more, death would always be there. It was the one thing that was guaranteed. If he ever reached a point that he couldn't handle, the Creator had given that contingency plan, so what the hell? Why not? He had absolutely nothing to lose and was enjoying the ride. Success was the journey, not the destination. Our destination was all the same.

Driving away, he felt totally free for the first time in his life. Rikki was perched on the passenger seat, enjoying the breeze from the window. There was no destination, no sense of economic slavery, no longing for something better, and no fear. Michael stopped briefly along the way so he could build a nice little campfire consisting of his driver's license, social security card, birth certificate, and other assorted registrations. He had no guilt and no sense of need of forgiveness. That was why he had no fear. Michael had become what he was meant to be, and now he was on his final journey in life, and as far as the beast control system was concerned, he no longer existed.

Traveling gave him a lot of time to reflect on all that had happened to get him here. Michael thought of all the guides that had been provided to show him the way. He thought of Butch, Al, and most of all, Jimmy—the three spirits that had given him assistance from the other side—although Tisha and Gene had definitely played a role in guiding his journey on this side. *Angel* was really the wrong term, but that was the best thing that would describe them. The biggest hidden truth of this world was that we were all spiritual beings here to experience the flesh. Before we agreed to come here, we already understood that the earth was a spiritual battleground and could be quite unpleasant at times. We had been here before and ascended higher in our spiritual awakening with each completed visit; no matter how joyous or miserable it might be, there was a lesson from it. Wonderful experiences like lovemaking and gourmet food could only be experienced in the third-dimensional flesh world of duality. We agreed to endure the suffering in order to experience those things. The source Creator sent specific souls here to help the others on their difficult journey through this reality. Sometimes these souls weren't exactly planning on coming back here, and they could be a little resistant. This made the complications surrounding Michael's birth make more sense.

He had a lot of time to think about all that Jimmy had told him on that day that should have ended in his suicide. It made more sense all the time. Although the demon inside of him had grown stronger over the years because of his drinking and blaming of his father, it had initially been created by his own ego, which took control of his free will. Once it took control, it led him away from his soul's purpose. He had incarnated to this world to serve others and not serve the self. Although he had done many good deeds in his life, they all ended up coming back to fuel his own ego. He smiled when he thought about the irony about his father. Had it not been for him, then Michael would have never become what he was supposed to be. Funny how it worked out that way.

Michael's ego had been the root of all his evil deeds. It was like a virus that led to all the other diseases like greed, lust, apathy, and narcissism. If not for the ego, the world would be a joyous place of abundant love and freedom. Not quite like any other virus. It was not a medical condition, but a spiritual one, and it could only be cured with the mind, not medications, which only really helped symptoms anyway. Humans were not born with it, but they were immediately susceptible to it after birth. The ego was artificially created by the Controllers; without it, they would cease to exist and not be able to control humanity. It is the ego that controlled the free will of humanity. This made complete sense the more that he thought about it. When he finally brought the demon out into the open, the only thing that was able to kill it was forgiveness, along with a very special crystal. Forgiveness was the only way to love. Love was the only way to the truth, but it took free will to do this, so it ended up being an endless cycle when the ego was in control of free will. It started to make his head hurt the more that he thought about it.

There were three things that must be open in order to find the truth: the heart, the eyes, and the mind. If any one of these were closed, than you simply lived a lie. For Michael, it was his heart that had become so closed off because of his worldly perception of all he had been through. When he achieved universal acceptance and forgiveness, it suddenly opened, thus revealing his true potential. Realizing his potential showed him the purpose of his soul.

Religions didn't work in truth; they dealt in comfort. Michael was supportive of anyone that took action with the intent of making a better world, as a lot of Christians did, but that was not really what the church provided. It had been a necessary tool of the Controllers for eons. He always used discernment in his questioning of religion, as with everything that he did. It just seemed odd to him that Jesus was teaching people to love and understand, while all Michael ever heard in churches was fear and judgment. The Bible even talked in many locations about Satan being in control of the earth, which was very true. Most Christians could not accept this fact even though the Bible told them so. The church's interpretation was why they believed such things. Being born again was also the fashionable thing to do in fundamentalist religions. Being born again was a regeneration in the church, but rebirth was the regeneration of the spirit. Michael had just been through the latter after a long dark night of the soul.

Michael knew that he could not change the world completely or all at once but he could gradually change it one misguided soul at a time. With all this new power, he would have to be careful. The Controllers would be on the lookout for him. They did not want the world to wake up to their evil agenda, so Michael would have to keep traveling around and be as discreet as he could. He knew that he would never be able to stay in one spot for too long, but Michael was in it for the adventure, not a sedentary lifestyle. The stakes would be high, and the danger to his life would be significant; but he could no longer stand back and continue to watch humanity be intentionally morphed into the self-destructive, self-absorbed, self-doubting, unconscious race of androids that it was becoming.

Life was a ride, but for an empath, it was the emotional roller coaster from hell. The ride produced different experiences that affected us based on how we perceived them. The problem was that society could influence our perception, and if society was corrupt, then so was our perception. We had the choice as to how much we let society influence us or whether or not we chose to obey or not. The perception of these experiences was what leads us to knowledge. Knowledge led to awareness, which wouldn't allow society to influence our perception. This was what led to wisdom, which in turn led to consciousness. It really came down to an information war, a war on our consciousness.

He looked over at Rikki enjoying the ride in her shotgun seat. "Are you ready for a trip into the unknown, old girl?" He reached over and scratched her ear with a smile, and she licked his hand to show her anticipation. He no longer thought about the next destination or the future. He was on a perpetual journey to today, and the future was still to be determined. "Let's go see how many of these manipulative controlling bastards we can irritate. Does that sound good, girl?"

She wagged her tail in excitement, not knowing at all what he had said but happy about the positive energy in the air. Michael let out a big laugh as he flipped his sunglasses on with his free hand and stared down the open highway. He was certain that he had the cure to humanity's problems now. Now, it was just time to walk the talk.

ABOUT THE AUTHOR

James Bartleson grew up in a small town in eastern Washington. After receiving his degree in civil engineering from the University of Idaho, he spent twenty years as a transportation engineer throughout the western United States. As a result of being born hypersensitive (known as empathic), he feels the pains of society much deeper than the majority. James thought of using real people and actual events as the basis for both tender and shocking stories that would open the world's eyes to the unconscionable dark influences that are affecting the human condition. In 2017, James's overwhelming desire to help humanity for the better caused him to leave his career as a professional engineer and begin the journey to become an author and an educator.

CPSIA information can be obtained
at www.ICGtesting.com
Printed in the USA
FSHW020132060721
82981FS